THE TINKER

Alan Reynolds

Fisher King Publishing

The Tinker
Copyright © Alan Reynolds 2014
ISBN 978-1-910406-09-0

Cover design based on a concept
by Leon Reynolds

All rights reserved. No part of this publication
may be reproduced or distributed in any form
or by any means, or stored in a database or
electronic retrieval system without the prior
written permission of Fisher King Publishing
Ltd. Thank you for respecting the author of this
work.

Published by
Fisher King Publishing
The Studio
Arthington Lane
Pool in Wharfedale
LS21 1JZ
England

The author would like to express his gratitude
to Rick Armstrong for his continued support,
guidance and friendship; also to Samantha
Richardson and Rachel Topping at
Fisher King Publishing for all their help.

Dedicated to my family and friends and to
everyone who has supported me in my
writing - your encouragement drives me on.

Much love

"We are what we pretend to be, so we must be careful about what we pretend to be."

Kurt Vonnegut

Chapter One

"More tea, dear?" said Denise Colesley, offering the china tea pot and hovering it over her husband's cup.

"What...? Oh, yes, thank you," replied her husband, the Reverend John Colesley, momentarily disturbed from reading through his notes for his forthcoming sermon.

"I don't know why you spend all that time on those, dear, no one listens. How many were in church last week? What was it, twenty?" she replied, filling her husband's cup and applying the milk.

He took his reading glasses off momentarily and looked at his wife. "That's not the point," he said, not sharply but in an understanding way. "People do get a great deal of comfort from church," he said raising the brimming cup to his lips and sipping gently.

He returned his spectacles and continued scanning the three A5 pages. Fairly short this week; ten minutes would be plenty.

Sunday morning, last week in May 1986 and the village looked immaculate. Drayburn, the small Cotswold hamlet nestling in a basin surrounded by spectacular hills, resembled a picture you might see on a 1950's toffee tin. It was as though some giant hand had scooped away the earth and gently lowered the houses into place. All made of typical Cotswold stone, properties were expensive and much sought after; several were second homes providing bolt holes for London Executives and at least one celebrity, none of whom would be in today's congregation. The small population, shy of fifteen hundred nearly all worked outside the village, Bristol, Cheltenham even Bath; commuting back every evening.

There was naturally a pub, The White Hart, on prime position at the top of the High Street which doubled as a hotel with fifteen so-called luxury rooms with guests happy to pay premium prices particularly at this time of year. Opposite the pub was a hairdressing salon and next to that the village store and Post Office which catered for most everyday needs. The larger weekly shop would mean a trip to the supermarket in Stonington - a small town ten miles to the north, the other side of the hill. There were a few other, boutique-style shops supplying arts and crafts and local produce as well as a couple of typically English Tea Shoppes.

The village school which catered for fifty or so 5 - 9 year olds was a short distance from the church, aptly named St James' Primary School, it had served the community for over a hundred years with four or even five generations of local pupils passing through its doors.

St James Church however dominated the village but not in an obtrusive way; it completed the scene. A quintessential English village without its church would just not compute.

The fifty-eight year old parish priest said farewell to his wife and left the vicarage to make the short walk to the medieval edifice. He never tired of this brief journey; past the row of three seventeenth century cottages to the right resplendent with their climbing roses clambering their way up the walls making a feature of the front porches; the small gardens, carefully tended, rich with the abundance of flowers. The early sun glinted off the pristine windows. In front of him Vicarage Road led towards the centre of the village, flanked each side by beautiful three story Georgian terraced houses in their typical Cotswold stone grey/ochre livery. Many had attic rooms which, it was recorded, used to be weavers' workshops.

Drayburn is from a bygone age; in fact the only nod towards the modern era are the ubiquitous double yellow lines. It is a popular tourist destination and visitors regularly clog the narrow streets; the one car-park, the other side of the village, is regularly full. Out-door TV aerials are banned by local by-laws to retain its old-world feel.

The vicar's passage did not require him to follow the road; the church was immediately to his left and it was a fifty yard walk to reach the low stone boundary wall of the church yard. In the warming sun he had dispensed with the need of a coat over his gown which fluttered behind him as he walked. Just gone seven thirty and with his first service, Holy Communion, at eight o'clock he would be in good time to open up and prepare the church for his early parishioners.

He stopped for a moment and looked up at the impressive spire; the sun in the east hidden behind it causing its rays to shoot either side. Earliest records suggested the church was built around 1182 although the spire was added much later. It is steeped in history with important references to the English Civil War and other conflicts.

Through the stone gateway and along the yew tree-lined path to the front porch passing the ancient grave-stones and chest tombs with inscriptions that had been erased by the ravages of time. Grass and wild flowers - the last of the blue bells, daisies of every description and poppies, gave added colour to the backdrop of the churchyard.

He was met at the door by the verger who was sweeping around the frontage trying to remove the vestiges of the previous day's wedding.

"I don't know why I bother," he said to the approaching figure who was viewing his labours with interest. "It'll all be back again next week."

"I'm sorry Jack," said the vicar. "I do remind them, but they just take no notice."

"It's just typical. Youngsters these days, got no respect." Jack Fleming a sprightly seventy year old spoke in the soft Gloucestershire brogue but with an edge that reflected his annoyance.

Weddings did however play an important role in the economy of the church; people came from across the county and beyond to get married in its beautiful setting and the financial contribution they brought was essential to its continued upkeep.

Two more figures approached and the vicar greeted them warmly.

"Hello Ted, Deidre." Mr and Mrs Lane, the first of the six bell-ringers and serious campanologists having rung the changes at the church for over fifteen years. They were quickly joined by the rest of the team and after a quick catch up they made their way into the church and took up their positions.

The vicar entered the church leaving the verger to his labours and started preparing for the service. He could hear the familiar tolls emanating from the bell tower alerting the village to the impending service. He reminisced for a moment and considered his good fortune. There is nowhere like this anywhere in the world, he thought.

By eight o'clock the first five rows were reasonably full with the congregation; the remaining sixteen rows were empty. The resident organist, Maisie Dailey who had been providing musical accompaniment for over forty years, played a gentle refrain. As the vicar now dressed in his white over-gown entered the nave from the vestry and walked to his position in front of the congregation the bells stopped and the minister started his service, welcoming the parishioners and visitors to St James'.

By quarter to nine the service had finished and the vicar was at the front door talking to the regulars and a couple of visitors who were staying at the White Hart. Everyone was given a warm welcome as befitting the Christian spirit. Major Blandforth, wealthy landowner and an important benefactor to the church, dressed in his familiar shooting jacket and plus fours and looking the very essence of the landed gentry was quickly to him. "Nice service Reverend, what. Will you be dropping by the Manor later?"

The vicar looked confused.

"Pick up the pheasants," clarified the Major seeing the disconnect.

"Yes, yes, of course. About three ok? Sundays do tend to be pretty busy," replied the vicar without any hint of sarcasm.

"Quite so, Reverend, quite so. Yes, that'll be fine I'll get Frank to bring a brace up to the house."

Frank Johnson was the Major's gamekeeper.

"Thank you, Denise will be very pleased," replied the vicar.

The Major walked away towards his Jaguar which was parked in one of the reserved spots at the end of the churchyard footpath. It took another twenty minutes of social discourse before the vicar was able to make his excuses and head back.

Down the footpath, out of the churchyard and a sharp right almost back on himself and the vicarage was in front of him. He was passing the three cottages to his left, deep in thought contemplating his next sermon when he was disturbed by one of his neighbours, Molly Ford, another of the many octogenarians in Drayburn. She was standing at the front door of her cottage dressed smartly ready for the next service in a two piece suit; an ornate hat strategically placed on her grey hair.

"Hello vicar, have you heard anything from Michael?" she called. "Will he be visiting this year?"

The vicar looked at her and knew straight away the target of her request.

"No, Molly, nothing yet but if he is coming this year then I guess it should be any day," he replied.

"Oh that's good. I have several jobs for him. You must let me know as soon as he arrives before he gets booked up," she said.

"Of course, Molly," replied the vicar. She walked back into her cottage and the vicar continued his short walk.

The vicarage was a substantial property also on three floors with leaded square windows giving it periodic character. It too was old, dating back to the eighteenth century. There was a large entrance hall with a room to the right which Reverend Colesley used as an office and also a meeting room with parishioners. There were three other rooms downstairs, lounge, dining room and a substantial kitchen to the left of the entrance hall. Upstairs there were two large bedrooms with en-suite plus a bathroom and two smaller bedrooms in the attic which were the children's; well actually they were young adults now. There was also a small four-roomed self-contained bungalow at the back of the vicarage they called 'the Lodge'.

The vicar used the side gate which led to the kitchen. The large lawned garden looked immaculate.

"Hello dear," said his wife as he walked in.

Just two years younger than her husband, she had dressed casually but smart, her natural dark auburn hair worn up, now flecked with a tinge of grey; she was attending a boiling kettle.

"How did it go?" she asked.

"Oh, very well. I counted forty which is up on last week," he said. "I think the fine weather helped; it's a glorious morning."

"The village will be packed with visitors later," she said.

The vicar went to the ancient wooden kitchen table and picked up the Sunday paper. John Colesley was a tall man around six

The Tinker

foot one and there were parts of the house where low beams were a potential hazard; the kitchen pantry was one and he rarely ventured in there. Having filled the kettle, his wife brought out a tin of biscuits and put two on a plate beside him. The vicar looked up and smiled in acknowledgement.

"Spoke to Major Blandforth earlier; he's got a brace of pheasants for us. Said I would pick them up after lunch," he said as his wife handed him a mug of coffee.

"Oh that's lovely, we can have them when the children join us. You haven't forgotten have you, dear?"

"Goodness no. Friday isn't it? It will be good to see them again. It seems so quiet when they're away," said the vicar as he drank his coffee.

"Yes, I do so miss them," said his wife. She continued. "William should be here by lunchtime. His train gets into the station in Bristol around eleven. The bus leaves... just a minute, I've got it here somewhere," and she rummage through a pile of papers next to the bread bin. She picked up a dog-eared envelop with writing on it. "Yes here it is... 11.30 to Cheltenham arrives in Drayburn at... 12.45."

"I could have picked him up from Temple Meads," said the vicar.

"I told him that but he said he was fine," said his wife. "Didn't want to trouble you."

"It would have been no trouble," he replied. "What about Daniella?"

"She will be a little later. The bus leaves Bath about two I think she said, so it will be after three I expect."

Denise took a drink of her coffee and stared wistfully. "I'm so proud of them you know," she continued. "Both at University, who'd have thought it; and doing so well."

"Yes, they've both worked hard. They deserve some success," said the vicar as he started reading his newspaper.

After glancing at the first page, he looked up. "Spoke to Molly Ford earlier. Wanted to know whether Michael will be coming this year."

"Oh I do hope so," said his wife. "I have a few jobs for him and I expect you'll need him too for the churchyard; the grass could definitely do with cutting back."

She got up and went to the sink and started washing her mug under the tap. "I've aired the Lodge and made up the bed just in case," she added.

"Yes, you're right about the churchyard," said the vicar. "Jack does his best but he's not as young as he was and to be honest I think it's starting to get too much for him." He continued to read his paper.

There were three services at St James on a regular Sunday - Holy Communion at eight; family communion at eleven and Evensong at six in the evening. Given the attendance at the early service the vicar was upbeat that the numbers would be an improvement on the previous week. The parishioners were on the whole wealthy and generous at collection time but the vicar knew he couldn't be complacent; the upkeep of the church was very expensive.

After the brief break the vicar was back in church for the next service and this time the pews were well-populated; at least seventy the verger confirmed later. The vicar was buoyed by the congregation and the hymns were sung with increased gusto. The small choir had joined the worshippers for the family service adding harmonies and depth to the tunes while Maisie extracted every ounce of sound from the ancient organ pipes. The sun sent shards of light through the stain-glass windows; memorials to

The Tinker

fallen heroes suddenly brought back to life.

The Reverend Colesley surveyed the scene. All was good; all was good.

After the service the vicar again mingled with the congregation as they left the church. Most were regulars but again there were some visitors from the White Hart who were taking in some spiritual refreshment before continuing their weekend retreat. Having satisfied his social responsibilities the vicar went back into the church and made his way to the vestry where the verger was counting and bagging the collection.

"One hundred and five pounds and a few pence," the verger said to the vicar's enquiry.

"Thanks Jack. Can you see to the money and bank it tomorrow as usual. I don't want to risk leaving it in the church overnight?" he said.

The money would be paid into the Parochial Church Council's account at the bank in Stonington.

"Of course, Reverend." He looked at the vicar. "You know I can't understand society today. I remember when we could leave our doors open, but now... It's such a shame."

"Yes, you're right Jack. I'm afraid true Christian values are a thing of the past."

The vicar watched as Jack put the money into a cloth coin bag and then into an innocuous looking supermarket carrier bag. "Can't be too careful," said the verger noticing his boss's interest.

"Right Jack, I'm off for some lunch, I'll see you this evening. Let's hope for another good turnout. Don't forget to lock up," he said with a grin.

The main church would of course remain open with residents and visitors wanting to look inside; some seeking the solitude for personal prayer away from the organised ritual of the morning service. There was a box just inside the entrance for donations. The vestry and office would however be denied to visitors.

The vicar walked through the nave and into the bright sunshine. As he reached the end of the path onto the small private car-park allocated for church-goers he noticed a yellow sports car driving towards him. He recognised the driver straight away. It stopped and a woman in her late thirties got out, leaving the engine running. She was casually dressed in cut-off jeans and a tight tee shirt. The obligatory designer sunglasses were perched on her nose.

"Hello Tina," said the vicar. "Lovely to see you again."

"Hello vicar," said the woman. "Glad I spotted you. Just wondered if you'd heard anything from that Michael chap at all. He did a great job servicing my boiler last year. Wondered if he would be around to help out again."

"Not heard anything but if he does come I'm sure he will. If he can spare the time that is. Seems like he's going to be very busy. I've had several enquiries already," replied the vicar.

"Oh...? Well, I'm sure he'll want to look after me," she said, hardly disguising the innuendo.

"Well if he turns up I'll mention you were enquiring," replied the vicar.

"Thanks," she said and smiled before returning to her car. The vicar watched as she manoeuvred herself into the driver's seat. She waved as the Triumph Spitfire turned around and went up Vicarage Road. The vicar could hear the noise of the engine echoing along the narrow streets long after the car had vanished from sight.

Back in the house Denise was preparing lunch, a light meal; the main Sunday dinner would be later, after Even Song. It had been tradition since the Reverend Colesley was given his first parish over twenty years ago in Cheltenham. It had been ten years since he took over at Drayburn; his predecessor was in his seventies when ill health forced his retirement and prompted John's appointment.

He had done much for the local community; the work of the local vicar was far more than just conducting church services. He was on numerous committees including the Parish Council and various ventures linked to the less well-off as well as Christian charities in Africa. Every October he volunteered to go to Uganda to work on an educational project helping to fund community schooling. The over-used term 'pillar of society' was deserved in the case of the Reverend John Colesley.

"Hello dear." His wife greeted him as he came into the kitchen. She spoke in a 'jolly-hockey-sticks' kind of way; posh/academia would be another description.

"You'll never guess who I've been talking to," he said, a rhetorical question he knew she could not answer.

"Who's that, dear?" she replied as she poured out two bowls of home-made mushroom soup.

The vicar sat at the kitchen table and started buttering a bread roll.

"Tina Ashworth," he replied.

"Oh yes. And what did she want?" she replied.

"Wanted to know if Michael was about. Something about servicing her boiler," he replied.

"Oh yes and a bit more besides, I'll warrant, a real man-eater that one. Is it her third marriage that just broke down I read in the paper?" she said.

"Must be. Let me see there was that film producer, then the director... What was his name?" he said.

"Lionel Fellows," offered his wife.

"Yes that's right and she's just split up with that young actor," he said. "So yes, three. Oh dear whatever happened to 'death do us part'?" he added.

"Well it's even worse nowadays with these... what are they called? Pre-nups. I mean it doesn't bode well if you have to sign a contract to say what will happen when you split up," she replied. "Where's the commitment in that?"

The vicar started drinking his tea. "Hmm," he said.

"Well I haven't seen much of her on TV since she left that soap opera. What was it she said? Something about new challenges," said Denise.

"Yes, I remember that?" said the vicar.

"She was on that series about the doctors last month, I noticed," she said. "Mind you they don't like her in the village. I was speaking to Mrs Audley in the hairdressers, called her a 'stuck-up so-and-so'. Happy to have her hair washed there apparently but goes into Cheltenham to have it styled and cut, something about not trusting amateurs. Right upset, Mrs Audley was."

But the career and goings-on of the village's TV celebrity had lost its interest with the vicar and he changed the subject.

"Do you need any shopping while I'm out later dear? I can call in at the store if you like," he asked.

"No, thank you darling. We had the delivery yesterday. It should see us through until the children arrive. You've just reminded me though, I must phone Brian at the store and warn him we'll need extra for the weekend," she said.

The delivery service offered by the village store was a boon to the locals many of whom were either house-bound or didn't own cars and given the twenty mile round trip to the supermarket a large proportion of the residents relied on this resource. Brian Davies, the proprietor, was more than happy to oblige; almost half his turnover came from his delivery service. He had even been

The Tinker

known to drop off a packet of toilet rolls to needy customers.

Just before three o'clock the vicar backed his five year old Ford Escort out of the adjoining stone-built garage and headed towards Major Blandforth's magnificent house. Known appropriately as 'The Manor' it was about a mile from the edge of the village, on a very narrow back road about ten minutes by car from the vicarage. The vicar negotiated his way through the crowded streets; as his wife had said, tourists were everywhere and the village store seemed to be doing a roaring trade with their ice creams.

There was a dirt parking area in front of the iron gates that led to the house and the vicar edged his Escort adjacent to the wall. He walked up to the two stone pillars that marked the entrance and through the opened wrought-iron gates. With a full time gardener the lawns and borders were immaculate and the old house appeared to gaze down on the vista with a deal of satisfaction.

The vicar made his way along the gravel path, a good fifty yards to the front of the house. It is a substantial property, eight bedrooms three bathrooms, large kitchen, four reception rooms set in grounds of at least ten acres. There was also a good size trout lake surrounded by woodland. The vicar looked up at the slate roof and its four magnificent stone chimneys with their terracotta flues. There was no smoke, fires would not be needed today.

The front door was open and the vicar rang the bell. Dogs barked from inside and the Major appeared holding onto two golden retrievers.

"Hello Reverend, come in," said the Major. "Hang on while I put the dogs in the sitting room," he added momentarily leaving the vicar in the hallway as he ushered the retrievers into the room on the right hand side of the hallway and shut the door. The dogs barked in annoyance for a few moments at being denied their freedom to roam the house but soon settled down.

The Major led the vicar into the kitchen where two dead cock pheasants were presented on the rustic oak table.

"How will these do?" he said, admiring the birds. "Frank shot them yesterday. You'll need to hang them for a few days but they look superb."

"They certainly do," said the vicar. "We are very grateful."

"My pleasure," said the Major lifting up the birds and handing them to the vicar. "Can I get you anything? Tea, coffee, something cold? The memsahib has made some fresh lemonade."

The vicar chuckled to himself at the nomenclature the Major had used for his wife whom he knew came from Cardiff and had no connection whatsoever with the Sub-Continent. The vicar had little detailed knowledge of the Major's former military history but he had served in India around the time of the partition which would probably account for the rather unusual address. The Major was renowned for his story telling and could keep guests entertained for hours if he was allowed.

"That's most kind, thank you, a lemonade will be fine. Never refuse the opportunity to sample one of your good lady's lemonades." said the vicar.

The Major went to the fridge and took out a large jug of greeny/grey juice and poured measures into two cut-glass tumblers which were waiting on the kitchen worktop. The vicar received the glass with gratitude and only politeness stopped him from downing the drink in one go; it was delicious.

"That's really excellent," said the vicar after his first taste.

"Yes," said the Major. "She makes a very good lemonade. Learned it out in India, don't you know, forty seven, forty eight. Didn't like it out there though, she didn't, can't stand the heat. She's upstairs now locked herself away in her studio, painting supposedly."

"I didn't realise your wife was a painter," said the vicar taking another sip from the refreshing drink.

"She's not," said the Major, and chuckled to himself. "But you have to indulge them in their fantasies don't you?"

The vicar watched the Major as he seemed suddenly locked away in a private moment as he too relished the thirst-quenching liquid. In his early eighties now but energetic and distinguished. With his white handle-bar moustache, ruddy cheeks and silver wisps of hair, he looked every part the typical Indian Army Major and was one of those people who by their mere presence appeared to command respect. It was almost as if he had been cloned; probably the breeding, the vicar thought. His father, the previous Lord of the Manor was a Viscount but Major Blandforth had not inherited the title on his death; it had gone to an elder brother who was also a land-owner, in Derbyshire. "He got the title, I got the manor," the Major had told him on several occasions. It was clear he thought he had got the best of the deal.

The Major re-focussed from his distraction and saw the vicar had emptied his glass. "Top-up, Reverend?" said the Major.

"I don't mind if I do, thank you. It's very warm this afternoon," replied the vicar.

"Humidity's up, storm later, if I'm not mistaken," said the Major, replenishing the vicar's tumbler.

The Major suddenly changed the subject.

"Wanted to ask, have you heard anything from that Michael fellow who comes to you in the summer?" he asked.

"No, nothing," said the vicar. "I never know whether he will show or not."

"How long has he been coming to Drayburn now?" asked the Major.

"This will be his sixth year. If he turns up," the vicar added.

"A strange state of affairs. Chap turns up, works for three months then disappears again without a by your leave," said the Major.

"Yes, very strange. Do you know I don't even know his surname? 'Just call me Michael,' he says. Very handy to have here in the village mind you, does great work around the church. Jack Fleming's not as young as he was and I think he's finding it a bit difficult. Mind you he would never admit it," said the vicar.

"Quite so, quite so," replied the Major. "Done some fine work here as well. The Memsahib has been on at me for weeks wanting to know when he'll be back. Got a list of jobs as long as your arm," he added. "You know it's so difficult to get tradesmen in when you need them and they charge you a fortune. They think just because we live in the village we're made of money, what." The Major was starting to go red.

"I know what you mean," said the vicar and he looked at his watch.

"Is that the time?" he said. "I should get back. The village is full of visitors and it may take longer than usual."

"Right you are, Reverend," said the Major.

He led the vicar back into the entrance porch. It was west-facing and the warm afternoon sun-bathed the frontage.

"Glorious day," said the Major. "Mind you there will be a storm later, you mark my words. I can feel it in the air. I can always tell," he added, emphasising the word 'will' to demonstrate his certainty.

The vicar watched the Major looking at the sky examining the very heavens.

"Well thank you again, Major," he said and shook him warmly by the hand.

"Think nothing of it," said the Major. "Oh, and you won't

forget to let me know if that Michael fellow turns up now will you? Plenty to keep him busy here," he added.

"Will do, and thanks again," said the vicar and walked up the path to the car carrying the two pheasants by the string binding their feet together. He heard the sound of dogs barking coming from the house.

Again the journey back to the vicarage was beset with delays as visitors negotiated the narrow streets. He saw the queues outside Betsy's Tea Shop and was pleased that the local economy was doing so well on this glorious day.

He arrived back at the vicarage and his wife was in the kitchen.

"Hello dear, how did you get on?" she asked.

"Very well," replied the vicar and he held up the two pheasants.

"Oh they're lovely," she said. "I'll hang them in the pantry. They should be ready by the weekend. We can have them next Sunday dinner, the children will like that," she added.

By six o'clock, the vicar was back in church conducting his final service of the day and this time St James was almost full with more visitors having swelled the numbers. The vicar was elated and the service was a huge success with everyone saying how much they had enjoyed it. The temperature had thankfully started to fall but had been replaced by a very heavy atmosphere and the vicar spotted several people in the congregation fanning themselves with the order of service.

As he mingled in front of the church with his parishioners he too noticed a change in the skies; a wind had got up and large clouds were forming in the distance to the north, Stonington way.

Chapter Two

It was eight o'clock before the vicar was able to leave the church and make his way back to the vicarage. The verger had offered to lock up for which the priest was grateful; it had been a long day.

With only just over three weeks until the summer solstice it was still broad daylight but the bright sunshine had been replaced by ominous black clouds. The vicar stopped at the end of the path and looked back at the spire silhouetted against the tumult. He hoped it would survive a lightning strike if the weather developed as the Major had predicted.

There were only a few people milling around now, clearly taking heed of the signs of the brewing storm and he quickened his pace as he made for home. Suddenly there was first rumbling of thunder in the distance.

As he reached the gate of the vicarage the first spots of rain stained the paved walk-way; large the size of golf balls, then heavier still. Within moments it was as if the gods were spraying the village with a giant watering can.

The vicar let himself in, his gown speckled with dark areas where the rain had hit.

His wife came into the kitchen from the hallway.

"Are you alright, dear?" she asked.

Behind him the first flash of lightning lit up the sky, a few seconds later the inevitable crack of thunder started with a loud bang then reverberated as the sound bounced among the surrounding hills.

"Yes, thank you," said the vicar. "I'll just change out of these wet things."

"Dinner will be ready when you come down," she said.

The vicar went up the wooden staircase; the floorboards were uneven and creaked as the weight of his stride bore down on them. The bedroom with its three lead-diamond windows overlooked the old church. It was as though the room had been designed specifically as a watch-tower to ensure the church came to no harm.

The room was quite dark now and the vicar switched on the light. He went to the middle window and looked out. The spire of St James appeared forlorn against the backdrop of the blackened skies. Another flash lit up the firmament as forked lightning skittishly zigzagged across the clouds urgently seeking a grounding. Strong in his faith the vicar felt in no danger but the magnitude of the following thunder clap made him jump. He watched for a moment wondering if the metal conductor was sufficient to protect the ancient tower. He closed the curtains to protect his modesty as he changed. He wondered if a higher being would protect his beloved church.

Suitably re-clothed in a light short sleeve shirt and slacks, as befitting an off-duty clergyman, sober and respectable, he went back to the kitchen just as his wife was serving the Sunday roast. Without any sustenance since lunch he was feeling hungry. He waited for his wife to sit down before saying some brief words. "For what we about to receive, may the Lord make us truly grateful."

A crack of thunder heralded the end of his expression of gratitude as if punctuating his prayer, he took it as an acknowledgement from above.

The storm outside showed no sign of abating; the rain was now coming down in torrents and posing an additional threat as the drains struggled to keep up with the deluge. After they had eaten the pair watched for a few minutes at the kitchen window in awe as nature played out its son et lumiére across the heavens.

They washed up and as usual on a Sunday, sat down to watch television. Luckily they shared the same tastes in viewing and enjoyed relaxing together on a Sunday night; it was their time, a break from the normal demands of others.

The storm was a distraction and it was difficult for either of them to concentrate. Then from no-where... darkness. Just a click, then nothing. The only sound was the relentless rain pit-patting on the stone path outside; the only light was from the fiery flashing of the lightning. Then there was noise, loud window-rattling noise, as the heavens played out their rumbling timpani.

The vicar's wife uttered a brief exclamation of surprise.

"Don't worry, dear" said the vicar, sensing his wife's unease. "Just a power cut. Pylon struck somewhere I expect. I'll get the candles."

The lightning lit the room as the vicar hunted for some temporary illumination. The comparative remoteness of the village meant that power cuts, although not regular, were not unusual. What was atypical was the time of year. Normally the problem would be in the winter following the seasonal blizzards.

After a few minutes the room was bathed in the soft glow of naked flames from three large thick candles.

"That's better," said the vicar as he surveyed his handy- work.

"I think I'll make us a cup of tea, dear. We won't be sleeping through this," she said.

"You won't be able to use the kettle," reminded her husband.

"It's ok, I'll use a saucepan," said his wife, not rising to any unintended sarcasm. John wasn't like that.

Denise Colesley took one of the candles to light her way to the kitchen and placed it on the wooden table where they had eaten earlier. The flickering flame cast eerie shadows on the wall but there was sufficient light to brighten the room and enable her to carry out her tea making duties.

She put a small saucepan of water on the gas hob and started the ritual. Two tea bags in the teapot and then waited for the pan to come to the boil. Lightning continued to illuminate the room in bursts of wavering brightness. As soon as the liquid was ready she poured the water carefully onto the teabags, went to one of the cupboards and took out a couple of mugs while it brewed. She added a small amount of milk to each of the mugs, then poured on the steaming tea, picked them up to return to the lounge.

As she turned she was facing the kitchen door. There was another flash of lightning.

She stared, her eyes wide in fear, unable to rationalise the vision. A dark shape, the silhouette of a man, a ghostly apparition behind the frosted glass... then gone.

"Ahhhhh." She let out a piercing scream.

One of the mugs fell from her hands and crashed onto the stone floor. The next flash of lightning and the face appeared again. John had joined his wife.

"Whatever's the matter?" he said. His wife had been struck dumb with fear. She was gazing blankly at the kitchen door; the only noise was the rain beating down.

Tap, tap, tap. The spectral figured appeared again and John slowly, cautiously went to open the door. He looked at the man in front of him unable to make out his features or form any sort of recognition. Another bolt of lightning and the visitor's face was lit as if by a photographer's flash gun.

Then, awareness...

"Michael!?" said the vicar.

It was three hours earlier when the man had stopped on the outskirts of Stonington at a regular truck stop on the busy trunk road which in Roman times was known as *Via Fossa*, the Fosse

Way. He could visualise legions of soldiers marching south to their base in Aqua Sullis from skirmishes in the Midlands.

It had taken him over five hours to do the same journey from his over-night stop in Evesham. No one bothered him as he ordered an all-day breakfast and took his fry-up to a table away from the chatting crews. One or two had recognised him having overtaken him pedalling vigorously along the unforgiving road towards his ultimate destination. There were pointed looks in his direction; he was clearly a topic of conversation. He ignored them. It had been hot and thirsty work; a litre bottle of water was devoured without drawing breath. His full beard glistened with moisture from the efforts of his riding and overspill from his drink.

After half an hour having sated his appetite and thirst, he left his table. There was a truckers' washroom out the back and he took the opportunity of freshening up before setting off. He returned to his cycle and secured another bottle of water in one of the panniers for the remainder of the journey; another twelve miles he estimated.

The cycle was unique. As well as the two containers either side of the back wheel which housed a change of clothing and toiletries, he had constructed a wooden trailer that fitted to the seat of the cycle and contained his survival gear - a small tent, sleeping bag and the tools of his trade. The added load meant it was hard going, especially on inclines; in the Cotswolds there were many.

He negotiated his transport onto the main road and pushed off, his ten-speed Derailleur gears taking the strain. A wind had got up from the south, opposing him, as if trying to bar his way as he pedalled relentlessly onwards towards his final stop.

The stiff breeze did little to reduce the temperature; sweat glistened on his forehead and dripped down his face; his tee shirt stuck to his chest. Traffic on this hot summer's early evening was relentless, day-trippers taking in the beauty of everything that the area could offer. They seemed oblivious to his presence and created concern for his own safety.

There were compensations; he felt at home on the open road, the trees magnificently luxurious and hedgerows full of life. He spotted several birds of prey circling for rodents; a Barn Owl flew across in front of him as he passed one of the many wooded areas. He rode on.

It was about eight o'clock when he detected the change. Nature seemed to be shutting down. He found a lay-by at the top of a long drag and took stock. He was high up having negotiated a steep incline that seemed to go on and on; another six miles, maybe less perhaps, an hour or so, he thought; but the skies worried him. He knew the signs. Living at one with the countryside for almost seven years he could tell. The billowing Cumulus with their Fractus companions would herald a thunderstorm. He watched from his vantage point as the storm built behind him, dark and foreboding. It wouldn't be long. He could see distant flashes, sheet lightning reflecting among the clouds as if playing hide and seek; now you see me, now you don't. It wouldn't be long.

He took a drink and retrieved his yellow oilskin from the pannier and fastened it around his shoulders. He was going to need it.

The traffic had gone; he was alone, others had detected the danger.

He cycled on, the road stretched out in front of him as straight as an arrow courtesy of Roman engineering. Another fifteen minutes, it was on him; first pitter-patter drops, teasing, tantalising, tormenting, then a deluge. In the distance he could see the lights of Drayburn guiding him home like a beacon; three miles said the sign post. The torrents poured down the gullies and, blocked by falling debris, created pools of flood water which stretched out into the middle of the road. Hitting them caused him to grind to a halt and threaten his stability. Occasional traffic roared past him spraying cascades of water to drench him. His bare legs and old trainers were soaked and despite his exertions he felt cold. Then in a moment his guiding lights were gone; it was pitch black. His battery powered lamp perched on his handle bars did little to highlight the road ahead. Lightning created weird patterns in the sky and lit the way, the distant church spire, like a needle pointing skywards, his beacon.

Rain, torrential, wet, cold, numbed his senses.

Another twenty minutes and he saw the junction ahead; the familiar sight of the garage on the opposite side of the road marked the turning. It was in darkness, another victim of the storm. He turned left off the main road that would continue onward and by-pass the village towards Aqua Sullis and the south. A small sign, 'Drayburn ¼ mile', it said, directed him; the only acknowledgement that the village existed to the unknowing world.

He was able to free-wheel down the steep hill into the centre. The houses unlit as if dead, but he knew the way; he wasn't to be denied. It would take more than a thunderstorm to deter him. He passed the White Hart on his left on the corner of the High Street. He could see people staring out of the window watching the storm; candles lit the tables inside, a welcoming sign of life. Water raced down the road in floods faster than he could ride and, where the drains couldn't cope, it swamped the pavement. He squinted through the cascade and suddenly it was there, in front of him, the church; its spire standing almost in defiance as the flashes of lightning danced around it mockingly, as if showing what almighty power it could unleash any time it wanted.

The last few yards and he had reached the vicarage. He got off his bike and breathed deeply taking in oxygen sending refreshing blood to his aching muscles. He stretched his arms and legs to enhance the recovery process.

He wheeled his bike and trailer and leant it against the boundary wall of the vicarage, under a tree. It would provide little protection for his transport. He left his gear on the trailer and opened the wooden gate to the right and walked to the kitchen door. He felt like he was home.

He knocked gently so as not to alarm the occupants. Tap, tap; tap, tap. He heard a scream from within.

A concerned face stood in front of him, bathed in the dim light of a candle. There was a momentary stare then, "Michael?" he said.

With his full beard and oilskin the man resembled more a trawler-man. He was ushered in and stood for a moment, the water draining down the yellow plastic from his face and hair creating puddles on the stone floor.

Then, as if by way of greeting, the lights returned. The man could see the vicar's wife picking up the remnants of a china mug off the floor.

"Michael, how good to see you again," said the vicar. "I didn't recognise you at first. The beard, you look so different. Here take off that raincoat and dry off. Would you like some tea?"

"Michael," said Denise. "It's good to see you again. You gave me such a fright."

"I'm sorry. Didn't mean to startle you," said the man softly. His accent familiar from previous visits but not regionally distinctive. There was great debate in the household. Denise thought she detected a hint of Irish but the vicar thought it was more Midlands, not the rather vulgar twang of Birmingham and the Black Country, instantly recognisable, but the more subtle tones of Coventry,

Nottingham or Leicester perhaps. Whatever, it was still a mystery. No-one, not even his hosts for these recent years had been able to ascertain any detailed background of their enigmatic visitor.

"Thank you, yes," he added as he released the fastening of his water-proof and dropped it to the floor. His tee-shirt was stained with water and stuck to his chest, his blue denim shorts clung to his lower torso like swimming trunks; Denise quickly averted her gaze from the outline. His legs were covered in hairs, coiled like barbed wire and were splattered with mud; his trainers sodden.

"Here, you must get out of those wet things," said Denise. "John, go and get a pair of trousers and a shirt from the wardrobe," and the vicar was duly dispatched upstairs and came back a few minutes later holding the necessary apparel. Michael stood there, water dripping down his neck from his bedraggled hair.

"You can change in the downstairs loo. There's a clean towel in there, use that. You know where it is," said Denise.

"Thank you," said the man and he took off his trainers and followed the vicar into the hall and to the aforesaid toilet, leaving a trail of footprints behind him. The downstairs washroom was a good size, regularly used by visitors, and there was plenty of space for Michael to dry himself and freshen up and after a few minutes he returned to the kitchen wearing the vicar's shirt and trousers.

As he came back into the kitchen Denise presented him with a steaming cup of tea.

"They almost fit you," she said and laughed looking at the baggy trousers. There were no more holes on the belt to fasten the buckle so Michael had tied it in a knot to hold them up.

Denise looked at him; he was an attractive man, about the same height as her husband, maybe an inch shorter, but lean and muscle-toned although not with the extreme of a body-builder's physique. She remembered last year he had been the main topic of conversation of many of the Ladies' Circle meetings. Not that she was involved in any licentious behaviour or lascivious gossip; her position as vicar's wife was respected by all, but out of her earshot she was certain that the chatter was far more risqué. She remembered that none of them could agree on his age - there was a lot of argument about that, but late thirties/early forties was the general consensus.

"Thank you," he said as she passed him his tea. She noticed his hands as he took the mug; white from the cold rain. Another rumble of thunder echoed across the valley, but more distant.

"Storm's passing," he said as he took his first sip.

"Thank goodness," said Denise. "I can't remember one as bad as that for some time," she added.

John returned with the man's wet things. "Denise will wash these through for you, won't you dear?" he said.

"Yes, of course. I'll have them ready for you tomorrow," she said.

"Thank you. I have spare but they will be damp too I expect," said Michael.

"Do you want anything to eat?" asked Denise. "I have some crackers and cheese."

"Yes, please," said Michael. "Thank you."

Denise went to the pantry and fetched the food. Then took three plates from the cupboard and served. The three of them sat round the table eating the savoury biscuits with a generous medium cheddar and some homemade pickled onions and chutney; not a feast, but to Michael it felt like one. They watched him eat; it was like he hadn't seen food in a while despite the fairly recent stop. There was an urgency as he devoured biscuit after biscuit.

The conversation was convivial but not too enlightening.

"How have you been?"

"Fine."

"What have you been doing for the past nine months?"

"This and that."

Not a deliberate cat and mouse game but Michael's way which the vicar respected.

They did learn of his recent travels and the difficulty of the journey, Evesham, Stonington.

"Wouldn't want to go through that again in a hurry," he proffered.

After consuming the cheese and another packet of crackers, Denise suggested that John took their visitor to the Lodge. It was still raining but with less ferocity, more a sharp shower.

"I have aired the rooms and the sheets are fresh on," she said. "Oh, take this bottle of milk and some bread. I'll get Brian to drop round some more supplies tomorrow if that's ok?" she replied. "Just let me have list of things you need."

"Thank you," said Michael.

John put on a raincoat and wellingtons and took the milk and bread from his wife. "I'll carry these for you," he said.

Michael slipped his still-wet trainers on his feet and thanked his hostess.

"You've been very kind. I'm very grateful," he said. "I'll check with you tomorrow and get to work," he said.

"Good night," said Michael, and he followed the vicar back to the gate to fetch his cycle and trailer.

The Lodge was the other side of the vicarage about twenty yards further down the footpath. It was once a store or barn of some sort but had been converted many years ago by the vicar's predecessor into a self-contained residence. Small and basic but comfortable and with every convenience. John opened the gate and waited for Michael to negotiate his cycle through and back up the path past the kitchen and round the back of the house.

The vicar took out a set of keys and unlocked the Lodge and put on the light. There was no entrance hall and the door opened directly onto a small sitting room which was equipped with a settee, a wooden dining table with two chairs. There was no TV but John had provided a portable radio which would ensure Michael had some entertainment if needed. He had little time for TV he had said in previous years.

"It's pretty well how you left it," said the vicar. "No-one has used the Lodge since; although I have on occasions retreated here when I want to concentrate. There's a certain solitude I find; good for writing sermons when I don't want to be disturbed."

Through the sitting room there was a single bedroom to the right with a tall-boy and a double bed. Next to that, a small toilet and shower then on the left a kitchenette which had a sink, drainer, cupboards, a fridge and a two-hob cooker and grill."

"I can get you a microwave tomorrow. One of the parishioners has a spare and asked if I knew someone who would want it," said the vicar.

"Thank you, very grateful" said Michael.

The vicar gave him the keys and wished him goodnight leaving Michael to sort himself out.

Michael had parked the cycle next to the front door and he went back outside to retrieve his two saddle-bags and took them into the Lodge. He would leave the rest of his things till morning.

The room smelt clean with just a hint of furniture polish. Nothing like the smells to which he had become accustomed.

He went into the kitchen and put the milk which the vicar had left on the draining board into the fridge. Then took his two bags and placed them on the work top and took out the contents. He had wrapped the clothes in a plastic carrier bag and had more or less survived the earlier deluge. He shook them to get them somewhere close to their normal shapes. The creases he could live with. He took out his toilet bag and took it to the bathroom. There was something he would need to do in the morning. Then there was his other bag, deliberately innocuous. He opened it up and checked. It was all there, the roll of fifty pound notes, his keep-money which would last him the summer with any earnings he hoped to make. He took the notes and put it back in its carrier and placed at the back of the bedside cabinet next to the bible. It would be safe there.

The vicar was back in the vicarage helping his wife with the washing up.

"Well that's a surprise," she said. "Fancy Michael turning up in all that rain. It must have been an awful journey. He did make me jump though when he appeared at the window. He looked quite... ghostly. Like an apparition almost." She shivered. "Brrr," she said out loud.

The vicar looked at her and frowned disapprovingly; he did not believe in such things.

"Yes, I don't know how he does it," he said changing the atmosphere. "I wouldn't have tried it in this weather. It's funny I was just thinking, the first time he came, I had no idea it would become a regular thing."

First week in June 1980, another Sunday, Reverend Colesley was walking down the yew-lined footpath and had reached the boundary wall when he spotted a man next to his bicycle sat on the bench seat opposite the entrance to the churchyard. He was drinking from a bottle and at first the vicar thought it was another vagrant but there was something different about him. He made

The Tinker

eye contact and instead of turning away and walking on, the vicar crossed the road to greet the traveller. "Have no idea why," he had often said when relating this story.

The man was dishevelled and unkempt with long hair and three days' worth of stubble. It was a warm day but the man was wearing an old raincoat, the vicar would recall.

"Hello," said the vicar. "Just passing through?" he asked.

"Not sure," said the man. "But I'll do a good day's work for a meal and a bed," he added.

Without thinking the vicar responded. "You better come with me," and he led the man to the vicarage.

"You can leave your bicycle there," he said at the gate to the house. "It will be quite safe."

The two of them walked up the garden path to the kitchen door and the vicar went in.

"Are you there, dear?" the vicar called out. "I have a visitor."

His wife came into the kitchen from the hall. The man was stood in at the kitchen door.

"Hello," she said.

"This is... sorry I don't know your name," he said.

"Just call me Michael," the man replied.

"Looking for work," said the vicar, "and a place to stay. Thought he could have the Lodge," he added.

"It's not very clean... and the bed's not made up," said his wife, clearly not enamoured with the prospect of a stranger around the house.

"I'm sure it won't take long to tidy it up and make the bed," said the vicar, not put off by his wife's apparent reluctance.

"I don't want to be any trouble," said the man.

"It's no trouble," said the vicar. "Could you rustle up some food, dear?"

He looked at his wife whom he knew had been forced into a corner.

"Very well. Sit down there. I'll see what I can find," she said but with little enthusiasm. If she was honest she admitted later that she felt uncomfortable. He looked like a tinker, she thought somewhat disparagingly. Despite her Christian beliefs this was perhaps a gesture too far.

The vicar joined the man at the table and wanted to know more about him.

"So... Michael, where are you from?" he asked.

Michael looked at the vicar. His eyes were a vivid blue, but it was not a penetrating stare just acknowledging the question.

"Came down from Stonington this morning," he replied.

It was not what the vicar was after but he realised he was not going to get too far with an interrogation.

"What brings you to Drayburn?" The vicar tried another tack.

"Stopped for a drink," said Michael.

Denise came in from the pantry carrying some bread and a slab of cheese. "I'll just see if we have any salad left," she said and went to the fridge and retrieved a wooden salad bowl with the leftovers from lunch time, a couple of tomatoes, lettuce and a quarter of a cucumber. She set out a place setting in front of the man.

"Would you like some tea to go with that?" she asked.

"Yes please, thank you," he said and started applying butter to a slice of bread.

"I'll just go and sort out the Lodge," said the vicar and he left the kitchen into the garden and headed to the annex.

He opened up. It was a warm night and the room was musty from being closed up. The vicar opened a window and set about making up the bed. The sheets and blankets were folded on a chair next to it.

The Tinker

Twenty minutes later the vicar was back in the kitchen of the vicarage and Michael was talking to Denise having finished his food. The salad bowl was empty and the cheese had gone.

She looked at her husband and seemed more relaxed now.

"Michael was telling me he can turn his hand to most jobs around the house, plumbing, electrical work as well as gardening. I told him there's plenty of things need doing around here and at the church which will keep him busy. I suggested he gives it a week and see how it goes. What do you think?"

The vicar was surprised at his wife's apparent change of heart.

"Yes... yes, if Michael is happy."

"That's very good of you. Thank you," he replied.

The week turned into three months and other villagers also made the most of 'the Tinker's' skills. No money changed hands for the church work or jobs at the vicarage - he insisted on that in exchange for his board and lodgings but he did charge other villagers which kept him in pocket money. Not that he needed a great deal; apart from the necessary toiletries he rarely spent anything. He didn't drink or smoke; in fact when he wasn't working he spent most of his time in the Lodge reading.

That was the start of a special relationship between Michael and the village. He returned the same time in successive years and was welcomed warmly in Drayburn; he was one of them.

1986 would be different.

Chapter Three

Michael lay in bed; thunder was still echoing around the valley but less frequent. The storm had blown itself out or moved on to wreak havoc on another community. His legs were stiffening as a result of his earlier labours but he was warm and comfortable. Different from the temporary roadside camp he had endured the previous day.

He drifted off but it was a fitful sleep; adrenaline still coursed around his body programmed by his survival instincts. He would not normally allow himself the luxury of deep sleep; it was conditioned and went back to an earlier life.

Dreams came to him, a reflection of past events or a portent of what was to come; he couldn't tell. There was one, a recurring theme which he knew all about... a bar, raised voices, threat, then blackness; it repeated time and time again; tonight there would be no exception. He woke with a start; the room was in total darkness. Soaked with sweat, he went to the window, opened it wide and inhaled. The air smelt good, the rain had released the pollen from a million plants and there was freshness as if it had been injected with additional oxygen. Behind the church he noticed an orange tinge to the sky, the hint of daybreak. Four a.m. he reckoned. He reached for his bottle of water and took a mouthful and returned to his slumbers.

This time he did fall into a deep sleep and woke again at 7.30 when he heard a tap on the door. Momentarily disorientated he put on his remaining pair of shorts and staggered to the door. He opened it and blinked in the bright sunshine; the vicar was standing there.

"Sorry Michael, didn't mean to disturb you but we wondered if you would like to join us for breakfast. Denise said she would do one of her special fry-ups."

"Yes, yes thank you. Can you give me a few minutes to freshen up and have a shower."

"Of course. Shall we say eight o'clock?" replied the vicar.

"Thank you. I'll see you at eight," and the vicar went back to the house.

Michael tried to clear his head; he was still feeling the effects of his night's sleep, like a bad hangover.

He went back to the bedroom and retrieved his wash-bag and took out a pair of scissors, then carefully started to snip away at his sea-dog beard. Now he was on 'home' territory again he would dispense with his traveller's appearance. The hair dropped into a carrier bag and once he had the facial hair reduced to medium stubble he could use a razor. He went to the bathroom and finished the job. His face felt raw but he was pleased with the result. His sun-bleached fair hair resembled an Australian Life Guard's, shoulder length but looked matted and dishevelled from the rain. A shower would sort that out; he might even pay a visit to the salon. Now that would certainly announce his arrival, remembering Mrs Audley's capacity for gossip from previous years.

Just before eight he had finished his ablutions, left the Lodge and knocked on the kitchen door. Denise opened it and was taken aback.

"Michael? You look so different. Come in," she said.

He was dressed in his second tee shirt, cut-off jeans and working boots and socks. Denise looked different too. She was encased in an apron but was definitely wearing makeup and just a hint of perfume.

The vicar came in and joined them as Michael was about to sit at the table.

"Morning Michael, how are you after that journey yesterday," he asked sitting opposite his guest.

"Fine, vicar thank you. Had a good night's sleep, works wonders."

"Was the bed comfortable?" he enquired.

"Yes, fine thank you," Michael replied.

Denise dished up the breakfast, eggs, tomatoes, fried bread, mushrooms with tea and toast, a proper Cotswold breakfast she said.

"So what have you got for me?" asked Michael as he made light work of his food.

It was John that answered.

"Well I thought you could give Jack Fleming a hand. He's struggling to keep the graveyard tidy at the moment. Not just the weeds but litter; it's becoming a bit of a problem," he said.

"I'll get onto it straight after breakfast," Michael replied and accepted another round of toast from Denise.

So by nine o'clock Michael followed the vicar into the church and down to the crypt underneath the nave where all the implements he would need were kept. Michael knew it well and most of the tools were in the same place he had left them the previous September. Some of them, like the long-handled scythe dated back to the eighteen hundreds but provided no challenge for Michael's expert hand.

There was not a cloud in the sky as Michael set to his labours and the oppressing humidity of the previous day had gone. He was glad of that; it was as though the previous evening's tempest had not happened. The only evidence was the puddles of water that lay in the pot holes of the road but they too would be gone soon, evaporating back to where they had come.

The verger arrived about nine thirty and could see Michael cutting back areas of grass from around the gravestones. The ground was sodden from last night's downpour and the water was beginning to seep through Michael's boots.

"Hello Michael," said Jack as he approached the visitor. "I didn't know you had arrived. When did you get here?" he asked.

"Last night," replied Michael, leaning on his scythe and taking a breather.

"What in all that rain?" said the verger as he walked up to Michael and shook his hands warmly.

"Aye," said Michael.

"Well it is good to see you again. We miss you when you go back, you know, the vicar, Mrs Colesley; we all do,"

"Thank you. It's good to be back," and he picked up a long-handled wooden corn rake and started putting the cut grass into piles for later collection. Jack Fleming continued into the church to report to the vicar.

The storm had been the major topic of conversation but Michael's arrival was about to overtake that.

First to spot him was Melanie Draper, one of Mrs Audley's stylists. A life-long resident of Drayburn she had married ten years earlier at seventeen and had regretted it ever since. Her husband who worked as a mechanic at the local garage on the by-pass was by her own admission a 'waste of space' and she was renowned for her outrageous behaviour and even more outrageous taste in clothes. Her present trend was 'Goth' and she had died her natural auburn hair jet black matching her nail polish, lipstick and eye make-up which made her look like a corpse. Her appearance had caused a great deal of consternation in Drayburn's only hair-dressing establishment. Several older folk had refused to be tended by her in recent weeks and had protested to Mrs Audley that she did something about it. "I will have a word," she had said but it had fallen on considerably-pierced deaf ears.

She was walking past the churchyard to start her ten o'clock shift when she noticed someone working around the gravestones. "It can't be," she said to herself but as he turned round she could see it was. Michael's tanned torso she would recognise anywhere; she had stared at it frequently enough in the past and imagined all kinds of possibilities. He had dispensed with his tee shirt and his wiry-haired chest glistened with sweat in the warm sun. She stopped in her tracks and crossed the road.

"Hello Michael," she shouted,

Michael stopped his grass cutting and acknowledged the greeting.

"Hello," he said, not making the connection and wiped his brow with his handkerchief to remove sweat from his eyes.

"It's Melanie... from the salon," she clarified.

"So it is. I didn't recognise you. You look... different."

Melanie wasn't sure if that was a compliment or not.

She looked at him up and down. "When did you get in?" she asked.

"Arrived last night," he said.

"Will we be seeing you in the salon?" she asked.

"Was thinking of getting a trim later. It's warm work," he said.

"I'm free at four," she said rather too quickly.

"Aye," said Michael. "Should be able to do that."

"See you later, then," she said and crossed back over the road with what seemed an extra skip in her step.

That momentary sighting had opened the flood gates. Within ten minutes of Melanie arriving at the salon it was across the village. Tina Ashworth was having her daily hair wash and made a mental note; she was not giving anything away. As soon as she had left Mrs Audley's she was in her yellow Spitfire and roaring down the narrow streets. She pulled up outside the churchyard and could see him some distance away around the side of the church. She was dressed casually, sunglasses of course, with cropped tee shirt, very short skirt and a pair of sandals. She carried a small handbag.

She walked up the path towards the church entrance and turned right. She could see Michael picking up bails of dead grass and taking them to a compost heap at the far end of the church yard. She watched him for a moment waiting for him to return to his spot. Something she was not used to doing. People generally waited for her.

She walked closer.

"Hello Michael," she said when he was in earshot. She lifted her sunglasses up so they were on her forehead and put her hand up the shield her eyes from the sun; she wanted eye contact.

"Hello Tina," he replied. Recognition was instant; there was only one Tina Ashworth.

"I heard you were back. Wondered if you would be able to service my boiler again. It worked perfectly all winter. I think you must have the magic touch, darling," she said. "I may have some other jobs for you too, a day's worth at least. If you're interested," she added.

"Aye," he said. "When?"

"Let me see," she said taking out her diary from her handbag to give the impression she was a busy person. It was blank if the truth be known.

"How about Wednesday?" she said not wishing to be too anxious.

"Aye," said Michael. "I can do that. Still at Ridge Cottage?"

"Yes," she said. "Fancy you remembering the name."

Michael had been programmed to remember detail in a former life.

"See you at nine," he said.

"Great, see you at nine," she repeated and she turned around and walked back down the path to her car. Michael could not see her smiling.

Around eleven Denise came up the churchyard path with a carrier bag. The vicar was talking to a couple of the parishioners in the church entrance and acknowledged his wife.

"Hello dear, won't be a minute," he said and continued his discussion.

Denise could see Michael and walked to the side of the church and called him.

"Michael, would you like a drink?"

Michael waved to her and put down his scythe. He picked up his tee shirt which he had draped over one of the grave stones and put it on; it stuck to him. He walked over.

Denise had put a table cloth on one of the larger chest tombs and was setting out three glasses from her carrier. A shadow from one of the Yew trees would shelter them from the sun.

"Hello Michael," said Denise. "I've brought some orange juice; it must be thirsty work."

"Yes, thank you," replied Michael and he took one of the glasses whilst Denise poured from a large Thermos flask.

She was wearing a summer dress with blue daisies, knee length; a straw sun-hat was covering her hair. There were streaks of white down her arms.

She looked at Michael's shoulders. "Don't you use any sun cream?" she asked.

"Never had the cause," said Michael who had finished the glass in one go. She poured another as the vicar joined them.

"Sorry about that, dear," he said. "Bible reading committee wanted to discuss Wednesday's passages."

The vicar looked at Michael as Denise poured another glass of squash and handed it to him. He acknowledged the drink and took a sip.

"I must say you have made such a difference already, a great improvement," he said.

"Thank you," said Michael.

The verger approached alerted by Denise's arrival. The vicar addressed him as he reached the small gathering.

"I was just saying, Jack, what a difference," said the vicar eying the piles of grass neatly positioned around the graveyard.

"Yes, I couldn't have managed it that's for sure," he replied and gratefully accepted a glass from Denise.

"I've brought a few bits to keep you going till lunch. I'll do some sandwiches. You can eat with us in the vicarage if you like, Michael," she said looking at him and handing out some buttered cream crackers. The drink had all gone.

"Thank you," said Michael.

By lunch time Michael had cleared the front of the church, all the right-hand side and half of the rear. He would finish today.

The back of the church was less populated with grave stones which made the work easier. Although bodies were buried there, they were the paupers' graves - for people who couldn't afford for their life to be represented in some way. It was as though they hadn't existed. Michael wondered how his own life would be remembered; what would it say on his tomb-stone.

Michael had often contemplated this, deep in thought as he worked; it's what kept him going, pondering issues of the day, personal things and stuff but rarely did he give himself the luxury of reminiscences. There were some things he was keen not to remember; they were firmly locked away.

He joined the vicar and his wife at the vicarage as arranged and enjoyed a healthy lunch of fresh cut sandwiches and salad. There was something special about local produce; it tasted different. Such a change from the fast food and instant cuisine that Michael was more used to.

"The children are coming home on Friday," said Denise. "They will be pleased to see you."

"How are they?" replied Michael, tucking into his sandwich.

"Fine, thanks. William's in his final year at Exeter. Just finished his Masters in Chemistry. Daniella's at Bath taking Law. We're very proud of them aren't we, dear?" she said looking at her husband.

"Yes, yes," said the vicar having been deep in thought and not really certain of the question.

"So you should be," said Michael. "So you should be."

"So, how is it going, Michael?" asked the vicar, changing the subject. "You seem to be making light work of the churchyard."

"Should finish clearing it this afternoon. Thought I would pop into the village later. I need to buy some more clothes and I want to call in at the salon and get a haircut."

"Of course, you come and go as you please. We're just glad to have you around," said the vicar.

Back at 'Split Endz', the trade name of Mrs Audley's salon, some changes were being considered. Having completed her morning clients, Melanie Draper needed a makeover she had decided, and quick; Michael clearly wasn't impressed by the punk appearance. Probably passé now anyway, she rationalised.

Janice Audley was a dominant character. In her late fifties now, she had owned the salon for as long as most residents could remember. It used to be a bakery before she set up a hairdressing business in the swinging sixties. Fresh from college in Gloucester she had grand ideas determined to knock the sleepy villagers into shape and drag them into the twentieth century. One of her ambitions was to bring haute couture to Drayburn and the salon would become the focal point for fashionable hairstyle in the area. At twenty eight anything seemed possible.

Now the salon had become the very antithesis of what Janice Audley had envisaged twenty years earlier. It was staid and conservative and Mrs Audley spent most her time applying blue rinse to the horsey set. Melanie Draper had at least brought some much needed new blood into the salon. She had even persuaded Mrs Audley to change the name from 'The Salon', its former creation, in an effort to modernise the business. It was no wonder that Tina Ashworth chose to go to Cheltenham for her cut.

At lunch time Melanie approached her boss.

"Mrs Audley, I've been thinking about what you were saying last week and you're right I don't think Drayburn is ready for a 'Goth'. Can you help me?"

Janice Audley was a bit taken aback by the sudden volte-face. "Of course, what do you want me to do?"

"I want to get rid of the black. Can you bleach it for me?"

"Yes, of course. When?"

"Well, now, if it's not too much trouble. I'll get some different nail varnish and a new top as well," she replied. There was a hint of urgency, almost desperation, in Melanie's voice which Mrs Audley couldn't fathom.

"Oh, ok," she said inwardly pleased at her stylist's image change. As she had said, it had not been universally welcomed.

Five minutes later and Janice with required rubber gloves, was applying the pungent smelling liquid to Melanie's hair. The sink soon becoming stained with black dye.

"It's going to take a while," said Janice which of course Melanie was well aware but with only one other client this afternoon she would let the chemicals do their thing while she worked.

As she waited for her hair to dry she took off the garish nail polish and started to apply a subtle pink shade then applied a lipstick of similar shade. She had already washed off her eye make-up.

"What time is your next appointment?" said Mrs Audley after she had finished her part. It had taken nearly an hour to wash out and apply the bleach.

"Two thirty. I want to pop next door to Marjorie's in a minute if that's ok," said Melanie.

"Yes, right, ok," said Mrs Audley still confused at Melanie's behaviour.

Marjorie Appleton owned the 'boutique' next door. She called it a 'boutique' so she could charge premium prices but really it was just a clothes shop which sold just about anything, provided it was made from cheese-cloth. It seemed to be the staple apparel of the area.

Melanie wrapped a tea-towel around her head resembling the 1940's fashion prevalent in black and white photographs and left the salon as Mrs Audley greeted her first afternoon appointment.

Melanie looked at the displays in the window then went to the front door. Marjorie Appleton was just opening up having taken her normal lunch hour in the upstairs flat.

"Hello Melanie, what can we do for you?" she said as she wandered back behind the small counter.

"I need a new top... change of image," she replied.

"I see," said Marjorie. "I did think the Goth look was maybe a step too far for Drayburn."

"Yes, I can see that. What have you got?" and Marjorie spent the next fifteen minutes showing Melanie the rather limited range

The Tinker

in her emporium. Eventually she settled for a peasant top, cheese-cloth naturally and paid the comparatively exorbitant price. It was going to be worth it she thought to herself.

Back in the salon and Melanie just had time to make some last minute adjustments before her two thirty arrived. She went into the small back room which acted as a staff area where the girls could have a coffee and cigarette. For the moment she left the top in the box but removed her boots and replaced them with a pair of sandals that she kept at work. She couldn't do much about her black skirt but if she shortened it a few inches it might just work and without thinking, or measuring, she took it off and went to work with a pair of her hairdressing scissors. She sat there in her knickers and white shirt and viewed her handiwork. Not bad she thought, not bad. She slipped back into the skirt and zipped it up. There were one or two threads hanging down which she pulled out but the end result would do; she just hoped it would have the desired result.

Mrs Audley put her head around the door. "Your two thirty is here," she said, then noticed something different.

"What have you done to your skirt?" she asked.

"Just thought it could do with some alterations. In this weather it's a bit warm," Melanie replied.

"Well there won't be much left if you take any more off," and she laughed.

"Anyway Mrs Blandforth's here," she said.

"I'll be right there," and Melanie Draper went back to work, her hair still covered in the tea towel.

"How are you Mrs Blandforth?" she said greeting the Major's wife, one of her regular clients.

During conversation the topic of Michael came up.

"I hear Michael's back," said the Major's wife. "I've sent

Horace round to the vicarage to see when he'll be free to do some work on the Manor. There's lots to be done," she added.

Melanie smiled. There were a few jobs she would like from Michael and it wouldn't involve cutting grass or pointing walls. She shivered at the thought.

Michael had returned to work and he was piling more hay onto his compost when another familiar voice disturbed him.

"Michael, old boy, heard you were back. Have you got a minute?"

It was the Major with little in the way of pleasantries.

Michael stopped his cutting and went to meet his visitor.

"Hello Major," said Michael.

"Just thought I would catch you before the rest of the village booked you up, what," he said in his familiar military tones. "Plenty of work for you at The Manor, don't you know. Could keep you busy most of the summer. Interested?"

"Yes Major. When?" replied Michael.

"As soon as you like, old boy. The Memsahib has been giving me terrible gip. I said to her, told her, we should wait for Michael, what!"

He appeared to end most sentences with this rhetorical question. Michael couldn't understand why.

"I've promised to do some work for Tina Ashworth on Wednesday... so Thursday?" Michael replied.

"Tina Ashworth you say? Well she'll certainly keep you busy you mark my words if half the rumours are true. Strange woman... Well yes, Thursday will have to do then. I'll tell the Memsahib. Perhaps she'll give me some peace now, what!" and he chuckled to himself. The Major made his goodbyes and left Michael to return to his labours happy with the knowledge that he had been

The Tinker

able to secure his services.

By three thirty Michael had met his self-imposed deadline; the churchyard was finished. It looked immaculate just like the earlier photographs of St James that were on sale at the Post Office. Michael was pleased with his work. Just as he was carrying his scythe and rake back towards the crypt, the vicar came out of the church and walked over to him.

"Thank you Michael, you've done such a wonderful job," he said looking at the picture-postcard grounds.

"A pleasure," said Michael with the tools of his trade on his shoulder, like an infantryman's rifle. "I'm just going back to the Lodge to shower and then I'm off into the village."

"Of course, you said you were going to. Oh, nearly forgot, I've put the microwave in the kitchen for you. May need a bit of a clean but seems to work ok," he said.

Michael looked at the vicar. "That's very kind, thank you," he said.

The vicar smiled. "It's a pleasure," he said. "Have you anything planned for dinner this evening?" he asked.

"No, nothing planned," said Michael.

"Would you like to join us? You would be very welcome," said the vicar.

"Yes, thank you. If it's not too much trouble," he replied.

"About six, I expect. I have a choir practice at eight," he said.

"I'll be there," said Michael.

There was a side entrance to the church which led to the nave but to the right a set of stone stairs led straight down to the crypt. Michael walked down, it was much cooler in the bowels of St James and Michael welcomed the refreshing change in temperature.

Having secured the tools Michael went back to the Lodge.

The window had been opened and the bed turned. The clothes he had worn the previous evening had been washed and were neatly placed on the end of the bed. Michael looked at them and made a mental note to thank Mrs Colesley. The microwave was on the top of the small work surface on top of the kitchen cupboard. Michael did a quick examination; it would do just fine.

He ran a shower, the water was tepid and revitalising and he soaked for several minutes before drying off and putting on his clean cut-off jeans, tee shirt and his trainers which had dried in the sun. He looked at the clock on the church spire; he hadn't owned a watch for many years. Three fifty it said. He went to the bedside drawer and put four fifty pound notes in his pocket then left the Lodge and headed into the village.

There were plenty of people about, day trippers, walkers and of course children, recently let out of school. The village store was doing a good trade. One or two folks he recognised from previous visits waived; others called out to him by name. "Hi Michael," they said.

He acknowledged the greetings with a nod of the head, no dramatic gestures.

His first port of call was the only men's clothes shop in the village. It was owned by Marjorie Appleton's husband, Edwin. Another long standing business, 'Appleton's' had been in the High Street since the thirties; Edwin had taken over from his father in 1976. Michael had been in the shop many times - the jeans he was wearing were bought there three years earlier. Michael had found them too warm for working in and had customised them accordingly.

Michael looked in the window, mostly traditional country gear, even shooting sticks, tweed jackets plus fours; it would be where the Major shopped.

A sharp 'ting' welcomed him into the shop as Michael pushed it open.

Edwin came into the shop from the back room and stared for a moment.

"Michael?" he said.

"Hello Edwin," said Michael.

"Good to see you again. Come for some clothes?" he asked.

"Aye, enough to last me the summer," he said.

The range wasn't great, but Edwin had at least modernised the merchandise and although Michael was not particularly interested in fashion, he wanted to look right. After twenty minutes he had chosen new shirts, tee shirts, slacks, jeans, casual shoes and underwear, enough to last him the summer as he had said. The trousers would need to be altered but would be ready the following day, after two, Edwin said. There was change from Michael's two hundred, not much, but sufficient for his next undertaking.

While Michael was considering his purchases, just up the road Melanie was making her final preparation for his arrival. Unfortunately it had not been a total success, in fact it had been something of a disaster. After looking after Mrs Blandforth, Melanie had re-rinsed her hair and started to dry it. To her dismay the jet black Goth look had been replaced by a strange orange colour. Melanie was horrified.

She wanted to burst into tears but Mrs Audley cheered her up, talking about her one-off fashion sense and brave choice of hairstyle. "A uniqueness," she called it. Melanie quite liked the sound of this and without any alternatives anyway she took out her top from her boutique box and took off her shirt, She thought about removing her bra but thought that might be a bit obvious and would certainly alert Mrs Audley. She put the top on and fastened two buttons in the middle then tied the bottom halves into a knot which revealed her tummy button and stomach. She decided that would do; she would leave the bra showing though; she was more than happy to advertise her ample wares. She dabbed on some perfume hoping it would mask the smell of the chlorine that still hung in the air. Then as a final goodbye to her Goth look she removed all but two of her ear studs.

Mrs Audley came in and looked at her.

"Wow, you look the business she said and I think the hair suits you," she said.

"You do?" said Melanie. "What about the skirt?"

"That as well. You have the legs to carry it off," said Mrs Audley in a knowledgeable way. Melanie reminded her of herself in 1967.

"What will your husband think?"

"Mark? Couldn't give a toss," she said. "I do what I want."

There was a defiance in her tone that took Mrs Audley aback.

Four o'clock and Melanie was looking at the clock anxiously. She hadn't told Mrs Audley about her latest appointment. Time went by and she started reading one of the fashion magazines left for clients wondering what had happened; the minutes ticked by slowly.

Then at four twenty the door opened and Michael walked in with his Appleton's carrier bags.

Melanie's eyes lit up. Mrs Audley was just finishing her last client and twigged straight away that the new customer was the target of Melanie's image change. Not that she blamed her. Ten years younger and she may have done the same thing.

"Hello Melanie," said Michael. "You look different."

Chapter Four

"Hello Michael," said Melanie. "Good to see you again."

Her eyes gave her away as she scanned his body, the customised jeans which left little to the imagination, the tight tee shirt seemingly glued to the contours of his chest.

"What would you like?" she asked, any 'entendres' were meant.

"I need a tidy up," said Michael running his hands through his long locks. He suddenly noticed the rather strange shade tint of Melanie's hair, then looked away trying not to stare.

"Let me take your bags," she said and put them behind the service counter. "Follow me," she said firmly.

Mrs Audley was cashing up; it had been an average day. Mondays were usually quiet and just the two of them were on duty. There were two other stylists who worked later in the week and on Saturday there was a full complement which included two juniors who were employed to wash hair and keep the salon clean.

"Hello Michael," said Mrs Audley as he walked past her to one of the three sinks at the back of the salon.

"Hello Janice," said Michael, more familiar than Melanie would have liked and she suddenly felt a tinge territorial.

There was a shelf stacked with towels and other apparel behind the sinks and Melanie picked up a black apron and placed it over Michael's head and tied it behind him. She took her time.

Each of the three wash basins had their own matching black faux-leather seat which tilted backwards to allow hair washing.

Melanie pointed to the middle seat.

"Sit here," she said assertively, still annoyed at Michael's casualness with her boss. He complied and sat down with his back to the sink. She put a towel under his head and guided it to the

51

wash area and turned on a spray. She checked the water ensuring it was not too hot.

"Is the temperature ok?" she enquired. She knew it was.

"It's fine," he said and Melanie went to work.

"I'm off now," said Mrs Audley. She regularly left Melanie on her own to lock up. Officially Melanie worked until six but if there were no clients booked in she would leave at five. Mrs Audley, as befitting an owner, did what she liked.

"See you in the morning," shouted Melanie and she watched her boss leave the salon.

Melanie was warming to her task and having rinsed Michael's hair she was now applying some shampoo.

"It's new. Do you like it?" she asked as she massaged the sweet-smelling foam into Michael's scalp.

"Yes," said Michael, his eyes closed as the head massage continued. It felt good. Melanie rinsed off the bubbles and leaned across the sink stretching over Michael, ostensibly to brush off some stray water. Her breasts were almost in his face. Michael opened his eyes and took in the view.

"Is that better?" she said.

"Much," he said.

"Hmm," she said.

The front windows had rather ancient Venetian blinds which were positioned so there was no direct vision into the salon from the street; no danger of being observed from the outside. Melanie was on a mission.

Melanie's hands wandered from Michael's head and started massaging his neck. He was still seated with his back to her looking up at the ceiling, his head tilted over the sink. He sat up slightly and leant forward to enable her to continue her work. She was an expert at head massage; it was one of her trademark services.

After a few minutes she stopped and wrapped the towel around his hair and started to rub gently; then led him to an adjacent position in front of a mirror where the haircutting would be carried out.

The salon was in an 'L' shape and this area was completely private. Behind was the entrance to the staff room.

"Would you like a coffee?" asked Melanie, "or something cold? There's some orange juice in the fridge," she added.

"Aye, orange juice will be fine," he said, and she left him in the seat staring at himself in the mirror, his hair hanging loose almost to his shoulders.

Through the reflection he watched her go into the back room, the door gently closing behind her of its own volition.

She went to the fridge and took the bottle of orange juice and diluted it a third/two thirds with water; then made a decision; it was time to move things on a bit, fortune favours the brave.

She lifted up her top and unclipped her bra dropping the straps down from her shoulders. She put it down on the table and went back into the salon and placed the drink on the shelf opposite Michael.

"Thanks," he said and picked up the glass and started to sip.

At first Michael didn't notice the less-than- subtle change. Then he twigged and nearly fell off the chair.

Melanie saw the signs.

"Getting very warm in here," she said nonchalantly and flapped her top in a fanning motion before continuing to clip away at the back of his hair. She waited to see the response. The atmosphere was electric. Both knew what was going to happen but not how it would start.

Feeling more and more adventurous Melanie put down her scissors and calmly undid the knot of her top, then the two buttons and dropped her blouse onto the floor. Then calmly picked up the scissors and continued cutting Michael's hair.

"This will be the best haircut you will ever have," she said. "Promise."

Michael couldn't believe it. He was used to being the object of female attention, a thing he didn't deliberately court; but this was different. He also remembered Melanie being flirtatious the previous year but didn't think any more about it.

Michael stared at her in the mirror as she expertly cut away at the back of his hair. It was a sight that would remain in his mind for a long time.

Satisfied with the back, she went around the chair, facing him and looked closely at his hair. "Just a tad off the fringe I think... Close your eyes," and she leaned forward, her breasts almost in Michael's face. "You can open them now," she said. She hadn't moved.

Instinctively he leaned forward a fraction and took her left nipple in his mouth and started to roll his tongue around it.

She moaned as the sensations, like mini electric shocks went around her body. She grabbed his head and pulled him towards her and fed each breast to him in turn. His hands were under the protective apron that she had placed around him and he started to move them but was admonished like a naughty schoolboy.

"Leave your hands where they are. Leave this to me," she said. Michael did as he was told.

She moved back for a moment and revolved the pedestal around, more room. He was now facing the staff room entrance. He watched as she reached behind her and started sliding down the zip at the back of her skirt. Slowly. Michael's face was beginning to redden; Melanie loved the control she had over him.

Her skirt dropped to the floor and she moved towards him again then knelt down on the floor at his feet and moved the apron to one side revealing his cut-off jeans. She put her hands to his chest and pushed him back in the chair. Her hands moved effortlessly to their task undoing the button at the top of his jeans; the sight of her breasts was already creating a stirring in his loins. She unzipped him and his penis bounced from its confinement. Alert and ready.

She leaned forward and took him full into her mouth wrapping her hand around his penis and started working him... up and down, up and down. He leaned back further to give her a better angle; it was his turn to groan.

Sensing he might finish before she was ready Melanie let go, stood up and took off her knickers.

"Stand up," she whispered.

He complied and she removed his apron then pushed his shorts down to his ankles. His penis stood firm and hard almost at right angles, ready. He stepped out of his clothes. She sat on the pedestal and opened her legs.

"I want you now," she said.

He needed no further bidding and he moved forwards. She opened herself with her fingers to guide him in and let out a gasp as he filled her. She had never felt anything as good. She raised her legs to deepen the penetration; her hands went to his buttocks to control his thrusts.

Michael knew what he was doing and gradually built up momentum until he could hold on no more and climaxed inside her. She let out a scream as she felt his juices flow.

He collapsed forward and lay on her to catch his breath.

Melanie stroked his head, his hair still damp from the unfinished styling, and from his more recent exertions.

"You've no idea how long I've waited for that," she said. "Every year I kept hoping that it would happen but I didn't know how. I promised myself if you showed up this year I wouldn't make the same mistake."

Michael disengaged and sat next to her on the adjacent pedestal.

"You should have said. I don't bite," he replied.

"I gave you enough hints," she said.

"I thought you were just flirting; you are married," he replied.

She got up from her seat and put her arms around his neck and kissed him.

"I'll tell you something which you may or not believe but it's true. I can't stand him near me. I wish he was dead, the useless piece of shit," she said.

Michael wasn't sure how to react. "What are you going to do?" he asked.

"If I had the money I'd leave him tomorrow," she said. "But I haven't so I'll have to put up with the tosser until something turns up."

"I hope it works out for you," he replied. She sat there for a moment without speaking then got up and walked to the toilet in the backroom.

Michael watched her and considered her plight. She was attractive with a great body and there was something about her that fascinated him but he had no intention of becoming her 'love interest', or anyone else's for that matter; it would cause all sorts of problems.

She came back after a few minutes and had freshened up. Michael could smell perfume.

She was still naked and suddenly let out a gasp.

"My God! The front door's still open. Now that would have been embarrassing," she said with a giggle. Michael was still on the pedestal and watched her.

She slipped on her skirt and wrapped her top around her

shoulders, walked through the salon and up to the front door. She peered through the slats of the blinds: the street looked deserted, turned the hanging 'open and closed' sign around and locked the door.

Melanie walked back to Michael who was starting to sort out his clothes which were scattered around the floor.

"Not so fast. I haven't finished with you yet," she said.

She walked up to him and flung her arms around his head and gave him a long lingering kiss. Her right hand moved downwards and found his penis and started rubbing gently. Michael opened his eyes, over her shoulder he could see the clock on the salon wall, 5.37. He didn't want to be late for his dinner at the vicarage but was now in a quandary. Given her earlier statement he didn't think she would take rejection well.

"It's a bit uncomfortable here. What about the back?" he said.

"Come on, then," and she took his hand and led him to the staffroom. It wasn't much better but at least there was a carpet on the floor. It was his turn to take charge. The kissing and Melanie's expert handling soon had Michael ready.

"Kneel down," he said. She complied.

"Now turn around."

She did.

"All fours," he said.

She cried out as he entered her, doggy style.

"Fuck me Michael, fuck me," she shouted. "Fill me... fuck me hard."

Her head tossed back and forth to the rhythm and she uttered a high pitched scream and collapsed on the floor just as she felt Michael's orgasm.

They were both panting now.

"God that was good," she said in between breaths.

Michael looked at the clock. He needed to be careful he didn't want to appear to rush off; there would be some expectation of post coitus cuddling, but he didn't want to be late.

"Yes," he said.

"Will I see you again?" she asked.

"Of course," he said. "I intend to be around all summer."

She planted another kiss. "I don't want you to go," she said.

"I need to be back at the vicarage at six. Mrs Colesley is making dinner," he said, deciding honesty was the best policy. He hoped with the implied consent to a rerun she would be understanding.

"Oh," she pouted." I was hoping for a bit longer."

"Later," he said. "I do need to go."

She got up and cupped her breasts. "Wouldn't you prefer to feast on these?" she said.

"Of course," he said "But they will be expecting me."

"Alright then," she said, recognising she may be pushing things; she had no intention of jeopardising any possible future liaisons.

Michael walked back into the salon and started dressing. Melanie followed him and started rubbing his buttocks playfully as he was trying to put on his shorts.

Michael was beginning to lose patience but kept his cool.

"My bags?" he said as he finished dressing.

Melanie went behind the counter and picked up his carriers and handed them to him. She was still naked and clearly not completely satisfied.

"How much do I owe you?" he asked.

Melanie looked him.

"For the haircut?" he clarified.

"It's on the house," she replied with a grin.

There was a pause. "Wish you didn't have to go," she added.

"Me too," he said. "I'll be in touch," and turned towards the door.

She walked in front of him and opened it.

"Hey, be careful, someone will see you," said Michael.

"I don't care," she said.

"I will be in touch," he repeated as he left the salon.

"You better," she said which sounded like a threat, and she watched him hurry down the street back to the vicarage.

Michael broke into a run. It was five minutes to six. Just about make it, he thought.

The church bells were chiming six as he walked up the path by the side of the vicarage and up to the kitchen door. He knocked and Denise answered it.

"That's good timing," she said, "I was just about to dish up."

She let him in and spotted the carrier bags.

"Oh, what have you been buying? You must show us later," she said. "And a haircut, if I'm not mistaken," she said eyeing his shorter style. His hair was still damp making it look even shorter. Melanie hadn't got around to drying it.

The vicar came in from the hall. "Hello, Michael," he said. "A successful venture?" he asked.

"Yes," said Michael but he had mixed feelings about his recent encounter.

"He's been shopping, haven't you Michael?" said Denise. "And been to the salon."

Michael lifted up the carrier bags to show the vicar.

"Appleton's eh. They will have cost you a pretty penny, I'll bet," he said.

"Not cheap," said Michael.

"Is it alright to freshen up. I won't be long," said Michael.

"Of course," said Denise. "Dishing up in five minutes."

Michael went to the downstairs washroom and quickly washed himself down. He could smell Melanie's perfume and other things.

He sat down at the kitchen table which the vicar and his wife invariably used for meals apart from special occasions or when the family were together for dinner. Denise had made a steak and kidney pie which she knew Michael enjoyed.

Michael waited for the vicar to say Grace before tucking in to his meal and formalities completed, the three started eating.

"Thank you for washing my things," said Michael, remembering his manners.

"You're welcome," said Denise. "Just drop off any clothes you need doing, I'll see to them. It will be no bother," she said.

"Thanks. Oh, and for the Microwave," he said looking at the vicar.

"Hope it will be ok?" the vicar replied.

"I'm sure it'll be fine," replied Michael.

"You've done a wonderful job in the churchyard," said the vicar. "I've had several favourable comments already. Mrs Grace from the Ladies Guild was most pleased. Stopped me at the gate, kept me talking for ages. She can go on a bit that woman."

"Thank you," said Michael. "I remember Mrs Grace. How is she?"

"She's fine. I think you'll have some work there as well shortly. She mentioned something about clearing her attic. Said she can't lift heavy things anymore. I said she could get in touch with you here."

"You'll need your own secretary at this rate," said Denise.

"I'm very grateful," said Michael and returned her smile.

The meal was convivial, or as convivial as Michael would allow; he would never let his guard down, not once. The vicar and his wife were familiar with his defensiveness when it came

The Tinker

to asking what he would see as intrusive questions, normal things like family, in fact anything to do with his past.

The couple accepted it as one of his foibles but it did nothing to quell their curiosity.

"What about tomorrow?" said Michael. "Anything else around the church, or here? Any decorating perhaps? Repairs?"

"The central heating at the church could do with some attention," said the vicar. "It was very cold some evenings in January I remember. One or two parishioners complained. I had to bring in some fan heaters but they are so expensive."

"I'll take a look," said Michael.

"The upstairs tap is leaking in the bathroom," said Denise.

"I'll check it tomorrow," said Michael.

"Thank you. I was saying to John how good it is to have you here," said Denise.

"It's good to be back," said Michael.

It was seven thirty as Michael walked back to the lodge. He had offered to help with the washing up but Denise was insistent. "You get yourself off, you've done enough for one day," she said.

He let himself in and took the carrier bags containing his new clothes and shoes into the bedroom and hung the shirts up in the small wardrobe. His shoes he placed on the floor next to the bed and his underwear and socks he put in a drawer in the bedside cabinet.

It was still broad daylight and early; Michael felt restless. His liaison with Melanie was on his mind. Given her marital state she seemed to be looking for a way-out. He would need to tread carefully, not raise expectations, but there was something about her. There had never been anyone since Colleen, nearly seven years ago now. He could still see her face when he closed his eyes. He would never allow anyone to get that close to him again, never. One night stands were fine, his longest relationship was two weeks but any signs of permanency would be met with 'goodbye'. It was the way it had to be.

He would take a walk and clear his head.

At the back of the Lodge there was a shortcut which joined the public footpath that led around the church. It was a fine summer evening and Michael needed to get out. He hated being shut in; something else that haunted him from way back.

He didn't often do jogging, didn't have the kit or inclination but enjoyed walking; he did a lot of it. He picked up his keys and locked the door. He turned left around the side of the Lodge and set off at a brisk pace. The narrow footpath from the vicarage continued past the Lodge with the churchyard wall to the right about four feet away. The dry stone boundary was festooned with creeping ivy.

After about fifty yards he joined the main footpath which led around the church and back towards the village. He was heading downhill in the opposite direction into open countryside. It was a familiar walk, one he had done many times before and never got tired of it. Incredible views which on this warm summer evening were at their best. The area was beautiful and green, freshened by the rain of the previous evening; trees, meandering streams encased in the vista of the surrounding hills and dotted by stone properties. The path linked Drayburn with Upton Winscliffe, a hamlet four miles away as the crow flies but much longer by foot.

After about a mile the path skirted the Major's land and as he was approaching the wall marking the edge of the estate he spotted a familiar face.

"Hello Michael," said the man.

"Hello Frank, wondered if I'd bump into you," Michael replied.

"Fancy some company? Just doing my rounds," said Frank.

"Aye," said Michael.

There was stile and next to that a gate with a warning notice 'Keep out, Private Land' painted on it.

Frank Johnson opened the gate and Michael walked through. There was another footpath in front of them which headed west, into the estate itself.

Frank was older than Michael, just turned seventy, and had the face of someone who had spent his life outdoors, red, weather-beaten. His clothes resembled that of the Major, tweed, but he was wearing wellingtons; the ground was still very wet. He was carrying a twelve bore shotgun under his arm, broken at the stock, as required for safety.

He shook hands with the visitor.

"It's good to see you again. The Major said you were back. Last night he said. How on earth did you manage in all that rain?"

"Not easy," said Michael.

"No, I bet," he said.

They crossed a small meadow and continued on the footpath towards one of the woods. They talked as they walked. Michael detected a change in his friend; he looked older and his stride seemed laboured as if he was in pain. Michael didn't comment.

"Having problems with poachers again, rabbits and pheasants. Caught a couple of lads by the lake last week. After trout I bet, but they got away."

"How do they take the pheasants?" asked Michael.

"Getting quite sophisticated nowadays, fancy traps, all-sorts. Trouble is the pheasant is such a stupid bird it don't take much to catch 'em," said Frank.

Michael was intrigued.

"In the old days they used to use tree bark, you know," Frank continued.

"Tree bark?" said Michael.

"Aye, you gets a piece of tree bark, like, and make a cone from it. You knows, like an ice cream cone but a bit bigger," said Frank.

"What sort of tree bark?" asked Michael.

"Birch is good but pretty well any tree will do."

Frank was demonstrating with hand gestures.

"You hold the cone together with something. I don't know, a piece of twine, grass, wood, vine, anything like that. You smear some tree resin on the inside of the cone, the stickier the better. Then you fills the end of the cone with seeds, grain, or raisins - they're really good, for bait. Then you puts the cone on the ground where the birds feed and lay a trail of seeds or raisins or whatever up to the cone. Most game birds, including yer pheasants will feed on the trail right up to the cone. Then they'll reach for the food in the end of the cone. The resin will stick to their feathers and it holds the cone to their head. The daft buggers will just sit there, not move at all. They won't struggle or nothing. Then you can walk right up to 'em and kill 'em."

"Get away," said Michael.

"It's right, as I'm standing here," said Frank. "And I've seen them do something similar using silver foil an' all would you believe,"

"Aye, I can see that. That would work, same principle," Michael replied.

Michael got on well with Frank and enjoyed his tales. He was his kind of man and they shared an interest in nature.

The Major's land stretched all the way from the Manor down into a dip where the large lake dominated the scene. It was surrounded on three sides by woods. The fourth side was open which allowed a view of the lake from the house. The two were approaching it through Toppis Wood which was the largest of the three. They were on the footpath leading to the lake from the boundary wall which cut through the trees. A roe deer crossed nervously in front of them. They both stood still so as not to alarm it.

They continued and talked animatedly as two friends would, catching up on news; all of it from Frank. He knew better than to quiz Michael.

"We've got a breeding pair of Great Crested Grebes this year. Magic watching them courting," the game-keeper said.

"Wish I could have been there," said Michael.

"Oh, they're still around. Got six chicks, if we're lucky we may see them," he added.

They were about fifty yards from the lake when Frank stopped in his tracks and put his arm out to hold Michael back.

"Poachers!" he whispered sharply. He stooped down and Michael followed.

"Can you see 'em... on the far side?" he added.

Michael strained his eyes in the failing light. He spotted the two figures crouched down seemingly engrossed in something in the water.

"They'll be using hand lines, I'll bet," said Frank. "We need to get round and come up behind them," he said.

"Ok, I'll give you a hand," said Michael "It won't be so easy on your own."

"Thanks," said Frank and the two of them continued crouch-walking, keeping in the shadows. It was twilight and quite dark now among the trees and they slowly eased their way around the wooded area that skirted the bottom edge of the lake. They could see the two poachers totally immersed in whatever they were doing and oblivious to Michael and Frank's presence.

At the far end of the lake the tree line was less than ten feet away from the edge; some of the overhanging branches dipped in the water with the weight of the leaves. There were fishing holes at intervals which were popular with fishermen paying a lot of money to pit their wits against the bream, pike and tench that populated the waters. Rainbow trout were the prize though and having spent a small fortune on keeping the lake stocked for paying customers; the Major was not about to tolerate a free ride. Frank shared his hatred for poachers.

They could see the two men at the next fishing hole; one of them was throwing a baited line out into the lake, the other seemed to be keeping watch but looking towards the Manor, not behind them. They had a basket with them presumably to keep their catch.

Michael and Frank were now only feet from them.

Frank pulled out two cartridges from his pocket and slotted them in the chambers of the shot-gun and slowly stood up. He gently raised the barrel and there was a click as it engaged. It didn't alert the poachers.

Without any hesitation he walked forward out of the protection of the trees; Michael was beside him. Both poachers were dressed in dark anoraks. The one on guard looked taller than the other and younger, early twenties possibly.

"Right lads, stop what you're doing. You're coming with me," said Frank holding his shotgun as a Wild-West sheriff might do.

Clearly startled, the men jumped to their feet and for a moment there was a stand-off as the two poachers wondered what to do.

"You ain't gonna use that thing, old feller," said the taller man. The other who had been crouching at the water's edge stood up and reached in his pocket. There was something about his demeanour that unsettled Michael. He was gypsy-looking with dark curly hair, matted and unkempt. Michael's natural instincts were on red alert. Suddenly the man pulled a blade from his pocket; there was a lunge as he made a move towards Frank.

Michael was on him in a flash, pouncing like a lion. The man's arm was bent upwards and behind his back there was a scream as his shoulder popped out of its socket. The knife fell to the floor. Michael gave the aggressor two swift punches to the side of the head and he dropped to his knees, crying in pain and holding his shoulder.

Michael picked up the knife.

"Do you want to try your luck?" Michael said to the other man.

There was another brief stand-off while he considered his options but having seen what Michael had done to his buddy he decided he would take his chances with the magistrates. He put his hands up in front of him in submission. "Nah, it's cool mate," he said.

"Right," said Frank who had taken control again. "You, help your friend up to the house. Now!"

The tall one managed to get his fellow poacher to his feet. He was in a great deal of pain and holding his shoulder. Frank marched them up the footpath towards the Manor. Michael threw the knife into the lake as far as he could then followed Frank and the prisoners.

An owl hooted in the distance disturbed from its roosting.

It took a good ten minutes before they reached the estate buildings. The first house they passed was Frank's, the old gamekeeper's cottage that came with the job and had been his home for many years. He could have called the police from there but wanted to report direct to the Major.

It was almost ten o'clock and dark now as Frank reached the front porch to the Manor. He went in and rapped on the front door urgently, dogs, disturbed from their slumbers, barked loudly from inside. The injured poacher sat on the floor of the porch with his mate stood behind him but there was no sign of resistance, just resignation. Michael was stood behind them, vigilant; although Frank still had his shotgun ready.

The Major came to the door and surveyed the scene.

"Caught these two down at the lake, after trout. We need to get the police and I think this one may need to get to hospital," said Frank.

"Right," said the Major, clearly taken aback for a moment. "I'll get on to it."

He returned to the door a few minutes later. "On their way from Stonington; twenty minutes they said. You can keep an eye on them out there; I'm not letting them in the house. Let me know when they've arrived," he said and shut the door. The Major hadn't noticed Michael.

The two men were seated on the paving next to the porch quiet and subdued and said nothing. The older one was groaning occasionally when he tried to move.

After about ten minutes seeing the men no longer posed any threat, Michael turned to Frank.

"If you're ok, I'll get off now," he said.

Frank was surprised. "Don't you want to hang around? The police may want a word, witness and all that."

"I'd prefer not to be involved Frank, if that's ok," he said.

"Yeah, ok Michael, whatever you want. See you tomorrow, eh?" said Frank.

"Aye," said Michael and he walked away towards the church in the distance. As he reached the vicarage gate he could hear the sounds of police sirens echoing from the other side of the village, getting louder.

Chapter Five

The following morning the Major was an early visitor to the vicarage. He parked his Jaguar on the grass verge next to the gate underneath the cherry tree. The ground was littered with white petals from the blossom like confetti. The church clock chimed the half hour, Westminster chimes.

Through the gate and up to the kitchen; as a regular visitor he did not have to use the front door.

Denise answered. "Hello, Major what a lovely surprise, do come in," she said and the Major took off his cap and went inside.

"Would you like a cup of tea; the kettle has boiled," she said.

"That's very good of you, don't mind if I do," he said.

"Thank you for the pheasants by the way," said Denise as she poured the boiling water into a tea pot. The Major sat at the kitchen table and Denise prepared three mugs. "John will be here in a minute just popped to the church to take some papers over to the vestry."

"It was Michael I've come to see," said the Major.

"He's at the Lodge, but he'll be here in a minute. He's doing one or two bits and pieces for me today before the rest of the village get hold of him," she replied.

The door opened and the vicar came in.

"Hello Major," he said, "I thought that was your car outside. To what do we owe this pleasure?"

"Just telling Mrs Colesley here, I was after Michael," he replied.

"Hope you don't want him to do any jobs. We have him booked today," and the vicar laughed. "He's in such demand."

"No, no, Reverend, nothing like that. Got him working at The Manor on Thursday." The Major looked at the vicar with a serious face. "So you won't have heard then?"

"Heard what?" said the vicar.

"Only caught two poachers last night down at the lake, him and Frank," said the Major.

"No, I hadn't heard," replied John. "Although now you come to mention it we did hear sirens last night about half past ten, didn't we dear?" he added, looking at Denise.

"Aye, that would be it." The Major took a sip of tea. "Saved Frank's life he did... Michael. One of them had a knife and went for Frank. After the shotgun apparently, but Michael took him down. Hell of a scrap according to Frank. The bloke never stood a chance, put him in hospital. He was in a bad way when the police came."

The vicar pondered on this information. "Well that's quite amazing," he observed. "Not that I condone violence in any way you understand," he added.

"Quite so," said the Major. "Mind you, I would have shot the blighters if I'd have got hold of 'em, that's for sure. We have the right to protect our property," he said. "Poachers, scum of the earth, what!"

"So where were they from? Do you know?" asked the vicar.

"Stonington, apparently, according to the police. Been caught before, right pair of hooligans by all account," replied the Major.

A shadow appeared at the kitchen door, then a knock.

"That will be Michael," said Denise.

She opened the door. "Come in Michael. We were just talking about you. There's someone who would like to speak to you."

Michael was dressed in his summer work gear, cropped jeans, rolled down woollen socks, boots and tee shirt. He was carrying what looked like an old army kit-bag.

"Hello Michael," said the vicar. "Would you like some tea?"

The Tinker

"Yes thank you," said Michael.

The Major stood up and went to Michael with his hand held out in greeting. Michael acknowledged and the Major shook it warmly. He searched for superlatives.

"Just came to say jolly good show last night, what! Frank told me how you saved his life," he added.

"Oh I wouldn't say that. Just glad I was there to help," Michael said humbly.

"No need to be modest. I shan't forget this. Been trying to catch the blighters for ages. It's not what they take; it's the principle. Straight forward theft, pure and simple. I'd hang 'em if it were down to me, like they did in the old days. They'll probably get a slap on the wrists, a fine, or community work, or some such rot. The magistrates over there are a right bunch of lily-livered liberals. Hang 'em that's what I would do, hang 'em, what!"

The three listened to the Major's tirade; he was starting to go red.

Denise poured Michael some tea. "A top-up, Major?" she said.

"What? Oh, yes, thank you, very nice," said the Major who was starting to calm down.

"Any way, just wanted to say well done, old boy. Jolly good show. Will see you on Thursday, yes?" said The Major.

"Thursday, Major, yes, about this time?" replied. Michael.

"Yes, come when you're ready, got plenty for you to do," said the Major downing the last dregs of his tea. "Well I'll be off," he said and walked to the door shaking everyone's hands as he left.

"Thanks again, old boy," he said to Michael. Then in a conspiratorial whisper added, "oh, and don't worry about the police. We didn't mention your involvement. Had a feeling you'd prefer it that way."

"Yes," said Michael. "Thank you," and the Major left and

closed the kitchen door behind him.

"Well you have certainly made a hit there," said Denise as she started to tidy up the kitchen table.

"Yes, well done," said the vicar, "but you could have got yourself injured or worse."

"Just instinctive," said Michael. "Anyone would have done the same. Now where's this tap you want me to look at," he added quickly changing the subject.

"I'll show you," said Denise.

"I'll leave you to it," said the vicar, getting up from his chair at the table. "Need to get back."

He looked at Michael. "I'll be at the church when you've finished here, Michael, and I'll show you the boiler."

"Right, ok, shouldn't be too long," Michael replied.

The vicar left and Denise showed Michael to the upstairs bathroom and the recalcitrant tap. Michael carried his kit bag containing his tools.

"This is the problem," she said pointing to a tap on the bath which was dripping and had stained the enamelling.

"Probably the washer," he said. "I'll take a look at it," and he went back to the kitchen and turned off the water at the stop cock under the sink. Back in the bathroom he opened up his kit bag and retrieved a wrench. Denise left him to it to continue her chores.

As he worked Michael was contemplating the latest turn of events. He had no desire to become the centre of attention; it was alien to him. Then there was the police. If the injured poacher was to make a formal complaint he could face charges. He thought this unlikely but he was very grateful for the Major's discretion. He needed to keep off their radar.

The poaching incident had consumed his thoughts. He had given no mind to his previous day's dalliance with his hairdresser.

Melanie had.

It was all she could think about. At the salon, Mrs Audley caught her daydreaming on several occasions and enquired if she was alright. "Oh yes," she said in a strange way, husky voice, eyes looking upwards. Mrs Audley thought for a moment she was on drugs.

Melanie kept re-running the event in her mind. On one occasion she had to stop herself from giggling when she escorted one of her clients to the chair, THE chair, where a few hours earlier she had been on the receiving end of Michael's passion. She shivered at the thought. She couldn't wait for a re-run and kept looking at her watch wondering if Michael would make contact with her. He had promised, she had convinced herself.

Then she had a sudden thought, did he have her phone number? She didn't know but if he did ring the salon it would show beyond any doubt that he must have been thinking about her, didn't it?

All these thoughts were going through her head. Michael had no inkling of Melanie's feelings or the potential consequences.

The tap in the vicarage bathroom was soon fixed and Michael went back to the kitchen and saw Denise to let her know. "Would you like a coffee before you start in the church?" she asked.

"Yes, thank you," replied Michael and he sat down at the kitchen table to wait.

"So what was the problem?" asked Denise. "With the tap," she clarified.

"It was the washer. I carry some spares. It's a common fault," he said.

He watched the vicar's wife go about her routines. Michael both admired and respected Denise, someone totally committed to her role in the community and to her husband. He wished he had found someone like her all those years ago.

She joined him at the table and produced a biscuit tin with chocolate digestives. "A treat," she said. "Don't normally have these; they get eaten too quickly."

"Thank you," said Michael.

She looked at him. Her hair was tied back giving her quite a stern look, almost matronly.

"The Major was very complimentary about your efforts last night. Never heard him so animated; he tends to be quite measured," she said.

Michael didn't reply straight away and Denise followed up with another question. "Weren't you frightened, tackling those poachers?"

"Didn't think about it," he said.

"No," she said. "They say the training never leaves you," she added.

"What do you mean?" said Michael.

"Army, police, military. We have been curious, John and I, your background. I said I bet you were military trained," she said.

He didn't respond for a minute thinking how best to answer the question. "Why did you think that?" he asked.

"Oh, just things you have said from time to time," she said. "The way you tackled that poacher... and you are very well organised. You have a focus. I don't think that is bred, certainly not in men," she laughed.

"It's not something I can really talk about," he said.

"No, of course," she replied. "We would always respect your privacy."

She paused and took a drink of her coffee before continuing.

"Let me tell you something which you won't know. We never speak of it, John and I, not even to the children."

She took another drink of coffee; Michael was staring into his.

The Tinker

"When I left school I went to Bristol University, studied psychology. Then after I got my degree I qualified as a counsellor. I worked with several different organisations and charities and did regular voluntary work with centres trying to help alcoholics. I also worked with people suffering from Post-Traumatic Stress Disorder, although it wasn't called that at the time; 'shell-shock' was the common term. This would be in the late fifties. I used to run surgeries once a week at a centre in Surrey that looked after servicemen who had been invalided out of the army through mental health. That's where I met John."

She sipped again; Michael was looking at her intently. She continued.

"John served in the army, in Kenya, during the Mau Mau uprising," she said.

Michael looked up. "Jesus," he said. "I had no idea."

"There's no reason why you would. We never talked about it," she said. "There are events he just couldn't talk about, The atrocities on both sides were unbelievable."

She stared into her coffee cup. "Some of the things that John saw, well frankly, no human should be witness to. One day he was referred to me and I spent a long time trying to get him to communicate. It took many visits. But, eventually, he gradually learned to trust me and opened up. That was also when he found religion. I took him to the local church a couple of times - he never believed in God and after what he had been through I'm not surprised. But I thought it might give him some solace, and of course it did. He was eventually discharged and applied to go to Theological College and was accepted. I kept in touch with him and one thing led to another, and well, here we are. Mind you it hasn't been easy. Even now he gets flash backs from time to time. He wakes up crying sometimes, but with his faith and the support around him he copes very well."

"I really don't know what to say. I really don't," said Michael.

"Well I only mentioned it because you display many of the classic PSTD symptoms. Avoidance is quite typical, particularly with anything that might be associated with a particular trauma. You won't go to the pub for instance, so perhaps there is something in your past that is associated with drinking or bars which you feel you need to block out. You have no relationships that you talk about anyway. So it could be you have been severely let down or you have experienced the tragic death of a close relative or partner perhaps. You seem to have shut down your whole past life."

She stopped while Michael digested this observation waiting for him to respond.

He got up from the table and downed the last of his drink. "Thank you for the coffee," he said. "I better get on, your husband will wonder where I've got to," he added.

"Just remember you can trust us, Michael, we do want to help," she replied.

"I know that, and thank you," he said.

He stopped and looked at her. "I'll think about what you've said. I do appreciate your concern," he replied, clearly disturbed by the accuracy of Denise's diagnosis.

Denise picked up the cups and started to wash them up and hoped that her disclosure would trigger some sort of positive response from Michael. It would take some time she thought.

Michael left the vicarage mulling over Denise's comments in his mind. He also thought about the vicar, now that was a turn up and no mistake. He was familiar with the Kenyan uprising and the ferocity of the fighting; many veterans had been left scarred. He could feel a kindred spirit.

Michael stopped and looked at the sky, it was another warm

The Tinker

day but cloudier and as he made his way up the footpath the church; the yew trees appeared to form a guard of honour. The churchyard looked on in all its splendour; the verger having continued Michael's earlier efforts. Several visitors were milling about looking at the church and taking photographs.

Michael went through the nave and into to the vestry where the vicar was sitting at his desk with a mountain of paperwork.

He knocked on the door. "Hello Michael. Come in, come in," he repeated. "Have a seat."

"Just came to take a look at the boiler," he said.

"Yes, of course. I'll take you to it in a minute. How did you get on at the vicarage? Were you able to fix the tap?" the vicar asked.

"Aye, no bother, just a new washer. Five minute job," he said.

"Oh that is good news. Denise will be pleased."

"Yes," said Michael. "Was there anything else?"

"No, no, nothing. Let me show you where the boiler is," said the vicar and he got up and led Michael down to the crypt where the gardening tools were kept. "It's over here," said the vicar pointing to a large gas boiler in the corner. "What do you think? Will you be able to fix it?"

"Don't see why not," said Michael. "It works on the same principle as your domestic boiler, just a bit bigger," he said.

"I'll leave you to it," said the vicar and he went back to the vestry.

As Michael wrestled with the innards of the church's boiler with the benefit of his inspection lamp, he was deep in thought. Denise's revelations about her husband and her observations about his own behaviour had been unsettling. He had managed very well on his own for almost seven years and it had kept him safe. He wasn't sure if he was ready for any disclosures, not yet.

By lunchtime Michael had traced the problem on the boiler

and was about to start putting it back together when Michael heard footsteps coming down the stairs. The crypt was dark and the three light bulbs which provided the illumination cast shadows.

"Michael?" said a familiar voice. "The Reverend said I would find you here."

"Frank?" said Michael.

The figure approached and Michael was able to properly identify his visitor.

He turned off his lamp and stood up. Frank went to shake his hands.

"Better not, they're filthy," Michael said. "How are you?"

"I'm fine which is more than can be said for those two scoundrels from last night," Frank said. "Wondered if you fancied a beer. Pop over to the White Hart, my treat. It's the least I can do to say thanks," he added.

"Sorry Frank, can't; need to keep a clear head here," he said.

"Oh, right, yes, I can see that," he said looking at the debris scattered across the floor of the crypt.

"Tell you what, I was just going to break off for lunch, get a sandwich. Could do with some fresh air," said Michael.

"Aye, I'll join you. I can tell you the latest about last night's events," replied Frank.

Michael wiped his hands on a cloth and walked with Frank back up the stairs.

"Just need to speak to the vicar," he said and Frank waited as Michael knocked on the door and went in.

"Hi Michael," said the vicar who appeared engrossed in more paperwork.

"Breaking off for some lunch. Boiler's fixed just got to put it back together, shouldn't be long," he said.

"Thank you," said the vicar. "Would you like to join us in the vicarage for lunch. I'm sure Denise will have enough to go round, and Frank if he would like."

"Thanks, that's very kind but I think the fresh air will do me good. I'll just get a sandwich," replied Michael.

"Of course," said the vicar. "What about dinner this evening? Have you got anything planned?"

"No," said Michael.

"Then you can join us then if you like. I'll let Denise know," said the vicar.

"Thank you, if it's not too much trouble," he replied.

"It's no trouble. Six o'clock suit?" said the vicar.

"Yes, thank you," said Michael, and he left the vestry and joined Frank who was waiting at the church entrance.

The two of them chatted as they walked into the village and Frank updated Michael on the latest news.

"Spoke to the police this morning. They came around about nine o'clock, two of 'em They're charging the two poachers. The Major spoke to you this morning about it, I think," said Frank.

"Yes, and thanks for the discretion, keeping me out of it. Appreciate it," replied Michael.

"That was the Major's idea. Mind you the police were a bit confused. Wanted to know who had attacked the poacher," Frank said.

"What did you tell them?" asked Michael.

"Told them he fell over," replied Frank.

"And they accepted that?" queried Michael.

"Not sure, but they haven't been back. The lads didn't want to say nothing. The one in hospital's ok, dislocated shoulder and a few bruises," said Frank.

They continued down the narrow road and turned right into the High Street; the White Hart faced them on the opposite corner. They walked past the salon, Michael giving no thought to his earlier visit, engrossed in conversation. Then it was past Mrs. Appleby's boutique and into the village store. As befitting a general store it stocked almost anything, newspapers, rows of canned and convenience foods, toiletries, a dairy section as well as sandwiches and snacks. It was also the village post office and so was always busy. Lunchtime and it was even more so; there were several school children around buying their tuck. They were queuing at the single till when a smart looking woman, another of the blue-rinse club, spotted Michael.

"Hello Michael," she said. "I heard you were back. Glad I bumped into you, wondered if you were free for a spot of gardening. The lawn is getting terribly long and my Albert can't manage it since he had his stroke."

Michael was trying to recall the woman.

"Mrs. Faulkner, Valley View," she reminded him.

"Yes, when?" Michael said.

"This week? If you're free that is," she replied.

Michael thought. "Could do Friday, afternoon, later on."

"Excellent. That's saved me a trip to the church; I was going to ask the vicar to ask you," she said. "See you Friday."

Michael acknowledged and Mrs. Faulkner took her place in the line three behind Michael and Frank.

"My, my, you really are in demand," said Frank. Michael smiled.

"Got to make a living," he said.

Eventually Michael reached the cashier with his sandwiches and fruit juice. Frank had also bought food and insisted in paying for both meals.

"Thanks," said Michael as they left and they headed back toward the church.

Just up the road from the store an anxious face was peering through the slats of the window blinds watching the two men walk away. There was a shiver of excitement and expectation when she had noticed them pass by earlier. Now the agony. Why hadn't he been in to see her? Melanie was desperate.

Frank and Michael sat on the bench opposite the churchyard and ate their lunch continuing their discussions.

"Just had a thought, how do you fancy a spot of fishing on Saturday... if you're not too busy, like?" asked Frank. "I've got a spare rod. We can take one of the boats out."

"Thanks, aye, its years since I've done any. Aye, I'd like that," replied Michael, in between mouthfuls of sandwich.

"Never knows you might be able to take the vicar back a couple of trout," said Frank.

"Aye, you never know," said Michael and he smiled.

"Right then, that's a deal," said Frank then glanced at his watch. "Is that the time? I'd best be off... I'll meet you by the stile on the footpath on Saturday, around 8.30 if that suits."

"Aye, that'll be fine. Thanks," said Michael, "But I'll probably see you on Thursday."

Frank looked puzzled.

"I'm working at the Manor," Michael said.

"Yes, of course. We'll catch up then," he said and the pair shook hands.

"Oh and if you fancy a beer tonight, I'll be down the White Hart. It's darts night. You can join in if you like. Always on the lookout for new members," said Frank.

"I'll pass if you don't mind, things to do. But I'll see you Thursday probably, and Saturday," Michael said.

"Right you are," said Frank. "And thanks again for last night. It could have turned out a lot different if you hadn't been there."

Michael watched Frank walk away; there was a distinct hobble in his gait, he noticed. Time to go back to work and he collected the sandwich wrappers and put them in one of the bins.

Back at the salon Melanie was considering the lunchtime snub. Why hadn't he been in to see her? He promised. "I'll be in touch," he had said. She needed another plan, she wasn't about to give up on her latest conquest. This one was special; a real man for a change.

Michael had put the boiler back together and went back to the vestry to see the vicar.

"Hello Michael," said the vicar answering the knock on the door. "How did it go?"

"Finished, vicar, it should be fine but I do need to run it just to check," he said. "Wanted to clear it with you first."

"Oh that's fine. You carry on," said the vicar.

Michael went to the control panel and started up the boiler. Within half an hour the radiators were piping hot. Michael had stayed in the church to monitor things and eventually the vicar came out of the vestry with sweat pouring down his face.

He went up to Michael. "Well I think we can safely say that the heating system is working."

"Yes," replied Michael. "I'll turn it off now."

There were a few other minor jobs needing Michael's attention, a sticking door, broken lock and some tidying up of the crypt and by five o'clock he had finished. The last hour Michael was serenaded by the choir who were practicing under the expert guidance of the vicar and the accompaniment of Maisie Daley on the organ.

Michael returned to the Lodge and showered and change before reporting to the vicarage for dinner. The vicar let him in as

Denise was draining vegetables.

"Come in Michael, I was just telling Denise about the great job you did on the boiler. I thought Maisie was going to pass out on that organ it was that hot. She complained so much we had to finish early." He laughed.

Denise had made chili con carne served with vegetables and jacket potatoes. The atmosphere during dinner was pleasant but in a restrained way, civilised rather than relaxed. It was the 'elephant in the room' scenario; everyone could see it but no-one was saying anything, so the discussion was about boilers, sweaty choirboys, and the Ladies Guild. Denise had a meeting that evening.

Michael offered to help with the washing up and this time Denise accepted the offer. "John has a committee meeting with the PCC tonight and I have my meeting at seven thirty," she said.

Michael was drying the dishes and Denise was washing up; the vicar had gone back to the church.

"So you're working at Tina Ashworth's tomorrow, John was telling me?" she said.

"Yes, servicing her boiler," he replied not intending any innuendoes.

Denise picked up on this. "Well you be careful, she's just got rid of husband number three so she'll be on the lookout for the next. A strange woman, that one," she said.

Michael grinned to himself; he'd had experience.

She sensed the time was right to ask the question that had been on her mind all through dinner. She didn't want to raise it in her husband's presence, recognising the sensitivity of the topic.

"Did you think any more about our discussion this morning?" she said and looked at him.

"Aye," he said.

Denise was hoping for a better response.

"Sorry, I'm not putting any pressure on you. I just want to help," she said.

"Aye, I know that. Now's not the time, though. It's for the best," he said.

"Ok, but just remember you are among friends here. You can trust us," she said.

"Aye, I know. I never doubted that," he said.

She quickly changed the subject. "Forgot to say, John said to help yourself to any books from the library if you wanted something to read while you are here."

"Aye thanks, I'll do that. I'll look now if that's all right. Not doing anything this evening," he replied.

"Help yourself, you know where it is," she replied.

Michael did. Over previous years he had regularly borrowed books from John's collection. Some of the religious tomes were not to his taste but there were some Dickens, Defoe and other classics and even some Ian Fleming which were more in his line. There were some military history books that Michael had noticed on previous visits which seemed incongruous for a priest but from this morning's revelations suddenly it became clear. He chose two.

It was just after seven when Michael left the vicarage and went back to the Lodge. He was in a dilemma maybe it was time to drop his guard. He had no reservations about trusting the vicar and his wife, it was a mental thing; he wasn't sure he could cope with the retrospection.

He let himself in. Denise had visited again by the look of it and tidied up; she had even made the bed. A skylight had been opened letting in the smell of the country, grass, trees, even horse manure rode on the wind. Small flying insects bounced against the glass trying to make their escape. A butterfly flapped frantically, trapped inside the room. Michael went to the window and opened it wide

The Tinker

and watched as it flew safely away. He took in the evening air - deep, deep breaths; it was refreshing, his mind and body seemed to respond to the healing oxygen.

He was sitting in his armchair reading one of his new books - 'Diary of a Nobody' by George and Weedon Grossmith. He was intrigued by the title; it seemed to sum up his life.

The church bells chimed eight, a sequence that lasted almost a minute. A noise made him jump; his instincts kicked in straightaway. A gentle knock, quiet, unassuming an almost hesitant knock.

Michael went to the door.

"What are you doing here?" he asked.

Chapter Six

Melanie would spend hours in between clients browsing through the magazines which Mrs Audley kept scattered around the salon for them to read. She lived vicariously through them, the glamour, the fashion. She stood at the doorway looking like she had just stepped off the pages of the latest edition.

She had spent most of the afternoon recovering her natural (almost!) hair colouring. The salon had been quiet and with Mrs Audley only having one appointment she agreed to help her, intrigued by her stylist's sudden fashion change. It had to be a man, but Michael? She thought probably not but did wonder given her behaviour the previous day.

Melanie and her husband Mark lived in one of the older properties in the village. It was in a row of terraced cottages on the north side not far from the by-pass which took the main Fosse Way around Drayburn. The church owned several properties in the village, mostly from bequests of previous residents and the Draper's cottage was one of those and specifically reserved for local married couples. With house prices in the area so high the opportunity of buying a house was generally out of reach for most villagers. The rent from the tenants also provided valuable income for St James'.

The garage where Mark Draper worked was the one on the corner of the junction with the by-pass and only a ten minute walk from their house. It was always very busy with passing traffic constantly using the petrol station, day and night. There was a flourishing service department which looked after the mechanical wellbeing of the vehicles of local customers and a small second hand car lot. Mark regularly worked long hours and tonight was no exception. Melanie had received a call at the salon to say that

The Tinker

he would not be home till after ten; the overtime would be very welcome given her propensity for spending money.

It wouldn't matter Melanie was not planning on staying in. "I will be out," she said when he phoned to give her the news.

It had taken her over half an hour to walk from her cottage on the other side of the village.

Michael looked at her clearly taken by surprise by his visitor.

"Came to see you," she said. "Aren't you going to invite me in?"

Michael opened the door wider and moved aside so she could enter.

"This is nice," she said before Michael could say anything.

"I thought you were going to pop by today," she continued as she walked into the room. "I did miss you, you know, yesterday, when you left. I kept thinking about you."

Michael was lost for words. He looked at her; her hair was down, a pale auburn rather than yesterday's rather garish orange. She was wearing makeup but sparingly, just enough to emphasise her cheek-bones, eyes and lips; a professional job that would not have looked out of place on a film set. She was wearing a short dark skirt, a white top complete with shoulder pads, which was all the fashion, and smart shoes. She had certainly made an effort; something that wasn't lost on Michael.

Melanie had a carrier bag from the village store. She opened it and produced a bottle of red wine. "Didn't know what you drank, so I got this," she said. "Hope you've got a corkscrew."

Michael looked at her. "I don't know," he said as he shut the door. "You better sit down."

Melanie sat on the other armchair on the opposite side of the fire place from the chair Michael had been sitting reading.

"What have you been doing?" she asked.

"Reading," he said.

"What are you reading? I haven't read a book for ages," she said. "Never get the time."

Michael sat down on his chair and showed her the cover. "What's it about?" she asked.

"Don't know," said Michael, "only just started it."

"Can we open this bottle," she said waving the wine. "I could really do with a drink."

Michael was feeling cornered. He had reservations about where this was leading.

"Why are you here?" he asked.

"I thought that was obvious," she replied looking at him intensely.

"But you can't just turn up. What if I had had visitors?" he said.

"But you haven't," she replied. There was a brief pause. "Why are you being like this? You didn't complain yesterday. I thought you liked me," she said.

"Look, it's been a long day," he said.

She wasn't about to give up now and got up from her chair. She went over to Michael, behind his chair, leaned over and put her hands on the back of his neck. Then she started to massage his shoulders.

"What you need is a bit of attention, not reading. I'll soon have you relaxed," she said. "I know you like it," she said.

Michael didn't move. Melanie could feel she was gradually winning this battle. Then suddenly he grabbed her wrists. "Ow!" she said. "That hurts."

"Stop it, right now," he said firmly. Michael got up from his chair.

"I said, it's been a long day. I don't want what you're offering,

The Tinker

is that clear?!" his voice was raised. "Now please go!!"

Melanie was taken aback by the anger; she had not seen him like this.

"I thought you liked me," she said as tears started rolling down her face. She wiped them away with the back of her hand.

Michael could see she was upset and calmed down.

"Look we had a bit of fun but I am not after any relationship. I can't give you what you are looking for," he said. "I'm not your way out, sorry."

For a moment Michael felt sorry for her; she had clearly gone to a lot of trouble only to be rejected so forcefully. She was still sobbing as Michael escorted her to the door.

"It's for the best," he said.

Melanie said nothing as she left the lodge and started her long walk back to her cottage. "You've not heard the last of this," she said to herself.

On the way through the village she decided to call in at the White Hart, maybe she would have better luck. She had spent a long time getting ready; it would be a shame to waste it.

She walked into the lounge and conversations stopped as twenty sets of eyes followed her to the bar. She sat down on one of the stools at the corner, her short skirt now almost at the top of her thighs. The conversations started again.

"What can I get you, Melanie?" said Tony Rollinson, the resident evening barman.

"Large vodka and tonic," said Melanie. "I need a drink."

"I'll get that," said a voice on the adjacent stool on the opposite corner. "And same again," he said handing a half lager glass to the barman.

Melanie looked at her benefactor, late thirties, smart, casually dressed, professional looking. "Thank you...?"

"Bradley, you can call me Brad," he said.

"Brad," she said.

Tony brought the drinks over and Brad paid. Melanie lifted her glass. "Cheers," she said.

"Why don't you come and join me; there's a spare stool," he said and Melanie walked around the bar and sat next to him.

"So what's your name?" he asked.

"Melanie," she replied.

"And what do you do Melanie?" he asked.

"I'm a stylist," she replied.

"You work around here?" he asked.

"Over the road," she replied. "You?" she said, having taken three large gulps of her vodka.

"I'm in sales, just passing through," he said.

"Where are you staying?" she asked.

"Here, I've got a room," he said.

"What are they like?" she said. "I've often wondered."

"Very nice. I can show you if you like," he said.

"Yeah, ok, just need another one of these," she said lifting up her empty vodka glass.

Brad called the waiter. "Another, Tony, when you're ready," he said.

"Be right with you," said Tony as he handed change to another customer.

Back in the Lodge and Michael was trying to settle back to his book but couldn't get the thought of Melanie out of his mind. He wondered if he had been too hard on her but given her vulnerability it was a case of being cruel to be kind. She would get over it he convinced himself, eventually.

Later as he was lay in bed he thought again about Denise's

The Tinker

revelations and the vicar's Kenyan experience. It was in his mind as he drifted off and it wasn't long before the first nightmare started - the usual one, a bar, voices, threat and darkness.

Wednesday morning and another glorious day. The sound of birdsong woke Michael at five a.m., the dawn chorus, and he dozed for a while, finally getting up around seven. He showered and changed into an old ripped tee shirt and shorts; it was going to be another warm one. He put a change of clothes in a carrier bag. He ate breakfast in the lodge not wishing to disturb the vicar. Denise had offered to cook him a fry up but having settled back into the village he wanted to be independent.

He was looking forward to the day ahead. He remembered the local celebrity, Tina Ashworth, from last year and her husband of three months; another actor he recalled, but couldn't remember his name. He would be about ten years younger than her, he thought, seeing them together. He paid little heed to their so-called status; it was just another job.

He had made two visits, the first was to sort out problems with a blocked sink; the second was to service the central heating boiler. Her husband wasn't around on the second occasion but on the first call he couldn't believe their behaviour. Hands all over each other. He remembered when he had gone to find them to collect his money after he had cleared the sink blockage. They were in the garden; he could picture them now on the sun-loungers, she was topless and had her hands down his shorts. He remembered attracting their attention.

"Hello, I've finished," he said, not venturing onto the patio trying to avoid any embarrassment. Tina just got up and went into the house without bothering to cover up.

"How much do we owe you?" she said.

He gave her the price and she paid.

He was just about to leave when she said, "we were wondering... can you service our boiler for us?"

So three weeks later he called again and completed the work. This time her husband was away in London, auditioning, she said. She kept going on about how she couldn't wait for him to get back, and what she was going to do to him when he did. Despite her words Michael thought she was coming onto him; it was her gaze, but he didn't respond. Those complications he didn't need.

As he was loading up his bike he also remembered Denise's warning from yesterday.

Today he would need his trailer to carry his tool-kit; it was a good half an hour's ride to Ridge Cottage. To most people it would be a challenging bike ride. It was on the way to Upton Winscliffe, the small hamlet to the east of Drayburn, about five miles away by road. The journey took Michael through the village turning right into the High Street, past the White Hart and the salon. Here the cycling was easy but the High Street was the start of a quite a steep downhill trek towards the bottom of the valley. After two hundred yards or so the houses became more scattered, replaced by trees and high verges. A sharp left-hand bend then the village sign, 'Welcome to Drayburn, Jewell of the Cotswolds', it said. It marked the end of the hill. There was a flat section - about half a mile, as the road followed the course of a stream before it started to climb again. About a half mile up the long drag the trees and high verge were replaced by fields and spectacular views, Ridge Cottage was on the right hand side surrounded by deciduous woods and a high stone wall. There was a ten feet tall heavy wooden gate with an intercom to the right. Michael pressed the button. "Hello", came the distorted response.

"It's Michael," he said.

The gates slowly opened.

The house was beautiful, a little larger than the vicarage, about half the size of The Manor. It had two floors but had an attic running the whole of the top floor which had been converted into bedrooms and a study. There were three skylights at intervals along the roof. The traditional ochre/grey stonework was immaculate. There was a small gravel drive which required Michael to push the bike to the front porch; it was impossible to ride on it. The front lawn and shrubs matched the care and attention of the rest of the property. There was clearly a gardener on the scene. Tina was not the sort of person to chip her nail varnish on menial duties. Her yellow Spitfire sports car with the distinctive number plate 'TNA 10' was parked in front of the stone-built garage to the right of the main building and immediately in front of the main gate. He could hear them closing behind him.

He reached the porch and parked his bike and trailer. Tina was there to meet him dressed in tiny shorts, slip-on sandals and a bikini top; her sunglasses were pushed back on her forehead, her bleach blonde hair tied back in a ribbon.

"Hello Michael. Lovely to see you again," she said.

She went to kiss him as an actress might do, but stopped herself. With the arduous journey, Michael was sweating profusely and his tee shirt was sticking to him.

"Would you like to freshen up?" she asked.

"If that's ok," Michael replied.

"Can you remember where it is? There are some clean towels on the rail."

"Yes, thank you," he replied.

"I'll get you a drink. Lemonade be ok?" she said.

"Thank you," said Michael.

He picked up his kit-bag and carrier containing his fresh clothes and walked through into the small reception area. It was a shrine to her art with citations and plaques. 'Best Up and Coming Actress award, 1972', 'Best Supporting Actress in a Continuing Drama, 1975.' There were various framed letters from adoring fans and autographs from more famous celebrities she had met at functions and opening nights. Nothing more recent. Michael had seen them before and took little notice as he made his way to the downstairs bathroom. He remembered the lay-out.

Hi took his clean clothes from the bag, stripped off and washed himself down. The soap's perfume was pungent, but not unpleasant and he felt refreshed as he dried off and changed into his clean clothes.

Ten minutes later he was carrying his kit bag from the hall into the magnificent kitchen.

"Oh that's better," she said as she watched him walk towards her; shorts, new tee shirt and sandals; he hadn't bothered with his boots for what was ostensibly an inside job.

"You can leave your stuff there," she said, pointing to the central heating boiler in the corner of the room. "I thought we could have our drinks on the patio. There's no rush," she said.

It was the same patio of course that Michael had witnessed the loved-up couple from the previous year.

"I've given Mrs Oxley the day off today," she said. "My daily," she clarified seeing Michael's confusion.

"Right," said Michael, not reading anything into this revelation.

Tina carried the jug of lemonade and two glasses out of the kitchen door and onto the large paved patio. Directly in front of them was a large lawn surrounded by shrubs and trees. The nearest neighbour would be over a mile away.

There were two sun loungers separated by a hard-wood table with a parasol protruding from it. The same sun loungers, Michael recognised, but the table was different.

Tina poured out two glasses and took out a handful of ice from a small ice-bucket and dropped them into Michael's glass. .

"Thank you," he said as she passed him the drink.

Michael was thirsty but refrained from downing the drink in one go.

Tina pushed her sunglasses into position and sipped on her lemonade.

"I do love it here," she said. "Bit cut off from London. My friends keep telling me to sell up and move back to Notting Hill but I refuse. My agent says it's costing me work, but I don't care," she said.

"Anyway why should I?" she continued as if justifying the decision to herself.

She was leaning on one elbow looking at Michael. Her bikini was gaping leaving very little to the imagination.

"You will have heard there have been a few changes since you were here last year," she said.

Michael was enjoying the lemonade.

"What would that be?" he said.

"Oh, you must have heard. It was all over the papers," she said.

Michael looked blank. "I don't read them," he said.

"I dumped my husband. You remember, Jason... Jason Lee Burn, the actor. You met him when you came to unblock the sink."

"I remember," said Michael.

"Piece of shit. Only caught him screwing some slag. In our bed for fuck's sake," she said angrily.

Tina enjoyed using expletives it made her feel like one of 'the people'.

Michael looked at her waiting for the rest of the story; he knew it was coming.

"Yes, I was due to go up to town for a reading for a part but

I could feel one of my headaches coming on so I phoned Aaron, he's my agent, from the station at Cheltenham and got him to re-arrange it. Wasn't much of a part anyway. I mean, do I look like I should be playing a prostitute in Victorian London?" she said. "It was only one scene as well. I told Aaron not to bother if that was the best he could do. I've got standards and a loyal fan base," she said, clearly getting annoyed. She stopped and took another sip.

Michael was sitting on the end of the sun lounger listening politely but not particularly interested.

"Anyway when I got back there were clothes scattered everywhere and I could hear noises from upstairs and so I went up to investigate and there they were as bold as brass shagging away to their hearts content."

· Michael looked at her. There was a comment expected.

"What did you do?" he asked.

"Told him to get the fuck out of my house. A fucking hairdresser for fuck's sake. Boy was I glad we had a pre-nup. I've learned my lesson I can tell you," she added getting somewhat agitated.

That had Michael's attention. "What, local?" he said. "The hairdresser?" repeated Michael, seeing Tina had lost the thread.

"Yes, one of the girls from the salon in the village. I spoke to Janice Audley to get her sacked but she couldn't apparently, no-one else to replace her."

Michael's interest was total. He was sitting up straight, looking at her although eye contact was difficult with Tina's shades.

"What happened?" he asked.

"Well I stopped going for a bit." Which was not what Michael meant but he listened anyway. "But it's such a trek into Stonington every day. I told Janice though, I wasn't having that trollop on my hair. So she always sees to me now."

"Which one was it?" asked Michael who had finished his

The Tinker

lemonade, "the stylist?"

"Melanie I think they call her, dressed up as a fucking Goth the last time I saw her," she replied.

Michael's decision to abandon any future trysts with the stylist now appeared totally justified.

She poured two more glasses of lemonade and lay back on the sun lounger.

"You best tell me what you need doing" he said,

"There's no rush," she said. "Enjoy your drink. Don't worry I'll pay you for the day. I could do with the company," she added.

Michael was still sitting on the sun lounger watching her lay out taking in the sun. Tina could feel his gaze; she enjoyed being looked at.

"Fair enough," he said and sat on the end of the sun lounger with his lemonade reflecting on the exposé regarding her ex-husband and the stylist.

Tina lay there for a few minutes soaking up the sun then suddenly sat up. "God it's hot today," she said and unclipped her top and dramatically dropped it on the parasol table.

"You don't mind do you?" she said.

"No," said Michael.

She picked up her lemonade and finished her drink. Michael watched her. As an actress and someone regularly in the public eye, she had obviously looked after herself; her physique toned, the result of hours with a personal trainer.

"Just popping to the little girls room. Would you like anymore to drink? I have a beer if you would prefer."

"I'm fine thanks," he said.

Tina went upstairs to the master bedroom; it was large and overlooked the patio and lawns at the back. The bed was queen-sized with an ornate wooden bed-head. There were cabinets either side with small antique looking reading lights on them. To the right was a walk-in wardrobe containing rows of dresses and other items of clothing, many of which she had acquired in her acting roles and had been allowed to keep. She had insisted on it; it was like a rock star's rider.

She looked through the window and could see Michael on the sun lounger. She went into the en-suite and took out a make-up bag from the mirrored bathroom cabinet and opened it. Inside was a smaller cellophane bag. She examined the contents then emptied a small amount, maybe half a teaspoon, of white powder onto the glass shelf beside the hand basin. She used an old credit card to put it into a neat line. There was a small straw also in the make-up bag and she used it to sniff the line until all the powder had gone. She pinched her nose and breathed in deeply and waited for the high to hit.

The effects of cocaine are short-lived, around half an hour in most cases which is why it becomes addictive; the need to continue the hits. Tina would not go down that route. One dose would be enough for her present needs.

She went down to the patio and went up to Michael and took his hand. "There is something I really need your help with," she said, and she pulled him gently and led him into the kitchen then up the stairs. They reached her bedroom.

Michael knew exactly what was happening but this was different from his experience with Melanie. Melanie was vulnerable and unpredictable whereas Tina was much more mature; there would be no emotional attachment.

She turn around and lifted his tee shirt over his head. She was no taller than his shoulders and she leaned forward and started kissing his nipples and massaging his chest. Her hands ran down his body to the top of his shorts. She wrestled momentarily with the button but it soon succumbed to her fingers and they continued their journey downwards. She gasped as she found his penis which had already warmed to its task. Before she could go any further Michael picked her up and carried her to the bed, and gently lay her down. He removed his shorts and she watched him move towards her. He tugged on her tiny pants and there was no resistance as he pulled them down her legs and dropped them on the floor.

He moved onto her and she held his hardness and guided him in. Tina screamed as he thrust into her. "Yes... yes... yes!" Then the explosion of feelings as she hit the heights of ecstasy. He quickly followed and rolled over onto his back.

They lay there recovering for a few moments before Tina turned her head and looked at him.

"You can forget the boiler for today," she said. "I have far more pressing needs."

It was five o'clock when Michael eventually left the house having spent most of the day servicing Tina Ashworth's pressing needs. She paid him his daily rate plus a bonus and invited him back the following week to work on the boiler. Michael was more than happy with his day's work. He pushed his bike and trailer to the gates and waited while they opened. Then it was the punishing ride back to the lodge.

As he was cycling up the steep gradient of the High Street, Melanie was about to leave the salon when she spotted him coming towards her. She quickly went back inside without any acknowledgment and watched him go by from the window.

Michael had noticed but was not too concerned. Interest from that direction had definitely cooled it seemed; he was not unhappy about that.

For Melanie it had been a difficult day and she was in a foul mood; Mrs Audley had to speak to her on more than one occasion for being sharp with clients. Her rebuff by Michael had affected her badly; she was not used to this treatment. Even her one-night stand with Brad the salesman had not softened the blow; he was not Michael. Michael was a real man; there was something almost animalistic about him, a physicality and intenseness that seemed to light the very fires of her soul. She wanted more despite her rejection; she needed a new plan.

It had been one a.m. when she got back to the cottage the previous evening and Mark was still waiting up for her.

"Where have you been?" he shouted when she came in. "It's one o'clock."

"Out," she said.

"Out where?" she said.

"Just out. I'm going to bed. I'm tired," she said.

As she walked passed him he grabbed her by the arm and pulled her back.

"I want to know where you've been," he said.

"Get your hands off me, you pig," she shouted.

He went to slap her. "You do and you won't see me again, ever," she screamed.

He let her go and she went upstairs and slammed the bedroom door and put a chair against the handle. Mark would be in the spare room, again.

Michael arrived at the vicarage and pushed his bike and trailer up the path to the lodge. He was passing the kitchen when Denise spotted him and came out to see him.

"Hello Michael. Would you like a spot of dinner with us? I've done enough," she said.

The Tinker

"Thank you," said Michael. "Can you give me a couple of minutes to get cleaned up?"

"Of course, dishing up in ten minutes," she said. "Fish pie," she added.

"Thank you," said Michael and he carried on to the lodge.

Chapter Seven

Sometimes the fates smile on us.

Clotho, the goddess who maps out our destiny, the spinner of the thread of life, weaves a path that keeps us safe; other times she takes us on a different road.

Brad Jackson's visit to Drayburn was entirely fortuitous. "Can you go down to Stonington and meet Matt Hastings?" Andy Gilbert, the sales director for Armitage Agricultural Supplies of Ellesmere Port had said. "Glenda's phoned in sick."

It was one of Glenda's customers and as a Client Relationship Manager she would regularly visit Hastings and other farmers in the Gloucestershire area to check service levels and pick up the occasional order. Brad had only recently joined the firm, less than three months ago and was still learning the ropes but had shown initiative and was impressing Andy Gilbert. "A chance to show us what you can do," he said when giving Brad the brief.

"Glenda usually stays at the White Hart in Drayburn, a nice place, peaceful. It'll give you a chance to get to know the area. Maybe pick up a new client or two," he had said.

So Brad was on a high as he made the journey down from Cheshire on Tuesday afternoon. It was another hot day and he felt good. The radio on his company Vauxhall Cavalier was clear and loud and he tapped his steering wheel to the music as it ate up the miles. The thought of a new car was one of the key factors in his career change; ten years as an assistant private investigator had been far from lucrative certainly not sufficient to have afforded him a new vehicle.

He had enjoyed the work, the unpredictability, the boring analysis, even the long hours, but economic pressures meant that some weeks he had no work at all. There was less call these days for a private investigator. So it was no great surprise when Barry Springer, the owner of Springer Investigations, called him into the office and gave him the dreaded news.

"I'll keep the job open for you if things pick up," he had said.

Brad mulled over these comments. Unlikely, he couldn't see things improving in the short term. Brad had thought of setting up on his own - he had considered it a number of times, but with no capital or contacts it would be a forlorn hope.

Anyway 'sales' wasn't so bad. Although early days, he had got off to a good start. He had the gift of the gab his manager had told him and had already made some new contacts which were beginning to bear fruit. It was his charisma; he had a way with words. "Charm the birds off a cherry tree," his mother had always told him.

The Cheshire Plain, the Black Country sprawl, the gentle hills of Worcestershire gave way to the rugged terrain of Gloucestershire and the Cotswolds. It was not an area he knew at all but he was armed with directions and would find his destination, no problem; he was good with maps. He used them all the time in his previous job.

The village was bathed in sunshine as he turned left from the by-pass. He slowed and admired the magnificent scenery for a moment, then, as any new visitor would, made his way watchfully through the narrow streets. The church spire was omnipresent, standing guard over the neighbouring cottages. He found the High Street with the White Hart on the corner just as his instructions had told him. The entrance to the car-park was just past the main building, on the left, down an extremely narrow covered alleyway. There were scrapes of paint where other less-careful drivers had misjudged the width. It was five thirty.

The parking lot was a small courtyard with bays for twelve

cars marked out on the worn cobbles next to the kitchens. The smell of food permeated the senses as Brad got out and stretched his back and legs. He retrieved his overnight bag from the boot of the Cavalier and went to Reception. It was an impressive hotel, typical olde-worlde, grade two listed he was told. As he waited at the desk he looked around. There was a large lounge/bar area to his left which he could see, led to the High Street. There was a separate restaurant ahead of him with a 'no-smoking' notice on the door. Brass ornaments hung from the black beams that ran the ceiling at what appeared to be every opportunity.

He completed the registration formalities and made his way up the narrow stairs to room 7, lucky seven, he thought. You never know.

Once he had settled in and stowed his gear, Brad phoned his wife from his room; he would add the cost to the bill and recover it from expenses. Having checked all was well at home, it was down to the restaurant for dinner. His meal allowance was reasonable; enough for three course dinner and he made the most of it, finishing off with coffee and brandy which he would pay out of his own money. It was still early, around seven thirty, by the time he returned to his room to change out of his suit. He put on his sports jacket and slacks, comfortable but smart; he needed to keep up appearances; you never know there could be sales opportunities. It looked the kind of place where all the locals would meet up for a beer in the evenings; he was sure he could pick out the farmers. He took a shower.

By eight o'clock Brad was back downstairs feeling refreshed. Not many people around so he introduced himself to Tony the barman and chatted to him in between customers. Brad got the history of the pub and some background about the community. As he had hoped, there were many farmers in the locality and Tony

The Tinker

had promised to introduce Brad to them in exchange for a drink. By eight thirty the bar was busier, possibly twenty customers; the restaurant too was doing a good trade. He was finishing his half of lager when a young woman entered looking like she had just stepped off the set of 'Top of the Pops'.

Brad, in common with most of the clientele watched her walk to the bar. She looked stunning, if a little 'tarty' he thought. She reminded him of some of the sights he had regularly seen in Liverpool City Centre on a Friday or Saturday desperate to get noticed by predatory males. The girl sat on one of the bar stools opposite him; he couldn't help staring.

"What can I get you, Melanie?" said Tony, the barman.

"Large vodka and tonic," said the girl. "I need a drink."

Without hesitation Brad made a decision. "I'll get that," he said.

He couldn't believe his luck when she agreed to join him. It was time to put on the charm. He was a long way from home and here was an opportunity that didn't involve selling agricultural products. This was far more interesting.

The conversation was briefer than he expected and for the price of two large vodkas he was escorting her up the stairs to his room. She was a little unsteady as she sat on the small armchair next to the TV but her voice seemed coherent.

"This is nice," she said. "Is there a mini-bar?"

"Yes, can I get you anything?" said Brad.

"Oh yes," she said. "A vodka will be fine for the moment."

Brad did the honours. "Tonic?" he asked.

"Thank you," she said.

"A four poster," she said looking at the bed. "Never tried one of those before," she added, taking her first sip of her drink. "A four-poster virgin," she giggled.

"We better change that," said Brad.

"Hmm, like the sound of that," she said and stood up.

Brad was sitting on the end of the bed as Melanie walked towards him. She threw her arms around his neck and engaged in a deep kiss. For Brad it was like being hit by an express train. He had never experienced anything like it before. She broke away and lifted her top over her head and dropped it on the floor. Then unzipped the back of her skirt and stepped out of it; she was naked. The fact that she was not wearing any knickers was not lost on Brad, but he wasn't about to complain.

So for the next couple of hours Melanie took out her frustrations on the unsuspecting Brad. She was insatiable and by midnight Brad had to call a halt, unable to cope with her demands any more.

"Have you got far to go?" he asked. "I can get you a taxi."

"It's ok, I only live up the road. I can walk," she said.

Brad wasn't too happy with the situation but she was insistent and so Melanie left the salesman and headed home. For all her exploits she still felt empty.

The next morning Brad had a full Cotswold breakfast and was looking forward to his ten o'clock appointment with Matt Hastings in Stonington. The farm was only about half an hour away he was told; plenty of time. He was in a buoyant mood. He still couldn't get over his evening with Melanie; it was a story he would love to have shared with his drinking buddies but nobody would believe him.

It was about eight fifteen when he checked out and took his bags to his car. Before leaving he needed to go to the village store to get a paper and a few bits for his journey. He had walked through the narrow alleyway that led to the car-park and was stood on the pavement waiting to cross the road when a man on an old bicycle and trailer approached from the direction of the church. The sun was bright, visibility perfect, recognition instant. "Michael!!"

He watched in disbelief as the man rode past oblivious to any possible threat.

Brad checked his watch, plenty of time, and went back inside. "Can I use a phone?" he said to the receptionist.

She directed him to the payphone in a small booth on the wall in an alcove next to the stairs. Not very private but would have to do.

Brad dialled the number he knew by heart. It rang out for what seemed like an eternity. "Springer's Investigations" came an indifferent voice on the other end of the phone.

"Kathy...? It's Brad. Is he in yet...? Right, can you get him, it's urgent."

There was a long pause. Brad fed another 50p into the slot on the front of the phone.

"Brad...? What do you want? Kathy said it was urgent," said the man.

"I've just seen him... Michael!" The phone went quiet. "Barry...? Are you there...?" said Brad.

"Eh... err... yeah. Are you sure?" Another coin went into the slot.

"Positive, I would know that face anywhere," said Brad.

Barry knew this to be true. Brad had a remarkable skill in recognising people and it had been an important asset to the firm, one that Barry missed greatly.

"Where?" asked Barry.

"I'm in a village in the Cotswolds called Drayburn, here on business. Staying at The White Hart. He rode past me on a bike not ten minutes since. What do you want to do?"

"How long are you there for?" asked Barry.

"I'm around this morning for a meeting in Stonington then back home," he replied.

"That's a shame... Any chance you could stay for another night, do some digging for me...? I'll make it worth your while," said the private investigator.

"Don't know about that I'm still on probation. Don't want to rock the boat," replied Brad.

"I'll cover any expenses," said Barry. "This could be the breakthrough."

Brad thought for a moment. "Ok, I'll just check with my boss and ring you straight back," he said and rang off.

He checked his pocket for change, a few coppers. He went to reception and changed a five pound note.

He dialled Armitage's and fed in another 50p into the coin box.

"Hi, is Andy Gilbert in?" he said to the telephonist.

"Andy Gilbert," came a voice after a moment.

"Andy...? It's Brad. Look is there any chance of me staying down another day? I've got one or two clients lined up and I think there's some business to be had."

He held his breath and hoped his lie didn't show.

"Yeah, ok, don't see why not, if you think it'll be worthwhile," Gilbert replied.

"Well I've potentially got another meeting after Matt Hastings, just waiting confirmation. Got to call at lunch time," he said. There was a pause.

"Yeah, ok. Look, ring me later and let me know how you got on. We'll see you tomorrow afternoon sometime," said the sales manager.

"Yeah, great, I'll give you a bell around four and give you an update," Brad replied and rang off.

Brad was worried. He couldn't afford to lose this job but he had an invested a lot of time in the search for Michael and if this was going to be the end, he wanted to be involved.

He went to reception and booked in for another night; luckily room seven was again available. Then he made another call to his long-suffering wife to say that he would be staying an extra day. She wasn't bothered.

As he made his way to Stonington to see Matt Hastings, Brad mulled over the abortive search for Michael, the hours and boring hours scouring electoral registers and military records. Nothing. It was as though he had never existed, but of course he had.

Then there were the 'possible sightings', a bar in Spain, another in Tenerife, even an olive grove in Crete but all met with the same result, a big fat zero. The reward for information, under the cover of a missing inheritance, had all sorts crawling out of the woodwork trying to claim the money. It had led to so many fruitless leads.

Brad began to question his own recollection; perhaps it wasn't him. The photo of Michael on a beach with someone who looked like a girlfriend was a few years old now, seven years, must be. But it was etched in his mind; he felt he knew every detail of Michael Curtiss.

Matt Hastings's farm was large, almost double the national average, nearly two hundred acres. He had an award winning dairy herd, sheep, pigs as well as wheat and barley crops and was naturally very keen to show his interim client relationship manager his enterprise. Brad was there for over two hours but the meeting with the farmer went better than expected and not only produced some good orders but also an introduction to a neighbouring farmer, Jim Randall.

Brad had explained to Matt the revised discount deals and the additional bonus for introducing new business, one of Brad's suggestions, which had resulted in a two o'clock appointment.

He had managed to collect some sandwiches at the farm shop before he left and ate them in the car while completing his paperwork before setting off to meet his prospective client.

Oakgate Farm was about two miles away. Brad arrived a few minutes early and was greeted by Jim, himself. It was a smaller business than the Hastings' set-up but nevertheless was still a sizeable venture. Again Brad's natural affinity with people paid dividends and the farmer signed up for a £3,000 order. Suddenly he was buzzing he had no qualms now about his extra day; he was sure Andy Gilbert would be more than happy.

As he headed back to Drayburn his thoughts moved to his task; how would he be able to confirm his sighting. He had an idea.

He returned to the White Hart around four thirty, registered again at reception and collected his key. His room smelt fresh and there was clean bed-linen. He looked out of the window and could see the salon; the phone number was on the fascia. He dialled the number.

"Can I speak to Melanie, please?" he said.

"Speaking," she replied.

"It's Brad... from last night," he said, in case she needed any clarification.

"Oh hello," she said without any real enthusiasm in her voice; Brad was disappointed at the response; there was work to do.

"I am staying on an extra night. Wondered if you fancied joining me for dinner tonight, my treat," he said.

"I think I'm busy," she said.

"That's a pity, I've got a bottle of champagne. It'd be a shame to waste it," he said.

"Aye, go on then," she said. "What time?"

"Seven thirty ok? Here, at the White Hart," he said.

"Ok, see you then. Look, I have to go, I'm with a client," she said and rang off.

This was not the same girl who couldn't get enough of him the previous evening; he couldn't understand why.

He made his call to the office and spoke to the sales manager who was 'over the moon' at Brad's success. "Tell you what, you can stay there all week if you can bring in those results," he said. "Anything lined up for tomorrow morning?" he added.

"I'm working on it," said Brad.

At seven thirty Brad was in the bar waiting for his dinner date, chatting to Tony the barman. Brad had thought about asking him about Michael but he was backwards and forwards with drinks and didn't want to broadcast his interest.

Earlier he had been across to the village store and bought a bottle of their cheapest champagne; he wasn't paying the White Hart's prices, and had put the bottle in the mini-bar to keep cool. He thought the hotel would not take kindly to a request for an ice bucket.

It was twenty to eight before Melanie walked through the door and into the bar. Brad was on a stool chatting to Tony and watched her. A different outfit from last night, very tight, 'spray-on', pink trousers, pink shoes, a black off-the-shoulder top and a white leather belt. Another of her fashion-statements. Once again the bar seemed to go quiet, like the old Wild West movies when the gunslinger walked in. Thirty pairs of eyes watched her entrance.

She was oblivious to the attention and walked up to Brad. "Vodka and tonic," please she said before Brad had time to ask.

"How are you?" he said. "You look nice."

"Thanks," she said. There was no attempt at a kiss or any other formal greeting for that matter. She sat on the stool next to Brad.

"Good day?" he asked.

"Average," she said.

"I've got a couple of menus. Is there anything you can recommend?" he said.

"You think I can afford to eat here?" she said sharply.

"Sorry... I wasn't... I didn't mean," Brad didn't complete the sentence and went back to the menu. Conversation didn't seem to be a priority; he hoped the vodka might do the trick. Tonight though it wasn't her body he was after.

They chose their meal and went into the dining room to eat. Brad had ordered another vodka for Melanie; he was sticking to his half of lager.

Gradually the effects of the vodka began to bear fruit and Melanie became more sociable. He discovered the reason for her coldness. It turned out that she had had another row at home when she announced to her husband that she was going out again. He hadn't had to work that evening. "Thought we could have an early night," he said.

She finished her second large vodka and Brad ordered a third.

She stared into her drink, her meal hardly touched. She had poked around her Chicken Supreme but certainly hadn't done it justice.

Suddenly she exclaimed, "all men are shits," and put her knife and fork down in an indication that she had finished eating.

"Why do you say that?" he asked.

"Only after one thing," she said. "Then they don't want to know you," she added.

"I'm here," he said.

"Oh yeah, I bet you're married and all, and you'll be buggering off back to wherever tomorrow," she said. There had been little attempt at conversation the previous evening.

The Tinker

"That didn't bother you last night," he said.

"Yeah well," she said unable to counter the argument.

Brad recognised that the evening was starting to free-fall and he needed to raise his question before Melanie freaked out all together. He wasn't expecting anything else tonight.

Brad ordered a coffee. Melanie seemed content sipping her vodka.

"Nearly forgot, there was something I was meaning to ask," he said. She was still staring into her drink. Brad continued. "I thought I saw one of my old army mates in town this morning," he said, as matter-of-factly as possible. Melanie didn't acknowledge. He continued.

"Yes, he was riding an old bike... tee shirt, shorts... pulling a trailer. Michael his name was."

This had Melanie's attention. Her ears pricked up; she thought quickly.

"No, don't know anyone round here called Michael," she said. "That sounds like Ted Saunders, does odd jobs round here. He's got an old bike with a trolley thingy."

Melanie was on alert. Someone enquiring about Michael could mean trouble for him. She suddenly knew she had a way in, back in Michael's good books. She would tell Michael someone was asking about him; he would be more than grateful then, wouldn't he?

Brad was taken aback by the answer. He was positive it was Michael, positive.

"Are you sure...? I could have sworn... It was the spitting image," he said.

"Certain," she said. "Anyway, thanks for the food... better get off," she said. "Hubby will be getting worried."

"But I thought..." said Brad. "What about the champagne?"

"Take it home for your wife," she said and rolled up her serviette and placed it on the table.

Brad just sat there as she got up and walked out. She had somewhere else to go.

Around ten o'clock two men walked into the bar. "Hi Mark," said Tony. "Haven't seen you for a while. What're you having?"

"Cheers Tone... two pints of lager... and two cheese and onion," replied the taller man.

"So how's it going up at the garage?" asked the barman as Mark took his first sip of his drink and opened a bag of crisps.

"Busy, very busy. Got the night off. Hoping to spend it with the missus but she's buggered off out again," he replied.

"She was in here earlier," said Tony. "Chatting to that bloke in the corner. They went into the restaurant. Haven't seen her since."

"Which one?" asked Mark taking another sip and scanning the bar.

"The one over by the window reading the paper. He was chatting to her last night as well," he said.

It appeared on the face of it that Tony had broken the cardinal rule of barmen, discretion; but he had no time for Melanie and her dalliances.

Mark turned his head and stared at the man as he drank his beer. He could feel his pulse quicken, he was getting angry. His mate Casey could see the signs. "Hey mate, calm down, eh?" he counselled.

"If he's been round my missus, he's in for a fucking kickin'," said Mark, who was now well down his glass.

He tipped back the lager and put the empty glass down on the bar. "Thanks Tone," he said. "Same again... and have one yourself."

The Tinker

Mark produced a five pound note and stared at Brad as Tony retrieved the change from the till.

"Is he staying here?" asked Mark when Tony presented him with his pint.

"Yeah," said Tony.

"Cheers," said Mark as he sipped the foaming top off his drink. He took out another handful of crisps.

Casey also worked at the garage with Mark and was privy to the difficulties he was having with Melanie. He was also aware of her reputation. 'Shag anything in trousers,' was a common description, but not in Mark's earshot.

After about twenty minutes Brad got up from his chair. Mark had hardly taken his eyes off him.

"Quick..." said Mark. "Let's go after him. I need a word."

Unfortunately instead of going back to his room, Brad had decided to go for a walk before turning in. It was a warm night and the fresh air would do him good. He also wanted to chew over the information Melanie had given him. He was positive that it was Michael he had seen, but why would she lie? She had no reason to.

Brad went through the main door of the lounge and turned left into the High Street. He had reached the entrance to the car-park when he was suddenly bundled off the street into the alleyway. It was more of a shoulder charge, like any you would see in a Saturday Rugby match, but it had the desired affect and Brad was on the floor. A kick in the groin followed, then two more fierce blows to the stomach. The heavy boots made a thudding noise as they landed. "That'll teach you to come around here and shag my missus," he said.

"I don't know what you're talking about," said Brad, trying to catch his breath.

"Melanie... I know what you've been up to. Don't try to deny it," said Mark.

Brad was curled in a ball waiting for the next blow. "I didn't know she was married," said Brad. "She wasn't wearing a ring. She said she was on her own."

Another kick landed before Casey managed to drag Mark away.

"That's enough... You've made your point. Let's get off," he said, trying to calm Mark down.

The two slunk away leaving Brad in a great deal of discomfort. He tried to get up but the pains in his stomach doubled him up. He took some deep breaths and gradually managed to get to his feet. Gingerly he made his way through the car-park to the side entrance of the hotel; he did not want the ignominy of going through the bar. He managed to hobble past reception and up to his room.

As beatings go he had survived worse. He took off his trousers and shirt to survey the damage. There were nasty bruises on his stomach and inner thigh; luckily the groin kick had only winded him and not scored a direct hit. He lay on the bed and took in the day's events.

Melanie meanwhile had other things on her mind. She needed to warn Michael.

After she had left the pub she walked along Vicarage Road and reached the church. The clock on the spire struck nine as she reached the gate and she walked up the path past the kitchen towards the lodge. It was still light and warm.

She was worried about the next bit. Given his reaction yesterday she knew he would not be expecting her; he could even be angry, but she knew it was important.

She reached the front door and breathed in deeply then tapped lightly and waited. Nothing. She tapped again. She could hear a

The Tinker

noise from inside then it opened.

Before Michael could say anything Melanie pushed by him and went inside.

"Sorry to barge in but I have some news for you. It's important," she said. "Then I'll go if you want me to."

Michael shut the door. "Can I sit down?" she said. Michael indicated with his head.

"Have you got a drink at all?" she said.

"Sorry," said Michael.

"Why are you here...? I thought I..." She cut in before he could finish.

"I think someone is after you," she said.

Michael stopped and looked at her. She was different somehow her attitude her voice, one of urgency, concern even.

He listened.

"I met this bloke at the White Hart. Seemed decent enough. Smart, northern accent it sounded like, said he was in sales. Brad his name was. Well we were chatting, like, when he suddenly says do I know anyone called Michael."

Michael looked at her. "Go on," he said.

"He said he had seen you go by on your bike this morning and recognised you. Said he thought you were an old army buddy."

"What did you say?" asked Michael.

"I told him I didn't know anyone called Michael. I made up some name. Said it was an odd job man called Ted something."

"What did he say?" asked Michael.

"I don't think he believed me at first... kept asking if I was certain. But I am sure I convinced him."

Michael was deep in thought.

"Thanks," he said.

"Is it ok if I stay for a while? I don't want to go home yet. Mark

117

threatened to slap me yesterday," she said.

"Aye, ok," said Michael.

"There is something else. I wanted to explain something, about yesterday. I'm not looking for a relationship. I was just looking for a bit of company, that's all. I thought you might feel the same."

Michael looked at her.

"Aye, I know," he said.

Chapter Eight

Michael stood up.

"I can get you a lemonade? I've no wine," he said.

Melanie sat on the armchair, her pink shoes discarded, her legs folded under her, like a cat curled up on its favourite seat. Any effects of the earlier vodka had gone.

"Thank you," she said.

Michael went to the kitchen and brought out two tumblers. "No ice I'm afraid but it's from the fridge," he said.

"That's fine," she said.

He handed her the drink and sat on the other armchair on the opposite side of the fireplace.

She stared into the drink for a moment wanting to make conversation but not knowing where to tread.

She looked at Michael. "So the people who are looking for you... are they... dangerous?" she said, and took a drink avoiding eye contact.

Michael thought before answering. "I don't know, but it's possible," he said. "Best you don't get involved."

"Can't help it," she said. "I am involved"

Michael pondered this.

"What are you going to do?" she asked.

"Nothing for now," he said. "I'll wait and see if anything happens."

"But you won't leave," she said. "Not yet."

"No, I plan to stick around for the moment," he said.

The church clock chimed half past the hour.

Michael looked at her; this was a different Melanie not the skittish girl from last night but relaxed, controlled. He was far from happy with the situation; the initiative was now with her but for the moment he would accept it. There was no immediate danger.

"Can I use the bathroom?" she asked, putting her empty glass on the floor by the chair.

"Yes," said Michael. "It's through there," he added, pointing to the door opposite.

Light was fading fast and the sounds of night creatures could be heard. Badgers, foxes had their distinctive resonances; then the owls hooting and calling. Bats, looking for insects, flitted past the windows. The night was alive.

It was still warm as Michael got up to draw the curtains. He liked to leave them open for as long as he could to view the goings-on outside his windows. He could see the clock on the church spire, movement too slow to detect but unstoppable, like time itself. He flicked the switch on the small table lamp and the room was bathed in a warm glow. Melanie came back into the room.

"This is nice," she said.

She looked at him. He was seated in one of the armchairs in his cut-off jeans and tee shirt. She went over to him and started to massage his neck again. Michael this time didn't resist and for several minutes relaxed as her expert fingers went to work.

"I think we have some unfinished business, don't you?" she whispered, sensing the time was right.

She stopped the massage and stood in front of him, undid the white leather belt and let it drop to the floor. Then lifted her top over her head and unclipped her bra.

Michael stood up and turned to her. She wrapped her arms around his neck and kissed him passionately. Then she pulled at his tee shirt; he lifted his arms up. His face was reddening.

She lay down on the rug in front of the empty fireplace and

The Tinker

eased down her pink 'spray-ons'. Michael took a cushion from one of the armchairs and placed it under hips to provide the right angle. Then entered her.

It had been everything she had hoped for, even better than in the salon. They lay there momentarily, breathless.

The clock chimed another half hour and Michael got up and went to the bathroom.

"You need to go," he said when he returned to the room. She was still lying on the floor.

"Can I stay?" she said. "I don't want to go home to that brute," she added. "I never want to see him again."

She sat up and Michael suddenly felt cornered.

"You know that's not possible. You really need to go. It's getting late," he said.

Melanie decided not to push it further, she remembered his reaction from the previous night and didn't want to jeopardise the possibilities of future meetings.

"Yeah, ok," she said. "You're right, I should be going."

She got up and walked to the bathroom taking her clothes with her. Ten minutes later she was back and ready to leave. Michael rose from the armchair where he had been deep in thought.

"Can I call again?" she asked. "I will let you know, not just turn up," she added.

"Aye," said Michael. "I'll be in touch," he said.

He opened the door and she leaned up and kissed his cheek.

"See you," she said and headed down the path past the vicarage for the two mile walk home.

Melanie was also in a reflective mood as she made her way through the village. She was on a high. As she saw it her relationship with Michael seemed to be back on track for now and with the promise of future visits there were opportunities to develop it even further. He was everything she wanted in a man. She imagined the two of them walking through Drayburn, arm in arm. Now that would be something, the jealousy, just imagine.

It had been a difficult time for her following the news of her relationship with Tina Ashworth's husband had leaked out. Her name had strangely been kept out of the newspapers but word soon got round the village that she was the 'other woman'. Melanie's marriage was already in difficulties, but it was Mark who begged her not to leave him; he promised he would change. Six months on however the relationship had all but collapsed. Mark was becoming almost paranoid in his possessiveness and Melanie had grown frightened of him.

She walked past the White Hart and up the hill out of the village towards the bypass. Another ten minutes and she could see the street light illuminating the entrance to the snicket, the shortcut that led to her cottage. The temperature had dropped but Melanie didn't feel cold despite her fairly skimpy outfit; she could still feel Michael inside her; his arms holding her as they made love. She shivered. The stars sparkled; she was suddenly reminded of a spandex jacket she had her eye on. She would need to go to Stonington for that; she couldn't imagine Mrs Appleby stocking one, 'mail-order I'm afraid,' would be her usual line. She chuckled to herself at the association.

She reached the lamp post and turned left into the alleyway. It was unlit but she could see the light at the other end of the path to guide her home. She didn't know how she would deal with Mark; she wasn't looking forward to another confrontation; he could go to hell.

She reached the cottage, opened the front door and went in, slightly anxious at the possible reception. Mark was fast asleep in the armchair in front of the TV which was still on. She turned it off and went upstairs to bed with the chair firmly wedged under the door handle.

Michael had endured another night of restless sleep; the dreams had returned. He had been awake since five, nothing unusual about that, consciousness brought solace from the nightmares. He lay listening to the sounds of the country that had triggered the arousal. To the untrained ear, birdsong was a discordant cacophony but Michael could pick out the distinctive trill of the Blackbird, the melody of the aptly named Song Thrush or the onomatopoeic call of the Chiff Chaff. They were all neighbours and appeared to be telling him it was time to face another day.

He thought again of Melanie; it troubled him. He could not allow anyone to have any control, any leverage that might threaten his independence; it could ultimately cost him his life. He didn't know whether she could be trusted, her behaviour too erratic; but he didn't have any answers yet. She may even prove useful if the enquirer turned up again. Sometimes making no decision is the right decision. Time would be the judge.

Thursday morning, Michael was eventually up around seven preparing for his day at The Manor. He was away by eight riding his bike and trailer. There was a cycle path, a right turn just past the cottages leading to Manor Road which avoided going through the village centre. Once past the houses, though, the road was very narrow and dangerous. There was barely room for a car to pass a bike and the banking either side rose to ten feet or more and was topped with hedges.

The hedgerows gradually fell away as Michael neared the Manor. Wrought iron railings marked the boundary, then the magnificent house, visible from the road to the right. He reached the gate and pushed his bike down the long gravel drive. He acknowledged David, the gardener who was busy tending the lawns. The Major was already about with his two gundogs and immediately went to greet Michael.

"Michael, old boy, good to see you. Beautiful day, what," he said. They shook hands warmly.

"Hello Major. Yes it is," Michael replied.

"Memsahib has been making some of her home-made lemonade. I expect you could do with a drink after that ride, yes?" he said.

"Thank you," said Michael.

There were a number of jobs that the Major had lined up for him but roof repairs were top of the list, several loose slates.

"The storm on Sunday caused a spot of bother old boy," he said to Michael, euphemistically describing the damage to the attic from the leaking roof.

"I'll get Frank to hold the ladder. He'll be up here in a bit," said the Major.

So Michael spent the day working on the roof of The Manor; it was a big job he explained to the Major during one of his several breaks; he would need to come back the following day.

"Take all the time you need. There'll be plenty more work for you while you're here," the Major assured Michael.

Luckily most of the slates were intact, just become dislodged, but there were some missing which would need to be replaced and Frank was dispatched to the builder's merchants in Stonington to buy the necessary replacements.

Michael enjoyed the Major's company. He was a great story-teller and whenever the opportunity allowed he would relate tales of his time in the army in India. He never questioned Michael's past and any curiosity in this direction was never pressed but the Major felt there was some affinity and thought there might be some

The Tinker

military connection. So during the afternoon while they waited for Frank to return with the slates Michael sat on the stone seating around the lawn at the rear of the house drinking the memsahib's lemonade and listening to the Major's tales. This was a good day.

Back at the White Hart the staff were clearing away the last of the breakfast things; ten o'clock and Glenda Gable, the house manageress was doing her rounds. She had finished room number six and knocked on the next room, believing the guest to have checked out by this time.

She used her master key to let herself in and was surprised to see the curtains still drawn. She went over to the windows and pulled the chord at the side to open them. Shoes on the floor, open suitcase on the armchair, she looked at the four-poster and could see a shape.

"Oh... I'm terribly sorry," she said. "I thought you had checked out, Mr Jackson... Mr Jackson?"

She went to the bed and put her hand to her mouth. His eyes were staring back at her... lifeless.

She ran out of the room and down the stairs to reception.

"Quick! Quick... Call an ambulance," she shouted.

The receptionist looked at her. "Glenda are you alright...? What's happened?" she asked.

"It's Mr Jackson... in room seven... I think... I think he's dead!" she managed to say.

The call was made.

The Manager of the hotel, Gavin Findley, was called from his office and he quickly took charge of the situation. The door to room seven was locked and Glenda was given some strong sweet tea for the shock.

It took half an hour for the ambulance to arrive from Stonington and Mr Findley took the paramedics up to the room. They were quickly able to establish that Brad had indeed passed away but the cause was not immediately obvious.

"Probably a heart attack," said the ambulance man. "But you'll need to call the police," he added.

"Is that really necessary?" said Findley. "You know, adverse publicity and all that."

"No option, unexplained death," said the paramedic.

Again the call was made and it was another half an hour before the police arrived.

Naturally there was a great deal of interest from the villagers as they watched the emergency services coming and going.

"What do you think it is?" asked Melanie to Mrs Audley in the salon. They were both looking across the road through the window; the slats were opened wider than usual.

It didn't take long for word to get round. Once Mrs Gable had been sent home to recover she called into the village store for some tablets for one of her headaches. "Stiff as a board, he was," she said to Joyce Dunwoody, the duty cashier.

News arrived at the salon shortly after.

"Have you heard the news? Someone's been found dead at the White Hart. Stiff as a board he was, according to Mrs Gable. Staring straight at her when she went in to clean. Gave her a right shock it did. She's been sent home, you know," said Annie Dalton, one of Mrs Audley's clients extracting as much drama from the situation as possible.

"Did they say what the name was?" asked Melanie who was working on the next chair.

"No, she didn't say but he was in room seven, apparently," said Annie.

"Room seven...?" said Melanie and she started thinking,

The Tinker

'couldn't be?' she asked herself.

At lunchtime the ambulance had gone but the police were still at the scene, interviewing staff. Melanie decided to take a closer look; the hotel was open for business. Over a coffee, Gavin Findley had been unofficially told by one of the officers that the initial findings suggested the death was 'unexplained' rather than 'suspicious'. The doctor at the scene had confirmed that the likely cause of death was almost certainly a heart attack but given the fairly youthful age of the deceased they would await a post mortem before making any final decision on opening a full investigation.

Melanie went to the bar and ordered an orange juice. Tony was serving as usual.

"Hi Tony, what's been going on?" she asked. "I heard someone's died."

"Yes," he said. "It was your friend, the salesman, Brad," he added.

The blood drained from Melanie's face. "What... when... how?" she said.

"Seem to think it's a heart attack. Mrs Gable found him this morning when she went in to clean. Stiff as a board he was, she said."

"I'd heard," said Melanie. "But not who."

She was trying to take in the information and took a sip of her drink; her hands were unsteady. She would need to speak to Michael and let him know. His secret, it appeared, was intact.

"The police were asking if we knew anything about him. They found his personal details in his wallet and have contacted his family," said Tony.

Melanie shuddered.

"It's ok, I didn't say anything about your meeting," he said, wiping a glass vigorously. "I expect they'll be wanting to speak to the waitresses at some stage as well but they won't say anything. I wouldn't worry," he added.

A favour courted now may well bear fruit in the future, he thought.

He paused. "Your Mark took an interest in him an' all. He was in here last night, heard you'd had dinner with him," Tony added.

"Who told him?" asked Melanie.

"Couldn't possibly say," said Tony continuing to polish the glass, holding it to the light to make sure there were no smears avoiding any eye contact with Melanie. He walked to the other end of the bar to put it on the shelf with the others, leaving Melanie with her thoughts.

She finished her drink and left the pub without acknowledging Tony who was serving another customer. Melanie was worried; even though she had nothing to hide, she didn't want to face any police interrogation. She did need to speak to Michael though. It would be another excuse to pay him a visit. She smiled at the thought; maybe things weren't so bad after all.

During the afternoon the death at the White Hart was the only topic of conversation. Melanie had a busy schedule with three appointments booked including Mrs Oxley, Tina Ashworth's daily.

The hourly bus service from Upton Winscliffe made its usual stop outside the Village store at three thirty. Freda Oxley was the only passenger; except for her days off she would always be on this bus. There were more people waiting at the bus stop to get on as it would continue its journey to Stonington. She got off and called into the store for some bits and pieces for tea before heading the short distance up the street to the salon.

"Hello Freda, take a seat. I'll be right with you," said Melanie, seeing her four o'clock appointment walk through the door.

"Would you like a cup of tea?"

Mrs Oxley gladly accepted the offer, picked up a magazine and sat in the small waiting area while Melanie was finishing off her existing client. Five minutes later Melanie went to the kitchen and made the tea and presented it to Freda.

"Just the usual, Freda?" asked Melanie as she stood behind Mrs Oxley fingering her hair.

"Yes please, dear," she said.

The washing was duly done and then it was back to the other seat for the trim.

"So how are things?" asked Melanie, opening up the conversation as she started to make small inroads into Mrs Oxley's greying hair.

"Fine thank you. I've just heard about all the excitement at the White Hart. Fancy finding someone dead like that. It must have been a hell of a shock to poor old Glenda Gable. Mrs Dunwoody was telling me all about it. Do we know anything about the poor man?"

"No, just a visitor I heard," said Melanie. She didn't want to pursue this gossip any further and there was a long pause as Melanie continued her work.

Freda Oxley of course knew all about Melanie and her affair with Tina Ashworth's now ex-husband, Jason. She had however remained remarkably impartial on the matter and although she didn't condone Melanie's activities, she didn't like Jason Lee Burns one bit and was glad to see the back of him. "Wretched gold digger," she called him. The gossip mongers had had their day and it was time to move on.

Mrs Oxley couldn't hold back any longer. "I think there's been some goings on up at the Ridge," she said, then looked around to make sure no-one could hear.

"Between you and me I think Miss Ashworth's got another man. I mean, the state of her bedroom this morning... well... and I had to wash all the bed-linen. Right state it was," Melanie was eager to hear the details.

"Go on," she said.

"Well, I thought it was a bit strange she gave me yesterday off... full pay and all, told me she was having a visitor... something about her boiler being serviced, she said."

Melanie's antenna was suddenly on alert.

"Boiler service. You mean like the gas man?" Melanie pressed.

"Oh no, it would be that odd job man hereabouts, Michael they call him, did it last year. She was saying how pleased she was with him. I remember her saying at the time. Mind you have you seen him? He could service my boiler any time," she said and started to laugh.

Melanie wasn't laughing. She felt a pain in her stomach and for a moment she thought she was going to faint.

"Are you all right dear?" said Freda, seeing Melanie in a state.

Melanie rushed into the back room and was sick in the sink in the toilet.

She took some deep breaths and went back to her client.

"Sorry about that, Freda. I think something must have disagreed with me," she said.

"Are you sure you are alright? You don't look too good," said Freda.

Melanie turned to Mrs Audley who had just finished her last client of the day.

"Mrs Audley, can you finish Freda for me I don't feel very well. I think I need to have a lie down," she said.

Mrs Audley looked at her. "My goodness you're as white as a sheet. Yes, of course, you get off."

Melanie said her goodbyes and grabbed her jacket from the staff room. She needed some air.

It was almost four thirty and her head was all over the place. The police cars had gone from the White Hart. She made her way over; she needed a drink.

Tony wasn't there; it was one of the restaurant waitresses covering.

"Large vodka, Louise," she said.

"Hi Melanie, I suppose you'll have heard about all the excitement here today," Louise replied as she got the drinks.

"Yes," said Melanie. She didn't want conversation; she needed to think.

She paid for her drink and sat by the window. "Stuck up cow," said Louise to herself as Melanie walked away from the bar.

Melanie was oblivious to any lack of courtesy, in her own world, deep in thought. She had already concluded it wasn't Michael's fault, she knew that. Tina Ashworth snaps her fingers and men fall at her feet. Melanie could understand the attraction. There was some satisfaction, though, knowing she had screwed her former husband; it lessened the blow somehow, but having Michael was unforgivable; he was spoken for. The question was, what was she going to do about it? She couldn't confront Michael; that would be totally fruitless. No, he was his own man; she admired that, strong and purposeful, took his pleasures where he could. It was Tina Ashworth, the so-called celebrity, all her doing. Melanie would give it a lot of thought.

On the bright side she now had an excuse to visit Michael. She hoped he would show his appreciation like only he could.

The colour had returned to her cheeks.

Having finished his chores for the Major, Michael was back at the Lodge around five thirty. He had made good progress with the roof but would return tomorrow to finish it off; the Major seemed more than happy with his work.

On his way back he remembered a stop he needed to make and called into Edwin Appleton's shop in the High street to pick up his trousers and jeans. He had been busy with the church boiler on Tuesday and with half day closing on Wednesday this was his first opportunity. He was greeted warmly by the proprietor.

"Hello Michael, good to see you," said Edwin as Michael entered the shop. With space at a premium it was cluttered with stock everywhere. Edwin, with his wife, were part of the 'horsey' set in the village and owned their own stables. Michael had regularly passed on the opportunity to join them at the yard for a ride.

"Hello Edwin. Come for the trousers," replied Michael.

"Yes, of course, they're in the back waiting for you. I'll just get them," said Edwin who went into a back room before returning with two carrier bags. "Do you want to try them on again, just to check?" said Edwin.

"No, I'm sure they'll be fine," said Michael and Edwin handed them over.

"Did you hear about all the excitement in the village this morning?" said Edwin.

"No," said Michael, only moderately interested; he tended not to get involved with gossip.

"All sorts goings on. One of the guests at the White Hart was found dead in his bed this morning, heart attack apparently. Ambulance, police, it was all happening," said Edwin.

Michael took in the information. "That's a shame," was about all he could muster in response.

"Yes," said Edwin, recognising that the conversation would

The Tinker

not be expanded further.

"Anyway, you know where I am if you need anything else while you're here. I take it you'll be staying for the summer as usual," he said.

"That's the plan," said Michael.

"Don't forget the offer is always open if you want to take out one of the horses, anytime," said Edwin.

"Thank you," said Michael. "I'll certainly bear that in mind," he added and left the store.

At the vicarage Denise noticed him pushing his bike along the path past the kitchen; the carrier bags from Appleton's were hanging from the handle bars. She went out.

"Hello Michael, would you like a spot of tea with us later? Just sausages. I've done enough to go round," she said.

"Thank you," said Michael.

"About six," said Denise,

"Aye, thank you. I'll be there," he said and carried on to the Lodge.

Later as Michael sat down to dinner with the vicar and his wife there was an air of excitement with the pending arrival of the children. Denise explained how she had been busy getting their rooms ready; then the topic of conversation changed.

"Did you hear the news about the body at the White Hart?" she asked, looking at Michael.

"Yes," he said. "Edwin Appleton told me."

"Very sad, don't you think, dying all on your own, away from your family. His poor wife, I can't imagine what she must be going through," she said. There was a pause.

"How did you get on at The Manor?" asked Denise changing the subject.

"Fine, spent most of the day on the roof, drinking lemonade

133

and listening to the Major," he replied.

"Yes, he can be very talkative when you get him on the topic of India," she said.

"I meant to mention, Frank has invited me to go fishing with him on Saturday. Do you think William would like to come?" asked Michael.

"Quite possibly. He does enjoy fishing but hasn't done any for some time. Not sure if he still has his rod and stuff," said Denise.

"I think it's in the shed somewhere," said the vicar. "I'm sure I remember seeing it there when I was getting the shears the other week," he added.

"Oh I do hope so. It will be good for him. I'm not sure how much fresh air he gets these days. He often used to go fishing with Frank when he was younger," said Denise. "I'll ask him when he gets in," she added.

Michael left the vicarage around seven thirty having once again thanked his hosts for their generosity and made his way back to the Lodge.

He could see someone waiting at the front door and as he got closer he could see it was Melanie dressed in what looked like her salon clothes.

"What are you doing here?" asked Michael as he approached.

"I've got some news about that bloke who was asking about you," she said,

Michael unlocked the door.

"You best come in," he said.

"Thank you. I won't stop though, I've got one or two things to sort out," she said.

She went straight to 'her' seat and sat down. Michael sat opposite; there was no familiar greeting.

"So what's this news then?" asked Michael getting straight to the point.

"Have you heard about the dead man at the White Hart?" she asked.

"Aye," he said.

"Well it was him, the bloke who was asking about you," she said.

"Hmm," said Michael.

"Well that's good isn't it? He can't hurt you now can he?" she said.

"I guess not," he replied.

He was in deep thought taking in the information. They wouldn't have sent just one.

Seeing Michael was pre-occupied Melanie chose her moment.

"Can I ask you something?" she said.

Michael looked at her. "What?" he replied but not really concentrating.

"Were you at Tina Ashworth's yesterday?" she asked.

"Why do you want to know?" he asked back in focus

"Mrs Oxley, the housekeeper was in today trying to gossip but I told her to mind her own business," she said. "I didn't think you would want anyone discussing your affairs," she added.

There was no response from Michael, he was still considering her earlier disclosure.

Melanie stood up.

"Anyway, I need to get off," she said.

Michael got up, surprised at her early departure but thankful she was not seeking anything else.

"Right," said Michael and he got up and held the door open.

As she reached him she leant forward and kissed his cheek. "I don't mind," she said.

"Don't mind what?" said Michael.

"You... with other women. I'm not the possessive sort," she said.

Michael was lost for words.

"Bye," she said and walked away.

Melanie walked back through the village. She was hoping for more from her visit to Michael but contented herself with having seen him with some good news. He would be more amenable next time, she thought.

More to the point was what she was going to do about Tina Ashworth. She would give that some thought. Nobody else was going to have Michael; he was hers.

Chapter Nine

Melanie stopped at the White Hart on the way home. It was still early and she had no intention of giving her husband any 'us' time. He said he would be home by nine. The bar was fairly empty, the hotel bedrooms less than half full; number seven was sealed off in case any further police investigation would be required. She wanted to be with Michael and thought about going back and seeing if he wanted any company, but quickly discounted that.

So Melanie sat in the corner of the hotel lounge reading one of the complementary newspapers but not really concentrating on the words. She was trying to work out possible retribution from that 'D list celebrity' as she called Tina Ashworth. Something would turn up; she would have her day.

Melanie remembered her first meeting with Jason Lee Burns, Tina's now ex-husband. She had sat in the very same seat - not a coincidence, she always sat in the same place when it was available; she considered it 'hers'. It would be the end of September, about seven o'clock and she had popped in with Mrs Audley for a drink after work. They had been busy at the salon with a wedding trying to look after the bride and four bridesmaids, she recalled. It had been a long day.

He walked in like he owned the place. There was a swagger that went with him, an arrogance bordering on the narcissistic. He was with two friends and sat on an adjacent table still wearing his sunglasses, indoors. "What a prat", she thought and almost giggled to herself. She remembered him staring at her, or that's what it seemed like; eye contact was impossible. He was certainly looking in her direction. Mrs Audley left after one drink but Melanie stayed on; it isn't every day you get stared at by a celebrity. Everybody knew Jason Lee Burns; he was hot property following his appearance in a costume drama on TV which had all the women swooning at his tight breeches and manly chest. Melanie wasn't the only one captivated by the series.

His two friends left and he immediately came to her table. "Can I buy you a drink?" he said in a Mid-Atlantic accent which he had no doubt been cultivating. He was from Leytonstone, so it said in the papers.

"Yes, yes please," she replied unable to contain her nervousness. "Vodka and tonic, please."

He returned to her table and engaged in conversation. She remembered being star-struck as he reeled all the famous names he had met or bumped into in the studios.

He asked her if she would like to go for a ride. "I've brought the Porsche," he said.

Melanie's heart skipped a beat.

"What about Tina?" she remembered asking him; they had only been married a few months.

"Oh she won't mind. We have an open relationship," he said.

So she accompanied 'the' Jason Lee Burns to the car-park and his Porsche. It was a surreal experience, but it quickly changed. As soon as they were out of the village his hands were everywhere and within ten minutes they were in a secluded lay-by. The car was far too small for any meaningful activity but Jason, as he told her at the time, was 'always prepared' and took out a rug from the boot, placed it down beside the car and asked her to lay down. Well you didn't say 'no' to Jason Lee Burns, and that was the start of a short but incredibly intense relationship.

It only lasted three weeks. She would phone him from the salon when no-one was around at allotted times, 'when the coast is clear' he would say. This one day they had made arrangements for him to pick her up on her day off. "How do you fancy coming up to the house," he had said. Tina was going up to 'town' for an audition, he explained. The invite was another dream-like experience. She felt like she was in her own soap drama.

It was a Wednesday morning and, at ten o'clock as arranged, Jason's orange Porsche pulled up outside the village store where she was waiting. They reached the house and she was immediately caught up in the magic of the place. He was the same age as her - how on earth did someone of twenty six manage to afford such a place, she wondered.

They went into the entrance hall and she remembered the awards and pictures in Tina's shrine. Melanie didn't feel in the least bit guilty at the time. It was as though she had been commanded by a higher being; someone who must be obeyed; the power of celebrity. He gave her a drink and took her upstairs. To go with his arrogance Jason Lee Burns was a selfish lover, caring only for his own gratification. He suggested 'something different' which she felt obliged to go along with. Neither of them heard Tina's car pull into the drive or the opening of the front door; they were too engrossed. When Tina finally entered the bedroom, Melanie was tied to the bed with Jason in full flow.

Melanie was seated with her vodka in the White Hart and suddenly felt a degree of satisfaction remembering Tina's face when she walked in. It was a picture, one of horror and disbelief. Jason turned around and was whimpering, begging for forgiveness. Melanie just shouted, "can someone fucking untie me?"

Melanie smiled again. Perhaps she had got her retribution in first; serves her right, the cow.

She was however worried when Tina left the room and came back with a knife. Just for a moment she feared the worst. But she just cut the ties and told her to leave. "Get the fuck out of my house, you slag," was her actual words.

Melanie finished her drink and checked the time, gone nine; she felt restless but didn't particularly want to go home. What she really wanted was to go back to Michael's.

The bar was getting busier but she was in no mood for any other company so, reluctantly, she headed back to the cottage.

Mark was in when she arrived. "Where the fuck have you been?" was his greeting as she walked in.

"Out," she said.

"Where?" he said.

"Wherever I want," she said. "I'm going to run a bath."

He grabbed her arm.

"Just you wait, my lady, I want to know where you've been. Not with that bloke again, I hope? I heard all about you and your romantic dinner at the White Hart. Well I sorted him out good and proper. He won't be shagging around anytime soon," he shouted. His face was distorted in hate.

There was a silence and Melanie stopped.

"What do you mean?" she said.

He let go of her arm.

"Oh, just gave him a bit of a warning that's all. Teach him a lesson," he said.

She stared at him.

"You haven't heard, have you?" she said.

"Heard what...?"

"He's dead," she replied.

Mark looked at her. "What do you mean, 'he's dead'?" he said.

"Just that. They found him dead this morning. They said it was a heart attack," she said.

Mark just stared at her.

"You're trying to wind me up aren't you?" he said, but he

The Tinker

could see by her face that she wasn't.

"You... you killed him," she said.

"No, no, I only gave him a kicking. I was with Casey, he'll tell you. He was ok when we left him. I swear," he said.

Mark was now looking very concerned.

"You better hope that the police don't find out then," she said.

Mark sat on the armchair in front of the TV and stared ahead contemplating this news.

"Now I'm going to have a bath. Then I'm going to have an early night. You can go fuck yourself for all I care, I want nothing more to do with you," she said and went upstairs.

Mark didn't take in her abuse.

Friday morning at the offices of Springer Investigations, Liverpool. It was early; Barry Springer had some work come in and wanted to make an early start; a possible insurance fraud. A day's observation, should be a good earner.

"Any news from Brad?" asked Barry.

Kathy Metcalf, his assistant, PA and general dogsbody was just unlocking the drawers of her desk.

"No, nothing," she replied.

Barry looked concerned. "That's funny. I thought he'd be in touch by now. Tell you what, try and get hold of him, you've got his new number. I'm just going to get my stuff together for the obs. It's going to be a boring day I can feel it," he said.

It was just one room with two desks. The larger one was Barry's a few feet from his was Kathy's. There were filing cabinets all around the room and a fax machine in the corner. The other office next door where Brad Jackson worked for all those years had been vacated to save costs.

Barry was in his late forties; chubby would be an apt description.

His ginger hair was thinning rapidly, almost at the same rate as his waistline was expanding, Kathy had joked. He smoked thumb-sized cigars which created a pungent odour around the office. Kathy regularly complained that it was all she could smell when she got home. It lingered on her clothes and in her hair.

Kathy had been at the firm for almost three years and was ten years younger than Barry. She had cropped blonde hair and a penchant for wearing trousers and bomber jackets. Barry had never seen her in a skirt.

In the corner there was a large cupboard where he kept the tools of his trade, cameras, lenses, recording devices, state of the art stuff and expensive, but necessary for his work. Barry was rummaging around as Kathy made the call. After about five minutes she came off the phone. Her face had a look of anguish.

Barry looked at her. "What on earth's the matter...? You look like you've seen a ghost."

"It's Brad..." she said. "He's dead."

"What?" said Barry.

"Spoke to his boss at Armitage's. He was found in his hotel room yesterday morning apparently. Heart attack, they think," she said.

Barry came away from the cupboard and went to Kathy's desk unable to take in the news. He was leaning against his own desk.

"I can't believe it, he was as fit as a flea. No, can't be right," he said.

"Well that's what the bloke from Armitage's says," she replied.

"Poor Annie, she must be frantic... and the kids. Can you get a bunch of flowers out to her?"

"Yeah, of course," she said.

Kathy called a local florist while Barry sat at his desk thinking. After she came off the phone Barry spoke to her. "I think we

The Tinker

need to get down there, something's not right," he said. "How do you fancy a couple of days in the Cotswolds?"

"Yeah, ok, sounds good," she said.

This was not an uncommon occurrence. Where required, they would often go as a couple, share the same room, share the same bed even. Looks less suspicious, Barry had said. It wasn't an issue; it was just work. There were no emotional attachments; Kathy's preferred partners were women.

Barry was thinking. "Can you get a call for me?" he said. "It's a Belfast number," he added.

"Of course," she said and he went to one of the drawers and produced a note book. He flicked through the pages, then stopped. He handed it to her.

"This one," he said. "Brendan Monahan."

All thoughts of the insurance job had gone, it wasn't urgent, a few days wouldn't hurt; this was more important and potentially far more lucrative.

As Kathy tried to get the call, Barry went to the small fridge in the opposite corner of the office which had a filter coffee making machine and two mugs on it. The coffee had been stewing since seven o'clock. He lifted the filter jug up to his assistant to indicate whether she would like one. She shook her head and he poured the last remaining dregs into a mug and turned off the machine.

Kathy put her hand over the receiver. "I've got Brendan Monahan for you," she said.

Barry put down his mug and took the phone from Kathy.

"Brendan...? Yeah fine thanks, You...? Look this may be nothing but I think it's possible that we could have a lead on Michael Curtiss."

Barry outlined the story of Brad's phone call and his subsequent demise.

"As I said it could be nothing but I think it could be worth following up. Brad was pretty insistent that it was yer man," he said, dropping into his native Irish accent.

"I'll need to bill yer for the time and exes, that ok?" he added. "Good, I'll report back to yer in a couple of days."

He rang off and looked at Kathy. "The Cotswolds it is then. You better find out where this place Drayburn is and book us a room, tonight and tomorrow. Brad was in a hotel there. The White Hart, I think that's what he said. Can't be many hotels in the village, very small apparently."

Kathy got the number from Directory Enquiries and called the hotel and made the reservation. "Mr and Mrs Springer," she said.

Meanwhile Barry had got out a large road atlas from his cupboard. This was like a bible to him and it was now looking distinctly tatty and dog-eared.

Kathy came off the phone and walked around to Barry's side of the desk where the map was open. "Here it is," he said, pointing to the place on the page. "About ten miles from Stonington, A46 about three hours with a bit of luck if the motorways are ok," he said.

So Barry got his kit together; he was thinking of this as another observation exercise, with maybe the odd enquiry, nothing to create any concern. If it was Michael he didn't want him to get spooked into leaving. Get in and out with the information, always safest way, he once said. Kathy meanwhile was tidying up and put the answering machine on.

It was a warm day, but cloudy, "good driving weather," said Barry.

"We'll stop off at mine, then go round to yours to get some overnight gear," he said as he locked the office.

Barry's pride and joy was his silver Jaguar XJ Coupe, almost eleven years old now but lovingly cared for. Kathy once told him him that if he'd given as much attention to his wife as he did to that car, she would never have left him.

It took about an hour to get themselves ready and by ten thirty they were on their way.

It was Kathy who started the conversation as they cruised down the M6.

"So what's the story about this Michael then, you've never said?" she said.

Barry looked across at her briefly then concentrated on the road.

"It was way before you joined us. About seven years ago a couple of guys walked in off the street. It was just Brad and me then. They'd just got off the ferry from Belfast... said they were looking for someone and wanted our help."

"Why did they choose you?" she asked.

"Good question. They said they'd done some research, whatever that means." he said.

"Did they say why they wanted this man?" she asked.

"No, they wouldn't go into details. Best I didn't know, they said. But it was obviously very important and they seemed to have a lot of financial backing. Somebody really wanted him badly."

"So how come it's taken all these years?" she asked.

"It's been the hardest investigation we've ever done. Brad spent months and months trawling though information, files, chasing leads. We even put an ad in the paper offering a reward on the basis that it was an inheritance search, but nothing." He continued. "Brad went all over the place, Ibiza, Greece, Tenerife. There were sightings of bar-staff, which we thought might be a possibility, you know someone moving from place to place. It made sense, but nothing. The problem was we didn't have a lot to go on; his background was very sketchy. We had a photograph, taken on the coast somewhere. He was with a girl who we were told was called Colleen... McBride."

"Can't you get in touch with her?" she asked.

"No, she's dead. I think that is what this is all about. But I didn't like to delve too much, just the information to do our job."

"So what do you know about this Michael then, apart from his picture?"

"British Army, almost certainly special forces. No record of him anywhere. Brad and me wondered if Michael Curtiss was even his real name but they insisted it was."

"Who are 'they' then?" she asked.

"The man you were speaking to is Brendan Monahan. He's the main contact. The other guy he came over with was called Jimmy, Jimmy Rafferty. Now he's a right head-case. Frightens me I don't mind telling you, but keep that to yerself," he said, again drifting into a slight Irish tone.

"IRA, I take it?" she asked.

"No, I don't think so. They said not. In fact they wouldn't say much at all if I'm honest, but paramilitary of some kind though, I'm pretty sure," he said.

After a stop for lunch they eventually arrived on the dual carriageway that bypassed the village around three o'clock.

"You need a left here, before the garage," said Kathy pointing to the Drayburn village sign.

Down the narrow streets, taking the same route as Brad Jackson had done just a few days earlier; they turned left into the High Street, past the hotel and into the alleyway which was signed to the car-park.

"Jesus," said Barry. "This is a bit tight," as he slowly negotiated the narrow passageway to the courtyard. He parked in a bay, got out and checked for any signs of scratches on his precious Jag.

Barry took a sports jacket from the back seat and put it on, Kathy had her leather bomber jacket. They took their cases from the boot and followed the signs to reception. There was no-one on duty and Barry rang the bell on the desk to attract someone's attention. It was Louise who eventually came to register them in.

"Mr & Mrs Springer... two nights bed and breakfast... room ten," she said as she took some details. "…Up the stairs and along the corridor at the end," she added.

They found the room. "Hey," said Kathy, as they went in and looked around, "this is not bad."

"Should be, the price they charge," said Barry.

"Lucky you're not paying then," she said.

She paused and looked at him. "So what's the plan then?" she said as she started to hang clothes in the wardrobe.

"Well, we'll have a cup of tea, then have a look around," he said.

Over at The Manor, Michael had spent most of the day on the roof; he had fixed all the loose slates and replaced the broken ones and it was now water proof. He had however found some crumbling masonry at the bottom of one of the chimney stacks which would need attention. He would call again on Monday and Frank was again detailed to collect the necessary materials from the builder's merchants.

It was a similar day to Liverpool, cloudier but still warm and the Major was on hand again to keep Michael supplied with lemonade and anecdotes. By two thirty Michael had done as much as he could and needed to leave to go to Mrs Faulkner's and her garden. The Major paid him for the two days, cash in hand. "In case you need some money for the weekend," he said. Michael thanked him.

Arrangements were made with Frank to meet at nine o'clock the following morning for the fishing trip at the stile where Michael had met him the night of the poachers. "There will be enough room in the boat if young William wants to join us," he said.

Michael made his way to Valley Drive which was only a quarter of a mile or so from the Manor. He was warmly greeted by Mrs Faulkner who was soon letting him know what she needed.

"If you can mow the lawn and clear the flower beds of weeds, that would be wonderful," she said. "My Albert just can't do it now," she said and started to go into great detail about her husband's hospitalisation and subsequent recuperation regime. Michael had to interrupt so he could start the work.

As it happened it wasn't too onerous and by just after four thirty he had finished. She paid him for the two hours and made arrangements for him to call back again in two weeks to cut the grass again.

Michael set off for the two mile journey back to the Lodge, but he was about to make a decision that would change his life. Instead of using the shortcut to the Vicarage as he had done on his way out that morning. he decided to call into the village and buy a bottle of wine. He had been invited to join the family again for dinner and with the children home he felt he should contribute in some small way.

Back outside the White Hart, Barry and Kathy had decided to have a look around the village. To anyone watching they would look like any other tourists with their cameras and local guide map, a fairly small document which they had picked up in a rack of brochures by the hotel reception desk. Barry had his Nikon

The Tinker

around his shoulder; what most people wouldn't have recognised was the added motor drive. It made the camera more cumbersome and was totally superfluous for most amateur photographers but it was an essential piece of kit for anyone wanting to take a number of pictures very quickly. "Just in case," Barry had said to Kathy when he was collecting his gear.

They crossed the road to go to the village store; Kathy wanted to buy some postcards for her mother. Inside there was a carousel of cards depicting the beauties of the Cotswolds, including the village of Drayburn and its wonderful church. "We must pay a visit while we're here," said Kathy choosing a selection.

Barry was on alert and looked around at fellow customers with more attention than would be normal; nobody took any notice of his apparent inquisitiveness. They were used to being stared at by tourists, especially Americans who often viewed them as a different species.

Kathy paid and joined Barry who was outside enjoying one of his cheroots. They were just about to walk down the hill when Barry grabbed Kathy's hand. "Over the road... quick!" he said and the two crossed over. Barry flicked his cigar into the gutter.

"In here," said Barry and they went into the alleyway that led to the car-park.

"What is it?" asked Kathy.

"Can you see that man coming up the hill on the bike, pulling the trailer?"

Kathy stared down the hill squinting her eyes to get a clearer view. "Where?" she said.

"There, coming towards us. It was what Brad said he saw... 'A man on a bike pulling a trailer', that's what he said. I want to get a closer look. Here stand in front of me," Barry said.

Kathy could make out the figure testing himself against the

steep incline. "Oh yeah," she said.

Barry took his camera from his shoulder and removed the lens cap. It was a small zoom lens - two hundred feet range, but would suit his purpose. He was standing behind Kathy and in the shadows of the alleyway. Michael would not see him as he approached the store. Click, click, click, ten frames in a couple of seconds via the rapid fire of the camera's motor drive as Barry went to work. He looked up to take a look to see if he could get any visual recognitions but Michael had got off his bike and was heading into the store.

"Do you want to go in and take a closer look?" said Kathy.

Barry thought for a moment. "No, not yet," he said. "Might be able to get a better shot when he comes out."

A few minutes later Michael left the store carrying a bottle of wine. More clicks.

Barry looked up for a second just as Michael was securing the bottle into one of the panniers on the side of the bike.

"It is him!" exclaimed Barry excitedly in a whisper.

"Are you sure?" whispered Kathy in reply, not turning to acknowledge her boss.

"Well ninety five per cent. We'll need to make a few more enquiries just to be on the safe side," said Barry.

More clicks.

"Shit, I've run out of film," he said.

"What, all thirty six?" said Kathy.

"Yeah, but I've got enough. We'll need to go over to Stonington tomorrow to see if we can get them developed. There won't be anywhere round here," he said.

They watched as Michael moved off and turned left into Vicarage Road.

Barry put his camera away and joined Kathy who was still

The Tinker

standing at the entrance to the alleyway.

"Don't you want to try and follow him?" she said.

"No, he'll be gone by now and I don't want to cause any alarms," he said. "We'll get the films developed and take it from there."

Barry was excited, not just at the possible culmination of the search but the claim of the ten thousand pound bounty he had been offered for a 'successful conclusion', whatever that meant.

"I think this calls for a drink, don't you?" he said.

"As long as you're paying," said Kathy and they went back into the hotel.

At Police Headquarters in Stonington, Chief Inspector Johns was reading the pathologist's report from the Coroner's Office on Bradley Jackson. There was the usual technical medical blurb which he skipped through and went straight to the summary. Death was due to a heart attack but there were signs of a recent trauma to the body in the form of blows to the abdomen and groin which may or may not have contributed to the attack. It would be impossible to be totally conclusive, it said, without further exploration. A more comprehensive report would be available in a few days.

Johns groaned. "An inquest, shit, why is nothing ever straightforward," he said to himself.

He called DC Rickstead to his office.

"Jeff, that death over in Drayburn, post mortem says it appears that he was beaten up before he died... not sure if that caused his death or not, coroner couldn't say for sure."

"Where does that leave us? Do we investigate or not? They can't keep that room sealed off forever," said Rickstead.

"Yes I know. Can you get back over there and ask around. See if anyone saw anything?" said Johns.

"Yes Guv, but we've pretty well done that already, sir," replied Rickstead.

"I know, but we didn't know about the beating then and that needs to be the line of enquiry. As you say we may not get anywhere but we need to be as thorough as we can. You never know someone might have seen something and not come forward," said Johns.

"I'll get on to it," said Rickstead.

"You can pop across tonight. Take Jenkins with you. It'll do her good to get out of here for a bit. Friday night, the hotel could be busier," said Johns.

Rickstead went back to the outer office where two other detectives were working.

"Hey Sam, you've got a hot date tonight," said Rickstead.

"I have? It's the first I've heard about it," she said.

"Yeah, we're going over to Drayburn, the White Hart. Seems our man in the bed may have been beaten up. Boss wants us to ask around, see if anyone saw anything," he said.

"And that's my hot date? Don't think much of that," she said.

"Got any better offers?" said Rickstead.

"No, not when you put it like that," she said. "Anyway, two chances in my book - slim chance, and no chance."

"Yeah, well you could be right but we need to go through the motions. Probably a waste of time as you say. Coroner will probably end up with 'natural causes'," he said.

Rickstead, lit up a cigarette, sat at his desk and started typing. At thirty two he was a couple of years older than his colleague, Samantha Jenkins, a recent addition to the small team.

"What time are we off then?" said Jenkins.

Rickstead looked at his watch. It was five thirty.

"About half an hour, just want to finish this report," he said.

Chapter Ten

Back at the vicarage there was a full house and a great deal of excitement. Both the vicar and Denise looked forward to the children returning from University as any proud parents would. The chatter was incessant as they caught up on news and gossip, this professor, that professor; names that stuck momentarily but soon disappeared from the memory banks.

William was mature for his years and at twenty four it was clear he had inherited his father's gene for premature balding. His fair hair lay in thin wisps lank and shapeless, personal grooming was not a priority. He wore student spectacles and was a shade smaller than his father not quite six feet and he was slim; he would rarely be seen without a 'Smiths' or other cool band tee shirt and faded jeans or cords.

Daniella was a younger version of Denise, bookish looking, again her glasses emphasising the rather studious appearance. The three of them were in the kitchen frantically disgorging all their news when Michael knocked on the door.

William answered. "Michael, how good to see you again. How are you?" he said with genuine warmth. He stood back from the door to allow him to pass and closed it behind him.

"Hello William, Daniella," he said looking at each in turn. "I've bought some wine, red, if that's alright," he said handing the bottle to Denise.

"Oh, that's very good of you Michael, you didn't have to, thank you. Have a seat. John's over at the church he'll be in shortly," she said.

A few minutes later the vicar returned from his duties and the family and Michael sat around the table catching up and discussing issues of the day. In Michael's case it was mostly listening but he felt more at home with the vicar and his family than at any time in his life. His own upbringing had been difficult with an abusive father and alcoholic mother. The army had rescued him; he could have gone in a very different direction.

In a break in conversation Michael raised the question of the fishing trip with William.

"Frank is lending me a rod," he said.

"That'd be great," said William. "It's years since I've been out with Frank. We used to go all the time when I was a kid."

"He reckons his boat will be big enough for the three of us," said Michael.

"Yes, it should be from what I can remember. Not sure where my stuff is," said William. "Do you know, Mother?" he said.

Denise was clearing the dishes and putting them on the draining board ready to be washed up.

"I'll give you a hand with those," said Daniella.

"Thank you, dear," said Denise. "I think your fishing rod is in the shed. That's right, John?" she added looking at the vicar.

"I'm sure I saw it in there a couple of weeks ago. We'll have a look after dinner," said the vicar.

By eight o'clock the errant fishing rod and reel had been found in the shed and dusted off and Michael arranged to call for William at eight thirty the following morning for the walk to meet Frank.

"Weather looks ok," said Denise. "You never know you might catch something for supper," she added.

"There're some big fish in there," said William, "but I never managed to catch one of them. A one pounder was the biggest I ever hooked," he added.

"I'll see you in the morning and thank you again for the dinner. It was very good," said Michael as he made his farewells and headed back to the Lodge.

It was another glorious evening and Michael had opened the window and the country smells again attacked the senses, so fresh, nothing quite like it. It was as though there was more oxygen in the air. He felt invigorated.

Earlier at the White Hart there was a great deal of activity.

The two DC's turned up about half past six and wanted to speak to the manager Gavin Findley who was duly summoned. He took them into one of the small downstairs meeting rooms.

"I thought this was all sorted," said Gavin when the police officers outlined their enquiry.

"Not quite," replied Rickstead. "We have reason to believe that Mr Jackson was beaten up shortly before his death." Gavin looked concerned.

"We need to interview any of your staff who were on duty that evening," added Rickstead.

"Yes of course. I'll get the duty roster."

Gavin left the room for a couple of minutes and came back with a clipboard.

"These are the staff," and Gavin handed over the list.

"Are any of these on duty tonight? We'd like to talk to them," asked Rickstead.

There were a couple of waitresses in the restaurant and Tony the barman. "And I was on duty that night, as well," said Gavin. "But I certainly can't recall hearing anything."

The officers duly interviewed the restaurant staff on the list and as expected it had proven a fruitless exercise.

"Well this is a waste of time," said DC Jenkins after the final interview with the waitresses. Rickstead agreed. "Come on let's get this done and get home," he said.

Tony Rollinson was the last to be interviewed; Gavin would

look after the bar.

DC Jenkins took over the interrogation.

"Come in," she said when Tony knocked on the door.

He was faced with the two officers.

"What's this about?" he asked.

"Sit down... Tony, isn't it? I'm DC Jenkins, this is my colleague DC Rickstead. I know one of my colleagues talked to you earlier in the week about Mr Jackson, the man who died in room seven," she clarified. "We have reason to believe he was attacked shortly before he died and we're asking a few questions to see if anyone can throw any light on this."

"Attacked? What, beaten up you mean?" Tony hesitated for a moment. "No, can't see that. Safe as houses round here. Who'd want to beat up a total stranger?" he asked.

"That's what we're trying to find out," said DC Jenkins.

The interview continued for about twenty minutes before the officers were satisfied with his statement and he was allowed back for his duties.

Seeing Tony leave Gavin returned to the room and confronted the officers.

"When can I open room seven?" Gavin asked.

"Not just yet, we may need to involve forensics. We'll let you know," said Rickstead.

The officers picked up all their paperwork.

"Right, back to the office, drop this lot off and it's off home for me," said Rickstead.

They thanked Gavin for his patience and assistance and left the pub.

"We'll be in touch shortly," said Rickstead as they left the room and headed for the car-park.

"What do you reckon?" DC Jenkins said as she fastened her

seat belt.

"We won't get anything here, even if they do know something, no-one's going to say anything," he replied as he carefully negotiated the car down the narrow alleyway.

"I thought the barman was bit... I don't know, just a feeling," said DC Jenkins.

"Yeah, I got that as well but apart from putting him against the wall and threatening to shoot him, I don't think we'll get anywhere. These communities just close ranks," he said.

"Yeah, you're probably right," conceded DC Jenkins.

Back in the bar Tony was concerned though. He remembered Mark Draper and his expression when he told him about the man and Melanie. He was quite capable, that was certain.

Melanie came in about eight o'clock. She had been home to change but didn't want to stay around the house in case her husband turned up. She ordered her usual and sat at the bar on a stool, her regular seat was occupied.

"Where's your Mark?" asked Tony.

"Work," said Melanie, sharply, as she poured the tonic into the vodka. "And he's not my Mark," she added with equal venom.

Tony moved closer and in hush tones said. "Yeah, whatever, but the police were in here earlier, saying that the man in room seven you had dinner with the other night was beaten up. They're making enquiries, asking questions and that. I mean it could be murder," he said.

Melanie didn't react and sipped her vodka.

"Nothing to do with me," she said, again with an edge.

"I know that, but I think your Mark should know," he said. "I didn't say anything, like," he quickly added.

"Why should he be interested?" she said not letting on her husband's disclosure. "And I told you he's not my Mark... Useless piece of shit," she muttered under her breath.

"No reason," said Tony "Just thought he might want to know, that's all."

Just then the man who was sitting in Melanie's favourite seat came to the bar with two pint glasses. Melanie took little notice, large man, chubby. She looked around at his companion; looked more like a bloke, she thought.

"Two pints of lager, please," he said, "and one for yourself," he added.

"Cheers," said Tony.

He brought the drinks and took the money.

"I don't suppose you could help me, could you?" Barry said as he put the change in his pocket.

"Depends," said Tony.

"I spotted a bloke this evening about five o'clock, on an old bike, pulling a trailer, looked like a tinker or something. He was the spitting image of an old army buddy of mine, Michael his name was. Don't suppose you know where I could find him do you. I'll make it worth your while. I would really love to catch up with him again. It's been a few years," he said.

Melanie heard the conversation and was on high alert and before Tony could say anything she interrupted.

She looked at the man. "What an old bike, pulling a trolley thingy...? Nah, that'd be Ted Saunders. Odd job man, been in the village for years. Nobody round here called Michael, that right, Tony?" she said.

Tony was taken by surprise at the intervention but straightaway picked up the gist.

"Aye that would be right," said Tony. "Old Ted, been here donkeys years," he added.

"Didn't look that old," said Barry.

"Figure of speech," said Tony. "People tend to call him 'old Ted'," he said.

The pair seemed convincing and Barry pondered the response as he went back to the table where Kathy was waiting for any news.

"Well?" said Kathy. "Any luck?"

Barry put the drinks down on the table and sat down.

"Well I don't know. It was strange. I asked the barman if he knew anything and that girl on the stool there interrupted and said it was some guy called Ted something or other, lived here for donkey's years apparently," said Barry.

"Maybe they're right, maybe it isn't him. I mean you've never actually met him, just that photo," she said. "Or... he could be using a different name," she added.

"Yeah, I guess that is a possibility, but... oh, I don't know... it all seems a bit peculiar. We'll get the pictures developed and keep an eye out over the weekend, maybe ask a few more folks, see what they say," said Barry.

Back at the bar Melanie was concerned that someone else was looking for Michael. "What was all that about?" asked Tony.

"Oh nothing, someone who should be minding their own business, not asking questions," she said.

"But why did you say it wasn't Michael?" he said.

"As I said people should mind their own business. We don't want people coming in here and upsetting the village, do we?" she said.

"No, but even so," said Tony.

Before he could say any more Melanie cut him off. "Listen if anyone else comes in looking for Michael just say nothing, right?"

"Yeah, ok," said Tony, feeling somewhat admonished and he went along the bar picking up glasses.

Melanie needed to make another house call; she was not disappointed at the prospect.

It was around eight forty five when Melanie arrived at Michael's lodge and knocked on the door.

Michael had showered and changed since his return from his dinner with the vicar and family and was reading his new book just wearing his tee shirt and shorts. The windows were still open allowing a pleasant breeze through the cottage. He heard the church clock sound the three quarters. Then the tap on the door.

He had a feeling it would be Melanie; no-one else visited.

He opened the door. "Hello," she said.

"Come in," he said, but not as coldly as he had on previous occasions.

"Thanks," she said. "I need to speak to you. Someone else was in the pub asking about you."

"Have a seat," he said.

Melanie was holding a carrier bag. "I hope you don't mind I've bought a bottle. I know you don't keep any in," she said with a smile, and produced a bottle of red wine.

He took it from her and went into the kitchen and returned with two glasses and the cork removed. He poured the wine and handed one to her.

"So what's the story?" he said, and Melanie revealed the conversation between the man in the pub and Tony.

"He said he saw you on your bike in the High Street," she said.

"What did Tony say to him?" he said.

"He didn't get a chance. I was at the bar and spoke to him before Tony could answer. Just told him it was that Ted bloke, same as I told the other chap, Brad."

"So what did he say, this man who was asking the questions?" he asked.

The Tinker

"Nothing he just went back to his table," she replied.

"What did he look like?" asked Michael.

"Biggish guy, fat... bit of a beer-belly, gingerish hair. He was with a woman, at least I think it was a woman. She looked more like a bloke, very butch she was," she said. "Do you know them?"

Michael was thinking. "No, I don't think so," he said.

"What are you going to do?" she asked.

"Don't know yet. They obviously don't know for certain who I am or they wouldn't be asking questions. I'll keep an eye out for them. I won't be around much tomorrow, I'm going fishing," he said.

"That's nice," she said. "Where?"

"At the Manor. I've been doing some work for the Major," he replied.

Michael took another sip of wine.

"There is another thing I need to tell you," she said. "That bloke Brad, the one they found in the White Hart."

"What about him?" asked Michael.

"It turns out he was beaten up the night before he died," she said.

Michael looked at her. "Beaten up? By who?"

"It was Mark, he did it. He told me last night. According to Tony, the police have been round the White Hart tonight questioning the staff again. A possible murder enquiry he said. Not that it concerns you, just needed you to know that the police are around that's all."

Michael was taking this in. "But why did Mark beat him up?" he asked.

"Someone saw him trying to chat me up and told Mark," she said. "I told you he was a nutter. I've had to barricade myself in the bedroom to stop him coming in," she said.

"Hmm," said Michael. "That's not good."

161

"I don't know what he'll do if the police find out it was him that beat the bloke up," she said.

"Where is he now?" he asked.

"At work. He said he'd be in around ten," she said.

"Have you got anywhere to stay, girlfriends? What about Janice?"

"Mrs Audley?" she said.

"I've not said anything to her," she said.

Michael was deliberately avoiding the obvious question she was dying to ask. Given the situation he could not afford any attachments.

"I think you should," he said.

The church clock struck the quarter hour. Michael got up and closed the windows; moths and other flying insects were beginning to make their presence felt.

He pulled the curtains and turned on the table lamp behind his armchair he used for reading.

"Can I stay for a while. I don't want to go back," she said. "We don't have to do anything if you don't want to."

"Aye, ok," he said.

His opinion of Melanie was changing. Tonight she was almost soberly dressed, for her anyway; in a casual top and skirt, again with only a hint of makeup. She was a stronger character than he had first imagined and he could empathise with the shambles of a home life she had to contend with. He had been witness to a similar situation as a child.

"Can I use the bathroom?" she said.

"Of course, you know where it is," he said.

She came back in and he was seated in his armchair drinking his wine in his shorts and tee shirt.

"I feel a bit overdressed. You don't mind do you? It's so warm," she said, taking off her top and unzipping her skirt.

"No," he said and she walked over to him in just her underwear.

She knelt down in front of him and put her head on his lap. Nothing more. They stayed there like that for a few minutes. Intimate company. Michael was again in deep contemplation.

It couldn't last long and the frisson of the moment soon overwhelmed them. They made love on the rug in front of the fireplace.

The church clock struck eleven and Michael and Melanie were still lying there on the floor.

"You need to go," he said. "It's getting late."

Melanie leaned up on one elbow. "You're a difficult man to love, Michael," she said. "You don't let your guard down for one minute, do you? Has anyone ever got through to you?"

"Just one," he said.

"She was a lucky girl," she said.

"No, not really, she's dead," said Michael.

"I'm sorry," she said.

Melanie picked up her underwear and clothes and made her way to the bathroom.

After a few minutes she returned to the living room where Michael had also dressed and was back in his armchair.

"I'll walk with you, if you like," he said. "It's a long way."

"No, no," she insisted. "I'll be fine. There's still plenty of people about. I walk all the time."

"If you're sure," he said. "I don't mind."

For a moment she imagined her and Michael strolling arm in arm through the streets like she had dreamed of for so long, but not tonight.

"It's ok, honest, Mark will be in bed with a bit of luck by the time I get in, starts early on a Saturday," she said. "Is it ok if I call again?" she added.

"Aye, ok," said Michael, and he opened the door and watched as she turned and walked along the path to the road.

He had enjoyed her company this evening; it had surprised him.

It took Melanie nearly half an hour to get back to the cottage. She was ready for a fight if necessary but wasn't looking for one.

She let herself in; Mark, once again, was asleep in the chair. There was a half empty bottle of scotch on the table; she didn't disturb him.

Saturday morning and Michael was up early again. As arranged, he met William at the vicarage and they set off down the footpath towards the Manor Estate. It was cloudy but still warm and no threat of rain. Michael was in his shorts and vest. William had a faded pair of jeans and a favourite 'Final Tour - Dead Kennedys' tee shirt, his rod under his arm and he carried a basket containing his fishing gear. It included a pack of sandwiches which Denise had thoughtfully made for them 'enough for the three of you,' she had said.

After about twenty minutes they reached the gate and stile to the estate and Frank was waiting for them.

"Grand morning," he said as he greeted them.

As they walked along the footpath into Toppis Wood toward the lake, Frank chatted to William wanting to know how things were at University. "Any girlfriend on the scene?" he asked.

William didn't respond. Michael tagged along behind them taking in the glorious countryside totally immersed in his surroundings and almost oblivious to Frank and William's conversation.

As they exited the tree cover the lake stretched out before

them; the scene was breath-taking. There was a slight mist rising from the shimmering surface as the sun's rays connected with the water; spectacular colours, browns, greens, mirroring the surrounding flora. Water-boatmen skipped across the top dodging predatory fishes creating random patterns; spiders webs glistened with early-morning dew; a perfect summer's day.

The fishing holes where Michael and Frank had confronted the poachers were empty. "No-one booked today. We'll have the lake to ourselves," said Frank.

Around the other side of the lake there was a small wooden hut where bits of equipment were stored. A rowing boat was tethered to a mooring in front. The door to the boathouse was wide open, Frank went inside and produced his spare rod and handed it to Michael.

"I've got a nice selection of flies here. Should see us through for today," said Frank producing a Perspex box separated into compartments with lures of different colours.

Resembling a scene from the pages of Jerome K Jerome, the three men made their way to the boat. William climbed in and Frank passed him the rods, landing net and other fishing gear; Michael was holding it steady.

Then they swapped with Frank holding the boat while Michael got in sitting opposite William. Finally Frank passed Michael the oars then boarded and sat in the middle. It wasn't a large lake, maybe two hundred yards across and with three sides bordered by woods it was reasonably sheltered from the wind, so within around five or six minutes with Michael on rowing duties they were in the middle.

"This is a good spot," said Frank looking at various landmarks on the bank, a large beech, a hawthorn bush and the top of the Manor House in the distance and triangulating from memory.

"Right, I'll keep the boat steady. William you cast left, Michael right, then we'll swap over," said Frank. "It's about fifteen feet deep here, deeper over there, nearer thirty," he said pointing to an area to the right about fifteen yards away. "But you can reach the bank under those trees with a good cast from here. The trout tend to swim quite shallow. They feed well this time of day. You never know you might even get the odd carp as well, they've been known to take a fly," he said.

Frank took the oars from Michael to make sure there was enough room to manoeuvre and lay them long-ways on the floor of the boat.

Given they were fishing from a boat, Frank had got short rods, four feet, which would still enable them to cast into the shallower waters by the trees where the fish would feed. Michael and William picked up their equipment and William expertly threaded the line through the five rings and tied on the leader, then the fly. Michael watched then followed suit; it had been a while.

William tried the first cast, a good distance into a shady bower and gently reeled in slowly. Michael watched his technique, then tried his luck. It wasn't the same distance but good enough for a relative novice.

While Michael and friends were enjoying their fishing trip, back in the village more serious matters were being considered. At the White Hart, Barry and Kathy were discussing their plans for the day.

"First thing is to get into Stonington and find a photographic shop," said Barry as they finished their breakfast. They went back to their room and collected their things, Barry took the film out of the camera and replaced it with another roll. He never allowed his camera to be without a film, habit.

The Tinker

By ten o'clock they had reached Stonington and parked up and after a browse round the small shopping centre found what they were looking for. The window was full of cameras and lenses; there was a notice offering four hour printing.

There was a loud clang from the doorbell as Barry and Kathy entered the shop. A man was fiddling with some stock behind the counter and turned to greet his customers.

"How quickly can you do a contact print for me?" said Barry putting the film cartridge on the counter.

The man picked up the cartridge and looked at it.

"Thirty six?" he queried. "I could have it for you by Tuesday," he said.

"That's no good. It says four hours in the window," said Barry.

"That's for basic printing not a specialised order," he said.

"I need it today; it's urgent," he said. "And I want a blow-up or two as well. I'll make it worth your while," he added.

The proprietor looked at his watch.

"Saturday is my busiest day," he said seriously and he looked at the roll of film, then at Barry. "Look, I'll see what I can do, but I can't promise."

"We can call back later," said Barry looking at Kathy.

"Ok, around two," said the man.

They left the shop. "What do we do for four hours?" said Kathy.

"We'll have a look round this place," said Barry.

"What will we do for the rest of the three hours fifty five minutes?" she said and started to laugh.

Back in Church Cottages, Melanie woke around seven o'clock and removed the chair from behind the bedroom door to get a shower. There was no sign of Mark in the spare room, the door

167

was still open and the bed looked like it hadn't been slept in. She went down stairs to see if he had gone to work; he was still asleep in the armchair more or less where she left him.

She shouted at him. "Hey, you... arsesole, you better get up you need to be at work in half an hour."

Mark suddenly opened his eyes, startled at the awakening. He tried to get up from the chair.

"Ooo shit, my head," he said. "Any chance of a cuppa?"

Melanie looked at him. "You make your own, I need the bathroom. Oh and the police were asking questions about the beating you gave that bloke at the White Hart."

"Shit," he said still trying to get his bearings.

"Yeah, right," said Melanie. "Don't worry, no one's saying nothing," she said.

"Where were you last night?" he said gradually getting himself together.

"Out," she said and went back up stairs and locked herself in the bathroom.

A moment later Mark followed her and banged on the door with his fist. "If I find you've been shagging around again, there'll be trouble," he shouted.

"Piss off," she shouted back.

He went back downstairs to the kitchen, boiled a kettle and made himself a coffee. Then he removed the dishes from the sink and washed his face; he was still dressed in his working clothes that he had slept in.

He dried himself off with a tea towel and having heard Melanie vacate the bathroom he went back upstairs. Before she could place the chair against the door he burst in on her. She had a towel around her head and was wearing a dressing gown fastened by a tie.

His eyes were wide as if he were on drugs. She just stared at

The Tinker

him. Without warning he made a lunge for the dressing gown and ripped it open.

"You need teaching a lesson, my girl," he said and started to unzip his trousers,

She stood there with the dressing gown gaping, her arms across her breasts, legs firmly pressed together.

"Don't you come anywhere near me, you bastard," she said her voice quivering.

He moved closer.

Melanie backed away slowly as he approached her then felt the shelf edge of the dressing table pressing against her, the limit of her retreat. Her hands fumbled anxiously flapping around the surface trying to find anything with which to defend herself. Her fingers detected a familiar shape, a pair of nail scissors. Mark made another move. She grabbed the scissors and in a single movement plunged them into his arm and he yelped in pain. She pushed him backwards causing him to overbalance and he fell onto the bed allowing her to make good her escape. Melanie ran past him back into the bathroom and locked the door.

"If you don't leave me alone, you bastard, I'll go to the police myself and tell them it was you who beat up that bloke. I want you out of here," she shouted. She was shaking.

"You slag," he shouted as he went downstairs. "You haven't heard the last of this," he said.

Mark went into the kitchen and examined his arm; it was only a scratch. He stemmed the bleeding and put on a plaster.

Melanie listened from the bathroom until she heard the front door go. Then she slowly went downstairs. Mark had gone.

Chapter Eleven

By two o'clock Barry and Kathy had had enough of Stonington.

"I think we've been in every shop," said Kathy "and I don't want to see another coffee as long as I live. I mean, what do people do around here all day?" she said.

"It is a bit dead," said Barry.

They made their way back to the photographic shop and the proprietor recognised them straight away.

"You're in luck," he said. "I've been fairly quiet today," and he produced a coloured folder from beneath the counter and opened it up.

Barry looked at it. "Have you got an eye glass by any chance?" he said, and the man produced a magnifier and handed it to Barry who scoured the small thumb-nail prints. He found three which were particularly clear.

"Can you do me three, ten by eights of these please?" and Barry gave him the numbers.

"Yes, I can do that. I presume you want them today?" he said.

"Yeah, it's urgent," said Barry.

"You're talking about seven fifty a print, high gloss," said the proprietor.

"Yeah," said Barry. "That's ok. Whatever it costs," he added.

The man looked at his watch. "Can you come back at four. If it stays quiet I should have them ready for you by then," he said.

Barry looked at Kathy and saw her face drop, another two hours to kill.

To pass the time they decided to head out of town and explore the countryside but arrived back at the car-park in Stonington just before four. They walked to the photographic shop where the proprietor was waiting for them, he handed Barry another folder.

The Tinker

"Managed to get them done for you, three ten by eights as marked," he said.

"Thanks," said Barry and he paid the man. "Can you let me have a VAT receipt, for expenses?" he clarified.

Barry and Kathy left the shop and headed to the car-park. Once inside the Jag, Barry opened up the folder and looked at the three large prints and showed them to Kathy; he was anxious to see the fruits of his labours.

"That's him... I just know it is." He looked at Kathy, his face reflecting the excitement he felt. "I'll get a couple of prints off to our friends on Monday. They'll know for certain. Then it's up to them," said Barry. "We've done our bit."

Barry turned on the ignition and fired up the Jag. "You know, I was thinking, if I wanted to disappear, I mean really disappear, what would I do?"

Kathy looked at him.

"An itinerant worker would do it," she said.

"That's my thinking an' all, but why would people lie?" he said.

"Don't know," said Kathy. "Maybe they weren't. As I said, he could be calling himself Ted whatsisname."

"Yeah, that's true I guess, but it was though... I don't know, all a bit shifty."

The car-park was starting to empty as shoppers had replenished their stocks and were heading home. Barry joined the queue exiting the parking lot.

"Well I think we'll have another look around the village. You never know we may spot him again," he said as they reached the car.

"I hope I never have to go back to Stonington again. I've seen enough quaintness to last a lifetime. Give me Liverpool any day," said Kathy.

"Amen to that," said Barry.

The visit to the lake was a special time for Michael. He had spent the best part of seven years moving from town to town, country to country always keeping one step ahead, but here in Drayburn he was among friends. It was the only place he returned to, a place of safety. He took in the scenery. The only sound was birdsong and the quarter hour striking of the church clock some way in the distance. Swallows and swifts skimmed the water picking up insects, the vivid flash of a kingfisher, the occasional disturbance of the water as a fish broke the surface, added to the beauty of the countryside. Even the Great Crested Grebe paid them a visit scurrying in the shallows followed by her five chicks in search of small fry. Here was a chance to be a person again.

There was little conversation on the boat, concentration was total as the three pitted their wits against the illusive trout. The occasional whisper, 'you might want to try across there; let out more line', words of advice from Frank, were the only attempt at discourse.

By lunchtime both William and Frank had caught fish but not the size you could take home and have for tea and had put them back. Michael was still to catch anything. They went back to the boathouse where Frank distributed slightly warm lemonade, kindly donated by the Memsahib to go with the sandwiches lovingly prepared by the vicar's wife.

During the afternoon the earlier sun was gradually replaced by clouds and despite Denise's optimism the weather was definitely breaking. It was around four thirty when Frank suggested calling it a day "before we get drenched," he said.

"Aye," said Michael. "Just one more cast and we'll head back.

The Tinker

There's a spot by that overhanging ash tree which I haven't tried yet. Frank looked at the spot. "Yeah, worth a go," he said.

Frank was stood up and fishing the other side of the boat as Michael made his cast.

"You're getting too good," said William as the line nestled on the water about ten feet from the shore and directly underneath the chosen spot. It was his turn to sit and watch.

Slowly Michael reeled in. Then suddenly the hit; a fish had taken the fly. The rod almost bent in half with its weight.

Frank turned around and saw Michael struggling to hold the rod, frantically reeling in the line.

"Hey, that's a beauty you've got there. Don't worry about reeling in, let some line out... There's no hurry. He'll get tired before you do. Let him run with it for a minute, then hit him again," said Frank sharing all his expertise.

William was ready with the landing net.

Michael let out the reel then locked it and pulled the rod sharply back. There was a tug as the hook pulled on the fish. Then... snap! The line broke. The sudden change of tension caused Michael to overbalance and he fell backwards crashing into Frank, sending him over the side. All the weight in the boat had now been distributed to Frank's side and with William unable to hold it steady, the boat capsized completely. Both William and Michael were overboard. Frank was quickly up and hanging onto the side of the upturned boat. Michael too was soon alongside, wiping water from his eyes.

"Where's William?" he said to Frank.

"Don't know... he's not surfaced," he said, scanning the area of lake directly around him.

"Wait there!" said Michael and he took a lung full of air and dived down. There was zero visibility in the murky waters.

173

Michael reached the bottom and felt around. There was weed and debris everywhere. He surfaced and took in more air and went back down widening the search. Then he felt a flailing arm. He followed it down and grabbed William by the waist but he wasn't moving. Michael went to his legs and feet. One of his sandals had become trapped in between the crook of two submerged branches. In a moment Michael had him free and pushed him upwards.

Frank saw William break the surface and made a grab for his tee shirt with one hand whilst still holding onto the boat with the other. He managed to pull William towards him just as Michael surfaced next to him.

"He's unconscious," said Michael. "Tip his head back."

With Frank trying to hold him steady Michael held William's nose and tried to breath into his mouth but the angle made it impossible.

"We've got to get him ashore... help me," said Michael and between them they dragged William towards the bank.

It seemed to take forever but it was less than two minutes when Michael felt the muddy bottom under his feet and he could stand up. Frank had been unable to keep pace with Michael and was swimming slowly in a sort of 'doggy paddle' style towards an adjacent fishing hole.

Michael had William by the tee shirt facing upwards out of the water. Once ashore Michael pulled him onto the bank then turned him over onto his stomach. He started to push on his back trying to expunge the water from William's lungs, then started CPR.

"Go and get help," shouted Michael seeing Frank had almost reached land.

Frank was still struggling to get himself out of the lake, the glutinous mud clawing at his waders and holding him back. He made a final effort then paused for a moment to catch his breath.

The Tinker

"I'm on my way," he said.

Frank started walking as fast as he was able around the lake and up the long footpath to the house, his sodden wellingtons making a squelching noise with every step. He used to be reasonably fit but, as he had complained to Michael earlier, his legs weren't as good as they used to be and it took him almost fifteen minutes to reach the Manor. The Major was cleaning one of his shot guns on one of the patio tables at the back of the house when he saw Frank struggling up the rise towards him clearly distressed.

"What's the matter, old boy?" said the Major, putting his gun down and walking towards the game-keeper.

Frank stopped and bent down with his hands on his knees, trying to get enough breath to speak; his legs were aching and he was in agony.

He inhaled deeply, once, twice, three times, before he managed to summon the energy.

"Quick... sir! Ring for an ambulance... There's been an accident... down on the lake," he panted.

The Major went inside and dialled the emergency service. "As quick as you can," he said.

Frank was seated on one of the chairs with his head between his knees taking in deep gasps of oxygen and clearly in some pain when the Major returned.

"You're soaking wet, old boy," said the Major. "What's happened?"

Frank was gradually recovering his powers of speech.

"The boat... capsized," he said and took a breath. "It's William... Michael pulled him out... but he... he looks in... in a bad way."

"Right," said the Major," I better phone the Reverend. The medics are on their way but they won't be here for a while."

"How are they going to get down to the lake...? They'll

Alan Reynolds

never get an ambulance down there," said Frank, his breathing stabilising.

"Don't know, old boy, they'll have to walk, I suppose," said the Major.

It was twenty minutes before the vicar arrived at the Manor house; he had been chairing a Bible group meeting.

"What's happened?" he said as he got out of his car.

The Major was about to say something when Frank interrupted. "It's William, there's been an accident, the boat tipped over," he said.

"What!? " said the vicar. "Where is he?" he said.

"Still down by the lake. Michael was with him trying to revive him," Frank said. "I'll take you down there."

"But you need to get out of those wet things," said the Major.

"No, Frank, you stay here. I'll find them," said the vicar, seeing Frank was in no state to go anywhere.

Frank gave the vicar directions. "You can't miss it," he said.

So the vicar headed down the long tree-flanked footpath that lead to the lake. It was downhill but it still took another ten minutes before he reached the waterside and could see Michael still sitting with William on the other side of the lake.

The vicar made his way through the trees to the place where Michael and William were.

"William!" said the vicar.

"He's ok," said Michael. "Just needs to rest; he's had a bit of a shock."

William opened his eyes. "Dad...?" he said, seeing his father standing over him.

"You ok son?" said the vicar.

"Yeah... I think so," said William." Feel a bit tired."

"That'll be the shock," said Michael. "We need to keep him

warm."

The vicar took off his sports jacket and wrapped it around William.

"What about the ambulance?" asked Michael. "He needs to be checked over."

"It's on its way," said the vicar.

"I've lost my glasses," said William, squinting to focus his eyes.

"Don't worry, we can replace them," said the vicar.

"It's ok, I've got a spare pair at home," said William.

It was another twenty minutes before the paramedics eventually arrived carrying their medical kits and a portable stretcher; they were led by the Major.

Michael gave them the background. One of them checked William's vital signs and put an oxygen mask over his face.

"Looks ok," said the medic, "but we'll take him in to get him checked over."

They gently moved William onto a stretcher and started the long haul back to the house.

By the time the stretcher party arrived at the house Denise and Daniella had arrived having been driven over by the verger. There was a commotion as the concerned relatives huddled around William. The effects of the oxygen were helping the revival process and he was already beginning to look much better.

Frank was still seated on the patio chair and attracted the vicar's attention.

"Reverend... " The vicar looked around. "He's a miracle this man," said Frank loudly, nodding towards Michael. "Went down twice to pull him out, he did. I thought he was gone when we got him to the bank. Saved his life, that's for sure."

The vicar grabbed Michael's hand. "We can never repay you,"

said the vicar.

"You don't have to," said Michael. "Only did what had to be done."

"A miracle worker, you mark my words," Frank repeated dramatically.

Denise went over to him.

"I can't begin to say thank you for saving William," she said.

"Anyone would do the same," he said.

"That's not true," she said. "It takes a special character."

She looked at him. "My goodness you're soaking wet... and covered in mud. You need to get into some dry clothes."

She turned to the Major. "Have you got anything you can lend Michael till we get back to the Lodge?"

"Of course, I'll get the Memsahib to find something suitable. Take a shower as well if you want."

"Thank you," said Michael.

So William went into the ambulance accompanied by Denise and Daniella. Michael went into the house with the Major to get showered and changed and the vicar stood talking with Frank and the verger.

By the time Michael reappeared, the vicar and the Major were in the porch of the Manor looking skywards; the threatened rain was cascading from the skies, just a summer shower. The verger had gone back to the church and Frank had recovered sufficiently to return to his cottage to change and put on his rain-proofs. He said he wanted to go back down to the lake later to salvage the boat and any fishing gear.

The vicar looked at Michael and stifled a laugh. He was standing there wearing a pair of tweed trousers, which looked like they had last seen the light of day thirty years earlier on a shooting party. They were several sizes too big around the waist and just about reached his ankles. The Major's wife had secured them with a large safety pin in the absence of a suitable belt. A check shirt which looked more like a night gown completed the ensemble. He was carrying a plastic bag with his clothes.

"Where're your shoes?" asked the vicar.

"In the bottom of the lake somewhere," said Michael.

"We'll get you a new pair. It's the least we can do," the vicar said.

"It's not necessary," said Michael. "I have spare."

"I insist... Come on I'll give you a lift back," the vicar said.

They said their farewells to the Major. "'I'll let you have the clothes back," said Michael.

"No rush," said the Major and the vicar and Michael headed back to the vicarage.

It was strangely quiet in the car both contemplating the events but from differing perspectives. For Michael the shock had brought back some of his demons. For the vicar he was thinking about the consequences if Michael hadn't been there.

The vicar dropped Michael at the gates of the vicarage, then headed to the hospital in Stonington to check on William. He would wait until he was ready to be discharged then bring the family back, he explained.

Michael went to the Lodge. Luckily his keys were still in the pocket of his shorts.

He changed into his cut-off jeans and tee shirt and took a drink of lemonade from the fridge. Suddenly he felt the need for something a bit stronger but without any alcohol around he would resist the temptation.

In the White Hart Melanie was having an after-work drink with Mrs Audley. She had said nothing to her about Mark's assault but Janice knew something wasn't right. Melanie hadn't been her normal bubbly self. After a glass of wine Melanie confided in her boss and told her of the attempted rape.

"You must go to the police," she said.

"Won't do any good, it's my word against his. A 'domestic' they'll call it," said Melanie.

"Well you can't stay there with him can you?" said Mrs Audley. "You can always stop with us, temporarily, if you like," she added as an afterthought, but Melanie detected the hint of reluctance.

"Thank you," she said. "I'll see how we go."

At seven o'clock Jack Flemming, the verger, came into the pub almost bursting with the news about Michael and his heroic deeds. He went to the bar and ordered a pint. It was Saturday night and it was fairly busy. The restaurant was fully booked and, with the exception of room seven, so was the hotel.

Tony was on duty together with one of the part time staff that worked Saturdays. He bought Jack his drink and change.

"Did you hear the news about Michael?" he said to Tony taking the first sip of his pint of bitter. "What would that be?" replied Tony

"Only pulled young Will Colesley out of the lake. Dived down three times before he managed to find him... Him and Frank Johnson managed to get him to the side... Michael gives him the kiss of life and everything. Young Will was already dead according to Frank... saved his life, he did, Michael."

Like Chinese whispers the story was already beginning to attract embellishments.

Melanie arrived at the bar to get another round in for her and Mrs Audley and caught the back-end of the verger's story.

"What was that about Michael?" she asked, and the verger, not for the first time, related the story with even more drama.

The Tinker

"A miracle the vicar called it," he said.

Just then Barry and Kathy came into the bar for a pre-dinner drink. Melanie spotted them straightaway. She turned to the verger who was sipping his pint; Tony was serving another customer. She whispered. "Please don't say anything about Michael in front of those two," she said. "I don't know who they are but they've been asking questions about him. I don't like the look of them."

The verger looked around and saw Barry and Kathy seated at the bar. "What those two...? They look like two blokes," he said.

"Yeah," she replied.

"Wonder why?" he said.

"Don't know but keep an eye on them, eh? We don't want to put him in any danger do we?" she said.

"Danger...?" he replied quizzically. "What danger?"

"Don't know, call it woman's intuition," she said and went back to Mrs Audley with a glass of wine.

"Do you mind, Mrs Audley, I have to go. Something's cropped up," she said.

"What's happened...? It's not Mark is it? What's he been up to?"

"No nothing like that," she said.

She left the pub and went across to the store to collect some provisions and headed down Vicarage Road towards the church. It had stopped raining, just a brief shower, but there was a moist feel to the air. It was also cooler. Melanie was dressed in her work clothes with a jacket over the top and as she walked down the narrow street, the clicking of her heels echoed around the houses. She had her make-up bag and a change of clothes with her; after the incident with Mark that morning, she had already decided she might not be returning to the marital home.

Through the gate and up the footpath to the Lodge. She knocked on the door.

Michael answered it. "Come in," he said.

"Thanks," she said and went inside. Michael closed the door and took her jacket, She put her bags down by the front door.

"Just been hearing about your exploits today. It's all round the White Hart," she said.

"Oh," he said.

"Yes, the verger was in there telling all and sundry," she said.

Michael looked worried.

"It's ok, I had a word and told him to keep it to himself. That strange couple were in the bar. You know the ones who were asking about you last night," she said.

"Thank you," said Michael.

"What are you going to do about them?" she asked.

"Nothing I can do," said Michael.

"I wish I knew what they're up to," she said.

"Best you don't get involved," he said.

There was a look of concern on her face. She changed the subject, seeing it was not going go any further.

"Have you eaten?" she said.

"No," he replied.

"I thought not," she said.

"I didn't know whether you had anything in so I went to the store and got some bits and pieces... not much. A bit of ham, some pasta and a cheese sauce mix and this," she said holding up a bottle of wine.

"Thank you, it wasn't necessary," he said. "I've got food in... just didn't feel very hungry."

"Well, let's go into the kitchen and see what there is. I'm starving," she said.

The Tinker

Michael wasn't about to argue. He was only just beginning to come to terms with today's events and how close he had come to causing William's death. If only he hadn't over balanced, if only he hadn't tried one last cast, if only they had been wearing life jackets. Questions running through his head he couldn't resolve or rationalise.

"Thank you," said Michael. "I'll pay you for the stuff," he said.

She walked through to the kitchen with her carrier bag and put it on the small work-top. She looked in the fridge there were the basics, milk, eggs, butter, some sausages.

"Where are the pots and pans kept?" she asked.

Michael directed her to the cupboard underneath the small cooker.

"Great, I can do something with this," she said, bringing out a frying pan. "Any olive oil?"

"Just what's there," he said.

"It'll have to be butter then. Can you open the bottle and pour us a glass and I'll crack on?"

Michael obliged and was then given his marching orders. "You go and put your feet up," she said. "It won't take long."

He could see Melanie beavering away in the kitchen from his armchair and any thoughts that she might be getting too close had gone. He didn't care now; the events of the day had affected him more than he had realised. It had resurrected old feelings, intense fear, isolation, anxiety - probably delayed shock; right now company was welcomed.

Melanie found plates and cutlery and within twenty minutes she was dishing up.

They sat together at the small table in the corner of the room. The curtains were still open with a skylight letting in some air.

Melanie brought in the wine and topped up the drinks.

"Thank you," said Michael.

"So what happened? On the lake," she said.

Michael played down the incident just saying that the boat had capsized and he had helped get William ashore.

"I hope he'll be ok," she said.

"He'll be fine. He was wide awake and talking when they took him off in the ambulance," he said.

She looked at him surprised at his casualness; it was almost blasé.

"This tastes good," said Michael after a couple of mouthfuls of pasta, changing the subject.

They finished their meal with just passing conversation.

"Can I use your shower after dinner," she said.

"Yes, of course," he said, "As long as you don't mind using the same towels I used this morning. They should be dry by now," he added.

"That's ok," she said. There was a pause.

"Mark tried to rape me this morning," she said.

"What?" said Michael and she described what had happened.

"What are you going to do?" he asked.

"Well I can't go to the police, they won't do anything. I told Mrs Audley, she said I could stay with her, but to be honest I think she was only saying it," she said. "I was hoping... that maybe I could stay with you... Just for tonight," she quickly added. "Until I can sort out something more permanent. I just haven't had the time today."

Michael looked at her. On another day he wouldn't even have considered it but today...

"Aye, ok. If you like," he said.

Michael washed the dishes while Melanie took a shower.

It was ten o'clock when Mark walked into the White Hart. The bar was now very busy and he had to queue to be served. Tony eventually got to him. "Evening Mark, what can I get you?" he said.

"Lager, Tone," he said.

Tony looked at him, his eyes were glazed and he looked unsteady on his feet. Tony hesitated for a moment. "You ok, Mark?" he said.

"Yeah, pint of lager," he repeated and Tony started pouring.

The queue had cleared and Mark managed to get himself on a vacant stool.

"One twenty five," Tony said handing over the drink.

Mark took a gulp then looked at Tony. "You seen that slag of a wife of mine?" he said, his voice was now starting to slur.

Tony looked at him. "No mate," he said.

"She's got another bloke again I know she has. I'm gonna fucking kill her when I get hold of her," he said.

"Now go easy, Mark, you don't want to go saying things like that. You know you don't mean it," said Tony.

"I fucking do," said Mark. "She's had it this time."

Tony was really concerned. He knew Mark was unstable and in a drunken state he would be quite capable. Tony thought quickly.

"Donna, can you look after the bar for a moment," he said to one of the other bar staff.

Tony went through into reception and picked up the phone. He took out a card from his pocket and dialled the number. It rang out.

"DC Rickstead," he said when the phone was eventually answered.

"No, he's off duty, can I help at all... I'm DI Johns," he said.

"I've got some information regarding the death at the White Hart," said Tony.

"I'm heading up that investigation," said DI Johns.

"I know who beat up the guy," said Tony. "I want to make a statement," and Tony gave the officer the details.

"Do you know where Mr Draper is now?" asked Johns.

"Yeah, he's in the bar threatening to kill his wife," replied Tony.

"Ok, I'll get someone straight over," said the Inspector.

Tony kept a close eye on Mark who was sitting on a stool at the bar seemingly talking to his drink. He was speaking incoherently. After twenty minutes he ordered another pint. Despite reservations Tony served him; he didn't want him leaving the pub. It was ten thirty and the bar was gradually emptying although over half the tables were still taken.

At 10.45 two officers came into the pub and went to the bar.

"Tony Rollinson?" one of them said. Tony saw them and ushered them through the door into the Hotel Reception.

He told the two officers what he had said to DI Johns on the phone.

"He's over there," he said pointing at Mark through the glass door.

"Ok, leave it to us," said the officer and the two policemen walked into the bar and confronted Mark.

His head was down, he was still staring into his drink and the interruption had spooked him.

He jumped down from his seat. "What do you fucking want?" he shouted at them. The bar went quiet.

"We need you to come with us, sir. We've a few questions we need to ask you," said the officer.

"Well you can fuck off an' all," he said.

"Come on sir, we don't want to cause any trouble do we?" replied the officer.

The Tinker

Mark made a move towards the nearest officer who quickly dragged him to the floor and placed a pair of handcuffs on him. Mark was kicking and screaming but eventually the two officers had him under control and took him outside and into the waiting police car. Tony went to the front of the bar and picked up the two stools that had been upturned. The hum of chat was gradually returning; there was only one topic of conversation.

Chapter Twelve

Seven o'clock, Sunday morning and Michael was awake. He looked at Melanie who was still sleeping; it had been seven years since he had felt the warm touch of someone beside him in bed. He would not normally allow anyone this close but somehow he felt at ease with it. Part of him, that part linked to his survival mechanism however was still on high alert. He could not afford to relax or lose focus; it had kept him alive.

The incident at the lake had disturbed him more than he had realised. During the night he had woken at regular intervals thinking about what happened and trying to rationalise it. He was assuming guilt and far from being a hero, he had convinced himself he was responsible for the whole debacle. It had also set him thinking about his own future. Circumstances had dictated that he had to be single minded of purpose; there had been little room for any emotion over recent years. People who would normally come into contact with him would say that he was a remote individual, not someone who would form attachments. It was different with the vicar and his family. They had never judged him, they accepted him like he was one of the family in the very spirit of Christian principles. William's near death experience had made him realise just how much he did care for the vicar and his family.

He shook himself from his retrospection, there was a call he needed to make. He got out of bed and made some coffee and took a mug into Melanie who was now awake.

"You can stay here if you like. I need to find out how William is. Won't be long," he said.

Melanie was also in a new situation; despite her dalliances this was the first time she had actually slept with someone other than her husband. It was good; she felt safe with Michael.

The Tinker

She sat up in bed and took the steaming mug that he offered.

"Ok," she said. "I'll make us some breakfast when you get back," she added.

Michael washed and dressed and left the Lodge to call on the vicar.

He reached the kitchen door and the smell of a cooked breakfast attacked his senses. Michael knocked and Denise answered.

"Michael," she said. "Come in, so glad you called. Would you like some breakfast?"

Michael went in. "I'm fine thank you. I've just had some." Which wasn't quite true. "Just come to see how William is."

As on every Sunday the vicar was preparing for the morning service and was seated at the kitchen table going through some notes. He rose and greeted Michael warmly. "Hello Michael. Are you ok after yesterday's drama? We've been hearing all about it from William. We were a bit concerned about you," he said.

"I'm fine, thanks. How is he?" asked Michael.

"He's ok, thanks to you," said Denise before her husband could answer. "We got back around eleven last night. William wanted to visit your place to say thank you but we said it was a bit late. We thought you might have had an early night," she continued.

"Yes," said Michael. "I did."

The vicar looked at him. "The doctors gave him a good check over and they were pleased with his progress; you got to him just in time. It was literally a matter of seconds, they said. There's no lasting damage, thank goodness, mainly shock. He's got to rest for a few days but he should be right as rain."

Denise interrupted. "He's in bed at the moment but I know he is keen to see you," she said.

"Like I said yesterday we will never be able to repay you," said the vicar.

"You don't owe me anything. I just did what needed to be done," said Michael.

"Would you like some tea?" said Denise.

"Aye," said Michael. He looked at the vicar. "I thought I could do some tidying down the crypt this morning, unless you have anything else for me."

"No, that's alright, Michael, you don't have to. There's nothing urgent," said the vicar. "You should get some rest."

"I'd like to get on with something. Can't be moping about," Michael said.

"Well that's up to you, but as I said, please don't feel you have to," said the vicar.

Michael finished his tea and went back to the Lodge. He would return to the church later to do some work; he was starting to feel restless.

Melanie had showered and was walking around the Lodge in her underwear when Michael walked in.

"Hello," she said. "Won't be a moment, I'll get us some breakfast. There are some eggs and the bread looks ok. I can do something on toast."

"Great," said Michael.

By nine o'clock Barry and Kathy had checked out of the White Hart and were loading the car with their suitcases. They had been awakened by the church bells announcing the eight o'clock service.

"Can't wait to get back to civilisation," said Kathy. "Couldn't live round here, do my head in. Quasimodo would have difficulty sleeping with that racket going on," she said.

Barry put the folder holding the photographs he had taken on to the back seat.

The Tinker

"Before we go I wouldn't mind having a look round the church," he said. "What do you think?"

"Do we have to? I've seen enough old relics to last a lifetime," she said.

"Won't take long," he said.

"Go on then, but don't hang around, eh?" she said.

Barry edged the car through the narrow alley and out into the High Street. He turned right then immediately left into Vicarage Road. The church spire was their guide.

Barry parked on the grass verge at the end of the churchyard wall, the allotted parking spaces were full, and got out. He took his camera from the dashboard shelf.

"Now that is pretty special you have to admit," said Barry looking down the footpath towards the church with the Yew trees performing their guard of honour.

"Yeah, I'll give you that," said Kathy.

"Come on," said Barry and he walked towards the church taking photographs as he went. They reached the porch that led into the church just as the vicar was returning to the vicarage for his morning coffee following the morning service.

"Morning," said the vicar. "Lovely day."

"Yes," said Barry. "It certainly is."

The vicar was about to walk on when Barry stopped him with a question.

"I don't suppose you know a bloke around here called Michael, do you? Rides around on an old bike pulling a cart," he said.

The vicar looked at him and was about to reply truthfully when he suddenly felt an air of threat about the inquisitor.

"Pulling a cart you say. What was the name again?" he said.

"Michael," said Barry.

"Doesn't ring a bell," said the vicar and walked away.

Barry watched him walk away. "Tha..." He tried to thank him but the vicar was already out of earshot.

Kathy looked at Barry. "Something's not right I'm telling you," said Barry. "Come on let's get out of here. I'll give the boys a ring when we get back and send them the photos."

"You could fax them a copy," said Kathy. "Save some time."

"Yeah, good idea. If they've got a machine..." said Barry.

They got into the car and drove away.

Back in the vicarage Denise was ready with the coffee when the vicar walked in. She sensed something wasn't right.

"Are you alright, dear?" she asked.

"I don't know dear. Someone, a man, definitely not local, was asking if I knew anyone called Michael who rode about on a bike pulling a cart," he said.

Denise looked worried. "What did you say?"

"I said I didn't. Don't know why. I'm not prone to telling lies, but I didn't like the look of him. There was something definitely wrong," replied the vicar who was clearly concerned.

"Where is Michael?" she said.

"In the Lodge, I presume. He hasn't come to the church yet," he said.

"Well you finish your coffee, dear. I'll pop round and see him in a minute and let him know," she said.

The vicar finished his coffee and returned to the church and Denise went to the Lodge.

After she had made them both some breakfast Melanie had decided to return home. She needed to do some washing and housework, she told Michael.

"I'll be fine, I can handle him," she said, although that was

The Tinker

more to convince herself. She was anxious about the possibility of facing her husband again. "I can come back later?" she said.

Michael thought for a moment; against his better judgment, he gave in. "It will need to be later. I'll probably be at the vicarage till about eight," he said.

"What about food?" she asked.

"I'll be ok," he said.

Melanie left the Lodge and headed back to the cottage.

A few minutes later there was a knock on the door. Michael was dressed in his work gear, shorts and old tee shirt; he opened it.

"Hello, come in."

"Thank you," Denise said.

"Can I get you a drink at all?" Michael said.

"No, I can't stop. I just wanted to let you know that someone was asking John about you at the church," she said.

"Oh," said Michael.

"Visitors, not local," she added.

"What did they look like?" he said.

"Oh, I didn't think to ask, but John will know," she said.

"Thanks for letting me know," he said. "I'm going over to the church later I'll speak to him."

"Look it's none of my business but if you are in any sort of trouble, well, you can talk to me. It might help," she said.

Michael thought about the offer. Many things had happened in the week or so since he had returned to Drayburn; maybe it was time to stop running.

"Let me think about it," he said.

She changed the subject. "Would you like to join us for dinner this evening? I know William will be keen to see you, and Daniella. We'll be eating early, about six. John has asked one of the lay preachers to step in for Evensong, given yesterday's events. We're having pheasant. The Major gave us a brace last week."

"Yes, thank you, appreciate that," he said.

"And I'll call round this afternoon and do some tidying up for you and change the bed linen. Daniella wants to do the pheasants," she said.

"Thank you," he said.

Denise left and went back to the vicarage. Michael accompanied her as far as the kitchen then he walked on to the church.

The church clock rang the half hour as Michael arrived; the vicar was in the vestry. Michael knocked on the door. The vicar got up and opened it.

"Michael," he said. "Come in. It's good to see you," he said.

"Mrs Colesley tells me someone was asking after me," said Michael.

"Oh... oh yes, strange couple. He was a big man, stout, ginger hair, I think there was a woman with him. At least I think it was a woman it was difficult to say. Didn't tell them anything... thought it was best," he said.

"Yes, thank you," said Michael.

"You will tell us if there is anything we can do?" said the vicar. "We do want to help, if we can."

"Yes, I appreciate that and your concern," said Michael. "But it really is something that only I can sort out."

The vicar looked at him. "The door is always open if you want to talk about it," he said.

Michael nodded in acknowledgement. "I'll get down to the crypt and sort out a few things".

"Right, well we'll see you later then. I think Denise would like you to come to dinner this evening. I've given myself a night off. Need to be with my family," he said.

The Tinker

"Yes," said Michael, "she has invited me. I look forward to it."

Michael left the vestry and went down to the crypt

Sunday morning at Stonington police station and DC Rickstead was in; DI Johns walked up to his desk.

"Just got an update on our Mr Jackson from the coroner," he said.

Rickstead looked up with an air of expectancy.

"Ruptured spleen and perforated intestine. It's a murder charge," Johns said.

Later that morning Mark Draper was interviewed again with a duty solicitor and confessed that he had beaten up Brad Jackson in a fit of jealousy. "Didn't mean to kill him, I only gave him a kicking," he said.

He was charged with murder and remanded in custody.

Melanie was walking back to the cottage. Tony Rollinson was in the lounge of the pub preparing the tables and spotted her walking by. He quickly stopped what he was doing, left the bar and caught up with her.

"Hi Melanie, thought it was you. What's happening with your Mark? Have they charged him?"

"Charged him? Sorry, don't know what you mean. Haven't seen the toss bag since yesterday," said Melanie.

"He was arrested last night for beating up that bloke who died... I thought you would know," he said.

"No, I've been staying with a friend," she said.

Melanie looked at him. "Where is he now?"

"Still at the cop-shop, I presume," said Tony.

"Thanks," said Melanie and she walked on up to the cottage. That at least solved one problem but she would telephone the police station to find out what was happening.

She got into the house, it was an absolute tip. Mark had clearly vented his anger on anything he could lay his hands on. Chairs had been tipped up, pictures broken. The TV was on its side. Melanie put her hand to her mouth in horror. She found the telephone among the rubbish and found the number of Stonington police station from the directory which was on the floor next to it. She was eventually put through to DC Rickstead who explained what was happening.

"Your husband has been held in custody, pending trial," he said. He told her that there had been no application for bail and Mark would be transferred to Gloucester prison after the formalities had been completed; she could visit him there. "You will need to phone this number and fill in some forms," he said.

"He won't be getting any visits from me," she said before hanging up.

She looked around at the mess then set to work with a bit of luck Mark could be out of her hair forever, she thought. There was a feeling of determination, optimism even; a chance of a new beginning.

Barry and Kathy had made good time and were back in Liverpool by one thirty despite having stopped off for lunch at one of the service stations. Barry eased the car onto the forecourt outside the office. He unlocked the door and Kathy followed. There was a small pile of letters on the floor which she picked up.

She flicked her way through them. "Anything exciting?" asked Barry as he opened the drawers of his desk. The light on the answer machine was flashing; Barry pressed it." You have three new messages," came the automated voice.

Kathy put the letters down on the desk. "Bills and chasers,

The Tinker

mainly," she said. "You're going to have to get some money in soon or you'll be in trouble," she said.

"We'll be ok," he said. "Especially if our man turns out to be Michael."

Barry replayed the messages. More people chasing money. 'When do you think we can expect payment?' said the first. "Shit," he said to himself.

"I'll get the kettle on," said Kathy, "while you get onto Belfast."

Barry rifled around in his drawer and took out the notepad with the phone number and dialled; it rang for over a minute. No answer.

"Don't think he's about," said Barry.

He dialled again. This time it was picked up on the third ring.

"Hello," said the voice on the other end, sharply.

"Brendan...? It's Barry Springer... I think we have found yer man," he said. There was a pause on the other end.

"Have you got a fax machine...? You haven't... No, ok. Can you get to one... great, give me a bell when you're there and I'll send over one of the photos, see what you think... Well if it's not him, it's his brother; that's all I can say. Not sure if he's calling himself Michael though. We asked around nobody's heard of that name. Somebody said his name was Ted somebody or other. I'll put the rest of the photos in the post but you're not going to get them till Tuesday at the earliest... No, I know there's no rush... Yes seven years... No, I suppose a couple of days won't make any difference. Unless of course he disappears again. Yeah ok... Speak again later."

Barry rang off.

"Any joy?" asked Kathy.

"I was right, no fax machine but the shop down the road's got one and he's going there to borrow it," said Barry. Kathy put a mug of tea down on his desk.

"Cheers," he said and took a sip.

It was half an hour before the phone rang.

"Hello Brendan," said Barry, hearing the Belfast brogue. "Ok give us the number. Ring us when you get it."

Barry took down the number and gave it to Kathy who started to feed one of the photographs into the machine.

Five minutes later the phone rang again.

"Brendan...? What do you think...? You do... that's great. What're you going to do...? No, no of course... no you're right, it is none of my business. Well if that's the case, can I just mention the err, subject of payment... You will...? Yeah that's great... by next weekend... Yeah I see, arrangements. Right, well I'll wait to hear from you then and I'll put all the photos in the post first thing," said Barry and he rang off.

"Well," said Kathy.

"It's definitely him. They're convinced," he said.

"Well that's brilliant," said Kathy. "Did they mention payment at all?"

"Yeah, they're bringing the cash with them when they come over," said Barry.

"Did they say when that would be?" said Kathy.

"Not definite, by next weekend, he said".

"Well that will certainly keep the wolf from the door for a bit," she said.

Later that afternoon while Michael was doing some odd jobs around the church and the vicar had gone for a walk with William and Daniella, Denise had gone round to the Lodge to tidy up and change the bed linen. It had taken about an hour and she had noticed the tell-tale signs.

The vicar was back in the vicarage when she returned. Daniella was preparing the pheasants, William had gone to his room. She went through to the study where her husband was working.

"Do you want a cup of tea, dear?" she asked.

The vicar looked up. "Yes, thank you. How did you get on at the Lodge?"

"Interesting," she said. "I think he's been entertaining... either that or he's taken to wearing perfume. Dior, if I'm not mistaken... Obsession."

"You would make a great detective," said the vicar smiling.

"Not really, Melanie was talking about it when I went for my cut a couple of weeks ago. She uses it. It is nice," she said. "You don't think...? Well it is possible," she said answering her own question. "She's certainly capable that one. I do hope Michael knows what he is letting himself in for. A bit too flighty if you ask me," she said and went to the kitchen to make the tea.

Later that afternoon Michael had completed the odd jobs and was back in the Lodge. It was clean and tidy, the bed had been made and even the fridge had been restocked with the basics. Michael smiled in appreciation.

By five thirty he had showered and changed and headed to the vicarage. He knocked on the kitchen door and it was William who greeted him.

"Michael," he said and flung his arms around him in an affectionate 'man-hug'. "I just want to say thank you for saving my life," he said.

Michael instinctively responded.

"That's ok, just as long as you're ok," he said.

"Come in," said Denise.

William had let go and Michael went in and sat at the table. "I have a beer in the fridge if you would like," said Denise. "We'll be eating in the dining room. We usually do when the children are here, there's more room," she explained.

"Thank you," said Michael, overwhelmed at the generous reception.

"Hello Michael," said Daniella who was basting the pheasant. "Thank you for saving William's life."

"Just glad I was there," he said.

After a great deal of chatter they eventually sat at the dining table in the large sitting room where the family would eat when numbers required. Michael knew the room but wasn't a regular visitor. There was a beautiful view of the church through the windows.

"You sit next to William," said Denise.

The vicar said grace and they started eating, full Sunday roast with pheasant. Michael had not eaten this well for many years. The chatter was lively and stimulating and Michael contributed far more than he had in the past, taking a particular interest in William and Daniella's studies.

"Did you go to university?" asked William at one point.

"No," said Michael.

The topic wasn't pursued.

"Do you think Frank found any of my fishing stuff?" asked William.

"Don't know. I'll ask him tomorrow, I'll be seeing him I expect. I'm working on the roof of the Manor repairing one of chimneys," said Michael.

The dinner finished with one of Denise's delicious apple crumbles.

William and Daniella left the table to go back to their bedrooms both had projects to complete. Michael insisted on helping with the washing up. "It's the least I can do after such a great meal," he said.

So Denise was at the sink while the vicar and Michael did the drying.

"So these people who were looking for you," said Denise. "Have you thought who they might be?"

Michael who was holding one of the dinner plates and giving it the serious attention of a tea towel, was slightly taken aback by the question; it was unexpected.

Denise could sense it was a sensitive topic but nevertheless pressed gently.

"You can trust us Michael, you know that don't you?" she said. It was a statement she had made before many times, but she wanted to emphasise, reassure; she was drawing on her years of counselling experience.

"Yes," said Michael. "I've never doubted that... but..." he paused for the right words. "There are some things that are best left in the past."

"Could you be in danger?" she asked. The vicar was an interested bystander and did not want to intervene.

"It's possible," said Michael. "But not likely."

"We would hate for you to have to leave," she warmly said.

"No, I won't be leaving. Not until the autumn anyway," he said.

Denise considered the response. "My offer still stands, if you ever need anyone to talk about it".

"Aye," said Michael.

After the drying up duties had been discharged Michael sat for a while with the vicar and Denise. They talked about future plans for the church and the work he was doing in Africa. "If you ever wanted to get involved, you just have to say," said the vicar.

"Don't you ever think about the future?" asked Denise.

Michael thought about the question; he found it difficult to answer.

"Not really. I don't make plans," he said.

"It just seems such a waste. You have so much to offer," she said.

"I hadn't considered that so," he said.

The church clock chimed the hour, Michael counted the strikes... eight.

"I need to be going," he said. "Thank you for the food and hospitality, oh, and for the cleaning today, very grateful," he said.

"My pleasure," said Denise.

William and Daniella were called to say goodbye.

"John's taking them back to Bristol tomorrow morning, college Tuesday," said Denise.

"When will you be back here?" asked Michael.

"We both finish our courses at the end of June, don't we Dan?" said William.

"Yes," said Daniella, "We'll be back around 26th or 27th."

"See you when you get back then," said Michael

"Hope so," said William. "Thanks for everything," he added, and proceeded to hug Michael.

Michael returned to the Lodge. He had a lot to think about. He went to the kitchen and poured a drink and sat in his armchair trying to make inroads into the book he borrowed from the vicar's library.

The church clock struck the half hour when there was a 'tap, tap' on the door. He got up and answered it.

"Hello Michael, is it ok?" said Melanie.

"Yes, it's fine, come in," he said.

She was carrying a small carrier and overnight case.

The Tinker

"I've brought some things; hope you don't mind. I wasn't taking it for granted," she said. "I can go back if you prefer," she added.

"No, it's fine," he said.

"I've got some news," she said as she took off her jacket. She was dressed casually in blouse and jeans.

Melanie produced a bottle of wine from her carrier. "I've bought some stuff from home that needs eating," she said. "I'll put it in the fridge."

"Ok," said Michael.

"Can you open the wine?" she said and Michael went to the kitchen drawer and retrieved bottle opener while Melanie transferred the contents of her carrier bag into the fridge.

"So what's the news?" asked Michael.

"It's Mark," she said, taking the first sip of her wine. "He's in prison."

Michael looked at her. "What for?" he asked.

"Murder," she said. "That bloke he beat up and died, turns out it was him that caused it. Spoke to the police myself this morning. He's confessed. They're transferring him to Gloucester tomorrow."

"Are you going to see him?" asked Michael

"Are you kidding? I hope he rots in there. With a bit of luck he'll get fifteen years and I'll never have to see his face again," she said. "Spent all day sorting out the house. Would you believe the wanker only turned the place over. I'll need to talk to the insurance tomorrow, see if I'm covered. He broke the TV and my new CD player," she said.

Melanie went into the bedroom and started unpacking her overnight bag which included a family photograph of what looked like her as a young girl with her parents, and a teddy bear which she placed next to 'her side' of the bed. Michael had followed her and was watching.

"Hope you don't mind," she said. "They go everywhere with me."

"No, that's fine," he said.

She hung up her work clothes in the wardrobe. Michael was having difficulty in taking in this encroachment. But for now he could live with it.

It was an early night but the time was not wasted. "It's amazing what you can do when you haven't got a telly," she said.

The following morning Michael was getting ready for his day at the Major's and Melanie was in the bathroom. He needed to say something to her; it had been on his mind.

She came out and went into the bedroom dressed in her underwear.

"I can't do this," he said to her.

"Do what?" she said.

"All this domestic stuff," he said.

"You seemed happy enough last night when I was sucking your cock," she said.

Michael ignored the comment. "You know I can't get involved. I need my space... and I will leave the village once my work is done. I can't afford any emotional ties."

"So you are just going to chuck me out is that it?" she countered.

"No... but I can't have you moving in. It won't work," he said.

"Oh I get it, like I said, 'all men are bastards', toss you aside once they're done with you," she said.

She picked up her picture and Teddy Bear and threw them in her overnight bag with the rest of the clothes.

"Right if that's what you want, I'm off," she said. "I'm not

The Tinker

sticking around where I 'm not wanted."

She walked to the front door.

"You can keep the stuff in the fridge," she said and left, slamming the door behind her.

Denise was at the kitchen window and saw Melanie walk by clearly upset. She tutted. "Oh dear," she said to herself.

Chapter Thirteen

Michael left the Lodge and headed to the Manor to repair the Major's chimney. It was another bright day but cloudy. There was no rain forecast according to the Major.

Michael walked up the path to the house pushing his bike and trailer and was greeted like a returning hero.

"Jolly good show on Saturday, what," said the Major after the initial 'hellos'.

"Thank you," said Michael.

"Hear the lad's fine. Phoned the Reverend yesterday myself just to check," said the Major.

"Yes, thank goodness," said Michael.

"Thanks to you," said the Major.

Frank heard the talking and came from the back of the house to welcome Michael.

"Michael, how are you after all the excitement on Saturday?" said Frank extending his hand.

"I'm ok," said Michael, his right hand now being vigorously pumped by the game-keeper.

"Well I thought it was a bloody miracle, I don't mind telling you," said Frank still shaking Michael's hand. "I couldn't have done what you did even forty years ago," he added. "I thought the lad was a gonner when I left you, I don't mind saying."

Frank let go but continued the dialogue. "Oh, while I remember, I managed to salvage William's fishing rod. It'd got caught on the side of the boat when it tipped over. "Fraid all my stuff's gone though," he said. "I'll drop it back when I am next over at the church, if you can let the reverend know," he added.

"Yes, will do," said Michael, who was starting to unload his work gear from his trailer.

The Tinker

"I'll replace your rod, Frank, don't you worry," said the Major. "At least the boy's all right."

The Major escorted Michael around the back of the house where a long ladder had been secured to enable him to carry out the repairs. Frank followed slowly pushing Michael's bike. He appeared to be limping.

Michael shook the ladder to ensure its stability and looked up at the roof high above them.

"I'll hold it steady while you're up there," Frank said.

"Shouldn't be too long," said Michael. "If it's straightforward."

Frank had got the sand and cement that Michael had specified and helped him mix the first batch on a large sheet of hardboard stretched across the patio to protect it. It was a laborious job mixing by hand and Michael had to carry the cement a bucket at a time to get it up to the roof, so several trips were needed.

As it happens it wasn't a large job and while Michael was on the roof carrying out the repairs, Frank was able to take over the mixing and keep the supply of material coming; the work was completed by lunch time.

The Major thanked Michael and paid him for the full day.

"Least I can do, old boy," he said. "Least I can do."

"I'll have some more work for you over the next week or so but shan't hog you. I know there's others in need of your attention, what," he said.

"Thank you," said Michael and he packed his gear and made his way back to the Lodge.

He parked his bike outside the vicarage and walked up the footpath. He was passing the kitchen window when Denise saw him and opened the door.

"Would you like a cup of tea, Michael? The kettle is on," she said. "John's taken the children to Bristol to catch their trains."

"Aye, thank you," he said.

He went in and sat at the kitchen table while Denise made the tea.

"It's so empty when the children go back, I do so miss them," she said as she brought the pot and two mugs to the table. The milk jug and sugar were already in place.

"Aye," he said. "I can understand that."

She sat down opposite him and poured the tea.

"That was a very brave thing you did at the weekend," she said. "It takes a very special kind of person to do what you did."

"Just did what I had to do," he said.

"No, it's more than that, much more..." she paused. "I've been thinking a lot about you since then and I would really like to help, if you'll let me."

She paused again, not wishing to rush anything. "Let me tell you about some of the work I did with ex-servicemen and see if it will help." She took a sip of her tea.

"Some of my patients were in a real bad way. Most common problems were flashbacks and nightmares... sound familiar?"

"Aye," said Michael.

"Then there was the general numbing of emotional responsiveness, again very common. In some cases there was a total dysfunction... rage, anger, violence towards wives, children even; behaviour became unpredictable, irrational."

"Aye," said Michael. "Been there."

"The detachment in your case is quite marked. You don't let people get close to you, partly in the belief, I think, that you will hurt them, mentally certainly and possibly physically... yes?" she said.

"Aye, about right," he said, drinking his tea but not making eye contact with Denise, just staring into the mug.

The Tinker

"The other part is that you fear getting hurt yourself, emotionally, I mean," she said. She paused taking the conversation slowly, a piece at a time.

"The constant running away is also interesting. You say nothing when you leave here, just say 'goodbye' and leave, and you never talk about where you go or where you've been. That would suggest that there is still fear. That, whatever caused the original trauma, is still a threat. Normally ex-soldiers are out of the firing line once they get home and it's a case of trying to put them back together again, as I had to with John. With the right treatment the effects of trauma can be gradually cured, although that is not the right word. You are never fully cured. It's not like flu or a broken leg which eventually mends; it's in the mind and can always recur whenever a trigger happens to set it off again. Some people do regress. It depends on the support mechanisms that surround them. That's why it has worked so well with John; he always has that support around him, and his faith of course."

Michael was listening. Denise was getting through; it was like she was in his head.

"I don't think that you will ever allow yourself the luxury of peace of mind until whatever is haunting you is properly resolved, over for good." She paused and took a drink of tea. "Those people that were looking for you, are they connected in some way?" she asked.

She waited for the usual rebuttal but Michael looked at her. "Aye," he said. "They could be."

"Why don't you share it with me?" she said. "As much, or as little as you want to tell me," she added.

Her voice was soft and soothing and Michael felt relaxed, almost in an hypnotic state. It was now or never.

"Aye," he said.

Suddenly his voice changed from that befitting an itinerant worker and the reclusive, recalcitrant persona he had adopted, into that of an army officer, articulate and fluent.

"My name is Michael Curtiss, ex lieutenant, British Army attached to the intelligence section, special operations."

He looked at Denise, his eyes were almost trance-like; she was shaken by this metamorphosis. She had heard about it in her research but never witnessed it at first hand. It was similar to schizophrenia which, she knew, could be triggered by severe trauma; but this was different. It was as though he had become trapped inside his own role play.

"Go on," she said, almost whispering and desperately hoping her husband would not return; she didn't want anything to break the spell.

"Curtiss is not my real surname, but the one I adopted for this particular assignment." His voice was clear and coherent and she could detect a slight hint of an Irish accent.

"Before I continue I need you to do something for me," he said.

"Anything," she said.

"Can you write this down and if anything should happen to me I want you to ring this number; they will tell you what to do."

She got a pen and paper.

He told her a a nine digit number and then said, "my code word is ER7258... That's all you will need say," he said.

"ER?" she queried.

"Stands for 'extreme risk'," he said.

She raised her eyebrows.

"I have a special bank account," he said. "And once a year they transfer my pay into it. As long as I draw that money out they know I'm alive, somewhere. I never have to contact them and they have no idea where I am, but I can access it anywhere in the world. It's sort of a witness protection scheme."

Denise looked at the piece of paper. "I'll look after it," she said.

"You were saying... special operations," she said. "When was this?"

Denise was trying to get him to access specific incidents which she knew could lead to difficulties. She would need to tread carefully; he could shut down again if it became too painful.

He looked straight ahead staring through the kitchen window as if he was reading from a video prompt.

"February 1979, we were getting reports of a group of loyalist extremists causing havoc in Northern Ireland..." He looked at Denise.

"They were responsible for many attacks and murders mostly based around Armagh. It became so bad locally the area was nick-named the murder triangle. We had a tip off that they were based out of a place called Glenbar Farm somewhere near the town, but it was very sketchy and we had little other information. We were never able to trace it. We nick-named them 'the Glenbar Gang'."

Denise watched his expression as he related the events. "Tell me about this gang," she said.

"They were like a vigilante group. They had some real nutcases among them, mostly UVF and UDA but also British soldiers and some members of the RUC... "

Michael paused; he continued to stare out of the window.

"The real worrying thing was we believed they were being bank-rolled by a prominent member of the British aristocracy. I volunteered to go undercover to try and infiltrate the gang and get information on the set-up, you know, where they were getting their weapons and any evidence on this guy who was providing the money..."

He paused again and drunk the rest of his tea which had now gone cold; it didn't register.

"This was a covert operation in every sense. The secret service were not involved, just my CO and a handler. The whole thing was managed by the Foreign Office."

Denise looked at him inquisitively, still trying to take in this new state. It was like a different person in Michael's body.

"You need to remember relations between the UK and The Irish Republic were difficult at the time and the Government were very keen not to upset them. We needed them onside to help manage the situation in the Province and to take action against the IRA. The Glenbar gang were causing real problems and becoming an embarrassment. There was a great deal of pressure being put on the British Government by the Irish to, how shall we say...? Sort it."

"Go on," said Denise.

It was like someone letting the lid off a pressure cooker. Michael was not about to stop now the box had been opened.

"The other problem was the whole secret service thing was in a mess at the time. No-one had any idea what was going on; there was no real strategy, everyone was just reacting to situations. We had SAS guys trying to infiltrate the IRA and being murdered, operations were being set up then closed down. Before that we had the MRF... the Military Reaction Force," he clarified. "Glorified executioners... They got shut down. Some of the people they were using were just thugs and criminals, little more than mercenaries. There was no proper security, utter bollocks... sorry," he said.

"That's ok," said Denise. "Just carry on, say whatever you feel. I've heard it all before." She smiled.

He continued. "This is why my part had to be separate and

The Tinker

secure. We didn't know who was involved and that included MI5 and MI6... It was very dangerous."

"Extreme risk," said Denise.

"Exactly."

"Out of interest, why did you volunteer?" asked Denise.

Michael thought for a moment. "Hmm, that's a difficult question. Looking back now, I'm still not sure."

Denise prompted. "Well, were you seeking excitement, was it a sense of loyalty, or duty... or were you running away from something?"

She wanted to understand this; it could help in the recovery process.

"Well, my mother had died a couple of months earlier," he said. "But I don't think that had any bearing on it. I hadn't seen her for some time. I only found out she had died when a neighbour managed to contact me. Never went to the funeral."

"That's sad," said Denise. "No other family, wife, girlfriend?"

"No, my father left when I was fourteen. I was an only child," he said.

"Sorry, you were saying about your motivation," she pressed gently.

"The bottom line was simple, I was a soldier. I was well-trained. It was something I felt had to be done," he replied.

"I see," she said. "Go on, you were saying about security."

"Yes..." Michael collected his thoughts. "There was a small section in the Foreign Office that reported directly to the Foreign Secretary, David Owen, at the time but Carrington also used it. It's known as E section. I was introduced to a chap called Huntington-Whitely who gave me an outline briefing but that was the only time I had any direct contact with London. We met in a coffee shop off Oxford Street. It was the first time I had ever been to

London... didn't like the place."

Michael took a long sip of water.

"As it happened he didn't have that much information, just a name really. He explained about the murders and intimidation going on in South Armagh. Opinion at the time was that it was the work of loyalist paramilitary. The intelligence services had no idea about the existence of this so-called 'gang'. Nobody had joined the dots; they thought it was just random action. He told me that his department had been contacted by a disaffected RUC officer, a chap called Brian Hanna, who appeared to know what was going on. He had managed to by-pass the usual covert channels, didn't trust them, and had directly approached someone he knew in the Foreign Office. He was to become my initial contact in Belfast."

Denise could see Michael was getting stressed; there were beads of sweat glistening on his brow.

"Would you like another cup of tea?" she said "Or a cold drink."

"Just a glass of water, please," he said and Denise went to the sink and poured water into a tumbler from the cold tap. She placed it in front of Michael.

Denise sat back down. "You were saying about your contact in Belfast," she said.

"Yes, Brian Hanna... a good man... wife and two kids. I stayed with them when I first got there until I found a place."

"When was this?" asked Denise.

"This would be June sometime. There was a lot of preparation and training before that. We created a complete dossier on me which mysteriously found its way into the police files in Belfast."

"Mr Hanna?" asked Denise.

"Yes. It said I had been up in court for stealing equipment from my employers, the local Gas Board. We had court reports, the works. The story was I had left the company under a bit of a cloud and set up on my own as a gas engineer. There was also a bit about my political leanings. I was suspected of having ultra-loyalist views and had been of interest to army intelligence but it had never been pursued. It was all made up, but we knew there would be some serious vetting if I was going to get accepted into the group. I had to look the part, I was even given voice coaching to make sure I got the accent right. I grew my hair long, kept a bit of stubble and dressed in old clothes which were bought locally. I chose the name Curtiss, it was my mother's maiden name."

"What about your military record, your real one I mean?" asked Denise.

"Michael Dugdale, according to his file, was killed on active service in West Germany in a car accident. So officially he doesn't exist."

"The telephone number you gave me, presumably that's this E section, you mentioned?" said Denise.

"Yes, my present controller. I've had four in the last seven years," he said.

"So... you were saying about your deployment... the preparation," she said.

"Yes. I knew Belfast, I did a nine month tour out there in seventy five. A very scary place, I don't mind telling you," he said.

"Weren't you worried about going back? What if you'd been recognised?" she asked.

"Little chance of that, we had been based in barracks and only went out on patrol in armoured vehicles. Foot patrols were far too dangerous at that time, and it was four years earlier. Things had changed, as I soon found out." he said.

"Changed? In what way? What was it like when you first got out there? How did you feel?" she asked, questions now pouring out trying to keep Michael focussed.

"I felt prepared. I had a good idea of what to expect... at least I thought I had, but it was much worse. Murders virtually every day, one after another with the army stuck in the middle just letting it happen."

"How did that make you feel?" she asked.

"Angry," he said. "Good people getting killed, on both sides, for nothing. West Belfast, the Catholic areas particularly, were terrible. It made me think of what Berlin must have been like after the war. The one positive thing was the peace movement which did have a lot of support but by the time I got there even that had fizzled out. It was like, I don't know... almost as though the people were resigned to it."

"So, take me through those first few weeks. Where did you stay? What did you do?" she gently asked.

"Like I said, for the first ten days or so I stayed with Brian... Hanna, the RUC constable. I owe him and his family a great deal. We used the cover story that I was a gas engineer, which is what I did before I joined the army. The story was that I'd moved across from Derry after my wife had died. Again we had documents, her name, death certificate, even my service records from my work with the gas company..."

Michael took another drink. He had emptied his glass and without asking, Denise got up and refilled the tumbler from the tap.

"Thank you," said Michael and took his first sip.

"Go on," said Denise. "The first few weeks, you were saying."

"Yes, I was glad about the preparation we put in, it paid dividends. I found out later that the RUC guys could get access to virtually any documents they wanted and pass it on to whomever. There was a lot of collusion with the loyalist paramilitary. No

The Tinker

wonder they weren't trusted by the Republicans. The army was no better. Luckily Brian was able to tip me off on what they were up to."

"So how did you managed to get accepted into the gang?" asked Denise.

"Wasn't easy and took a while, it was about a month before Warren Point when I made the breakthrough."

"Warren Point? I've heard the name," said Denise.

"August, seventy nine. I will never forget that day. It was an atrocity. The worst single loss of life inflicted on the army by the Provos since the troubles started. Eighteen men killed, six wounded... a roadside bomb." Michael looked down at the table. "Same day they murdered Mountbatten."

"Oh, I remember that," she said.

"The anger in the loyalist community was immense and everyone on that side of the fence wanted revenge."

Michael took another sip of water.

"Go on..." said Denise.

"After I'd arrived in Belfast Brian managed to get me fixed up with a few service calls. He got hold of some tools and a small van which I paid for. This was a good start as it gave me access to houses and I soon got to know one or two locals. It's amazing what you can pick up while you are having a cup of tea after you've serviced a boiler."

He smiled for the first time since he started his recollection.

"I moved into this pretty awful flat, Brian knew the landlord. It was in Albert Street just off Sandy Row, home to UDF and UDA, real Unionist territory. One of the victims of Warren Point actually came from around there. It was virtually a no-go area for the RUC, the people pretty well policed themselves and I based myself there. This would be mid-June, I guess. There was this local pub, The Duchess of York... we just called it 'the Duchess'. Brian suggested it. It was a place where loyalist extremists were known to hang out."

"So what happened?" asked Denise.

"Well, as I said, I started doing a few service jobs and gradually word got round. I became quite busy actually. Even managed to pay my own way... Didn't touch my float."

Michael could see Denise was confused.

"I had this reserve of cash I could use, my 'float'... couldn't risk a bank account. It was literally stuffed inside the mattress," he explained.

He took another sip of water. "I made a point of visiting the Duchess, at first three or four times a week then every night around nine o'clock - a real local. I soon got to know the landlord, Gerry Donahue, we hit it off pretty well. He was a big George Best fan. Always boasting he knew his family, followed United, so I used this."

He took another drink.

"I soon got to know who the hard-cases were. They would come in the pub three or four at a time and the bar would go quiet. They would sit in the same places. From a security point of view it was not a clever move. A Provo could come in at any time and take them out with an automatic. It did happen in a pub quite close by. What a stir that caused, four killed. The retribution was terrible, but that's another story."

He looked at Denise who returned the eye contact.

"Go on... the pub... you were saying about contacts," she said.

He continued. "Yes. On my rounds I tried to get the topic around to 'the troubles'. You know, mention a murder, or some topical political thing... 'Did you hear about? What do you think about?' that sort of thing. Sometimes people would clam up but other times they would start venting. There was one name, Brendan Monahan, that kept cropping up. He was clearly very influential around there, almost like the Godfather. He seemed to be the chief law-enforcer. There were kangaroo courts, the lot. He also had some close friends who were a bit tasty, certainly not people you would not want to mess around. There was this one chap, Jimmy Rafferty who was a real thug, at least four murders for certain but probably many, many more. He was the main henchman but it was Monahan who was pulling the strings."

Denise took in this information. "So you were saying you were gradually getting known locally. What happened next?" she asked.

"Well it was quite strange really. I had been in my flat and doing work in the area for about six weeks or thereabouts, early August I guess. I was using the Duchess pretty well every night by this time. The plan was going well, I was treated like one of them. Several were customers and word was getting round. They were becoming quite hospitable. They would tell me about their families, football, anything in the news. It was quite easy to get my views across, I was among friends. So if a Catholic was murdered I would go, 'well that's one less to worry about'. Or if one was caught by the authorities, I would say things like, 'I hope they hang the bastard'. That sort of thing." Michael apologised again for the expletive.

"That's ok, please go on," said Denise.

"That was the mind-set of the whole area, frightening really when you look back. It was like Nazi Germany and the Jews all over again."

Michael paused, collecting his thoughts. "Where was I? Ah yes, the Duchess. This one night I was at the bar as usual when this guy came up to me and offered to buy me a drink. I accepted, it was the polite thing to do, but I also had this thought, intuition if you like, that this was the one I had been waiting for. So he puts this pint down next to me and says, 'why don't you come over and join us?' I walked with him to this table in the corner and he introduced me to these four guys who he had come in with. Then he said, 'by the way, the name's Brendan.' Just like that. This was it."

"How did you feel?" asked Denise.

"Honestly...? I was shitting myself, but this was the introduction I'd been working on for all this time. It was a strange sensation being introduced."

"Weren't you worried that you might have been a target?" asked Denise.

"Not really. I knew that they would have done some investigation before they approached me. If they had really thought I was some spy or something I would have been dead already."

Denise looked at him shocked at the thought.

"So what happened?" asked Denise.

"Well, I sat right in the middle of them which was quite intimidating at the time; no-where to run, but I had to keep the façade that I was not uncomfortable in their presence. So I shook hands with them, one by one. Made some joke about were they all Manchester United fans, something like that, very relaxed, nothing controversial. I needed them to make the first move... then I would know."

Michael paused and took another drink.

"Go on," said Denise who was now completely immersed in his story.

"It went much better than I had hoped. Brendan sat opposite and said they had heard good things about me and that they may have some work and would I be interested. I remember saying, 'yeah, I could be if it helps the cause', or words to that effect.

The Tinker

I wanted them to think I was keen but not too enthusiastic that would cause suspicion. Right out of the blue Brendan asked if I could rig a boiler up so it would explode."

"What did you say?" asked Denise.

"I told them I could, theoretically. He said that there was this guy they knew that was one of the people who had murdered the four UDF guys, the ones I mentioned earlier. They knew where he lived. They wanted me to go into the house and tamper with the gas so it wouldn't look like a bomb. They would get me into the house, I just had to do the rest."

"What happened?" asked Denise.

"They said they would contact me when it was time and a couple of days later I was told to meet them at this address. It was off one of the side streets of the Lisburn Road. I parked the van around the corner and two of the guys were waiting for me. They had keys and everything. They let me in and I did what I had to do and was out again in under twenty minutes."

Denise listened to Michael describe the scene, the drama being played out in front of her was like nothing she had experienced.

"So you actually did what they wanted?" she said.

"Yes. It wasn't easy I can tell you but I spoke to my handler and they told me to do whatever it took. What I was doing would save more lives in the long run. The next day it was all over the local papers, 'man killed in gas explosion' said the headline. The RUC had discounted any paramilitary activity. There was no trace of explosives and they blamed a faulty boiler. Several of the officers were aware of what was going on; they just turned a blind eye."

"How did you feel about being responsible for this man's death?" she asked.

"It's just one of the things that haunts me," he said. "It's something that will always be on my conscience but I did what needed to be done."

"Would you like another drink?" asked Denise.

Just then John returned from his taxi duties.

"Hello dear, hello Michael," said the vicar as he came into the kitchen.

"Would you like a cup of tea, dear? Michael has been telling me some stories from his past," she said.

The vicar took the hint and having taken the mug from Denise he went into his office. The break had been useful for Michael, it had given him to gather his thoughts before continuing his story.

Chapter Fourteen

Michael continued his story.

August 21st 1979, a Tuesday, Albert Street, Belfast.

It had been over a week since he had carried out the work on the boiler of the unfortunate IRA gunman that resulted in his demise. Despite everything he felt uneasy about it; killing in a war zone on active service was one thing but carrying out what was literally a death sentence on some unsuspecting catholic was something else; considering it as part of the job was not easy. The newspapers didn't help, 'just preparing breakfast' it said, and Michael could picture the poor Danny Flynn lighting his gas stove with catastrophic results. Michael closed his eyes and tried to concentrate on the job in hand.

His handler had been ecstatic. "Great work," he had said, "sounds like you're in".

Brendan Monahan was even more effusive, treating Michael like a brother. The evening after the explosion, the mood at the Duchess was more than up-beat. Michael was at the bar around nine o'clock as usual talking about the chances of United for the coming season with Gerry Donahue when Brendan and two of his associates came in.

"Michael," he said. "What're yer having? It's on me," he said and hugged Michael for what seemed longer than appropriate.

"Come and sit down with us. Yer one of the lads now," he said.

Michael followed Brendan to the table and was greeted warmly by Ryan O'Dowd and Dory Flanagan, who Michael hadn't met formally before but had seen in the pub with Brendan. Jimmy Rafferty was on drinks duty.

The chat was lively, any strike against the Provos was good but getting the last of the four that had taken out the UDF men, well that really was a result. There were rumours going around that the other three had been beheaded with a butcher's knife, presumably by Jimmy Rafferty; the brutality designed to put fear into the community. It certainly had done that. As the stories of past exploits rolled on it became clear that Rafferty was a psychopath and appeared to wallow in the killings; the reputation he had built up was well-founded.

Towards the end of the evening Brendan had a cursory warning for Michael. "Whatever yer do, make sure yer check yer van before yer start it up in the morning. Yer should be ok but yer never know there could be a feckin' grass who could tip off the boyos."

"Yeah, thanks Brendan, will do," Michael said.

Michael looked at Monahan, a product of the ship building yards of Harland and Woolf whose great cranes dominated the distant skyline. Some people just exude menace, Monahan did that and then some. He was in his forties, tough looking and hard, straight from the script of a gangster movie. Stories about him were the stuff of local folk-law and Monahan did nothing to deny the rumours. It created fear and respect, a valuable commodity in these troubled times.

It was Gerry, the barman, who provided Michael with some background, not through any pressing, just in casual chat. He told Michael that Monahan had worked his way up from a riveter to shop steward before being paid off following an industrial injury; the cash he invested in property. He now owned more than twenty houses, according to gossip, and half a dozen shops, and was on his way to creating an empire. Money seemed to be in plentiful supply, Michael observed.

So that Tuesday Michael walked around the corner of Albert Road as usual to a piece of wasteland where he parked his van. He had a service call that morning twenty minutes away. He could

The Tinker

see someone hovering around the vehicle and at first he thought it could be someone planting something nasty but as he got nearer he could see it was Brian Hanna, in casual clothes.

"Can we go somewhere?" said Brian.

He was fidgety and on edge; Michael could tell straight away that something was not right.

"Aye, come back for a coffee," said Michael.

"No, you can't go back there. Leave the van and come with me, now," said Hanna. There was an urgency in his voice and Michael complied.

They walked down a snicket and into an adjacent road where Michael could see Brian's car.

"We'll take mine. I'll take you back to the house. You can stay for a couple of days until we can sort out what's happening," he said.

They got into Brian's car and headed out to the officer's house.

"What's going on?" asked Michael, as they pulled away and headed north.

"We had a tip off last night that the Provos think that the explosion at Danny Flynn's house was not an accident. We've got nothing specific but I thought it would be a good idea to get you out, just in case," he said.

"I can't do that, not now. I've got Monahan's trust. I don't want to jeopardise all the hard work. If I get pulled now it'll blow everything," Michael was insistent.

Brian slowed down and pulled into a parking bay.

"What do you want to do?" asked Brian.

"Not sure yet but drop me off close to the flat and I'll speak to Monahan. Actually thinking about it, this could work in our favour. He may provide me with some protection," said Michael.

"I don't like it, Mikey," said Brian. After a few moments

considering the situation he relented. "Aye, ok but you will be needing this, just in case," he said and pulled a Browning Automatic Pistol from his pocket. He opened his glove box and took out a couple of small boxes. "Forty rounds to go with it."

Michael knew the weapon well, it was a favourite in the Irish Republic and many had made their way north of the border. Where Brian had got it he didn't think to ask. "Yeah, ta. Feel a bit better with that," he said.

Brian turned the car around and headed back towards Sandy Row, then dropped Michael off outside The Grapes public house, another safe haven for dissident loyalists.

"Thanks Brian, for everything. I'll be in touch," said Michael as Brian pulled away towards his base.

Michael checked his bearings. He still had the service call but that was the last thing on his mind. There was a telephone box on the corner of the street right outside the pub, Michael went in and looked up a number. Michael dialled and fed coins into the slot. "Gerry there?" he said when the phone was answered. There was a pause. "Gerry...? Michael... I need to get hold of Brendan, it's urgent. Do you have a number...? Great, thanks. See you tonight."

Michael dialled the number he had been given by Gerry Donahue. It was answered on the third ring. "Brendan...? It's Michael... Curtiss... aye. I think I might have some trouble."

Michael outlined the conversation he had had with Brian. Brendan knew Hanna's information would be reliable. He was considered a valuable asset to the loyalist cause and had given them many helpful tip-offs in the past. There was silence from the other end of the phone as Michael relayed the information.

"Right," said Brendan. "We need to get yer away. From my experience these tip-offs are usually good but often a step behind. They could well have already worked out what happened and it

The Tinker

won't take them long to find out who might have rigged the boiler. They can be very persuasive, the boyos." There was a pause while Brendan considered the appropriate course of action. "Where are yer now? The Grapes... yeah yer'll be ok in there. Wait for us inside. I'll be about half an hour."

Michael hung up the phone, left the call box and knocked on the door of the pub; it didn't officially open for over two hours. Michael could see a shape in the glass-paned door opening bolts. A thickset man in a vest and old-fashioned brown corduroy trousers opened the door.

"Yeah?" he said.

"My name's Michael," he said. "Brendan Monahan said I should wait for him inside."

"Yer better come in," said the landlord. "You the gas man?"

"How did you know?" said Michael.

"Word gets around," he said.

"Can I get yer something...? On the house," said the landlord.

"No, thanks," said Michael. "I'll just wait if that's ok."

"Suit yerself, but it was a good job yer did on that Provo. Folks round here appreciate that dedication," he said.

The landlord left to do his landlord tasks, Michael sat in the corner of the dismal room and looked around. It was dark and gloomy, the obnoxious concoction of beer and cigarettes still hanging in the air in a blue fug. The table was sticky to the touch, the residue of the previous evening's consumption. Michael fiddled nervously with the Browning which was in his jacket pocket; he was definitely worried now. It was quite clear that word had got out about his involvement in the killing and, as Brendan had intimated, it would only be a matter of time.

It was nearer three quarters of an hour before there was a sharp rap on the door. The landlord appeared from the cellar behind the bar and went to open it.

"Come in Brendan," said the landlord. "Yer man is sat over there," he indicated with a nod of his head towards the corner. Michael was already on his feet.

"Michael," said Brendan.

"Brendan," said Michael in acknowledgement.

"We need to get going," said Brendan and the landlord opened the door and let the two men out.

"Good luck to yers," said the landlord to Michael who nodded in acknowledgement.

Outside the pub there was a plain white van with its engine running. Michael ran to it with his head down, opened the passenger side door, folded down the front seat and got in. There was a bench running behind the front seats and he sat down on it, not the height of comfort.

Brendan got in and it pulled away. Dory Flanagan was driving and Michael exchanged greetings.

"So what's the plan?" asked Michael.

"Well it seems yer man was right. We've been to yer flat and there was something nasty waiting for yer when yer lifted the seat of the bog," he said.

"What!" exclaimed Michael.

"Yep in the time you were out they've planted a booby trap on your toilet seat. Oh and yer van was rigged as well."

"Jesus," said Michael.

"Yep, you'd have been able to talk to him face to face if yer'd gone back to the flat," he said.

"They must've been watching me leave," said Michael trying desperately to remember seeing anyone acting suspiciously outside. His mind was mush; he couldn't.

"I've made a few calls and fixed up a place for yer," Brendan

The Tinker

said. "We've cleared yer room and the van; your stuff is in the back."

Michael looked behind him; there were a number of carrier bags with clothes poking out the top and his tool-bag from the van.

"We've got rid of the device as well. That was one of my properties yer were in. Can't afford unnecessary repairs," he said and laughed. Michael hadn't realised Brendan was his landlord. Brian had said the owner was a contact but hadn't named him.

"Thanks," said Michael.

Michael was beginning to appreciate the resources at Brendan's command. He knew about the IRA's expertise in bomb making from his tour of duty in '75 and the difficulties some of the Army teams had in defusing them.

"Where're we going?" asked Michael.

"We've got a place just outside Armagh. It's a farm we use, sort of a base. Yer'll be ok there. It'll not be safe for you to return to Belfast. When things cool down we could get you somewheres in Derry if yer like, or yer may want to go across to England," he said.

"It'll take us a good hour to get there, depending on how many checkpoints we get stopped at," he added.

Brendan looked at Michael. "Are you armed?" he said.

"Yeah," said Michael.

"I shan't ask what a gas man is doing with a gun," he said.

"Brian gave it me this morning. He said I might need it," Michael replied as innocently as he could.

"OK we need to hide it quick. They're not too thorough unless we give them cause but just to be on the safe side. Pass it over. Yer can have it back when we get out of the city," said Brendan.

Having little choice in the matter, Michael passed over the

Browning and bullets that Brian had given him and Brendan rummaged around behind the dashboard and stowed it.

"It'll be safe there," he said.

Michael was still feeling uneasy. He was without any defence and being driven to who knows where. If Brendan had any hint of suspicion about him this would surely be his last day on earth. Michael stared straight ahead as the van steered its way through the city watching the dereliction, burned out cars and army checkpoints. Saracen Armoured cars flitted around the streets with heavy wire mesh protecting their windscreens, more befitting a scene from a war zone. The van got stopped once but it was no more than a cursory glance through the window and they were waved through.

It took nearly an hour and a half to do the forty odd miles to Armagh. Michael had only passed through it once before so this was new territory. There had been little conversation during the journey, Michael spent the time watching the road ahead in between Dory and Brendan thinking about what he might do if he had to escape in a hurry. He drew no conclusions; there was no escape. As they drove south it was much greener than Belfast but the countryside masked a dangerous terrain. This was bandit country, a regular terrorist hotspot because of its proximity to the Irish border.

About five miles outside Armagh they pulled into a lay-by and for a moment Michael thought this might be it; his senses were on high alert. There was an old five bar gate on the left and a trail beyond which to the untrained eye looked just like a farm track that tractors would use to access a field. It was the only indication that there was any human activity but the trail was well worn, Michael noticed; clearly in regular use. It was a mild day but rainy and the mid-August sunshine was shrouded with cloud. Brendan got out and Michael watched anxiously but Brendan just opened the gate and the van passed through; then he closed it behind them.

The van pulled up outside a large nineteenth century property. There was a grassy area in front of the main farmhouse which was used as a car-park where three fairly ancient vehicles were stationed. The house was in a hollow and certainly not visible to any casual walker, there were no trees just grass and sheep roamed freely about unperturbed by the new arrivals. Brendan got out and lifted up the seat so Michael could get out. Brendan handed him back his gun and ammunition.

"Just in case," said Brendan.

"Thanks, "said Michael, not able to display his relief.

Brendan watched his partner open the back of the van, then turned to Michael who was stood eyeing things up. "Go on, Dory will bring the bags. Get yerself inside and we'll fix yer up with a bedroom."

Michael walked to the front door. He looked at the fading exterior, definitely in need of attention. Some of the brickwork was crumbling and the paintwork was peeled back or missing in several places. There was a name plate on the wall, 'Glenbar Farm'.

Michael just stared at the sign. This was it. The farm they had been tipped off about, it had to be. He was actually here. He felt strange but couldn't afford to show any recognition.

He opened the door. The inside was in a similar condition and desperately in need of remedial work. A middle aged woman came from another room which he later discovered was the kitchen and greeted him.

"You must be the new lodger; I'm Flora O'Dowd. This is my house, yer very welcome. Michael, isn't it?" she said.

"Aye," he replied, "Thank you."

He looked around his new surroundings. The room was large and quite typical of its type, stone flooring with red tiling, a wooden table and four chairs - lathe-back, rustic design; to the right was a large Welsh dresser with plates and other crockery. A single light bulb hung from the ceiling with no lamp shade. There were a couple of worn old-fashioned armchairs in Gainsborough style facing a roaring open fire, giving the room a cosy feel. The atmosphere though, was far from cosy. The room was stiflingly hot and there was something about the place which gave Michael the creeps. There was a momentary déjà vu. It was like he had walked into a haunted house with evil spirits lurking in every dingy corner.

Brendan came up behind him and spoke; it made him jump.

"I see yer've met Flora," said Brendan who went up to the woman and gave her a hug as a child would give to his mother.

"Flora my lovely, how the devil are yers?" he said.

"Ah Brendan, less of the Blarney. So what're we doing then?" she said.

"Well, this is Michael I told yer about."

"The gas man?" she interrupted.

"Aye," said Brendan. Michael looked at her. Word was definitely getting out. "He'll be staying for a while and I want yer to really look after him. We'll be going back to Belfast this afternoon but will be back tomorrow. Can yer fix us up with some coffees and a biscuit or two?" he said.

"Aye," said Flora. "Make yerself comfortable Michael... Yer very welcome here, so y'are."

"Thank you," said Michael.

"Come on Michael, let me show yer around," said Brendan.

They walked through the room to a door opposite. To the left was a flight of very steep stairs. It was dark and Brendan put on the

The Tinker

light. There was no stair carpet just wooden steps which creaked under the weight of the men as they ascended. At the top there was a landing and a corridor, left and right. Brendan went down the right hand side; the ceiling was low and they had to stoop, past a couple of rooms and opened the door at the end.

"This is your room. I'll get Dory to bring yer stuff up later," he said.

It was a good size bedroom, the white emulsion was beginning to yellow but it was clean with a large double bed and a wardrobe. There was also a Victorian-style white china washbasin with towels hanging from an adjacent rail. A single window let in some natural light; Michael looked through and could see outbuildings at the back of the farmhouse. There was a small chair next to the bed and what looked like a portable TV with a circular aerial protruding from the top. Brendan saw Michael looking at it.

"Don't think yer'll get much of a picture but it might be a bit of company," he said. "Let me show yer the rest of the place; there's something I want yer to see," and they went back downstairs.

There were three mugs of coffees and a plate of Digestives waiting on the table when they got back to the living room. Dory had placed the carrier bags on the floor by the table.

"I'm going to show Michael the workshop. When you've finished can yer take the bags up to the end bedroom. Then we best get back," Brendan said to Dory.

Brendan ignored the drinks and asked Michael to follow him outside.

At the back of the farmhouse there were several out-buildings. The first one looked more substantial than the others which were of timber construction. Chickens scurried out of their way as they walked to the door. Guano was everywhere requiring the men to skip over the ground to dodge the mess. The building was padlocked and Brendan took a key from his pocket and opened it. Inside it resembled an old smithy with various implements hanging from the walls. There was an old but working bellows, a couple of compressors, a generator and there were bags of fertiliser and other farm chemicals, in one of the corners.

Michael looked with interest. "I was hoping we might be able to use your engineering skills while yer here," said Brendan.

"Aye, don't see why not," said Michael.

They went back outside and Brendan locked up and they walked back to the farmhouse. The coffee was lukewarm but Flora had brought in a plate of sandwiches and a refill.

"This will keep yer going till you get back," she said.

"Thanks Flora," said Brendan and the three sat down and started to eat.

"I'll leave yer a set of keys for one of the cars," said Brendan looking at Michael. "I don't expect yer to stay here all the time, yer not a prisoner, but be very careful, Armagh can be just as dangerous as Belfast if yer go to the wrong places... There's a bar on West Street, so there is, called O'Hanrahan's, yer'll be safe there if yer want to go out. I need to get back otherwise I would introduce yers to a few people. The barman's name is Shaun, Shaun O'Reilly tell him Brendan sent yers, yer'll be well-looked after."

"Thanks, I'll be fine," said Michael.

"OK, but if yer do go out make sure yer close the gate," said Brendan. "Don't want the sheep getting out," he joked.

An hour later Brendan and Dory left and were on the way back to Belfast leaving Michael to settle in. He went up to his room to sort out his belongings. He took out his clothes and stowed them in the wardrobe. He checked his tool bag; they were all there. His Browning was in his jacket pocket, he took it out and placed it in

The Tinker

the drawer of the bed-side cabinet.

Michael realised straight away he had a problem. His float of almost £5,000 was still in the mattress in the flat. Somehow he needed to get it; he would need cash if he was going to continue his mission. This was not like on the TV where characters would eat at the finest restaurants, stay in the best hotel rooms and produce money at the drop of a hat to bribe potential snitches. The real world meant everything needed to be paid for, his drinks at the bar, rent, everything. He needed to make a couple of phone calls.

"Flora," he called to his landlady. She came out from the kitchen. "I need to pop into town to get some bits and pieces. I won't be long," he said.

"Well, yer be careful young Michael, there'll be all sorts of people looking out for yers, to be sure," she said.

"Aye, I will, and thanks," he said.

He left the farmhouse and looked at the cars, then at the key ring. 'Ford,' it said. There was a five year old Escort which had definitely seen better days. He walked up to it and tried the key. It turned and he got in. It smelt like it had been transporting chickens, and cigarettes. Michael wound down the window to let in some air. It was still a cool day for late August.

The car started fine and he drove the quarter mile down the track and came to the gate. He stopped the car got out and opened it, drove through and closed it behind him.

It was a right hand turn to Armagh and the road was lined with trees and hedges until he reached the outskirts of the town. As the houses gave way to shops, he saw what he was looking for and stopped directly outside the red phone box. He checked his pockets for change; he had a few coins plus his pocket float of about three hundred pounds.

He dialled the number that went direct to Brian's desk at police headquarters.

"Hanna," he said when he picked up the phone.

"Brian, it's Michael," he said.

"Mikey...? You ok...? I've been sat here worrying." Brian turned towards the wall and whispered hoping that no-one was eavesdropping.

"Aye, I'm fine but I need you to do me a favour," said Michael. "I'm in Armagh, at a farmhouse called Glenbar. Be careful how you use that information, I'm not sure whether this place is on the radar or not up there."

"Aye, I shall say nottin'," said Brian.

"You were right the Provos had rigged up my flat... and the van. Monahan's got me out of town," said Michael.

"Jesus," said Brian.

"Monahan tells me that it's safe now and they've got my stuff out but I need my float," he said.

"Float?" queried Brian.

"Aye, my money, close on five grand," said Michael.

"Right, yes I can see that," he said.

"I need a favour. Do you think you can get it for me? It's in the mattress at the top by the head board. You'll need to push it forward and it's under the lining, you'll see," said Michael. "I assume you'll be able to access the flat ok."

"Aye, I can do that, but how do I get it to you?" he asked.

"You'll have to see Monahan and give it to him," said Michael.

"Do you trust him?" asked Brian. "He's going to ask questions about that sort of money."

"I'll just say I don't trust banks or something, but I've got no alternative really. He does seem to want to help me though. I mean he didn't have to get me out. He obviously went to some trouble so he must think I might be useful to him," said Michael.

"Ok, I'll pop round later. Ring me tomorrow and I'll update you," said Brian and he rang off.

Michael made a second call, a London number. He checked his coins, three pounds. He hoped it would be enough.

The phone rang and a voice answered. "Daniel," it said.

"Michael," he replied.

"Go ahead," said the voice.

"I've been moved from Belfast to a farm outside Armagh called Glenbar Farm... That is the Glenbar Farm. There's no doubt Monahan is the main player. He seems to be in complete control on the ground. I don't know how long I'll have to stay here but I will make a service call again tomorrow," said Michael.

"Right... call logged; keep safe," said the voice and Michael hung up.

Michael turned the car around and headed back to the farm. He would return later.

Flora the landlady turned out to be an excellent host. She was in her fifties with a round figure and smiley disposition. She seemed pleased with the company. There were no other guests. Over dinner Michael found out that the farm would be used quite regularly usually for three sometimes four days at a time. She was clearly of the Unionist cause but didn't appear to know what was going on in any detail. Michael was very careful not to be seen to be too inquisitive. Word would get back to Brendan and he did not want to jeopardise the mission by being too hasty.

It was eight o'clock and Michael needed to get out. "I'm going back into town," he said to Flora. I want to give the bar a visit. Whereabouts is it?" he asked.

Flora obliged with directions and Michael changed into his smart casual gear before heading off to O'Hanrahan's.

The town was quiet. Tuesday night, there were a few people

milling about including some American tourists judging by the accents. Michael was able to park in the main street just around the corner from the bar and as he turned into West Street he could see the sign about half way along on the right hand side. He crossed the road and went to the entrance. The ubiquitous smell of beer and cigarettes attacked his senses as he walked into the pub. It was different from the bars in Belfast. There was something homely about it. Although there were bare floor boards, it seemed to have its own distinctive atmosphere. Smoke hung in the air. The drinks counter was not large but there was an impressive array of beers on tap and numerous optics and bottles of liquor on the shelves. There was a picture of the Queen and the union flag framed on the wall behind.

It was surprisingly busy; all the tables were taken and Michael had to push his way gently to the bar. He could hear singing coming from another room. The barman eventually reached Michael to serve him.

"Beer please," said Michael. "Are you Shaun?"

"Aye," said the barman.

"Brendan asked me to pass on his regards," said Michael.

"Ah, he did now did he? Well make sure you return the favour. This one is on the house, then you're on your own," he said.

The barman handed him the drink "What's yer name?" he said.

"Michael," he replied.

"And where are yer from Michael?" he asked.

"Derry, originally" said Michael.

"Good to meet yer, Michael. Yer very welcome here," said Shaun.

"Thanks," said Michael.

"Do you like the music?" said Shaun.

"Aye, that I do," said Michael.

The Tinker

"Go through to the other room, you'll have a great time so you will," said Shaun.

"Thanks, I will," said Michael.

He walked in the direction of the music. It was a girl's voice as clear as a bell, accompanied by a simple guitar.

He walked from the bar into a corridor - past the toilets, then another room, the lounge, was in front of him. In the North West of England it would be termed a 'snug'. It wasn't large but had its own small bar on the right hand side as you went in; a young lady in her twenties was cleaning glasses in between serving. There was a small stage on the opposite side of the room and about twenty people, over half of whom were standing, were listening intently to the strains of a ballad. The Gaelic lyrics had their own resonance which seemed to add to the emotion of the refrain. Some were in tears as they listened to the haunting voice. Michael looked at her. She was the most beautiful thing he had ever seen.

Someone got up from one of the bar stools and Michael sat down and put his beer on the counter and just watched. He was transfixed.

She finished the number and there was warm applause as she made her way to the bar. Michael was still on the bar stool as she walked towards him. Their eyes met. He was smitten.

"Hi," she said.

"Hi," said Michael. "Can I get you a drink?"

"Thank you, just an orange juice will be fine," she said.

"I'm Michael," he said.

"Colleen," she said.

Chapter Fifteen

Michael and Colleen started swapping stories and something magical happened; it was as though they had known each other for years. She performed a few more numbers during the evening and as she was singing she stared at Michael; she was singing just for him. As well as the voice of an angel, she had an inner beauty; she moved with the poise of a ballerina, her skin was alabaster white, hair black, shoulder length parted in the middle, emphasising her high cheek bones and green eyes. She was wearing a green gathered top and black skin-tight velvet trousers. Michael was in her thrall.

It was eleven o'clock before the landlord called time. Colleen thanked the audience and her guitarist and returned to the bar.

"Well I better be off," she said.

"Can I give you a lift home?" he said.

"No, but you can walk me if you like. It's not far," she replied.

So Michael thanked Shaun and walked the beautiful Colleen back to her flat.

"Just here," she said as they approached a row of detached houses on the edge of the town. "I have the top flat," she said.

Michael was hoping for an invite. "Can I see you again?" he asked.

"I shall be in the bar again tomorrow night," she said. "About eight o'clock, I'm not working," she said.

"Would you like something to eat," he said. "I can buy you dinner."

"No, a drink will be fine," she said. "I'll see you tomorrow."

She pulled him closer and kissed him, then turned around and entered the building without looking back.

Michael walked back to the car unable to shake the memory

of this girl from his mind. He had never felt this way before. He tried desperately to concentrate on matters in hand. Getting the money from Brian was a priority, and finding out who was funding this operation. He mulled possibilities. Brendan Monahan certainly had money if the rumours were true but he wasn't 'Mr Big', Michael was sure. He seemed more 'on the ground' than a strategist. Not that he wouldn't be a dangerous character. There was no doubting his ruthlessness and with his team of enforcers he would be capable of anything.

Michael got to the car and his mind was back to Colleen. He looked forward to seeing her tomorrow.

It was after midnight when Michael got back to the farm. The front porch was illuminated by an outside light. The door was unlocked. Flora had said they tended to leave it open so guests could come and go as they pleased. Michael wasn't sure this was a good idea given the area.

Michael got into bed but couldn't settle so decided to watch some TV to see if that would take his mind off things. He turned the set on and after a few seconds a feint coloured image appeared. Michael fiddled with the aerial until a semblance of a picture emerged.

A presenter was announcing the late evening local headlines.

"*Police and army personnel are investigating an explosion in Albert Street, Belfast. Initial reports suggest it was a terrorist attack and security forces are linking it to the killing of Danny Flynn earlier this month. It is believed there has been one fatality.*"

Michael stared at the screen unable to take in what he was seeing. Despite the grainy picture he could tell immediately. It was his flat, in ruins, like something from the Blitz. One fatality it said.

"Jesus, no," he said out loud. "Not Brian."

He put his hands in his head and straight away thought of Brian's wife Siobhan and his two children Rhea and Charlotte. He remembered their hospitality and how close a family they were, laughter everywhere. They were a joy to be with and now there was an overwhelming possibility he was dead.

The following morning Brendan, with Jimmy Rafferty, Ryan O'Dowd and Dory Flanagan turned up at ten o'clock. Michael had hardly slept; he had assumed the inevitable and knew Brian's death would be down to him.

"The feckin' Provos have done it this time," said Brendan as he came through the door. "Flora can you make us a coffee I need to have a chat with the lads," he said.

"What's happened?" said Michael, deciding not to let on that he had seen the news.

"They've only gone and feckin' blown up my house in Albert Street," he said.

"Which house?" asked Michael.

"The one you were staying in... and Brian Hanna as well. Don't know what he was doing in there but he must have set off another device. We didn't check everywhere," he said. "There must have been more than the one in the bog. We were lucky. Pity about poor Brian. He was a good man," he said.

Michael was devastated having had the news confirmed.

"This calls for serious retribution, eh lads?" said Brendan.

"That's for sure," said Jimmy.

"Do we know who did it?" asked Michael.

"Not yet but believe me when I find out they will wish they had never been feckin' born," said Brendan, the anger and hatred boiling over in invective.

"Well I think we should just target a bar and be done with it. We know where they hang out," said Jimmy.

The Tinker

"Aye, but not the ones who planted this," said Brendan.

Michael was watching as emotions were getting the better of them.

"Just a minute," said Michael, as the four started talking over each other with ideas and counter ideas. It went quiet.

"This calls for cool heads and a proper strategy," said Michael. He had their attention. "Yes, you can create carnage but what'll that achieve? It may make you feel better for a while but you know what, it'll happen again. The Provos will just strike back and you'll never get anywhere."

"I say we bomb the bastards," said Jimmy, interrupting Michael.

"Just a minute," said Brendan. "Let the man speak."

"I assume you have scouts out," said Michael.

"Scouts?" said Jimmy. "What the feck is that all about, feckin' boy scouts?"

"Shut up, Jimmy," said Brendan. "I'm listening," he added looking at Michael.

"You've got contacts, that's what I'm saying. Use them," Michael added. The four men were staring at him.

"Look, this tit-for-tat that's going on will never work. Lots more good people, innocent people will get killed," replied Michael, "and the RUC and army will be watching you guys like a hawk. You'll leave yourself wide open to getting caught."

"You sound like a feckin' politician or one of them peace protesters," Jimmy said and looked at Monahan. He continued his rant. "They should have tought about that before they bombed Brian Hanna. He's got a wife and kids you know."

He turned his attention to Michael again who was beginning to regret his intervention.

He pointed his finger at him in a sign of aggression. "And

don't yer worry about the feckin' army, or the RUC, they won't be bothered. We'll be doing their job for 'em," he added.

Brendan stepped in. "No, Michael's right. This is about justice. We need to find out who did this. Let's give it a few days and see if any of the lads can come up with a name or two. It's worth a try, we're in no hurry."

Jimmy was far from happy that Brendan had ostensibly taken Michael's side. There was a cleaning bucket by the side of the table and he kicked it towards the fireplace in anger. Water sprayed everywhere. Flora came in wondering what all the noise was.

"Will yer take a look at yerselves," she said. "All this commotion and you Jimmy Rafferty what are yer doing kicking my feckin' bucket? Yer can clean up the feckin' mess."

Jimmy calmed down after this rebuke from the mighty Flora and went into the kitchen to fetch a mop and cloth. Michael watched the antics with interest. Flora O'Dowd was certainly a powerful woman and definitely not to be crossed.

Brendan resumed control and outlined a plan. He endorsed Michael's idea of a more focused hit on the perpetrators of the bombing rather than declaring all-out war. That's not to say there would not be some serious tension on both sides of the divide in Belfast for some time.

After emotions had calmed and the coffees had been drunk. Brendan ushered the group outside while Flora cleared the cups.

Michael joined them; the white van they arrived in the previous day was parked at the front of the house.

"Right we need to get this stuff in the workshop out of the way and head back," he said. "We've got work to do."

Jimmy opened the back of the van and there were crates and wooden boxes, some small and some bigger ones. Michael counted ten of the larger and about twenty smaller; he lost count

The Tinker

as they carried them into the workshop.

"Michael, you need to look after these for us... valuable merchandise, cost us a pretty penny I can tell yers," said Brendan as the boxes were stacked in the corner by the small window.

"Sure," said Michael. "Is there anything I can do?" he asked.

"Not for the moment. Just keep yer head down. We'll be back tomorrow. I may have some work for yers then," he said.

Michael looked at the boxes. He had a pretty good idea what they contained but would love to know where they came from.

A few minutes later Brendan and his associates left and headed back to Belfast. Michael had work to do.

"Just popping into town," he said to Flora after they had gone.

Michael used the old Escort again and pulled up outside the phone box. He checked his change; he would need plenty.

He dialled the number. "Michael," he said when the call was answered.

"Go ahead Michael," said the voice.

"Brian Hanna has been killed," he said.

"Yes, we have been advised," said the man.

"I lost the float in the explosion. I'll need funds," said Michael.

"Ok that... Call back in one hour; we will have instructions. Any information on Hanna?" asked the man.

"Provos... retribution for Danny Flynn is the word. They were after me," said Michael.

"Ok that. Are you still in A?" said the voice cryptically.

"Yes. There has been a delivery this morning, almost certainly weaponry. Will get more information when I can," said Michael.

"Quantity?" asked the man.

"Counted ten large boxes, possibly rifles. Other boxes... ammunition, small arms, about twenty," he said.

"Ok that," said the man. "Call back in one hour."

The phone went dead and Michael left the call box. He had some time to kill so decided to return to O'Hanrahan's bar. Shaun was behind the pumps serving a customer when he walked in. Suddenly he was reminded about Colleen.

"Hi Shaun," said Michael.

Shaun acknowledged. "Be with you in a sec," he said.

Michael looked around half hoping she would be in. There were a few people around, talking or just quietly reading the newspapers. He noticed the headline, 'RUC Officer killed in Albert Street blast'. He ordered an orange juice and some sandwiches. He felt rotten.

An hour later he returned to the phone box for instructions.

"You'll need to open an account at the Ulster Bank, Market Street and phone back with the account number. We will replace the float in two hours," said the voice.

The money transfer system at that time was unsophisticated and getting money to Michael would not be straightforward. The main problem would be hiding where the money had originated. The British Government could not be seen to be funding covert operations. To cover this, a number of dummy companies had been set up to facilitate the movement of money. The cash would be transferred in from a holding account then bounced around the companies then wired out to the recipient.

Michael found the branch as advised and was able to open a current account on production of his driver's license; he gave his address as Glenbar Farm. He said he would collect his cheque book but he knew in reality this wouldn't happen.

He phoned back his handler with the details and the wheels were put in motion for the float to be replaced. It would be available for collection the following day.

Later Michael was back in the town and making his way to

The Tinker

O'Hanrahan's. He was still trying to get over the death of Brian Hanna but the thoughts of Colleen was lessening the blow. He arrived just after eight and ordered a beer. In the back lounge area another band was warming up and Michael listened to their practise session. By eight thirty the bar was packed but there was no sign of Colleen and Michael was fearing she wouldn't turn up. Then as he was staring into his beer in deep concentration, he heard a voice. "Buy a girl a beer?" she said.

Michael turned around and his face gave him away as it changed to a broad grin. She looked stunning wearing a plum coloured sparkly V-neck top and jeans.

"Shall we go through to the back," she said. "There's a good céilidh band on tonight."

He picked up the drinks and followed her into the lounge bar at the back of the pub where Colleen had performed the previous evening. They sat together and carried on where they left off; their body language totally in tune. He smiled most of the time, more than he could ever remember smiling before. Colleen did most of the talking which was just as well as he would have to make up a credible story about his life as a self-employed heating engineer. He learned that she was a professional singer hoping to get a recording contract and was even considering moving to London to further her career. She was coy about her personal background but then so was Michael.

Halfway through the evening the band called her on stage and she obliged. One of the group gave her a tin whistle and she burst into the old Irish standard, 'Toss the Feathers'. At first a solo, then the band joined in before finishing the tune with a duet with the fiddle player, like two musicians duelling with the notes. It brought the house down. Michael couldn't believe how talented she was.

At the end of the night Michael offered to walk her home

again. This time she linked her arms in his and they walked slowly back to her house.

"Would you like to come in?" she said.

He followed her through the front door and up the stairs to the top floor flat. She opened the door and led him inside. It was a spacious apartment, the decor tasteful and elegant. There was a large settee with a coffee table and what looked like a Persian Rug, fronting the fire place; dining table, two armchairs in chintz pattern.

"Have a seat," she said. "I'll make some coffees."

Michael sat on the sofa. Looking at the ornaments and bits and pieces; there was definitely money about. This was not the flat of an impecunious musician.

Colleen brought in a coffee jug, milk and two mugs on a tray and placed it on the small table. The lighting was low and atmospheric. Colleen went to a cabinet and pressed a button and the room was bathed in the distinctive sounds of traditional Irish music sung in Gaelic.

"This is a beautiful place you have here, so it is," said Michael as he watched Colleen pour the coffee.

"Thank you," she said. "I rent it from my father."

That was the first time she had mentioned her parents. He decided not to enquire further.

"When's your next concert?" he asked.

"Saturday in Portadown. You could come if you like," she said.

"I would love to. I'll have to let you know though," he said.

She sat next to him and for a moment there was just silence as they listened to the haunting melodies coming from the hidden speakers. He looked at her and out of the blue just said, "you are the most beautiful thing I have ever seen."

She put down her mug on the coffee table and took Michael's

and placed it alongside it. She looked him in the eyes and he thought he would melt. She leaned forward and kissed him. At first tentative, almost sisterly like, then more intense. Her arms were round his neck pulling him towards her with increasing urgency. Then she stood up, held his hand and gently pulled him from the sofa and headed towards the door on the opposite side of the room. There was a short corridor and she opened the first door on the right; her bedroom.

She led him to the bed and stood for a moment as they kissed again. She broke away and lifted her top over her head. She didn't wear a bra and Michael moved down to her breasts and licked her nipples one after the other. She groaned with pleasure as she took in the sensations. Then she moved away momentarily and unbuttoned Michael's shirt, undid the buckle of his trousers and unzipped him.

"I want you now," she said and he gently picked her up and placed her on the bed.

It was almost three o'clock before Michael left the flat. Colleen had invited him to stay but with one eye on his mission he thought that arriving back for breakfast may open up questions.

"I'll let you know about Portadown," he said as he left.

The roads were empty as he drove the old Escort back to the farm. His mind was still back with Colleen; she had affected him like no one he had ever known.

The following day Flora made breakfast; it was again just the two of them. Until now Flora was not the most loquacious host and the meals they had had together previously had been spent pretty well in silence. Today, though, she made conversation and Michael learned something of her background. She and her late husband had been in the farm for over forty years. Her husband had been murdered by the IRA in 1972. They were tenant farmers she explained, it belonged to the land owner, Lord Ansty.

Michael pricked up his ears. This could be the connection he had been waiting for.

"I don't know him," said Michael.

"Been very good to me," she said. "Even helps me out from time to time... money I mean. Since Paddy died he has always been there for me," she said.

"So, does he come here?" Michael asked.

"Jazus, no," she said. "Brendan sees to it all. There, I've said enough, so I have".

"It's ok," said Michael. "I understand."

"I'll need to go into town today to get some provisions in. I tink Brendan will be coming back tonight with the boys. Eat me out of house and home, so they do," she added.

"I can run you into town, if you like," said Michael.

"No, to be sure, I have someone who comes for me. I phoned him this morning, so I have," she said.

It was around eleven when an old pickup truck pulled up and Michael watched as she set off. He went to his tool box and retrieved the equipment he would need. There was something he was desperate to check.

He left the house and went to the outbuilding where the boxes were stored. The lock proved no barrier, Michael using a special tool to open the padlock. He had no idea how long Flora would be away and he moved quickly to the boxes. Anything that would indicate country of origin would be of value. Lifting the lids again would be straight forward and with a crowbar he gently levered the top from one of the boxes. Rifles, Armalite AR18's, American standard issue. They were loose rather than neatly packed which they would have been if they had originated from the factory. The boxes were just containers.

He had enough information and he carefully replaced the lid and left the building, checking footprints and anything else that might indicate an intruder. It was raining which would aid the concealment.

Michael needed to call in this information and also collect his float; he would need the money if he had to leave in a hurry.

Without waiting for Flora to return he headed into town and went to his new bank to pick up the money. There were little formalities, the cashier remembered him from the previous day and with the funds having arrived earlier he withdrew all but £1 of the cash. He wrapped it in a carrier bag and put it in his jacket. Then he went to the phone box and made a call.

It was answered on the first ring.

"It's Michael."

"Go ahead," said the handler.

"I've got more information on the boxes... American standard issue, Armalite AR18's. Provos use them. Consider possible confiscated merchandise... I think someone is selling captured weapons from the stores."

"Ok, that," said the voice.

"You may want to check out a Lord Ansty... That's Alpha, November, Sierra, Tango, Yankee. Owns Glenbar Farm."

"Ok that," said the voice.

Michael did not notice the old pickup truck going past or the silver-haired woman taking an interest in the occupant of the telephone box.

After a short shopping expedition to get some toiletries, he returned to Glenbar, Flora was already back at the farm. She greeted him with a coffee and some biscuits.

"Thank you," said Michael as he was handed the mug.

"So you've been in to town, so you have," she said.

"Aye, just getting a few things," he replied holding up a plastic carrier bag with his purchases.

She kept her council; she was not too concerned about seeing him in the call box, just curious, but for the time being decided to keep it to herself.

The afternoon dragged, Michael couldn't settle; boredom was setting in big time and he was getting restless. For someone always on the edge, hanging around an old farmhouse miles from anywhere was proving difficult. He had not been idle in his short stay at the farm. He had already serviced the central heating and was starting other odd jobs around the place that needed doing. There was no shortage; the farm was in a serious state of disrepair. Flora was grateful for the work he was doing and had commented as such to Brendan. However for now, he couldn't shake off the memory of last night and his time with Colleen. He was desperate to see her again but was having somehow to put these feelings to one side.

In the end Michael, to save him going completely mad, fixed a dripping tap in the bathroom and unblocked one of the outside drains that had been flooding. The dead starling that had caused the blockage was unceremoniously dropped in the dustbin.

Brendan and his three associates, Ryan O'Dowd, who Michael discovered was in fact Flora's nephew, Jimmy Rafferty and Dory Flanagan eventually arrived back at the farm around seven. The group were warmly greeted by Flora.

"You sit down, while I get yers a bite to eat," she said. "How long are yer going to be here?"

Michael was seated at the table watching the group settle in.

"Just tonight, Flora," Brendan replied.

Brendan looked at Michael and explained. "Me and the lads

are back up north the morrow, back here on Sunday afternoon sometime," he said. "I'll be bringing a guest with us I'd like yers to meet. He's also an engineer... well, sort of." The three lads laughed when they heard the description. Michael was none-the-wiser.

Flora bought in a plate of sandwiches and salad accompaniments. "There's a crate of beer in the scullery," she said, and Jimmy got up and fetched it.

"Hope you're not too bored down here," said Brendan to Michael who was sitting opposite him at the table. Brendan was tucking into one of Flora's cheese and pickle specials.

"Believe me t'is better than being back in Belfast, so it is. You're a very wanted man," he added. "Flora tells me about all the work you've been doing about the place, she's very pleased. The old house has been in need of some attention for some time. His Lordship will be pleased an' all."

"Lordship...?" said Michael.

"Ah, nottin'. Just someone who's got an interest in the farm, that's all." Brendan quickly backtracked; he was giving nothing away.

Michael was keen to hear what was going on in Belfast and Brendan gave him a brief update. Despite a great deal of investigation they had got no further forward in identifying the perpetrator of the Albert Street bombing and Jimmy's suggestion of planting a device in a bar was becoming more attractive. Retribution was still the main objective. Brendan's other concern was whether his insurance company would pay up; he wasn't sure if acts of terrorism was covered under the policy. This had wound him up even more, thinking that he might have to pay for the damage from his own money.

After they had eaten and settled in Brendan made a suggestion.

"Who fancies a game of seven card brag?" he said, taking a pack from his pockets.

"Aye," said Jimmy.

"Count me in," said Ryan.

"Aye," said Dory.

"What about you Michael?" said Brendan as the four pulled up chairs around the table.

"Aye, go on," he said, "Yer'll have to remind us of the rules though. It's been a while."

So there he was, playing cards for pennies with the lads with a few beers but Michael was still uneasy. Despite his, so far, benevolence, he trusted Brendan about as far as he could throw him. There was no doubting he was a dangerous individual.

As the alcohol was consumed the talking got louder and more open and Michael picked up some useful information. He discovered that the weapons were to be distributed to various people across East Belfast and Derry over the weekend. Michael made a mental note of the names and places. It was hoped there would be another consignment the following week.

It was Brendan who proffered the information. He leant forward and whispered.

"Keep this to yerselves, lads, but I have it on good authority that the Provos will be getting another visit from our friends in the constabulary tonight. We should be in for a good haul," he said.

Jimmy looked at Brendan, then at Michael.

"Ah, get over yerself. Michael's one of us... That's right enough isn't it Michael?" said Brendan.

Michael pretended not to be listening and was looking at his cards in concentration.

"Eh, what?" said Michael.

"I was telling young Jimmy here, you're one of us now,"

Brendan repeated.

"Aye, that I am. Sure haven't I got catholic blood on my hands?" Michael said.

Jimmy looked at Michael. He wasn't too sure but bowed to Brendan's authority.

"Whose deal is it?" said Michael.

Jimmy picked up the conversation. "So what about the money?" he said.

"Aye, I have it, so I have. Met yer man himself at lunchtime in the Clarendon," Brendan said.

Michael knew the Clarendon, one of Belfast's most expensive hotels.

"And what are you doing in the Clarendon?" asked Jimmy. "Getting a bit above yerself if I'm not mistaken. I can remember when you were just popping rivets, Brendan me lad," he said.

"That was another life, Jimmy, and one I am not going back to," said Brendan. "I mean can you see his Lordship coming down the Duchess?" he said and burst out laughing.

Jimmy saw the funny side.

This was more information for Michael to store in his head. His Lordship, presumably Ansty was definitely funding the gang.

The following morning around nine thirty the lads loaded the weapons onto the van and headed off.

"We'll be back Sunday afternoon," said Brendan. "Don't do anything I wouldn't do," he said as they drove off.

Michael needed to go into town again.

Chapter Sixteen

So Friday morning Michael headed back into Armagh. His first port of call was the telephone kiosk to report in the information from the previous evening.

"Ok that," said the man. "Well done. Will follow up. We need to consider exfil," he said.

"Negative," said Michael. "Now I'm in I can get more information. I'm being introduced to someone on Sunday described as 'an engineer'... possible bomb maker. We need to identify him," said Michael.

The line went quiet.

"Ok that. Review Monday," he said.

"Be in touch," said Michael.

Unbeknown to Michael, his information had already proved extremely valuable. With the main players identified, other agents were now watching Brendan Monahan and the so called 'Glenbar Gang'. The collusion between the RUC and the Loyalist Paramilitary groups, long since suspected had not only been confirmed but some of the officers involved were now known. Lord Ansty was more problematic. He owned Ballygall Castle, a large stately home and estate just outside the small town of Moy. An outspoken antagonist of the republican movement, he had vigorously opposed any dialogue with the nationalist paramilitary groups whom he considered no more than murderers. Neither would he countenance labelling captured terrorists as political prisoners or prisoners of war. His speeches in the House of Lords were unequivocal. For the moment Section E decided to do nothing.

He left the phone box and looked at his watch, eleven ten; it was still too early to return to the farm. Despite Brendan's words, to some extent Michael did feel like a prisoner but it was something he would have to endure. He decided to take a chance and got back in the Escort and headed to Colleen's flat.

He parked outside the house and went to the front door. There was a buzzer for the top floor with a small intercom. He pressed it and hoped.

"Hello," said Colleen. Michael was elated.

"It's Michael," he said.

There was a click as the front door opened and he went upstairs, Colleen was waiting for him at the door and she moved to one side so he could enter and closed the door behind her.

"Sorry to call unannounced. I didn't have a number," he said.

She went up to him and put her arms around his neck and kissed him deeply.

"I've missed you," she said. "I was so hoping you would call. Come in and sit down."

"I've been wondering how I could see you," he said, "so here I am."

She smiled.

"Would you like a coffee?" she asked.

"Aye," said Michael. "That would be good."

Colleen went into the kitchen returned with two mugs of coffees. She sat next to him. She was wearing a pair of jeans and a tee shirt.

"Sorry for the scruff appearance," she said. "I do have to do my own cleaning," she added and smiled.

"I hadn't noticed," said Michael as he sipped his coffee.

"I wanted to say lots of things but my mind has gone blank," he said. "But I would love to go with you to Portadown tomorrow night and I thought perhaps we could go out for lunch somewhere. Go up to the coast maybe, if you're not busy."

Colleen thought for a moment. "Yeah, I'd love to. Its ages since I've been to the coast, apart from work that is. I'll need to be back in the afternoon to get ready," she said.

"Ok, that's great," he said.

It went quiet for a moment and she just looked at him for a second, but the gaze; he would never forget that look.

"Would you like to go to bed?" she said.

"Yes, I would like that very much," said Michael.

"Me too," she said, and Colleen retraced her steps from Wednesday night and led Michael into the bedroom and started to undress. Michael did the same and in a moment they were in bed and locked in an embrace that Michael wanted to last forever.

They stayed there all afternoon until Colleen eventually said, "I'm feeling hungry would you like me to do some dinner for us... unless you've got to get back for something."

"No," he said. "I don't have to get back."

"That's good. You can talk to me while I'm cooking," she said.

Colleen got up and put on her jeans and tee shirt and went to the bathroom. Michael lay there for a moment, never wanting to leave her for one minute.

"Bathroom's free," she shouted, as she walked past the bedroom to the kitchen. Michael took the hint and got up. Opposite the bathroom was another bedroom and the door was open. There was a piano and a guitar on a stand and other musical paraphernalia.

Michael went into the kitchen where Colleen was starting to peel onions.

"Something quick," she said watching his interest.

"I saw your piano. Do you play that as well?" Michael asked.

"Yes, and guitar. I use both for composition," she said. "Depending on what sound I am looking for."

Michael was intrigued and listened as she explained the way

she wrote her music.

Then the question she needed to ask and Michael was dreading. "So Michael," she said as she stirred. "You haven't told me, how long are you staying in Armagh?"

The topic of residence had not cropped up in conversation but Michael knew it would come.

"If you'd have asked me that question two days ago I would have said possibly less than a week, but now..." he tailed off.

"Where did you say you were staying?" she said, as she continued stirring a pan which was giving off wonderful smells. She was making no eye contact almost afraid of the answers she was getting.

"A farm, the other side of town," he said.

"Glenbar Farm, by any chance?" she said.

"You know it?" he said with some surprise.

"Yes," she said. "My father owns it."

Michael was lost for words for a second.

"Your father is Lord Ansty?" he said.

"You know about him?" she asked.

"Not that he was your father but I knew he owned the farm, Flora told me... So you're his daughter," he said in disbelief.

"Yes, but I don't broadcast it. I have very little to do with him now. We have too many different views. We just end up arguing, so I don't get to see him," she said.

"What about your Mam?" he said.

"She does what me Da tells her. I phone her most days just to catch up but she's stuck in that huge house with just the staff for company. Da is always away."

Michael still couldn't take this in.

"You need to be very careful Michael. I'm not sure what you are doing but it will be dangerous. My father is a very powerful man, politically I mean," she said. "He is a big loyalist supporter. I spent many days in Stormont when I was growing up. He would often take me there with my Mam."

"And now?" asked Michael.

"He's away in London a lot," she said. "But I know he has some particularly nasty friends. I have met one or two. They come into the bar some nights. There's this one guy, Brendan. I could tell you some stories about him. Do you know him?" she said.

"Yeah," he said.

"Don't trust him whatever you do. He's responsible for a lot of murders," she said.

Michael was deep in thought.

Colleen dished up the dinner and they continued talking but the topic had moved away from politics. Not once had Colleen asked Michael about his involvement or why he was at the farm.

After dinner Colleen suggested they go back to the bar again to see another band who were performing that evening.

"Aye, that'll be great, but I'll need to get back to the farm and change. Shall I meet you there at eight o'clock?" he said.

Michael was beginning to worry what Flora might think if he didn't turn up at all.

"Aye... You can bring your toothbrush as well if you like," she said.

"Aye, thank you, I will," he said.

It was just after six when Michael left for the farm. Flora, as Michael had expected, was interested in his movements but merely from a domestic perspective.

"So where have you been Michael, me lad?" she said. "I didn't know whether you would be wantin' anyting to eat or not," she added, clearly upset at the lack of courtesy.

"Sorry Flora. I've been in town. I've no way of contacting you

The Tinker

without a phone," he said.

"To be sure, and I tought you had done a runner," she said.

"No," said Michael. "Nothing like that. But I will be away overnight," he added.

"Aye, I get it right enough. It'll be a lassy... sure, am I not wrong?" she said. "It always is. Well you mind what yer doing Michael, my lad, there's danger out there, sure there is."

"Thanks Flora, and I'm sorry for not letting you know. I think I'll be away tomorrow as well. Going to Portadown to see some music," he said.

"That'll be young Colleen McBride. Right?" she said.

"How did you know?" asked Michael.

"Sure, she's singing there tomorrow night. I've known Colleen since she was a baby. Her Da use to bring her here sometimes," she said. "Beautiful girl, voice of an angel... And is she the interest you have?"

Michael looked down.

"I knew it," Flora said. "Well she's a lovely girl, so she is. Now you don't go hurting her, or there will be trouble," she added.

"No Flora, I never would," said Michael.

By half seven Michael was showered and changed and ready to leave. Flora was waiting for him by the front door.

"Now you hear what I'm saying, young Michael. Just you be careful and you look after that lovely girl," she said.

"I will," said Michael. "And thank you, for everything."

"Now get away with yers. I'll see you Sunday sometime," she said.

Michael had taken Flora's words to heart and his Browning pistol was in his jacket pocket with half his float. Once in the car he hid the gun and the money in the dashboard glove compartment.

He arrived at the bar at just before eight and minutes later

Colleen walked in. It was as though a ray of sunshine had lit up the room and she walked straight up to Michael and kissed him warmly. It was like there was no-one else in the room. Shaun the barman took more than a passing interest.

"Hi Michael, and what would you be having," he asked.

"Just a lager," said Michael. "And a glass of red wine please," added Colleen.

Colleen smiled and sat on the chair next to him at the bar and linked her arm in his. Shaun produced the drinks. "Shall we go through," she said after a few minutes hearing the band starting up.

Friday night and the place was heaving by nine thirty. Everybody joining in with the singing, mostly traditional Irish numbers but without the political rhetoric. It was as though the place was somewhere to get away from 'the Troubles'.

At the end of the night Michael went to his car and collected a small overnight bag containing his toiletries and his gun and money, then walked Colleen back to her flat. He was happy to leave his car in the street; it would be safe enough. They went into the flat together and Colleen made them both a coffee. It had been a great evening and Michael had let his hair down for the first time in a long, long time singing to the familiar songs. He felt free and invigorated. Colleen was his future, he was sure. He never wanted to be apart from her.

Later they slept in each other's arms and for Michael his world would never be the same again.

The next morning was warm with the late summer sun glowing from a cloudless sky. Colleen and Michael laughed and joked as they enjoyed their first breakfast together and prepared for their day by the seaside. Colleen had already suggested a venue; Dundrum Bay where she used to go as a child.

The Tinker

"I'll take my camera," she said. "There's some beautiful scenery."

Michael drove the old Escort and Colleen provided the directions, through Tandragee, Banbridge, Castlewellan before coming into the small town of Dundrum where they stopped for coffee. Then they headed to the headland where Dundrum Bay meets the Irish Sea. There was a small sandy beach and they stayed there till early afternoon lying in the warm sunshine holding hands like a pair of sixteen year olds. Colleen gave her camera to a passing dog-walker who took a couple of photos.

"I'll get them developed in town this afternoon when we get back," she said.

They left around two and headed back to Armagh, stopping at the chemists in the High Street to drop off the film. "Can't wait to see them," said Colleen. "I'll pick them up on Tuesday," she added. Monday was Bank Holiday.

Then it was getting ready for the evening's gig in Portadown.

It was almost one a.m. by the time Michael parked outside Colleen's flat having returned from the concert. It was an amazing night watching Colleen work the audience and she left the stage to a standing ovation. Michael was so proud and as he locked his car he realised that this was probably the best day of his life.

Sunday would be different.

Michael felt wretched having to leave Colleen to go back to the farm. Colleen too was desolate that Michael was having to leave.

"When will I see you again?" she asked.

"Tomorrow, I'll be around tomorrow," he said as he drove away.

"Be careful," she shouted to him but he wouldn't have heard.

Michael was trying to think of a way out. Brendan would be

an issue but if he was serious about providing Michael with a safe haven then where better than with Colleen; he would be ok there, surely. He would speak to his handler at the Foreign Office, arrange for passage for the two of them; London perhaps, Colleen kept talking about moving there to pursue her music. Yeah that could work, he thought. He had earned the right. Yes, that's what he would do.

The Belfast lads hadn't arrived when Michael returned to the farm and Flora made a fuss of him and wanted to hear about the concert in Portadown. She made him a mug of coffee and sat down with him listening to the story.

At just after three o'clock the white van pulled up and Brendan got out of the passenger seat Dory Flanagan was driving, with Jimmy Rafferty, Ryan O'Dowd in the back plus another man which Michael assumed would be the bomb maker.

The group entered the farm and Flora was waiting for them with mugs of coffee and more homemade biscuits.

Brendan was last in and made the introductions. "Flora, this is Billy Reavey... Michael..."

The man nodded in acknowledgment. Michael weighed him up, another hard man in the same mould as Jimmy Rafferty and by all accounts from the same area of Belfast, even went to school with him, he discovered later.

After a catch up Brendan spoke to Michael. "Why don't you and Billy go to the forge and he'll tell you what he needs," he said.

So Michael led Billy from the farmhouse to the outbuilding where the weapons had been stored. Brendan gave Michael the keys.

Once inside Billy explained that Brendan had decided to go with Jimmy's idea of a bomb which would be planted in one of the IRA's known hang-outs.

The Tinker

Michael was in a dilemma but in the end was left with no alternative but to comply. Billy described his idea of a briefcase device of some kind explaining it needed to be small enough to be easily transported but powerful enough to do some damage.

"I know nothing about putting bombs together," Michael said in the hope it might let him off the hook. "But I can make some sort of case for yer."

"You're the gas man, right?" said Billy.

"Yes," said Michael.

"Then you know about circuits, right?" said Billy.

"Yes," said Michael.

"In which case yer can make us a bomb," he said.

Billy had been carrying a duffle bag since he arrived and was holding it like a pet dog. He put it down on a workbench and opened it.

"One circuit board," he said putting the said item on the bench.

"Detonator," he said and placed it next to it.

"We have Semtex - enough to bring down a building... We just need it to go off," he said.

"I thought you were the bomb maker," said Michael.

"Aye, that I am, but I need somtin a bit special for this job," he said.

He delved back in his bag and produced a briefcase.

"Now if we was to reinforce the sides and bottom and fill with the plastic and bits, we could rig the detonator to the opening fastener so that when it was opened... whoosh," he said, making a dramatic gesture with his arms.

"Aye, that would do it," Michael said.

"Can you do it for us... or not?" Reavey said.

There was a sinister tone in the 'or not'.

"Let's give it a go," he said.

So Michael with Billy the bomber worked that evening until eleven o'clock with a brief stoppage for food and eventually came up with the prescribed device. Billy was elated and went to the farmhouse to get the rest of the lads who were engaged in another round of Brag.

"Show 'em yer handiwork," said Billy when he walked in with Brendan and co.

"Yer man's a genius," said Billy who was now officially Michael's best friend.

This concerned Michael as the last thing he wanted was to make him a valuable asset. He would never be out of their clutches.

Nevertheless Brendan was impressed with the results. "Right, now we can get the bastards that did for poor Brian," he said defiantly.

The lads stayed over that night but returned to Belfast the following morning, August 27th 1979, Bank Holiday Monday.

Michael was able to get away and see Colleen. He was hardly through the door when she had grabbed his hand and led him to the bedroom. She had missed him she said.

They lay in bed talking for ages, swapping childhood stories. Then out of the blue Colleen leaned up on one elbow and looked at Michael. "Why don't you move in here," she said. "With me."

Michael sat up, slightly taken aback by the unexpected question. "Are you sure?" he said.

She smiled. "Yes, I'm sure," she said.

"In which case... yes. I really want that... more than anything," he said. "I'll need to sort out a couple of things first," he added.

"Yeah, I guessed you would," she said.

"I need to go back to the farm tonight, but tomorrow," he said.

She smiled. "Ok," she said. "Better make the most of you while you're here then," and she grabbed hold of him, pulled him

The Tinker

on top of her.

It was around five o'clock when Michael arrived back at the farm. There was no sign of the lads.

Flora again welcomed him warmly.

At seven thirty there was the familiar sound of the van pulling up outside.

Brendan stormed into the room, his face displaying terrifying anger.

"Get us a drink, Flora, my love," he said.

"Whatever's wrong?" asked Flora seeing the despair on Brendan's face.

"It's the feckin' Provos again," he said, as the rest of the group sat down. Billy the bomber wasn't with them.

"Yer won't have heard, will yer? It's just been on the news. They've only gone and blown up a bunch of soldiers not far from here, Warren Point... twelve dead they said," he said. "Bastards, there'll be hell to pay for this I reckon."

"What are you going to do?" asked Flora. Michael was just watching and listening. He was in no doubt there would be serious repercussions.

"Don't know yet. I'll speak to yer man first before we get too carried away," said Brendan.

Michael recognised this would be Lord Ansty.

Dory came in having picked up some stuff from the van. He spoke to Brendan.

"Just put the news on to see what was happening and you'll never guess... they've blown up Mountbatten an' all," he said.

"What?" said Michael. Brendan just stood in disbelief.

"What...? Lord Mountbatten, as in THE Lord Mountbatten?" Brendan said.

"That's what it said. Something about a fishing boat down near

Sligo," said Dory.

"But that's in the south," said Jimmy.

"Aye," said Brendan. There was a long pause, the lads were looking at him. "I think it's about time we showed them bastards in the south a thing or two. Dory, can you go into town and give Billy a ring and tell him to forget the bar for now. I've got a bigger target in mind."

"What's that?" asked Jimmy.

"Well the Garda Síochána do feck all about it, so maybe it's time they had a taste of their own medicine. We'll get Billy down here and plan a hit in Dublin or somewheres. The bar in Belfast can wait for the moment," he said.

Events were now moving very quickly and Michael was concerned. He needed to phone in the latest development but he would have to wait. It would raise suspicions if he were to leave now.

Tuesday morning and the mood was sombre. Brendan had taken the TV from Michael's room into the kitchen to get the latest news but the reception was even worse and they couldn't get any picture; they just listened to the commentary to a background of white fuzz. More details were being given on the deaths of the soldiers and Lord Mountbatten.

"What're we going to do?" asked Jimmy.

Brendan looked at him. "I need to go back to Belfast and see yer man and talk it over with him but my plan stands. We'll look for somewheres suitable in Dublin and give the boyos a little surprise of their own," he said.

As they were preparing to leave Michael had a quiet word with Brendan.

"Look, I've been here a week already and I'm crawling up the walls. I've found a place in town, near the bar where I can stay."

he said. Brendan looked at him with a degree of suspicion.

"You'll still be able to get hold of me and I'll still be on hand to help you out," he emphasised.

Flora was close by and had heard the conversation and intervened on Michael's behalf.

"Now you be letting the man go. He's under my feet here, so he is. Hasn't he done enough for yers?" she said.

Michael was on a knife edge. There was silence as Brendan looked at Flora, then at Michael; he appeared to be weighing up the consequences.

"Aye, all right. But you tell us where we can get hold of yers and make sure you let Shaun at the bar know as well," he eventually said. "I may need you again in a day or so. Make sure you're ready."

"I will... and thanks," said Michael.

"Well you keep a sharp eye out Michael, me lad, the Provos have long arms and if they know you're down here they'll find you, sure enough," he said.

Jimmy, Dory and Ryan got into the van as Brendan said goodbye to Flora with a flamboyant hug.

He turned to Michael and shook hands. "Now you watch yerself," he said, and he got in the van and drove away.

Michael felt a weight lifted from his shoulders but he couldn't afford to relax for a moment. The Provos were still looking for him and if for one minute Brendan thought Michael was double-crossing him he would be killed; there was no doubting that.

"Thank you Flora for that. I'll get me things together and be off. You know where Colleen lives?"

"Aye, that I do," said Flora.

"Then you will know where to contact me. I'll take the car and leave it in town. I'll give the keys to Shaun at the bar," he said.

"Aye, that'll be fine," she said.

Michael collected his gear and loaded the Escort; then said goodbye to Flora.

"Thanks for everything," said Michael and kissed her cheek.

"Ah be off with yers, yer'll have me in tears so yer will," she said.

"I'll be around," he said.

"Not if yer have any sense you won't," she said cryptically. "And you make sure you look after that lovely girl."

"I will," said Michael and he headed up the track for the last time.

Before he drove to Colleen's flat he need to make a call.

He pulled up at the red kiosk; it was busy. Michael waited anxiously as a man in his thirties talked animatedly emphasising words with hand gestures that the recipient of the call could never see. Michael wondered why people did that. He drummed his hands on the steering wheel impatiently. His palms were sweating, leaving hand prints on the plastic. It seemed longer but after five minutes the caller put down the phone and left the kiosk.

Michael went in before anyone else could claim a turn. There was a foul smell of cigarettes and body odour. He dialled the number and held the door of the callbox open a few inches to let in some fresh air.

The phone was answered straight away.

"It's Michael... I have an update."

"Go ahead,"

"They're going to hit Dublin," he said.

"Ok that," said the man. "Any more detail?"

"They have a device they're planning to leave in a bar. No more information at this stage."

"Ok that," replied the man.

Michael continued. "There's a possible drop of more weapons this week from the constabulary... funding via the head man."

"Ok that," he said. "Be advised priorities have changed... finding perpetrators of recent events taking precedence."

"Understood," said Michael. He paused.

"Anything else?" said the man.

"Request evac," said Michael.

"Ok that... wait," he said.

There was a pause. "Have you contingency?" asked the man.

"Heading south, then ferry home," he said. "There will be another passenger," he added.

"Clarify," said the man.

"Will evac with company," he said.

"Ok that," he said. "Contact when home for further instructions."

"Will do," he said and hung up.

Michael considered the conversation; they were obviously happy with Michael's contribution; there had been no further instructions. He would discuss it with Colleen but the sooner he got out of Ireland, the better.

He arrived at the flat and Colleen's face beamed. Michael was carrying his hold-all.

"You're staying?" she asked.

"If you'll have me," said Michael.

"Oh, I'll have you all right," she said and she flung her arms around him.

Michael went in and put his bag by the side of the sofa. Colleen went to the kitchen to make a drink.

A couple of minutes later she returned with two mugs and sat next to him. Before she could speak; he dropped the bombshell.

"I need to get out of Ireland..." he said. "And I want you to come with me."

For a moment she just sat there drinking her coffee in a state of shock.

"So you are in trouble?" she said.

"Yes, I can't go into detail but... yes, I am in trouble. There are people after me," he said.

"When do you have to leave?" she said.

"I should be ok for a couple of days but the sooner the better," he said.

"And where are you heading for?" she asked. She was huddled over her drink in a defensive way, her head down, elbows tight to her side.

"London..." he said, "but there is no way I want to leave you."

"Am I in danger?" she asked.

"I don't think so, no," he said.

"I have a lot of things to do. I have concert commitments, all sorts, here," she said.

"You have an agent?" he asked.

"Yes," she said.

"You could get him to cancel. You'll get more work in England," he said. "And a recording contract," he added.

"I have thought about that possibility... but not just now," she said. "Let me think about it."

She got up and took her mug into the kitchen. Michael could hear the running of water.

She came back into the room. "Ok," she said. "Let's do it."

Michael got up from the sofa and put his arms around her. "I love you," he said.

"I love you too," she replied.

Brendan Monahan was seated at his desk in his office in Belfast. It was on the top floor of a bookmaker's shop which he also happened to own. He was putting together his plan of action to deal a major blow against the Republicans; he was meeting his Lordship later to discuss options, when his phone rang.

"Sergeant Drago... always a pleasure. What can I do for you?" he said.

Brendan listened intently, his face contorting with anger as the story unfolded.

"So let me get this straight... you've been in Brian Hanna's locker... Are you sure?"

He listened.

"So Brian was an informer... definite...? And Michael Curtiss is a British agent."

There was a long pause. "Feck!"

Chapter Seventeen

Brendan had made a couple of phone calls and was at his desk holding a pencil in his hand doodling on a note pad. It helped him think. He suddenly broke it in half and threw the bits at the wall. He stormed out of the building and went to his car and drove off. Ten minutes later he was sitting in the bar of the Duchess with Jimmy Rafferty. He had ordered a double whiskey which Gerry Donahue bought over.

"Have a seat a minute, Gerry, you can join us. You need to know this," he said.

The Duchess was quiet, having only opened ten minutes earlier. Those in desperate need who had been queuing waiting for the pub to open had been served and were scattered around the room sitting in silence.

Brendan outlined the story from his RUC informer.

"I never trusted the bastard," said Jimmy. "Do you want me to do him? It'll be a pleasure," he added.

"No, I've been thinking this through. I've got a much better idea. Meet us back here in an hour and get hold of Ryan and Dory," said Brendan. Gerry had returned to his bar duties.

The more he thought about it the more it made sense. He got back to his office and picked up the phone; suddenly there was an impetus. He was clear on the solution.

"Colin Drago please?" he said when the local police station answered.

"It's Brendan, what's the latest code word for bomb threats from the Provos?" he asked.

"Thanks... got it," he said and replaced the receiver. Now came the tricky bit.

He went into his drawer and pulled out a black notebook. It had

274

The Tinker

details of his contacts and a few other things as well. He thumbed through and found the number. It was a bar on the Crumlin Road in the Ardoyne area, about as Republican as you could get.

He dialled the number and waited anxiously for the pick up; necessity breeds strange bedfellows.

It seemed to take forever but eventually it was answered.

"Yeah!" came the stern response.

"Donny Mulligan..."

"Who's calling?"

"Tell him I have some information about the gasman," said Brendan.

There was a long pause.

"Mulligan," came the voice.

"I have something you want, you have something we want... I am suggesting a trade," said Brendan.

"I'm listening," said Mulligan.

"Code word 'Genevieve' just so you know I am genuine. I have the whereabouts of the gasman, can you give me the name of the person responsible for Albert Street? I will call back in one hour."

Brendan hung up. He had no wish to be engaged in any dialogue with a Provo.

As it happened, the Brian Hanna murder was not really an issue any more. If Brendan had found out he was an informer he would have shot him anyway. It was the principle and the fact that one of his houses had to be demolished and the insurance company were playing hard-ball.

He called back at the appointed time and on this occasion Mulligan answered.

"I am taking a chance here," said Mulligan. "It could be a set up."

"It's not, you have my word. Call it a temporary truce to sort out some business," said Brendan.

"I can go with that," said Mulligan. "You have information about the gasman?"

"Yes. Can you give me what I need?" asked Brendan.

"Aye, it's a bargain. Sure, the man was on his own, not a sanctioned hit," said Mulligan.

This was not strictly true; the hunt for the so-called 'gas man' had been a priority objective for the local IRA leadership. However they were having real problems with one of their men who was becoming something of a loose cannon and therefore a liability. They quickly recognised this would be an ideal opportunity for them to clear up the mess without any active involvement on their part; a win-win situation. Much the same tactic that Brendan Monahan was using.

"Right, the man you want is called Michael Curtiss. He is in Armagh and you can find him via Shaun O'Reilly at O'Hanrahan's. It's a bar on West Street. He's got a place somewhere close by," Brendan said.

"O'Hanrahan's, you say? Right... got that," said Mulligan.

He continued. "Ok. You need to speak to Declan Weaver. Most evenings he will be at the Shamrock Club in Woodvine Road... I take it you're not planning a bomb. We have kids in there," said Mulligan.

"You have my word on that," said Brendan.

"Can I have the courtesy of your name?" asked Mulligan. "You seem to have mine. You never know it could help avoid any misunderstandings in the future."

"You can call me Brendan," he said and hung up.

Brendan had called Jimmy and explained what was going on. Jimmy wanted to take care of Michael himself but could see the logic in Brendan's plan. "This way we deal with Curtiss and I get the bastard that blew up me house," he said.

That evening Jimmy Rafferty and Ryan O'Dowd went west down the Crumlin Road, an extremely dangerous place for a loyalist paramilitary. They found the Shamrock Club on Woodvine Road and went in.

It was quiet. There were Irish Tricolours everywhere and various IRA regalia behind the bar. Jimmy was not one to be easily fazed but this was not a comfortable environment. He ordered two pints of Guinness and they stood surveying the scene and drinking their stout.

"Not seen you in here," said the barman.

"No, we're looking for Declan, Declan Weaver," said Jimmy.

"Aye, thought you might be. Mulligan said to expect someone," said the barman. "He's over there," he said pointing to a man in his forties reading the racing pages of the evening paper and wearing a light coloured raincoat. He was also enjoying a pint of the black stuff.

There was no one in the immediate vicinity and Jimmy went to the man. Ryan gave the barman a ten pound note. "Keep the change," he said and watched.

"Are you Declan Weaver," said Jimmy.

The man looked up. Whether or not he realised what was about to happen no-one would ever know. He just nodded in what appeared to be an air of resignation. Jimmy took out a pistol from his jacket and shot the man twice in the head. He put his gun back in his pocket and walked out the door with Ryan following.

"Well that's one job done," said Jimmy. "Now let's see what the Provos do," he added.

Donny Mulligan was a product of West Belfast and a staunch

Republican. He was a brute of a man, frequenting boxing clubs in the Ardoyne and Falls road. Now in his forties, he was over six feet tall, if on the podgy side, but would still be a match for most all-comers in a fight. He had joined the Provos following the Battle of the Bogside in Derry in 1969 and had been a very active member, responsible for numerous murders both sectarian and British Soldiers. He ran a small off-license with his wife, Bridie.

It hadn't taken long for him to gather two of his boys together, Finny Hennessey and Patrick Scullion. Hennessey had a butcher's shop along the Shankhill Road and had an awesome reputation. Rumours were abound that he used his knives on victims in a most dreadful way. It was believed that brutalised bodies found by the authorities were almost certainly down to him. Scullion was a second-hand car dealer who had a car-lot close to Finny's shop and was a local enforcer. They were both known to the authorities, and potential targets of the UDF. Donny Mulligan knew he could rely on them for this job which on the face of it was fairly straightforward, "find yer man, kidnap him and take him back north." There were questions to be asked and information to be had, they were sure.

They borrowed a three year old Volvo from the forecourt of the car-lot, the vehicle had been on sale for £1,500; the sticker was still in the window when Scullion turned up outside the off-license. Hennessey and Mulligan were waiting when the car pulled up. Mulligan was carrying a black hold-all which he put in the boot. He got in and peeled off the 'for-sale' notice.

With Scullion at the wheel they headed south arriving in Armagh around six. He parked in the main street outside a burger restaurant and the three went inside to get some food and discuss tactics. Despite the hour the eatery was fairly empty and they found a seat away from the window and the four other customers.

Seeing the sinister-looking men one couple immediately got up and left. Mulligan did not notice.

"We need to find the bar," he said. "West Street according to our friend Brendan."

"What if it's a set-up?" asked Hennessey. "They get us out of Belfast and into a loyalist bar. Spells trouble in my book," he added.

"No, I don't think so," said Mulligan. "I tink yer man was genuine."

After further discussions on tactics, they went to pay the bill and Mulligan asked the girl at the cash desk for directions. "Ah, yer nearly there, so you are," she said. "Across the road and next on the left."

The three followed the directions and sure enough they could see the bar.

"I'm going in on my own," said Mulligan. "Don't want to frighten anyone. A cool head will get us what we want."

He looked at the lads as he pushed open the door. "If I'm not out in five minutes you come in," he added.

So Donny Mulligan walked into the Protestant pub and could see Shaun behind the bar.

"What about yers?" said Mulligan who had attracted Shaun's attention.

The Belfast accent was obvious and Shaun had a feeling he knew who he was and what he wanted. Brendan had phoned him earlier and detailed Michael's perfidy. Shaun was told to comply with any request concerning Michael's whereabouts. Shaun would oblige; Michael was now a traitor and could expect no help.

"I believe you may know a friend of mine, Michael Curtiss," said Mulligan.

"Can I get yer a drink? On the house," said Shaun, ignoring

the question.

"A shot of Irish would hit the spot," said Mulligan.

Shaun poured a measure of Paddy's Irish malt into a small tumbler.

"Ice?" said Shaun.

"In a good malt...? Yer kidding," said Mulligan and he knocked it back in one go.

"Put another in there will yers," he said. "I'll pay for it," and he put a five pound note on the table.

Shaun obliged.

"Keep the change," said Mulligan as again he hit back the drink.

"Now as I was saying we need to find Michael and Brendan said you know where he is," said Mulligan.

"Well that depends. I know where he might be," said Shaun.

"Well you better tell us where that is," he said.

Shaun was in a quandary. In his phone call Brendan had merely said that Michael had left the farm and got a place somewhere close to the bar, not much else. However, Shaun was aware of Michael's friendship with Colleen and had no intention of putting her in any danger. He liked her enormously, and she drew in the punters.

Mulligan didn't like the delay; he thought Shaun was being obstructive.

"Well, let me tell yer how it is... Shaun, is it?" he said.

"Aye," said Shaun.

"You can give me what I want and this bar will never have any trouble from the lads... never, if you know what I mean. The alternative is that one day, next week, next month, next year maybe, you will be opening up the bar and the roof falls in. You understand what I'm saying?" he said.

The message was clear.

"All I know is that he has a place round here somewhere, close to the bar. That's all I know. He just comes in. He's just a customer. I don't know his domestic arrangements."

"Will he be in tonight?" asked Mulligan.

"I have no idea. I don't have access to his social calendar. He wasn't in last night. In fact he hasn't been in since last week," said Shaun who was looking increasingly anxious. He tried another tack. "Look, I don't know what more I can say; I've told you everything I know," he said.

Mulligan watched Shaun's face for any signs of wavering or that he might be telling a lie. He wasn't totally convinced.

There were two other people in the bar and they could see the discussion was getting more and more threatening. They drank up their drinks and walked out, worried they might get caught up in some cross-fire. Finny and Patrick came in wondering what was causing the delay.

Mulligan saw them.

"Yer man here says he doesn't know where he is... and I'm not sure I believe him," he said. It was just the four of them. Shaun could feel the level of threat rise.

Scullion went back and locked the bar door.

"Come on lads. I've told you everything," said Shaun as the three Provos walked towards him.

He leaned forward against the bar, his hands rummaging the shelf below. He felt what he was looking for and made a grab. It was the twelve bore shotgun he kept there for emergencies and before the Provos could come any closer he raised it.

"Right lads that's enough," he said. "I said I don't know where Michael is. I would tell yers if I did. He's a feckin' spy," he said.

Mulligan looked at his associates. They stopped their approach.

"What do you mean a spy?" said Mulligan.

"Only what Brendan told me. Working for the British Government."

"Oh this gets better and better," said Mulligan. "We do so want to speak to yer man. Now there's something yer not telling us, I am sure of that, and it would be in your best interests to give us what we want."

"And I'm telling yers to get the feck out of my bar," said Shaun.

"Oh dear we seem to have come to a bit of an impasse," said Mulligan.

The dialogue had distracted Shaun and before he could move Mulligan had pulled a pistol from a shoulder holster and fired a round at the barman. It was a deliberate shot, the shoulder blade; Shaun dropped the gun and grasped the top of his arm in agony.

"Now the next one will be between the eyes," said Mulligan pointing the gun at his face. Shaun slumped to the floor behind the bar.

Hennessey lifted the flap on the counter top that gave access to the serving area and went around the other side of the bar. Scullion joined him and they dragged Shaun out from behind the counter and into the customer space. He was still holding his shoulder blood oozing between his fingers.

"Right lads, the knees," said Mulligan. "Now that really is painful, specially from behind... shatters the kneecap so it does."

He looked at Shaun and held his cheeks together with one fist. "You know there are blokes in Belfast who can only limp along now, pitiful sight so it is. Ain't it lads?" he said looking at his two associates.

"Are yer right or left-handed, Shaun? We would hate to deprive yers of yer ability to earn a decent wage."

Shaun was shaking with fear, his face had turned white. There was blood down the front of his shirt and his hands were red from holding his shoulder.

"No... no... there is something," he moaned pitifully.

"Now that's more like it," said Mulligan.

"He... he ha... has a g g girlfriend," he stammered.

"And where does she live?" asked Mulligan.

"T... Tandragee R... Road, third house on the left... top floor flat," said Shaun.

"And what's her name?" he asked.

"C... Colleen," said Shaun.

"Now you could have saved yerself a lot of grief if yer had told us that in the first place," said Mulligan.

He took the pistol off Hennessey, aimed it at Shaun and shot him between the eyes.

"I keep me promises, so I do," he said. "Right lads, let's get out of here."

They walked out of the pub back to the car as cool as you like; there were few people about now all the shops were closed.

Scullion took the driver's seat again; Mulligan, the passenger, with Hennessey in the back of the Volvo.

"Right, let's find this girlfriend... what was her name?" said Mulligan.

"Colleen," said Hennessey, as they pulled away.

"Aye that was it," said Mulligan.

Scullion spotted the sign to Tandragee. "It must be down here," he said slowing down at a junction.

Meanwhile in the flat, the scene of domestic bliss was being played out. Michael was on the sofa reading a newspaper. The photographs of the day out at the coast were in a folder on the table. Colleen had collected them from the chemists earlier and they had spent a few minutes looking through them swapping memories of the day. "I will put this one in a frame," she said when they came to the one of the two of them taken by the dog-walker. She had put it on the top of the folder to remind her.

Colleen was in the kitchen and suddenly announced. "Oh dear, we've run out of milk." She opened the fridge wider and looked around. "We could do with some cheese, and bread as well," she said. Michael put down his paper.

"I'll go into town and get some," he said. "Won't take a minute."

He picked up his jacket from the back of one of the chairs. "Do you want to go to the bar later?" he said.

Colleen came back into the lounge. "Aye, that would be nice," she said.

"Ok, we'll take the Escort. I promised Flora I would leave it in town. Then I can drop the keys off with Shaun. He said he would get them back to her," he said. "I'll have to see about getting a new one," he added.

"You won't need to. We can use mine," she said.

"I didn't know you drove," he said.

"Well now, how's a girl going to get to the gigs?" she said.

"I thought you guys had roadies and limos," he said.

"Aye, in yer dreams. I'm not David Bowie," she said. "It's parked round the back," she said.

He went over and kissed her. "Won't be long," he said.

Taking Shaun's directions the lads found the property and parked outside.

"Right boys, this must be it. Now just a thought, if this guy is security forces, he will be good and probably armed so go careful and watch yerselves... Ok, check yer weapons," he said and the men took out guns from their pockets and released the safety catches.

They went up to the front door and Mulligan spotted the buzzer.

"What do we do?" said Hennessey.

"See if anyone is home," said Mulligan and he pressed it.

To their surprise there was a click and the front door opened. Mulligan pushed it and slowly entered the building; Hennessey and Scullion followed.

"I don't like it," said Hennessey. "It might be a trap."

The stairs were in front of them and they made their way up to the top floor one step at a time. Mulligan was leading and had his gun drawn, the others followed. They reached the the flat and couldn't believe the door was ajar a couple of inches.

"I don't like this," said Hennessey not for the first time.

Mulligan pushed the door open slowly. It made a creaking sound. He looked back at Scullion who was directly behind him. Hennessey was at the rear covering their backs.

"Michael?" Colleen called from the kitchen.

Mulligan entered the lounge just as Colleen came out of the kitchen. She looked at the men and gasped.

"Who are you?" she asked "Get out of my house."

Mulligan raised his gun.

"Where is he?" he said.

"Who?" said Colleen.

"Yer man, Michael. You just called his name," said Mulligan.

"He's not here," she said.

"Oh dear that's such a shame and we've come all this way. Looks like we'll have to sit down and wait for him," said Mulligan.

Colleen was petrified. Mulligan walked towards her and grabbed her arm. "Sit down," he barked.

"Patrick, check the place make sure there's no one else here," said Mulligan. Scullion left the lounge and made the search.

"All clear," he said on his return.

"So you're Colleen. I can see why Michael has taken a shine to yer, sure I can... such a pretty young thing, so y'are," he said. He looked around the room. "Nice place yer have, so it is."

"What do you want? Why are you here?" she said.

"We need to have a chat with yer man," said Mulligan.

Just then the buzzer went.

"Yer better let him in," said Mulligan, "and no messing, eh?"

Colleen went to the intercom and pressed the button to let him in.

"Michael get out now... They're here," she shouted.

Mulligan grabbed her around the waist and threw her onto the settee.

"Now look what yer've done. Yer've made me angry, so yer have," he said and he slapped her hard across the face with the back of his hand. She landed on the floor and tried to get up. Blood was coming from her mouth. Mulligan grabbed her by the hair and dragged her back onto the sofa. He had the gun pointing to the side of her head just above the ear, her head jerked right back by Mulligan's grip.

Hennessey and Scullion were either side of the door waiting for Michael to appear both had guns drawn. Suddenly he was there in the doorway and saw Colleen and Mulligan.

"Leave her alone," he shouted. "She's done nothing wrong. I'll come with yer," he said.

Colleen's eyes were wide with fright. Michael was trying to suppress his natural instincts. He walked into the room towards Mulligan. He had not seen the other two men.

Scullion was holding a black hood and before Michael could move he had forced it over his head. Hennessey grabbed Michael's arms and tied them behind his back; their guns were

The Tinker

back in their pockets. There were muffled pleas and rants which were incoherent.

"Leave him alone," shouted Colleen.

"Now I've had enough of you young lady," said Mulligan.

He looked at Michael who was being held like a rampant stallion by Hennessey and Scullion, desperate but futile.

Mulligan lifted Colleen off the sofa by her hair. She was screaming. "Let go of me you bastard," she shouted.

"Jazus, but you're a nightmare," said Mulligan and without a moment's hesitation he put the gun to her head and pulled the trigger.

She dropped like a stone onto the floor, blood was seeping from her head and started to soak into the carpet.

Michael sank to his knees, recognising what had happened. Hennessey and Scullion just looked at Mulligan.

"Jazus Donny, what have you done now?" said Patrick.

Anger surged through Michael's body like he had never known, but his training kicked in. Feigned compliance; it was what Michael had been taught in military school when faced with captive situations.

When Michael returned from the shops he had noticed the Volvo with the Belfast license plate parked in front of Colleen's flat. Intuition told him something wasn't right and as a precaution he took the Browning from the glove box of the Escort and slipped it into his sock, just above the instep of his shoe.

Unwittingly by distracting the men, Colleen had probably saved Michael's life. They had been careless and not searched him.

Michael was still on his knees, the hood over his head, but not tight; he could see the floor. He had stopped struggling and had gone limp which had allowed the cord around his wrists to slacken. He started to work the ties; Scullion and Hennessey were still looking at the body of Colleen as she was lay on the floor; her eyes staring vacantly at them.

"Come on Donny let's get this finished. We've got to get the feck out of here," said Scullion.

"I tought we were taking him back with us," said Hennessey.

"Change of plan," said Mulligan.

Michael sensed the end was very close.

Mulligan looked at Patrick. "Let me have a look at the fecker. He can see his girlfriend at the same time. He'll be joining her soon enough, sure he will," he said and Scullion took the hood off. Hennessey was holding Michael's shoulders.

Michael could see Colleen but all thoughts were geared towards survival... and revenge. The cord was now loose and he reached for his gun, very slowly.

Mulligan walked towards him.

"Now you see what yer've made us do, yer fecker. That'll teach yer to go blowing up our friends," he said.

Michael let out a scream. "Jazus, no...! Why did yer have to do that?" he said, which momentarily caught the lads off-guard.

Like a panther striking an unwary prey, in one movement Michael pulled the gun from the improvised holster and from his kneeling position shot at Mulligan then turned and fired at Hennessey then Scullion before they could move.

Michael got up. Mulligan was conscious but groaning; the bullet had hit him in the groin and travelled up through his body; his gun was on the floor. Michael kicked it away and grabbed him by the hair.

"Yer bastard. What's this all about, eh? Is this what yer so-called 'cause' is all for... killing defenceless women?" and Michael raised his gun to Mulligan's head and shot him in the temple.

The Tinker

He checked the other two Provos. Hennessey was already dead, Scullion unconscious but still alive. Michael finished him off with another head shot.

Michael had to move quickly. The shots would have alerted people and the police would be around any minute.

Michael put his gun in the pocket of his jeans and went to the bedroom. His duffle bag was still packed. He picked it up and left the flat. Michael hurried downstairs. There were a few houses down the Tandragee Road but were spaced apart before the greenbelt on the town border took over; he checked left, and right it was deserted. He opened the door of the Escort, flung the bag, including his gun and money onto the back seat and set off.

Armagh was less than ten miles from the Irish border; ironically he would be safer there. The direct route would be the A3 which would take him to the town of Monaghan but instead he decided to use the back roads. Crossing the border would not be difficult, terrorists went back and forth on a regular basis; it was time to leave the province.

As it happened the commotion at the bar had taken up all the police activity and it would be sometime before the carnage at the flat was reported. The owner of the house had come home and noticed Colleen's door was not shut properly and had gone in to investigate to be greeted by four bodies.

Chapter Eighteen

Denise looked at Michael. He had been speaking for over two hours and looked exhausted. She had filled his tumbler with water several times. This was a convenient time for a break.

"I need to be excused," he said.

Denise looked at the clock on the kitchen wall. "Yes, goodness look at the time. I need to get the dinner on, John has a meeting this evening. You can stay and eat with us if you like, I have plenty," she said.

"Thank you, yes please," he said.

The vicar was still in his study but seeing Michael walk towards the downstairs toilet, the vicar got up from his desk and went into the kitchen.

"Everything alright, dear?" he said and sat down.

"Yes, it's going very well," said Denise. She was rummaging around in the fridge and not making eye contact.

Michael came back and sat opposite the vicar who looked at Michael with a degree of concern.

"You ok, Michael?" he said.

"Aye," replied Michael.

Denise had taken out some cold chicken and salad and was washing lettuce at the sink.

"Just some chicken and salad," she said "I can do some baked potatoes if you like," she added.

"Yes, thank you," said Michael.

He had gone quiet again and Denise was concerned that he might regress and withdraw further.

"How do you feel?" she asked.

"Drained... emotional, if I'm honest. It's opened up a lot of locked doors," he said. He put his head in his hands and rubbed

The Tinker

his eyes in an attempt to restore his energy levels.

"Well after dinner, if you feel up to it you must tell me the rest. John has a Bible reading meeting at seven," she said.

The conversation at the table while they ate was strangely muted. The vicar was only too aware of the emotional roller coaster that Michael had been through; he had been there himself. There was no mention of his revelations with Denise and the discussion centred on possible work for Michael. Gradually Michael relaxed and the vicar could see his change of demeanour and the tone of his voice.

"I have another boiler to service tomorrow," he said. "Molly Ford at the cottage."

"Well she'll keep you there all day. Talk the hind leg off a donkey can Molly," the vicar said which lightened the atmosphere.

So after they had eaten and washed up, the vicar went off to his meeting and Denise made two coffees.

Again they sat at the kitchen. The weather was still warm with blue sky flecked by white fluffy clouds. The trees, visible through the kitchen window, moved gently in the breeze.

"I have to say I cannot even begin to imagine how you must be feeling," she said as she put down the coffees on the table and sat down. "I have heard some harrowing tales in my time but that was something else," she said.

"It's been tough," he said.

"You were saying that you had to leave Northern Ireland. Do you want to tell me what happened next?" she said.

"Aye," said Michael, who was continuing to drift into his Irish accent quite frequently now having been transported back there by Denise's counselling skills.

"So how did you get away?" she asked.

"That was fairly straight forward. I headed down to Dublin and caught the ferry to Liverpool. Left the car at the terminal. I had a passport, not in the name of Michael Curtiss, Michael Beresford. I still use that name when I go abroad. It was the escape name I was given when I started the assignment," he said.

"What about the contact with the Foreign Office?" asked Denise.

"As soon as I got back to England I phoned in. I told them what had happened and they told me to go to London. So I stayed at a hotel near the station in Liverpool for one night then the following day took the train and met up with my handler for a debrief. It was the same coffee shop off Oxford Street. I gave him more detail on what had happened but it was not what I expected. As I said earlier because of the Warren Point and Mountbatten investigations my mission was now low priority. I also found out that there was all kinds of shit... sorry, flying around. As I said, Colleen was Lord Ansty's daughter and of course he wanted a full enquiry into what had happened, and how his daughter had become involved. The police had worked out that the Provos had killed her but they didn't know who had killed the Provos. Also I didn't know at that time that they had killed Shaun. My handler told me about it."

Michael paused and drank his coffee.

"You can imagine the press locally were having a whale of a time - five murders in one day... made the national news, but I discovered later that the F.O. buried the investigation in the national interest. Ansty had of course found out from Monahan what had happened. He was furious and was blaming 'their operative'... me, for Colleen's death. Which of course was true."

Michael looked down at the table in a state of despair, then covered his face again with his hands. Denise was pleased that he was able to display that emotion; it was a positive sign. She was certain that he had never properly grieved; something he would

The Tinker

need to do if he was ever going to move on.

"You know," he said looking at Denise. "In some ways I wish I hadn't met her; she would still be alive now. She's always in my head; I can't seem to let her go."

"You may never will. The way you described it, the intensity; it was so vivid. Not everyone has that experience but in a way that's something to celebrate. The only solution to cope with it is to compartmentalise it. I can show you how to do that," said Denise.

"I might take you up on that, but part of me doesn't want to let her go," he said.

"Yes, I can understand that but it's not about letting her go but being able to move on," said Denise. She changed the subject. "What about the farm and, what was his name, Brendan? Surely something happened there. That's why you were sent in the first place."

"Yes." He gathered his thoughts. "After my tip-off the security services had the gang under surveillance and raided the farm just after the next arms shipment arrived."

He looked at Denise with an ironic smile.

"Would you believe Brendan and Jimmy weren't there; they'd gone back to Belfast. They were picked up later but never charged, lack of evidence. Jimmy Rafferty had killed at least six people to my knowledge," he said. "The rest of them, O'Dowd, Flanagan, Billy Reavey and a couple of others I hadn't met were charged with fire arms offenses, even poor Flora... although she was let off. I was glad of that, I liked her, and she was good to me. Some of them were convicted. Ryan O'Dowd got four years, Reavey and Flanagan two, although how they worked that out I'll never know."

Michael took a drink of his coffee.

"They did manage to trace the arms back to the RUC though, which lead them to the officers who had supplied the weapons and were on the take. That was my information so I had made some difference. I can take some comfort in that. The Glenbar Gang were effectively closed down and the tit-for-tat killings became less frequent."

"Did you feel the sacrifice was worth the result?" she asked.

"Not personally, no. Nothing could ever justify Colleen's death. The F.O. were extremely pragmatic, the gas explosion and the killing of the Provos were just... collateral, I think he called it, my handler. I would never face charges. It's just something I have to live with."

Denise looked at him. She had heard similar tales from returning soldiers who had killed. It had affected them in a similar way.

"And you cope with that?" she asked.

"Yes, pretty well. The Provos never cause me a moment's thought after what they did to Colleen. I will never mourn those bastards' deaths. Sorry, not very Christian," he said.

"You did what you had to do. You would have been dead otherwise," she said.

"The gas thing I think about from time to time. But that was the job," he said.

"Yes, the job of a soldier is quite unique," said Denise. "When did you become aware you might be in danger?" she added.

"Pretty well straight away. It was obvious Ansty wasn't going to let it rest and of course Brendan Monahan would be fired up as well. They clearly knew I had been a plant and I'd got away. My handler told me that they had been tipped off that money was on offer for my, how can I put this...? Execution."

Denise looked at him with some concern.

The Tinker

"I thought I would be ok, my section handler said they'd arrange for a change of identity but I had forgotten about the photograph. It meant they, whoever 'they' were, could identify me."

"What the one at the beach?" said Denise.

"Yes. I was told that the police had taken an interest in the picture but it had mysteriously disappeared. I think Ansty has it. So I had to get away. I didn't know who I could trust. I thought I might have become expendable. I just told them I would sort myself out and left it at that. Officially I didn't exist, my military record had been wiped out and obviously I couldn't work for them again so the F.O sorted this bank account arrangement for me I mentioned earlier. That at least gave me a bit of freedom. So I decided I would hit the road."

"What about Lord Ansty? What's happened to him?" asked Denise.

"Nothing, as far as I know... seems to be untouchable. I mean they know about his involvement. Whether anyone has said anything to him or not I don't know but he hasn't been arrested or anything."

Denise considered this. "We talked at the start about the effects of post-traumatic stress. How has all this affected you, mentally I mean?" she asked.

"That was when the problems really started. I was never particularly outgoing but the isolation meant I became more and more withdrawn. I was paranoid about being discovered. I kept changing my appearance, like the big beard." He smiled.

"The one you arrived here with?" she said. "Gave me quite a fright."

"Yes, sorry about that," he said. "I avoided towns and lived off the land for a while, camping out in all weathers, although I was not by any means penniless. I had this thing about being cornered in a hotel. Daft now looking back; I could have saved myself a lot of uncomfortable nights."

"What about after you left here, the winters, where did you go?" she asked.

"I went all over the place including Spain, picking fruit and Greece, olives. I worked in a beach bar in Ibiza and Tenerife, but the only real respite I had was here. I felt safe... and a sense of belonging," he said.

"But you never let anyone in here either, emotionally I mean," she said.

Michael looked down. "I know. It was self-imposed, a safety mechanism I suppose. I had this persona that had kept me safe so I stuck to it."

"Why didn't you stay here, permanently I mean, if you felt safe?" asked Denise.

"I did consider it and I did stay here longer than anywhere else but I thought that sooner or later someone would find me. I never stayed anywhere for longer than a few weeks. I found myself getting restless," he said.

"But how long are you going to keep running?" she asked.

"That's a good question... I really don't know. I have a lot of thinking to do," he said.

"Well you can stay here for as long as you like, you know that," she said.

"Thank you," he said.

Denise got up and took the empty coffee mugs to the draining board. Michael was still staring at the table.

"Do you think these people will come after you?" she asked.

"If they know I am here, almost certainly. I thought they might have given up. It's been nearly seven years. But when I heard that people have been asking about me, well I guess they must be still looking," he said.

"How do you think they traced you here?" she said.

"I have no idea," he said.

"Well I'm sure no-one in the village would say anything. Anyway, no-one knows anything about you, your background I mean. Although I think one or two do find you fascinating. Especially the ladies... 'the enigmatic Tinker'," she said.

Michael chuckled to himself. "Is that what they think?" he said.

"Well I know Melanie Draper carries a torch," she said. "Mind you she does have a bit of a reputation."

Michael smiled again but wasn't saying anything.

The church clock struck nine. Michael looked at the clock on the kitchen wall, as if to check.

"I should go," he said. "I have taken up enough of your time."

He got up from his chair and looking at her he said, "thank you, thank you for everything."

"I just hope it has helped. We do care about you," she said. "You know that."

"Aye," said Michael. "I do."

Denise got up and kissed him on the cheek.

"You take care of yourself Michael," she said.

"Aye, I will," he said as he opened the door, left the vicarage and made his way back to the Lodge.

Back in the room, Michael couldn't settle and for the first time in seven years felt in need of some company. He put on his jacket and with the money he had from the work for the Major went for a walk along Vicarage Road into the village. He saw the pub with its lights glowing, beckoning; one or two were drinking outside making the most of the warm summer's evening. He took a deep breath and walked inside. He looked around; there was the usual hub-hub of chatter. Monday night was not normally busy but over half of the tables were taken.

This was the first time he had been in a pub for over seven years, since his visit to O'Hanrahan's with Colleen. Suddenly the memories returned and he started to feel nauseous; his hands were shaking and he was sweating. He reached the bar when he heard a voice. "Hello Michael."

He turned to his right; it was Melanie.

Michael looked at her.

"Are you alright?" she said.

"Yes... thank you. Can I get you a drink?" he said.

She got up from the stool and joined him. "A vodka and tonic, please," she said. "I've never seen you in here before," she added.

"I've never been in before. Not in the bar anyway," he said.

Michael had done some decorating and plumbing at the White Hart the previous year but in the hotel, never in the pub area.

Tony Rollinson came out from the back.

"Michael, what a pleasant surprise. We don't normally see you in here," he said.

"No," said Michael. "Got bored staring at the walls," he said.

"What can I get you?"

"A lager and a... Vodka and Tonic?" Melanie interjected.

"I'm glad you've called in," said Tony as he put the drinks in front of Michael. "Gavin was saying he's got quite a bit of work, if you're interested like. I told him you were back. I was going to pop over to the church and see you," he said.

"Yeah, thanks. I'll call in tomorrow lunchtime and speak to him," said Michael.

"Yeah, he'll be in around one," said Tony.

"Cheers," said Michael.

Melanie was watching Michael. There was something different

about him, and he was talking in a strange accent.

She picked up the tonic bottle and poured it into the vodka.

"Thanks," she said. "Are you sure you're ok? You sound different," she said.

"Yeah, not been in a pub for seven years," he said as he picked up his drink. "Sorry about yesterday," he said. "There's some stuff I'm trying to sort out."

"That's ok. Do you want some company?" she said.

Michael looked at her, skin tight black satin trousers, heels, white top, looked new.

"Yeah," he said. "That would be good."

They found a vacant table in one of the corners which was out of the way and as a result, quieter. It was separated by two small armchairs. Michael could hear the background music which was inaudible closer to the bar. They sat down and Melanie moved closer.

"You're different," she said and rubbed his arm in an affectionate way.

"Different?" he said, as he took his first sip of lager.

"Yes," she said. "I can't work it out but you told me you never went into bars, so that's a start," she said.

"Yes, I did say that, and I haven't... not for seven years," he said, taking a sip of his lager.

"So why now?" she asked.

"Been doing a lot of thinking," he said. "I need to change a few things."

"Anything to do with those people who were asking about you?" she said.

"Sort of... indirectly," he said. "It's because of that I find it difficult to trust people."

"Well maybe it's about time you did," she looked down. "I

know what people think of me round here. I've probably deserved the reputation, but I do care about you Michael, I really do," she said.

"I don't know why. I haven't treated you that well," he replied.

"No you haven't, Michael," she said and smiled with a deliberate feigned pout.

"Sorry," he said and he took another sip of lager.

"What's the news on your husband?" he asked.

"Oh, the tosser. He's been remanded in custody pending trial in September. He wants me to visit. I told him to fuck off," she said. "Don't want anything to do with him. The sooner he's out of my life the better. Got an appointment tomorrow with the lawyer in Stonington. Filing for divorce," she said.

"Well if it's what you want," said Michael. "Then it's for the best."

"It is," she said and took a sip of her vodka. "Come on Michael, now it's your turn," she said.

"What do you mean?" he said.

"Well, why are these people after you? Did you rob a bank or something? Upset the mafia? It must be pretty big for people to be looking for you," she said.

"Aye, it is. I can't go into details," he said.

Melanie's face showed disappointment.

"Is it about that girl you were involved with?" she pressed; she wasn't letting go.

Michael looked at her. "As I said I can't go into details."

"Come on then, tell me about you, your background. At least you can tell me that."

Michael thought for a moment.

"What do you want to know?" he asked.

"Your name for a start, where are you from, why you disappear

The Tinker

every September, but keep coming back," she said.

Michael was not going to be as forthcoming as he had been with Denise but he felt it was time to share some things.

"Aye, ok. Let me get you another drink," he said. "Same again?"

"Michael, you're infuriating," she said. "But, I'm not letting you get away that easily. Yes, another vodka please. You can tell me when you get back from the bar."

So Michael bought another round. He looked across at Melanie while he was waiting for the drinks. Despite all her bravado he could sense her vulnerability. In some ways they weren't that dissimilar.

He went back to the table. The bar was busy now and several regulars had spotted him and waved or said hello, including Janice Audley.

"Your boss is here," he said as he returned and put the drinks down on the table.

Melanie waved as she caught Janice's eye. "More gossip," she said.

"So go on," said Melanie, "where are you from?"

Michael looked at her, hesitated for a moment then said, "East Midlands," he replied. "Near Derby."

"Any relatives?" she asked.

"No, just me?" he said.

"What do you do? I mean before you started running away," she said.

"Heating engineer," he said.

"Really? So how does a heating engineer get caught up in skulduggery?" she asked.

"It's a long story, and I can't go into it in detail," he said.

She looked at him, quizzically.

301

"Very intriguing," she said, "Ok, I'll let you off," she added, recognising she was not going to get any further with this line of enquiry.

"So, what's your name, your real name I mean?" she said, changing the question.

Michael looked at his beer as he took another drink to give him thinking time.

"Beresford, Michael Beresford," he said. "That's what's on my passport," he added.

Melanie poured the tonic into the vodka and took a drink.

"Michael Beresford," she repeated. "So where do you disappear to when you leave here?" she asked.

"Varies, depends on what I feel like doing... go abroad, take a holiday," he said, which was still on the vague side for Melanie's liking.

Recognising that her attempt at small-talk was not really getting anywhere, she tried another direction.

"What about the future? Is it going to be more of the same, going place to place, stopping for a while then moving on?"

"I don't know, possibly," he said, which was more promising than 'probably'.

Melanie had tried to open a real dialogue before but Michael clammed up very quickly so this conversation had been the most productive they had had. Melanie thought it was a step in the right direction.

"Isn't it all a bit selfish though?" She decided she would push another button.

"I hadn't really thought about it," he replied and took another sip of his beer.

"But isn't that it? You don't care about anyone else. You do use people you know," she said, but not in an angry way.

The Tinker

These were some home truths that needed saying. Michael looked at his drink and rubbed his fingers up the glass, clearing the condensation.

"I guess it could appear that way, but I never make promises," he replied.

"No you don't, that's for sure," she replied and finished her vodka.

"Same again?" he asked.

Michael went to the bar which was now crowded and he made his way to the front to be served.

He ordered another vodka for Melanie and a small lager for himself.

He went back to the table and put down the drinks and excused himself to go to the men's room. Melanie watched him go through the door to the toilets and wondered whether she was actually getting anywhere with him. There was no shortage of men trying it on; she could guarantee a proposition pretty well every time she went to the pub, mostly from guests; she was too well known around the village. But it wasn't what she wanted. It was Michael who she found irresistible.

Michael came back and sat down. "Do you want to come back to the Lodge?" he said.

Melanie was in a quandary. She wanted him like mad but after the way she had been treated she wasn't going to make this quite so easy.

"I'm not sure," she said. "Not if it means being discarded once you've done with me like you did before."

"No, you're right, but I can't make any promises. I can't say what will happen. It could actually be dangerous," he said.

Far from putting her off, the thought of danger and adventure was like a moth to a flame. It was after all what drove her to him in the first place. Anything was better than this sleepy village where people lived in their quaint cottages in a sheltered 'wholemeal' world.

"I'll need to pop back home to get some stuff," she said.

"Ok, I'll walk you," said Michael.

With four large vodkas now consumed, Melanie was not as steady on her feet as she might have been but managed to stand up. Janice Audley was standing at the bar with her husband and another couple and saw Melanie and Michael walking towards her.

"Goodnight you two," she said. "Don't do anything I wouldn't do," she added and laughed loudly; she too would not have passed a breathalyser.

They got outside the White Hart and Melanie linked arms with Michael. It was another warm summer's evening and as they climbed the rise out of the village towards the rumble of traffic on the bypass, the remnants of the day were still just visible on the western horizon. The hills to the east were in total darkness and just the odd twinkling of light from a farmhouse gave any indication of civilisation. Once at the cottage she left Michael in the sitting room while she went upstairs and packed an overnight bag and some other bits and pieces plus her clothes for the following day. Melanie had managed to clear all the mess left by her soon-to-be former husband. Then they set off back to the Lodge.

The fresh summer air and exercise had had a sobering effect and by the time they headed up the path of the vicarage Melanie was feeling fully awake and ready for anything. She would not be disappointed.

Later, Michael was in a deep slumber but the dreams had come back. Denise's counselling and the talk with Melanie had brought all his demons to the surface.

"Why did you do that, yer feckers? Why did yer have to kill her?" he shouted in a strong Irish accent. Melanie woke with a start.

She turned on the bedside light. He was wet with sweat. "Michael are you alright," she said.

At first he wouldn't wake and Melanie was worried. The church clock struck the quarter hour, she checked her wrist watch, two fifteen.

"Yer bastards," he shouted again and Melanie shook him and he suddenly woke up, totally disorientated. "Colleen?" he said before coming round.

"Eh... what...? Jazus," he said.

He put his hands over his eyes.

Melanie stroked his forehead. "I'm going to make a cup of tea," she said. "Then I want you to tell me about your dream."

A few minutes later she returned to the bedroom with two mugs of teaming liquid. Michael appeared to be dozing.

"Michael, drink this," she said.

He made a groaning sound then opened one eye. He shielded his face from the glare of the bedside lamp.

"What...?" he said.

"Here I've made you some tea. You were having a nightmare," she said.

He slowly raised himself into a sitting position, still heady from the deep sleep. He put his hands to his face and rubbed his eyes with his fingers.

"What time is it?" he said.

"Just gone quarter past two," she said.

"Oh, Jazus," he said. It was the Irish accent again.

He took the mug from Melanie, still not fully conscious and sipped.

"That's hot," he said and put the mug on the bedside table. "What are we doing having tea at two o'clock in the morning?" he said.

Melanie put her mug on her side table and got back into bed. She put her arms around him and said, "you frightened me you know."

"Sorry," said Michael. "I was dreaming."

"I know," she said. "It was scary. You were screaming."

"Sorry," he said again. "I didn't mean to wake you up."

"That's ok, I know that. I was worried," she said.

Michael was trying to think when someone was last worried about him; he couldn't remember.

She looked at him. "You watched her being killed, didn't you?" she said.

Michael picked up his mug and took a drink.

"I was there, aye," he said.

"And this was in Ireland?" she said.

"Aye," he said. "How did you know?"

"You were speaking in an Irish accent," she said. Then a realisation. "You were in the army? I'm right, aren't I...? It would explain a lot of things," she said.

"I can't talk about it," he said.

"No, I know, I understand. It makes sense now," she said sitting drinking her tea.

Michael was now wide awake and reflective.

Eventually, they both finished their drinks and Melanie turned out the light. She curled up behind him in the spoons position and held him till he went back to sleep.

The church clock struck seven and again Melanie got up. She went to the bathroom then went back to the kitchen to make more tea. When she returned to the bedroom Michael was still sound asleep but looked peaceful; it was as though he had not moved.

"Michael... wake up, it's gone seven," she said.

He stirred. "Eh... what?"

"I've bought you some more tea," she said. "You'll need milk later," she added.

Michael looked at her. "Thanks. Sorry if I scared you last night," he said.

"That's ok. Are you alright this morning?" she said.

"Aye, much better," he said as he sipped his drink.

Once Michael finished his tea he took a shower while Melanie prepared some toast.

"You'll need more bread as well," she said as he came into the kitchen with a towel wrapped around his waist. "Tell you what, I'll do a list of things you're running out of and if you want, I'll pick them up at lunch time. I'll need some cash though."

"Aye," he said. "Let me know how much, I'll cover it."

He looked at her. "Thanks, and for last night."

He wanted to say more but couldn't think of the right words.

"Go on, go and get changed before I whip that towel from you," she said and started laughing. "I'll make us some dinner tonight if you want," she said.

Melanie felt more confident with Michael; the previous evening had been a watershed.

"Aye, thanks. I'm working at Molly Ford's today," he said.

"What, from the cottage?" she said.

"Aye," he said.

"Well you be careful there. Got a right reputation. She'll have your trousers off given half the chance," she said and started to laugh again. The whole atmosphere had changed from previous visits.

"She must be eighty," said Michael.

"Eighty four, to be precise, but you know what they say, many a good tune played on an old fiddle," she said.

"Ah, get away with yers," he said in a strong Belfast accent. Melanie just looked at him.

"Are you sure you're ok, Michael?" she said.

"Sorry," he said. "I don't know where that came from."

"Hmm," she said.

By eight thirty they had gone their separate ways with the arrangement that Melanie would come back after work and cook dinner for the two of them. It was everything that Melanie had wanted and even the sight of Tina Ashworth having her roots done didn't cause any angst with her. A week or so earlier and she wanted to kill the so-called celebrity but now, water under the bridge. Michael was also beginning to recognise that things had changed between them.

Chapter Nineteen

In another part of the British Isles however, events were unfolding which would seal the future for both Melanie and Michael.

Tuesday morning and in his Belfast office Brendan Monahan stared at the grainy fax copy of the photograph that Barry had taken of the person he believed was Michael Curtiss. He was waiting for the morning post to be delivered which would bring the original photograph which would be far clearer and confirm his suspicions, but deep inside he was sure this was the man, everything fitted.

Over the last seven years since he said goodbye to Michael Curtiss at Glenbar Farm, things had gone well for Brendan. In addition to escaping any sanction for his not-inconsiderable involvement in the loyalist paramilitary, he had met and married a Belfast lawyer and settled in the upmarket area of Helen's Bay on the coast. It was a large property, six bedrooms with views over the ocean. Now with two children aged three and eighteen months he had left the world of politics and violence and concentrated on his property empire which continued to flourish. He was well known in the community - he owned a good portion of it, and was not without influence. His wife even suggested he stood for local election and maybe even Westminster. He had considered this; he still had a loyal following which he could count on if necessary. For the moment though he was happy with his lot.

The Glenbar Gang had dispersed, some were in jail, but Jimmy Rafferty was still around. Brendan was amazed how he had escaped the wrath of the police, and the IRA for that matter; he had a considerable amount of blood on his hands. So when Brendan called him to say that there had been a credible sighting of Michael, Jimmy was only too willing to help him in the task.

It was almost midday before the mail arrived and Brendan discarded the rest as soon as he saw the cardboard envelope - 'photographs - do not bend' it said; it had a Liverpool postmark.

He opened the envelope with a letter-opener shaped as a dagger and gently pulled out the photos. There were three, high quality pictures, one of which had been blown up. It confirmed everything he wanted to know. It was Michael Curtiss, beyond any doubt.

He picked up his phone and dialled a London number. "House of Lords." Was the reply from the switchboard.

"Lord Ansty's office please," said Brendan.

"Brendan Monahan."

"David?" asked Brendan when his lordship answered. He was one of a select few who was allowed to use his given name rather than his ennobled one.

"I have managed to track down yer man," Brendan said with a sense of satisfaction.

"You have? Are you certain?" he said.

"As sure as I am sitting here. I have a photograph of him in a village somewhere working as some sort of itinerant… Aye, yer not wrong, it does serve the bastard right. The question is what do we do about it?"

"At any cost you say? Aye, I can do that. When? OK tomorrow night at the Clarendon, six fifteen. I'll be there." He rang off.

Jimmy turned up about half an hour later and Brendan was able to outline the conversation with Lord Ansty. Jimmy had aged in the last seven years and Michael would not easily recognise him. He had shaved his head completely to overcome the natural hair-loss he was encountering but he was still fit, slim and wiry looking.

"At any cost?" said Jimmy as Brendan was briefing him.

"Aye, yer man wants him dead, sure enough," said Brendan.

The Tinker

"I'm meeting his Lordship tomorrow night at the Clarendon and I'll be letting him know what my plans are."

"And what would they be?" asked Jimmy.

"Well you and me are going to go and see our friendly private eye and find out where this village is and how we can get there. He will want paying as well, no doubt. Then we go find that bastard, Michael once and for all," said Brendan.

Jimmy smiled.

The following day Brendan was at the Clarendon to meet Lord Ansty. He had arrived just after six, carrying a briefcase, and found a corner in what used to be the great hall but where they now served coffee and afternoon teas at exorbitant prices. The seats were red leather studded wing-backed, very ornate and in keeping with the decor. Brendan looked at the ceiling with paintings in the style of Michelangelo, all cherubs and Greek Gods. He was admiring the artwork when he was disturbed.

"Brendan?" It was his Lordship.

"David," said Brendan and he stood up and they shook hands.

Lord Ansty was tall, distinguished-looking, with thick grey wavy hair, he was wearing a smart tweed suit and brown leather Church Brogues. He sat in the seat opposite, a similar design to Brendan's. They were separated by an ornate heavy coffee table.

From nowhere a waiter appeared.

"Welcome, your Lordship, your usual?" he said.

"Hello Ewan. Yes that will be fine, thank you. What about you, Brendan?"

Despite his Irish roots he spoke in a distinctly 'upper-class' accent; it was in the breeding.

"A pint of Guinness," replied Brendan.

"And a pint of Guinness," repeated his Lordship to the waiter.

"So you managed to track him down then?" said Ansty.

Brendan took out a folder from his briefcase. "Yes, I have brought you these."

He opened it and handed him the three photos. Ansty studied them carefully.

"Yes," he said. "I can see what you mean. I never met the man of course, but he certainly looks like the one in the photograph."

"Aye, everything fits... the itinerant worker thing, moving around, very difficult to find," he said.

"And this private investigator, what is his name?"

"Springer, Barry Springer," said Brendan.

"Yes, Springer. He found him, right?" said Ansty.

"Yes, a fluke really, it seems one of his former associates just happened to be in the village on business and spotted him," said Brendan.

"Hmm," said Ansty, as he put the photographs back in the folder and handed it back to Brendan. "I hope there are not going to be any loose ends. I mean you will need to be very discreet. I wouldn't want my name implicated in any way," he said.

"No, I will ensure there will be no fall out," said Brendan.

"So what do you plan to do?" asked Ansty as the waiter brought the drinks.

There was a lull in conversation as the waiter poured just a thimble full of water into a whiskey glass heavy with ice and half full of a yellowy-orange liquid, a vintage Bushmills. His Lordship took a sip and rolled it around his tongue like a mouth-wash, looking every part the connoisseur.

"Thank you, Ewan," he said and the waiter left them. Brendan was already into his stout, white foam moustached his top lip. He wiped it with the back of his hand.

"As I was about to say. I'll be taking Jimmy with me tomorrow. We're booked on the seven o'clock ferry to Birkenhead, so we are."

"What, Jimmy Rafferty?" said Ansty.

"Aye," said Brendan.

"Well I hope you know what you're doing. He can be a bit... troublesome," said Ansty.

"Nah, he'll be as good as gold," said Brendan. "I would trust him with me life," he added.

"You may have to," said Ansty.

He took a drink of his whiskey and continued. "So that means you'll be in Liverpool... what, about four o'clock?" said Ansty.

"Aye, I phoned Springer this afternoon. He's going to wait for us," Brendan said.

"No doubt he will want paying," said Ansty.

"I think there is an expectancy there," said Brendan.

"So, what do we do?" said Ansty. "Can I leave it with you to, how shall I put this...? See to things."

"Yes I will see to everything," said Brendan.

Ansty looked around to ensure there was no-one looking and produced a paper bag from the inside of his jacket.

"Take this, there's five hundred which should cover any out of pocket expenses. I assume you will be hiring a car and staying in a hotel. Let me know if you need any more," he said.

"Thanks, I will," replied Brendan.

"Right, business concluded. Ring me as soon as you get any news, and needless to say I will be extremely grateful for a satisfactory outcome. We might even discuss your political ambitions if you ever decide to stand. I am sure I can get you selected as a candidate," he said.

"Thanks," said Brendan.

This was the cue for Brendan to leave; his Lordship would finish his Irish malt and just have time for dinner. He would fly back to London on the nine o'clock to Heathrow.

Brendan quickly tipped back the rest of his Guinness and made his farewells.

"Stay in touch," said Ansty as Brendan stood up.

"Will do," he said and walked towards the exit. He was deep in thought.

The next morning, an early start, and Jimmy was waiting at the ferry terminal at seven a.m. with a small rucksack. Brendan, with a suitcase and holdall, had taken a taxi from his house on the coast.

"Not sure when I'll be back; three, four days at the most," were the last words he said to his wife before he left and got into the waiting car at 6.15 a.m.

It was cloudy when they left Belfast but as they got closer to the English mainland the skies cleared and it was a glorious summer's day when they docked in Birkenhead. Brendan and Jimmy were taking in the sun, standing on the passenger deck as it pulled into the harbour.

"We'll have to get you a hat if it stays like this," said Brendan.

Jimmy saw the funny side and grinned. "Aye," he said and rubbed his shaved pate.

First priority was to get a vehicle. As usual there was a car hire franchise housed in a temporary unit next to the terminal. The choice wasn't huge but there was a nice Honda Accord which Brendan went for straight away. "This won't let us down," he said to Jimmy as they stowed their luggage in the boot.

It was a hot day and with the car having been in the open, the temperature inside was stifling. Brendan wound down the windows to let in some air. He put the heater on cold and full blast.

With a four day hire Brendan was given a free road map but

before setting off he consulted the route to the Private Investigator's office. Jimmy looked over his shoulder.

"There," he said pointing at the map. Their previous visits had been by taxi.

Jimmy did the navigating and it was gone four thirty when they found themselves in familiar surroundings.

"Around here somewheres," said Brendan as he meandered around the Business Park looking for Springer's office.

"Yes, there it is," he said as he made a left turn and spotted the building. There was a silver Jaguar parked in one of the two allotted spaces; Brendan parked the Honda next to it. The area was shaded from the sun which by this time had passed over to the other side of the building and it was cooler.

Brendan stretched his back as he got out of the car. Jimmy opened the boot and took out Brendan's holdall. They approached the door and Brendan pressed the bell to the side. There was movement and footsteps. The door opened and Barry Springer greeted them warmly.

"Brendan, Jimmy how are yas, great to see ya again. Come on up," he said, and he let them in and led them up the flight of stairs to the office.

"Take a seat. Erm, can I get you anything?" said Barry.

"No, yer ok. We had something on the ferry," said Brendan, as he and Jimmy sat down. Jimmy was holding the holdall on his lap.

"How was the trip? What is it eight hours?" asked Barry as he sat at his desk.

"Aye," said Brendan.

"Right," said Barry. "I have everything you need," and he opened the folder in front of him.

He showed the pair more photographs including some smaller ones, six by four. "I took a few of the village so you can get an idea of the place. This is the pub called the White Hart. It'll be worth staying there. You'll be on the ground, as it were. Nice rooms, not too expensive," he said, showing a picture of the pub.

"There're more pictures of the man you're looking for," Barry said, handing Brendan another picture. Brendan looked at the photograph with interest.

"Do you know where he's staying?" asked Brendan.

"Not exactly, but I would check around the church somewheres. It's the kind of place that would take in tramps and the like. The people we asked were a bit, I don't know, erm... coy, as if they didn't want to say anything. Someone said his name was ..." He looked at his notes which were in the file. "Ted Saunders. Whether he's using that as an alias or not, I don't know."

"So where is this village?" said Brendan.

"Drayburn. It's in the Cotswolds not far from Stonington," said Barry.

Brendan was none the wiser. Barry took his well-worn road atlas from his desk and opened it on top of his file. He flicked a few pages and turned it around so Brendan could read it. "Down the M5... Take this junction here. There's Stonington and... there you are, Drayburn."

Brendan nodded. "Aye, got that," he said.

Barry put all the pictures and notes back in the folder and closed it.

"So, you happy with that?" asked Barry.

"Very," said Brendan. "Yer've done a great job, so yer have."

"That's good, after all this time. It's just a pity that Brad Jackson couldn't be here to see it. Spent months on the case he did. It was him who spotted the fella. Got himself killed down there," said Barry.

Brendan looked at Barry. "What do you mean?" he said,

thinking Michael might have been involved in some way.

"Haven't got all the details but it seems that he was beaten up by one of the locals. Probably shagging his wife. I told him it would be the death of him. Chase anything in a skirt would Brad... still," said Barry as he drifted into his thoughts.

"I see," said Brendan.

Barry hesitated for a moment and cleared his throat. "Is this a good time to discuss payment. I mean you did say on the phone that I would be ok for the, erm, bounty," he said.

"Ah yes, so I did," said Brendan. "Jimmy has it here for you."

Jimmy opened the holdall and before Barry could move, produced a Beretta 92 complete with suppressor and shot the private investigator in the head. The noise was a sharp pop, like a Champagne cork leaving a bottle but quieter. Barry would not be celebrating. The force of the bullet had sent him backwards in the chair and he was slumped to the side with blood oozing from the entry point just above the eyes. The exit had taken out the back of his head and sprayed the wall in a red mess.

Brendan picked up the folder from the desk while Jimmy wiped the door handle and anything else that they may have touched. Jimmy produced a cigarette lighter but before he could light it Brendan whispered to him sharply.

"No, don't do that! You'll have the fire brigade here in minutes. Let's just get away. There'll probably be no-body about till tomorrow and we'll be long gone," he said.

Jimmy looked at Brendan. "Aye," he said recognising the logic.

Brendan put on a pair of gloves and opened up the filing cabinets.

"Here give us a hand," he said to Jimmy. "Make 'em think we was looking for something," he said and he started to scatter files around.

The office looked like a tornado had hit it by the time they had finished. Brendan checked there were no obvious references to them or their mission; there were no files in the name of Ireland, Brendan or Michael that he could see.

"Right let's get out of here," said Brendan.

As it happened Kathy, Barry's assistant, was on a job in Wallasey and would not return until Thursday morning.

They left the building and headed off toward the motorway; five p.m. and the traffic getting out of Liverpool was relentless.

"So, do we head down to the village tonight or wait till tomorrow?" said Jimmy.

"No, we'll find somewhere near. What's the name of that town that was close by?" he said.

"Stonington?" said Jimmy.

"Aye, that's it. It'll give us a fresh start tomorrow. Don't know about you but I'm banjaxed," he said.

Following Jimmy's directions they arrived in Stonington just after eight thirty and found a hotel on the High Street, The Crown, an old English coaching inn according to the information in reception. They decided on two rooms; two men sharing they reasoned may give rise to false assumptions and gossip. They had no intention of drawing attention to themselves.

Tuesday proved fruitful for Michael. As well as servicing Molly Ford's boiler, his meeting at the White Hart with the manager Gavin Findley was very successful and resulted in several week's work decorating and some routine maintenance. They even discussed Michael taking on the maintenance contract on the hotel long term but for the moment Michael did not want to commit himself further than the work he had been given. "Let's see how we go," he had said.

As he was just over the road he called in at the salon and invited Melanie back to the pub for lunch before she left to see her solicitor and they sat in the bar eating sandwiches and catching up.

"We had Tina Ashworth in earlier; you should see the state of her hair," Melanie said. She couldn't help herself.

Michael smiled but said nothing.

"What do you fancy for dinner?" she asked.

Michael couldn't recall anyone asking him that question but somehow it didn't seem out of place.

"I don't mind. I'll leave it to you," he said.

"And there I was looking for inspiration," she said. "Well you can help me choose then," and smiled.

In fact she had been smiling all morning which hadn't gone unnoticed by Mrs Audley.

"Somebody obviously had a good time last night," she said when they were having their mid-morning break.

"I'm not saying anything," Melanie said and smiled again.

With dinner more or less sorted Michael returned to the lodge lumbered with two bags of shopping. He had been co-opted as basket carrier in the Village Store while Melanie dropped in suitable provisions. He was now rueing his decision to leave his bike at the vicarage. Melanie meanwhile had caught the bus into Stonington for her three o'clock appointment.

As he walked down the path to the Lodge, Denise was in the garden knelt weeding the borders of the lawn in front of the kitchen.

She looked up hearing someone approach and shielded her eyes from the sun so she could identify the visitor.

"Hello Michael," she said. "That was good timing you have given me the perfect excuse to give up the weeding and make some tea. Would you like a cup?"

"Aye," said Michael. "Thank you."

Denise got up from the grass and walked towards the kitchen door which was open.

"Come in," she said. "You will have to excuse the mess. It's been one of those days."

Michael followed her. The kitchen looked 'lived in', a basket of laundry, unopened mail, newspapers, plates and cups waiting to be put away. The evidence of a busy day in the life of a vicar's wife.

"Have a seat... if you can find some room," she said and removed a pile of papers from the table.

"John's been working on his sermon for Sunday. Gone round to the Major's place," she said. "Wanted to have a chat apparently."

Michael sat down and put his bags of shopping underneath the table as Denise filled the kettle.

Denise looked at the bags. "Hello, someone's been stocking up," she said. "You've got enough stuff to feed an army," she said.

Michael felt embarrassed. "Well it's not all for me," he said.

"I thought as much, let me guess... Melanie Draper?" she said, as she brought the coffees to the table and sat down.

"Aye," said Michael rather sheepishly.

"Good for you," she said. "It's what I was saying yesterday, time to move on."

She took a drink. "So, how do you feel? After yesterday, I mean," she said.

"I had nightmares last night, terrible ones. It was like being back there," he said.

"Was Melanie with you?" she said. "Sorry I didn't mean to pry. I was just wondering what she made of it all."

"Aye, she was and she was... well, great, really great," he said and took a drink of his coffee.

"I've known Melanie a long time and I know she has a reputation for being a bit flighty, but I think underneath all that she is a bright girl. She could have gone to college you know, but got mixed up with that dreadful husband of hers. I knew that would all end in tears. Got himself charged with murder, I hear. What's she going to do, do you know?"

"She's seeing a solicitor. This afternoon in fact... getting a divorce," replied Michael.

"Well thank goodness for that. I always thought she was too good for him," she said. "And you. How do you feel? About her, I mean," she asked. "If you want to tell me, of course. It's none of my business." Denise wondered if she might have been too intrusive.

"Aye," he said. "It's early days. Just see how it goes."

"Well, I guess this could at least give you the chance of experiencing closeness with someone. I mean you have nothing to lose," she said.

"No, that's true," he said.

"A bit of advice," she said. "Try not to compare Melanie with Colleen. Think of it as something different, otherwise you will never move on. It was what I was trying to say yesterday. The compartmentalisation process. If you can think of Colleen like a picture album which you have in a drawer. Every now and then you will get it out and have a look at it. Then you can put it back again. It means you will be able to keep her in your heart without it preventing you from moving on. Does that make sense?" she said.

"Aye," he said. "It makes a lot of sense."

"It's not easy, but it can work," she said. "It's about taking control of your mind, rather than the other way around."

Michael looked at his coffee then picked up his cup and finished it. This was a conversation he couldn't have had only two days ago; progress, he realised.

"Thanks," he said. "I best get off and leave you to get back to your weeding," he said.

"Yes, weather's on the change. Storms again by Thursday according to the forecast," she said.

She picked up the two cups and placed them on the draining board. Michael picked up the shopping and followed Denise out of the kitchen. She turned around.

"You know... you and Melanie; it might just work. I hope it does... You are both lost souls," she said.

Michael walked back to the Lodge. "Lost souls," he repeated to himself, and considered the meaning.

Back at the Lodge, he put the shopping away and spent the rest of the afternoon pottering about and tidying around, not something he was familiar with; he had never done nest building before.

The church clock struck five and he suddenly thought that Melanie would be on the bus which arrived about ten past. He would take a wander to the Village Store and buy some wine and meet her. This was definitely new territory, emotionally; it was just something he felt he wanted to do.

As he approached the White Hart he could see the small single-decker coming down the hill from the by-pass. He waited at the bus stop and could see her standing up waiting to get off.

"Hi," he said as she walked towards him and instinctively she kissed him.

"Hi," she said.

"Thought I'd get some wine," he said.

"Great," she said and linked arms with him.

"How did it go?" he asked.

The Tinker

"Fine, he should get the papers over the next few days. The sooner that tosser's out of my life the better as far as I'm concerned," she said.

Chapter Twenty

They walked to the Lodge and Melanie cooked dinner while Michael read a magazine he had bought from the store.

Later as they washed up together they were chatting. "I could do with going back to the house later," she said, "just to pick up a few bits. We could pop into the White Hart on the way back if you like."

"Yeah, ok, that would be good," he said.

So around nine they walked up to the cottage to collect Melanie's things, then called at the pub on the way back. It was busy again with the restaurant doing a good trade.

"Busy tonight," Michael remarked as Tony served the drinks.

"Yes, hotel's full. A coach party of day trippers," he said. "They'll be wandering around the village tomorrow, you mark my words," he added and raised his eyebrows.

Michael picked up the drinks.

"Gavin's booked you up with some work, he was telling me," said Tony just as Michael was about to deliver the drinks to Melanie who was sitting at one of the vacant tables.

"Yeah," said Michael. "Start next Monday."

"Well it'll be good to have you around," said Tony.

"Cheers," said Michael.

Tony noticed the new expression; Michael seemed different somehow.

Michael and Melanie were chatting when one of the regulars approached them.

"Michael...? How are you...? Don't see you in here very often," said the friendly voice.

"Frank," said Michael. "Good to see you."

"And Melanie," said Frank.

The Tinker

"Hello Frank," said Melanie.

Frank pulled up a chair and joined them. "Shan't keep you a minute," he said. "Has the vicar spoke to you at all?" asked Frank.

"What about? I've not seen him today," said Michael.

"Oh, right, well are you about anytime tomorrow? I think the Major would like a word with you, if you're not too busy, like," said Frank.

"Aye," said Michael. "Doing some bits and pieces around the church then servicing Mrs Kitchen's central heating, but should be around sometime during the afternoon."

"Yes, ok I'll let him know," said Frank.

There was something about Frank's demeanour, something wasn't right.

"Are you ok, Frank?" asked Michael.

Frank looked at the floor. "Not specially," he said. "Talk tomorrow, can't discuss it in here," he added.

Frank got up from his chair, with difficulty Michael noticed and as he walked back to the bar Michael saw he seemed to be dragging his leg.

"He doesn't look too good," said Melanie.

"No," said Michael. "Wonder what that was all about."

On Wednesday Michael completed his chores around the church and serviced Mrs Kitchen's central heating. She was very grateful and mentioned she would recommend him to all her friend in the Ladies Circle. He was going to be very busy over the summer.

It was mid-afternoon by the time he dropped his trailer with his kit at the vicarage and cycled over to see the Major. The sun was still beaming down and he wondered if Denise's forecast of an imminent change was right. He could detect no evidence; trees were still, no sign of a wind which would denote a difference in air pressure. His arms were tanned from the outdoor work and his hair almost straw-colour, bleached by the sun.

The Manor looked magnificent as he parked his cycle at the end of the drive and made his way to the front of the house. The Major and Frank were sitting on one of the ornamental benches which were positioned next to the front door with two glasses in front of them.

"Michael," said the Major as he approached; he got up and greeted the new arrival warmly.

"Would you like some of the Memsahib's lemonade, freshly made this morning?" he added.

"Thank you Major," said Michael.

The Major went inside the house. Frank stayed seated, there was a walking stick next to him resting against the bench.

"Hello Frank," said Michael and he walked over to him and shook his hand.

Frank didn't get up but responded to the greeting. "Hello Michael, have a seat," he said.

Michael sat down on the bench opposite rather than invade Frank's personal space - the bench would not sit three comfortably. After a few moments the Major came back with a jug of the Memsahib's finest and a glass. He did the pouring honours.

"Thanks," said Michael as the Major handed him the heavy tumbler.

"Thanks for coming over, old boy," said the Major. "Wanted a chat."

Michael took a mouthful of lemonade.

The Major continued. "Got a bit of a manpower problem, don't you know," he said.

Frank was staring at the floor.

The Tinker

"Yes... Frank, do you want to tell him?" said the Major.

Michael looked at Frank. "The Major's right," said Frank. "I've been having problems with my legs, you see, for a month or so, but it's been getting worse. At first they would just stiffen up at the end of the day but since that do at the lake at the weekend... well, it's most of the time. The doctor's been giving me painkillers and that but on Monday I had some tests at the hospital in Stonington, got the results yesterday morning..."

Frank stopped for a moment looking quite emotional.

"The thing is, I've got cancer," said Frank. "Not to put a too fine a point on it... I ain't got long."

Michael didn't know what to say. "I'm so sorry Frank, I really am," he said.

The Major took over. "That's why I wanted to speak to you. Frank's been with me for... how long would it be Frank?"

"Thirty four years," said Frank.

"Almost part of the family," said the Major. "It leaves me with a bit of a problem, you see. I don't want to go advertising the job in the paper and start talking to people I don't know. This is a very special position, what."

Michael could see where this was leading.

"I spoke to the Reverend yesterday, see what he thought and we both agree you would be the ideal man... What do you say old boy?" said the Major.

Michael looked suitably surprised. "I don't know what to say," he said. "But I don't know anything about being a game keeper."

"Don't worry about that. Frank has already said he would teach you all you need to know... Won't you Frank?"

Frank nodded.

"We could send you to college if you like... This job is about the man, you see. Look, you're military, yes...?" Michael nodded. "Cut from the same cloth you and me, what? You like your independence, well, you can have that. I don't interfere with what Frank does. You'll have your own cottage." The Major was desperate to get his man.

"That's a very generous offer," said Michael.

"Well I don't expect an answer straight away. The Reverend said you were pretty busy," said the Major.

"Yes," said Michael. "Word seems to get around," and he smiled.

Michael thought for a moment; it was too big a commitment to give an answer. "Look, can I give you a decision at the weekend. There's a lot to think about?" he said.

"Of course, of course, old boy. Just let me know," said the Major.

Michael finished his drink, said his farewells and went back to the Lodge with a lot on his mind.

Melanie, having finished work for the day, arrived back at the Lodge around five thirty carrying a shopping bag from the village store. Michael let her in.

"Hi," he said and she kissed him. "How was your day?"

"Good. Thought we would have some chicken tonight," she added, as she went into the kitchen and emptied the bag.

Michael still hadn't quite got used to the idea of being looked after but he was happy for her to take charge of the domestic arrangements. He was wondering whether to tell her about his job offer from the Major. This responsibility of involving someone else in his decision making had never crossed his mind before; it was a strange feeling.

Over dinner the discussion revolved around gossip at the salon and whether Melanie should buy the outfit she saw in the

Boutique. "Just like Madonna wears," she said. Michael was less than enthusiastic.

"You want to look like Madonna?" he said.

"No, but she does wear some great clothes," she said.

"Yeah," said Michael, "almost."

She laughed. "I don't see you complaining," she teased.

"No, that's for sure," he said.

It went quiet for a moment, then he decided to say something.

"I went to see the Major this afternoon," he said.

"Of course... Frank, how is he?" she said.

"Not good... He's got cancer," he said.

"Bad?" she said.

"Yeah... he said he's not got long to live," replied Michael.

"Oh, that's terrible. I like Frank, he's a real gentleman. Not many of his sort around," she said.

She thought for a moment contemplating the news. "You never know what's just around the corner, do you?" she said. "It just goes to show, you have to make the most of every day."

"Yeah," he said.

Michael decided not to say anything more until he was certain that he would accept the gamekeeper's job. It would mean a great deal of change, part of him enjoyed the freedom of having no responsibilities and he wasn't sure if he was ready for such a commitment.

Thursday morning and Michael had arranged with the vicar to help the Verger with some maintenance work around the graveyard. He was cleaning around some of the ancient gravestones removing moss and weeds; he was wearing just a pair of shorts. It was stifling hot but the dry heat of the last couple of days had been replaced by a heavy, humid atmosphere and he was drenched in sweat. It looked as though Denise's prediction about the weather had proved correct.

The village was busy with tourists and there were several admiring glances at his body glistening in the sunshine from a coach party of ladies that had stopped to see the church. One even proffered a wolf whistle. Michael just looked up and smiled.

He was about to finish for lunch when the throaty exhaust of a Triumph Spitfire echoed around the buildings; it came nearer. Michael looked up and could see the yellow sports car with its number plate 'TNA 10'.

It stopped and the lady driver approached him. She took her sunglasses off for a moment to speak.

"Michael... I'm so glad I caught you, can you come to the house as soon as you can, I've got a leak in my sink in the kitchen. I tried calling a plumber but they are just too busy. You're my last hope," she said. "I've managed to turn the water off," she added.

Michael looked at her, tee shirt cropped just below her breasts, tiny shorts and sandals.

"Aye," said Michael. "I can get over this afternoon."

"Oh, you are such a darling," she said effusively. "You've saved my life."

With that she walked to her car and drove off. One or two tourists had recognised her. "Wasn't that Tina whatsername? You know the one off the telly... Can't stand her. Stuck up cow," said one loud enough for Michael to hear. He smiled at the accurate assessment.

Michael had popped back to the Lodge and washed himself down then joined the vicar and verger in the vestry for lunch; it was mercifully much cooler in the church. Michael had said nothing about the job offer from the Major and the vicar didn't raise the topic.

The Tinker

He set off to Tina's house around two o'clock and arrived at the gates which swung open before he could press the intercom; she had obviously been waiting.

He pushed his bike and trailer over the gravel drive to the front of the house and Tina came out straight away.

"Thank you so much. You're a god-send you really are," she said.

A fresh smell of perfume hit him as he carried his toolbox through the front door.

"It's over here," she said as she led him to the kitchen. The layout of course was familiar to him from his previous visits.

"What's the problem?" he asked.

"It's the sink. There was a pool of water underneath it this morning after I'd washed up the breakfast things," she said.

Michael looked at her; she was still in her skimpy top and shorts.

"I've been in town all week. Been reading for a lead role in a new TV series... My agent is very optimistic," she added. "Well, I came back last night so I haven't used the sink for a while. It's Mrs Oxley's day off. She would normally look after the dishes," she said, hardly drawing breath.

Michael opened up the cupboard and looked at the underside of the sink unit.

"Here's your problem," he said. "The seal's gone on your down pipe. Soon fix that," he said.

He rummaged around in his tool-kit for his wrench. The seal was soon repaired and tested. Michael was lain on his back tightening up the join and applying some sealant. His head was under the sink with just his torso and legs sticking out. Tina was staring at his shorts and thinking of other needs.

He extracted himself from the confines of the cupboard and

almost choked. Tina was standing there totally naked.

"I have a bonus for you," she said.

Michael was in a dilemma. In a way there was a certain irony considering what happened just a couple of weeks' earlier but he was not about to jeopardise his relationship with Melanie.

"I can't Tina, sorry," and he picked up his tool kit and walked past her and out through the front door. She stood there speechless, not used to being denied. He pushed his bike and trailer down to the gate which was locked and for a moment thought he might be penned in but he lifted the manual latch and let himself out and cycled away.

In twenty minutes he was back in the village and as he pedalled up the long incline of the High Street past the White Hart on the right he did not see the two men sitting in the bar talking. One of them stared in his direction, then the other.

Earlier that day Brendan and Jimmy left Stonington after breakfast and headed to Drayburn. As they pulled away from The Crown they were discussing a plan of action.

"What do we do when we get there?" said Jimmy.

"Have a look round. Find this hotel place that yer man was talking about... What was it?" said Brendan.

"The White Hart I tink he said," said Jimmy

"Aye, that's it. Can't be many pubs, it's only a small place," said Brendan. "We'll need somewhere to stay in any case. It may take us a day or two."

"He may have gone," said Jimmy.

"Aye, that's always a possibility," said Brendan. "We'll give it a couple of days and see what we find."

They arrived in Drayburn mid-morning.

"Well there's yer pub," said Jimmy as they came to the top of

The Tinker

the High Street.

"Aye, not much else here," said Brendan.

"You can always get yer haircut," said Brendan looking at the salon.

"I don't tink I'll be needing that today," said Jimmy rubbing his head.

Brendan went left and saw the archway just past the hotel with the sign, 'Hotel Car Park'. He turned into the narrow entrance.

"Leave the stuff for now, let's see if they have any rooms," said Brendan.

Tony Rollinson was walking past reception as the two men made the enquiry.

"Have yer got two rooms for a couple of days?" said Brendan to the receptionist.

Tony's ears were alerted by the Irish accent. Most tourists tended to be from America or Australia with the odd coach of Japanese and their cameras, so the unfamiliar brogue did attract attention.

"You're in luck," said Mandy Fletcher, the regular receptionist. "Yesterday we were full but we have had some visitors leave this morning," she said, making polite conversation. "Sign here for me please," she said.

"Thank you, Mr... Keane," she said, reading the name from the register. It was one of Brendan's many alias's. "Two nights, bed and breakfast," she confirmed.

"And for you, Mr Boyle?" Jimmy had also used a false name. "Would you both like a wake-up call or newspapers?"

Brendan shook his head and paid in cash for the two rooms, avoiding the need for credit cards. In fact neither had any identification on them; it was standard practice for 'a job'.

Having acquired accommodation and taken their luggage to

333

their respective rooms, Brendan suggested that they had a look around and get the lie of the land. They left the White Hart dressed casually in jeans and tee shirts and stood looking down the High Street. There was the boutique and a couple of other shops, then houses before the road disappeared into what looked like countryside.

"Nothing down that way," said Brendan. "Let's take a look in the Village store."

"Why don't we ask someone?" said Jimmy. "Sure, haven't we got the photograph?" he added.

"Not just for the moment. It might alert someone. We have no idea what he's doing here," replied Brendan.

They walked across the road and into the store. Brendan bought a bar of chocolate. Jimmy just followed looking menacing; his bald head and rugged features made him look sinister and one or two locals avoided eye contact. He was used to it and paid no regard.

They headed to the top of the High Street, past the Salon, and turned left.

"Where does this go?" asked Jimmy.

"It's called Vicarage Road, so that might be a clue," he said somewhat sarcastically which was lost on Jimmy.

They walked down the narrow street towards the church.

"Will yer take a look at that," said Brendan as the scene opened out before them bathed in beautiful sunshine. "Yer have to admit it's a wonderful sight, sure it is," he said.

"We ain't come here to sight-see," said Jimmy not sharing his partners love of things ecclesiastical.

"What an earth do people find to do all day?" remarked Jimmy.

"It makes yer wonder," said Brendan. "Let's get back to the hotel and get a drink."

The Tinker

So Brendan and Jimmy wandered back to the pub and stayed in the bar until after lunch just watching people going about their routines from a vantage point by the window. It wasn't very interesting and by two o'clock Brendan was getting restless.

"I'm going for another walk. You coming?" he asked.

"Nah, I think I'll go up to my room and put my head down for an hour," Jimmy replied.

"OK, I'll see you later," he said and Brendan walked back towards the church. There was something that Barry Springer had mentioned and he thought he would explore a bit further.

Brendan reached the church and went into the nave. He looked at the stain glass windows commemorating fallen heroes from both World Wars and walked up the aisle to the transept. To the left were steps to the vestry. Brendan waited for a while, taking in the splendour of the architecture, then walked back towards the door. The air was still heavy and with the sun streaming through the windows the humidity levels had caused Brendan to perspire. He took out a handkerchief and mopped his forehead.

After about ten minutes or so the vicar appeared from the vestry and walked towards the entrance to the church. Brendan was reading some of the literature that was on display. He caught the vicar's eye.

"Hello Father," he said. "Wonderful church you have here, so you have," said Brendan.

"Thank you," said the vicar. "We like it. Just visiting?" he added.

"Aye, that I am," he said.

"What part of Ireland are you from?" asked the vicar.

"North... near Belfast," he said.

"I thought I recognised the accent," said the vicar.

"Aye," said Brendan. "Very proud of our heritage, and our

Queen," he said, clearly disclosing his political leanings. "And I can't be doing with that priest in Rome."

The vicar made no comment.

Brendan looked at the vicar. "I suppose you get all sorts around here," he said.

"What do you mean?" asked the vicar still mulling over the last comment.

"Well, tramps and the like, looking for free hand-outs," said Brendan, trying to disguise his real motive.

The vicar looked at him in a quizzical way.

"Not really, no," said the vicar, suddenly recognising the danger. Denise had not disclosed all of Michael's revelations but had mentioned that it had Irish roots.

"Well it's nice to have met you Mr...?" the vicar said, indicating he wanted to address the visitor by name.

"Michael," said Brendan, "Michael Keane."

"Michael," repeated the vicar, and he walked down the path between the yew trees to the churchyard wall. Brendan watched him like a hawk. The vicar for some reason sensed he was being observed and instead of heading towards the Vicarage turned left in the opposite direction. This road came to a dead end before turning ninety degrees right then running parallel to Vicarage Road; it was lined with more residential houses. The vicar went around the corner and waited for five minutes before retracing his steps.

There was no sign of Brendan and the vicar made his way home.

Brendan went back to the pub frustrated at his lack of information; he was hoping for more from the vicar but was careful in not pressing too vigorously. He still had no idea of Michael's place or otherwise in the village.

Jimmy was still in his room when Brendan returned and he knocked on the door louder than he probably intended. There was some delay in the answer.

"What the feck is it?" asked Jimmy, clearly disturbed from his sleep.

Brendan ignored him and walked in.

"Well I found the church but we'll get nowhere there... even spoke to the vicar himself but he was giving nottin' away... if he knew anything at all, that is," he said. "I'm going back down to the bar and keep an eye out," he added. "You coming?"

"Aye, I'll join yers in a minute or two," Jimmy said.

Tony Rollinson noticed the Irishmen again in the window seat appearing to be looking out at the High Street.

"Strange... been there most of the day," he said to Mandy Fletcher when he was taking some bottles from the store room to replenish the bar. She had also seen them.

Around five o'clock he noticed them suddenly get very agitated for some reason but couldn't hear the conversation.

The vicar meanwhile had returned to the Vicarage and called out to Denise.

"Are you there dear?" he said.

She came into the kitchen from the hall.

"Hello darling, would you like some tea? I'll put the kettle on."

"Yes, thank you," said the vicar.

"I've just had a strange conversation," he said as he sat down and took off his shoes.

"Well it wouldn't be the first," she said as she filled the kettle.

"No... this was different," he said. "You know you mentioned that the problems Michael had experienced originated from Ireland?"

"Yes," she said.

"Well I've just been speaking to a chap with a strong Belfast accent," he said. "Sounded like that Reverend Paisley."

Denise switched on the kettle and looked at him. He had her undivided attention.

"Oh dear," she said.

"Well it may be nothing of course, but this chap asked if we'd had any tramps around here looking for hand outs," he said.

"What did you say?" asked Denise clearly concerned.

"Well... nothing but then he said his name was Michael, and I'm sure he was testing me for a reaction. You know it's just a feeling, but it was the way he looked. I certainly wouldn't want to mess with him that's for sure. Something sinister about him."

"I don't like the sound of that at all," said Denise. "I'll keep an eye out for Michael. I saw him go out earlier... I'll let him know what's going on," she said.

"Right," said the vicar and he took his tea and went to his study.

Back in the White Hart, Brendan and Jimmy were back at the window seat again. It was Brendan who saw him first, pedalling up the High Street following his visit to Tina Ashworth's blocked sink.

"Jimmy...!" he said excitedly "Will yer take a look at yer man there. It's him as sure as I'm sitting here," he said.

"Jazus... You're right, so you are. The bastard," said Jimmy. "What do you want us to do?"

"Quick, follow him, see where he goes. He's not going very fast, but don't let him see yers," said Brendan. "Quick, get on with it!" he said.

Jimmy got up and rushed through the front door almost knocking down a lady coming in.

"So rude," she said as he pushed past.

The Tinker

Jimmy was easily able to keep Michael in view as he headed down Vicarage Road. He saw Michael stop outside the Vicarage and open the gate. Then spotted him push his bike and trailer up the path, past the Vicarage kitchen and towards the Lodge. Jimmy crouch-walked left and had a good view. He watched closely as Michael parked his bike outside and unlock the door.

This was it.

Jimmy almost ran back to the White Hart; he couldn't wait to tell Brendan the news. Brendan was still in the window seat anxiously awaiting Jimmy's return.

"It's him alright... and I knows where he lives. It's next to the church," he said.

"Well that figures," said Brendan.

"So do you want to go over and take him out now?" said Jimmy.

"No, no, can't do that. We'll wait till it's dark and he's asleep. Then we'll pay him a call," said Brendan.

Chapter Twenty One

Melanie walked along the path to the Lodge as the church clock struck the three quarters.

Michael had just got out of the shower when she knocked on the door and he went to answer it in just a towel.

"Now that's how to greet a girl when she's just finished work," she said and leaned forward and kissed him. "God, it's so hot," she said.

She went into the kitchen and put her bag down on the work top.

"I'll just go and shower. I need to freshen up and cool down," she said.

Michael followed her to the bathroom and watched as she took off her clothes.

"How was your day?" she said as she operated the over-the-bath shower.

"Aye, good," he said. "What about you?"

"Yes, good, very good," she said.

The water cascaded downwards but with no great power, being gravity fed. Melanie pulled the shower curtain across to avoid flooding the bathroom and got in. Michael stood at the door and watched still dressed in his towel. His interest was becoming obvious.

"Would you like me to join you?" said Michael.

"Then we won't get any dinner," she said as she let the cooling water drain down her body.

"Yes, you're right," he said and left her to it.

Michael changed into his shorts and sat in the lounge waiting for Melanie. The window was open and Michael noticed the curtain beginning to twitch, at first gently, then more vigorously

The Tinker

as the wind increased. He went over and looked out towards the church. The sky had changed colour; large clouds were gathering to the south. He watched them billowing angrily like a sailcloth on a yacht, huge white cumulus with yellow tinges. It was still hot and Michael pulled the window to, not fully closed, allowing in some air.

Melanie came back into the room in a light blue tee shirt and what looked like running shorts.

"What do you think?" she said as she twirled around in the middle of the room.

"Looks great," he said.

"Bought them at lunch time from the boutique... just in. All the rage in London apparently," she said.

"Very nice," he said as she finished her modelling.

"I'll go and get the dinner on, got some quiche. Thought we could have it with jacket potatoes, what do you think?" she said.

"Sounds good to me," replied Michael and Melanie disappeared into the kitchen. Michael could hear the rattle of pans and dishes.

Melanie was still in the kitchen when there was a knock on the door. Michael opened it.

"Denise," he said "Good to see you, come on in."

"Can I have a word," she said. "Hello Melanie," she added, seeing her coming out of the kitchen.

"Hi Denise," said Melanie.

"In private, if that's ok, Michael," said Denise.

"Don't mind me," said Melanie. "I'll sort out the dinner," and she returned to the kitchen.

Denise went back outside the front door and Michael followed.

"What is it?" asked Michael "Nothing wrong with the children?"

"No, nothing like that... no," she replied.

341

Denise looked over her shoulder concerned that someone might be watching or eavesdropping.

"It may be nothing, but John came back this afternoon and said that an Irishman had been to the church and was asking strange questions," she said.

"When was this?" said Michael.

"Don't know exactly, around two-thirty, three o'clock, I suppose," she said. "John thought he looked like a gangster," she added.

"What sort of questions?" he asked.

"He asked John whether we had any tramps looking for hand-outs. He said his name was Michael. John thought he might be testing him out, you know, looking for a reaction," she said.

Michael was deep in thought.

"What are you going to do?" she said.

"I don't know yet," he said.

"Well you will be careful, won't you," she said. "Would it be worth calling the police?" she said as an afterthought.

"They couldn't do anything. In any case, asking strange questions is not a crime," he said.

"No, I guess not," said Denise realising that it was probably a ridiculous suggestion but it was an indication of the helplessness she felt.

"Are you going to be alright?" she asked.

"Aye," said Michael.

"What about Melanie? Are you going to tell her?" she asked.

"Not just yet. I've not said anything to her about Ireland, not in any detail anyway but she does know that people have been asking after me." He looked down. "I don't want to worry her unnecessarily," he said.

"Right, ok," she said. "But you will let us know if there is

The Tinker

anything we can do... anything," she repeated with a look of concern. "If you need to use the phone, you just have to say." Then she had another thought. "What about your friends in London? Wouldn't they be able to help?"

Michael thought. "Not really. Probably a bit late now anyway," he said. "Look, don't worry. If I need anything I will ask, I promise," he said.

This did little to reassure Denise but she couldn't do anything else. "Ok," she said, "I'll leave you to your dinner. Pop in tomorrow morning for a coffee, if you're around," she said.

"Yeah, I will," he said, and Denise walked back to the Vicarage. She was still worried and felt frustrated at not being able to do anything; she was desperate to help. As she reached the kitchen she looked up at the sky. The clouds had completely obscured the sun; it had grown quite dark. It looked like the forecasters were right.

John was seated at the kitchen table.

"How did you get on, dear?" he said as she walked in. The kitchen light was on.

"Well I told him, but as he said there isn't much he can do," she said.

"Well if he's been in Special Forces he'll know how to look after himself, that's for sure," said the vicar.

"I do hope so," said Denise.

Back in the Lodge, Melanie was still in the kitchen when Michael came back from his chat with Denise.

"Everything alright?" she said.

"Yes," said Michael. "Nothing to worry about."

Michael went into the bedroom. His pannier from his bike was on the floor. He rummaged around in the bottom of the left hand side and found what he was looking for. He took it out, checked

343

the magazine; the Browning Automatic Pistol was fully loaded. He put it in the drawer of the bedside cabinet next to him... just in case.

They had their meal and discussed the day. Michael decided not to say anything about his trip to see Tina Ashworth; there was history there.

"What do you fancy doing tonight?" said Melanie. "Do you want to go to the pub?"

"Yeah, we can have a stroll up there later. Maybe Frank will be about it'll be good to talk to him," said Michael.

Going out as a couple, something alien to him for so long, was beginning to feel like the most natural thing in the world. His whole life had turned around since his revelations to Denise; it had been like some immense exorcism; he owed her a great deal.

Just before nine o'clock Michael noticed a further change in the air pressure; it was like a warm wind. He went to the window and the first spots of rain were starting to streak the glass. He pulled it shut and turned to Melanie who was reading a magazine.

"Well if we're going to the pub then I think we're going to get wet," he said.

Melanie looked up just as the heavens opened its sluice gates; she put down her read and joined Michael at the window. They watched as the rain increased in intensity. It bounced off the churchyard wall on the other side of the footpath that skirted the Lodge. Already pools of water were beginning to form in the pot-holes. With little rain for over two weeks the ground was rock hard and water was running off in whatever direction led downward.

Melanie linked her arms in Michael's then looked up at him.

"Well we can't go out in this. How do you fancy an early night," she said and gave him a long and lingering kiss. He responded.

"Seems like a much better idea," he said and she led him by the hand to the bedroom.

Back at the White Hart, other people were taking an interest in the weather.

"Jazus, will yer take a look at the feckin' rain," said Jimmy who was in Brendan's room discussing tactics for the task ahead. "Not seen anything like this in Belfast," he said.

Brendan joined him looking out over the High Street. The rain was flowing down the gutter in torrents as each drain filled so the water raced down to the next one; the High Street was in flood.

"Well I tink yer man can wait a bit, don't you?" said Jimmy.

"It's too early yet anyways. We'll wait a while, till its proper dark. Let's go and wet the old whistle, what do you say?" said Brendan.

"Aye, sounds good to me," said Jimmy and they went down to the bar.

It was strangely subdued, people staring at the rain. Then at nine thirty came the first clap of thunder, more a rumble really, in the distance but audible.

Tony was talking to Mrs Audley who had made it with her husband just before the storm started.

"Sounds like another big one. Remember that storm a couple of weeks' ago?" he said.

"I'll say," she said. "Didn't think we would see another like that so soon."

"Yeah," said Tony. "Been strange, apart from that shower on Saturday, we've had over a fortnight of brilliant weather, and now this. It makes you wonder if there's someone controlling it."

"What do you mean?" said Mrs Audley.

"Well these scientists messing around and all that. I mean, you don't know what's going on, do you? I've got a mate who works at that listening place in Cheltenham. You know... hush, hush and all that." He tapped the side of his nose twice with his forefinger. "The things he hears about. Not that he tells me anything of course," said Tony as he continued dispensing their drinks.

He was giving Mrs Audley the change and noticed the two Irish guys waiting.

"Yes gents, what can I get you?" said Tony.

"Two pints of the black stuff," said Brendan.

Tony went to the Guinness tap and started the process - that's how it felt. Pouring the famous stout was almost an art form according to Tony.

"Tanks," said Jimmy as Tony handed the drinks over and took the money.

"So have you had a good day?" Tony asked.

"Aye, yer could say that," said Brendan obviously not wishing to engage in any conversation. He looked at Jimmy and they left the bar area and went over to one of the window seats and sat down.

Back in the Lodge the church clock struck; Michael counted eleven. He and Melanie were lying in bed watching the incredible light show being played out before them. Flashes lit the bedroom like Strobes followed quickly by thunder. The bed faced the window and Michael had opened the curtains so they could watch the storm. Michael found it fascinating.

"Did you know you can tell how far away the storm is?" said Michael.

Melanie was not comfortable in thunderstorms and was holding onto Michael for protection.

"I can't remember, I've heard about it. Don't you have to count or something?" she said.

The Tinker

"Yes, five seconds is one mile. So it's quite simple, you watch the lightning then count slowly in seconds. Then as soon as you hear the thunder, stop counting and divide the seconds by five. I'll show you. Wait for the next lightning," he said.

A few minutes went by then suddenly the room was lit like a flash gun. Michael started counting. "One and two and three..." He got up to nine then the thunder echoed around the valley. "There you are, just under two miles away," he said. "Quite close."

"That's clever," she said. "I didn't know that."

"Useful if you are caught out in the open, happened to me a few times. There was this one time in Italy... Sorrento, if I remember rightly, an amazing storm, beautiful, but scary I can tell you," he said.

"You must tell me all about your exploits. I would love to know," she said.

"Yes," he said "I will."

She snuggled up closer. "I'm glad I'm with you," she said. "You make me feel safe."

Michael could see the irony but said nothing.

Back at the White Hart it had gone midnight and Brendan and Jimmy were back in the room getting prepared. It was still raining but not as strongly, just the odd rumble in the distance.

"Storms passing... Let's get this done," Brendan said.

Jimmy had a small hold-all containing the tools of his trade, including two Beretta 92s, one each.

The pair went downstairs and through the reception area; the bar was closed. Tony was finishing washing the last of the glasses and noticed them leave; dark clothing, they looked like commandos; he wondered where they might be heading at this hour.

They went through the hotel exit to the car-park and down the covered way into the High Street; turned right, then left into Vicarage Road. Neither of them spoke, completely focused on their mission. Jimmy had the hold-all over his shoulder. Flashes of sheet lightning were visible in the distance illuminating the hills behind the village. The rain was now a steady flow rather than the torrents falling earlier.

They reached the gate of the Vicarage and opened it.

"Along here," whispered Jimmy.

The Vicarage was in darkness as they walked up the footpath and past the kitchen window. The Lodge was in front of them.

"We'll take a look around. Don't want to force the door; one of the windows might be easier," whispered Brendan.

Brendan walked up to the front door, turned to the right and reached the corner of the building, only a few yards; Jimmy followed, checking backwards every few steps to make sure they weren't being trailed. Brendan peered around the corner of the Lodge to the left and looked ahead. There was the footpath that went between the Lodge and the churchyard wall. They turned and walked slowly along the path and crouched when they came to the first window just three or four paces down. Brendan leaned up slowly and peered through. The curtains were not fully drawn and he was able to see inside; the room was empty. They continued about ten feet and reached the bedroom window, the skylight was wide open. Again they crouched down below the sill then walked to the end of the building, another five feet or so and stood up to check their bearings. They turned left past the bathroom, again the skylight was open. Then to the other end of the building, back up past the kitchen until they reached the front of the Lodge once more. They had completed the recce of the place.

Brendan beckoned Jimmy to get closer for the briefing.

The Tinker

"We go through the first window," he whispered. "If he's asleep he'll be in the bottom room; that looks like the bedroom. There are no other doors so he can't get out. This one's the living room, I tink," he said.

Their eyes had now become accustomed to the dark and visibility was reasonable.

A flash of lightning lit the surrounding area, then a few seconds later the thunder. Melanie counted... fourteen... nearly three miles. Michael was fast asleep.

The rain started getting heavier.

"Jazus," said Jimmy "It's feckin' pissing down."

Another flash of lightning. Melanie was counting again... ten. It was coming back, inexorably.

Brendan walked slowly to the living room window and crouched down again. The rain was starting to get really heavy now. "Feck," said Jimmy. "We could do without all this."

"Aye... come on let's get this thing over with and get out of here. I'm for heading home," said Brendan.

"Amen to that," said Jimmy.

Jimmy took a crow bar out of his hold-all, then passed one of the Beretta's to Brendan who put it in the waistband of his trousers. Jimmy pocketed his gun then started wrenching at the window pulling it downwards and lifting the frame from the casement. There was a crack as the frame splintered. The window opened towards them.

Melanie lay awake waiting for the next flash of lightning. A moment later the room was bathed in white light. One and two and three... Then another noise... different. The thunder clap that followed the flash felt like it was rattling the ceiling. Melanie was alerted. The other noise... coming from the living room.

"Michael," Melanie whispered. "Wake up... Something's

wrong."

"Eh... what," said Michael.

"Shhh," whispered Melanie. "I think someone's trying to break in," and before Michael could do or say anything, she had got out of bed and was heading out of the bedroom in just a pair of knickers. It was an instinctive reaction and without any thought for her own safety.

She slowly pushed open the door to the living room and put her hand around the frame searching for the switch. Her fingers ran up and down the wall. It was an unfamiliar house but there was definitely a switch somewhere; she found it. There was another flash of lightning which bathed the room in bright light. Melanie peered around the door. She could see two men, one being helped through the window by the other.

She thought quickly then flicked the switch and went into the room.

"Hey, who the hell are you? What the fuck are you doing in my house?" she said and crossed her hands over her breasts to protect her modesty.

"Get out of here before I call the police," she shouted.

Jimmy was in and had his gun; Brendan quickly followed and stood up. Melanie saw the weapon and screamed.

"What're you doing? What do you want? I've got no money," she shouted.

"Where is he?" shouted Brendan.

"Where's who?" shouted Melanie." I'm on my own... this is my house," she said and dropped her arms briefly. The sight unsettled the men.

There was a moment of uncertainty as the men considered this. Brendan looked at Jimmy: Melanie was very convincing. She stood there having drawn back her hands to cover herself, but a significant distraction none-the-less.

Jimmy was still pointing the gun at Melanie. Brendan was looking around the room, looking for signs.

"Look," she said, more rationally but almost pleading. "I've no idea who you're talking about. I told you... there's no-one else here. You've got the wrong place."

It was a stand-off and Jimmy made a move for Melanie.

"I don't believe yers. Yer lying. I know he's here," he said. She flayed her arms her fingers scratching Jimmy's arm. He managed to grab her hair and dragged her to the middle of the room. Melanie dropped to the floor kicking and screaming.

"Get off me, you bastard! Let me go!" she shouted. "What do you want? I don't know what you're talking about? I'm on my own here," she shrieked. "Don't hurt me."

While this was going on Michael had slipped on his shorts, tee shirt and plimsolls, pushed up the sash window in the bedroom and got out. He crawled in the mud back along the footpath until he was outside the lounge window. It was open, hanging off its frame.

He could see Melanie's performance confronting the men.

"Good girl," he whispered. Then watched in horror as Jimmy dragged her down.

Michael was totally invisible in the dark whereas the men were bathed in the light of the sixty watt bulb hanging from the living room ceiling. They were also distracted by Melanie's performance.

Michael stood at the open window the rain had already drenched his hair, his tee shirt was sticking to his body.

He raised his gun at Jimmy.

"Leave her be, Jimmy, put that gun away!" he shouted.

Brendan and Jimmy turned around and before they could move Melanie got up and ran back to the bathroom and locked the door.

She crouched on the floor, breathing heavily. She hoped she had done enough; it was down to Michael now.

Jimmy swung around and aimed a shot at Michael which shattered the window then turned to pursue Melanie.

"Leave her," said Brendan. "That's the bastard we're after."

They both ran towards the window. Brendan slowly put his head through and looked right, then left. He could see Michael walking away from the Lodge towards the main footpath.

Michael had a plan; he had been working on it in his mind for a few days. He had even rehearsed it on his last walk.

A flash of lightning scarred the sky and seemed to light up the whole village. The thunder followed before the count of five. Another lightning flash and it seemed to hit the church spire; there was a loud crack and a flicker of what looked like a blue flame which ran down the side of the church to the ground. The conductor had done its work. Michael stayed in sight; he needed to draw them away from the Lodge, like a Lapwing drawing a falcon from its chicks.

Both Jimmy and Brendan had got back through the window and were now pursuing Michael. The rain was back to its earlier intensity. Michael stopped momentarily to make sure they were following; a gunshot would be unlikely to hit him. It was worth the chance.

"Come here, yer bastard," shouted Jimmy and they were now in hot pursuit down the footpath. Michael was a good thirty or forty yards in front running in a zigzag. The only illumination was from the regular flashes of lightning. The ground was waterlogged. Michael splashed through the puddles, the cold water swamping his footwear and attacking his muscles.

Meanwhile Melanie was still hunkered down on the floor of the bathroom listening to what was going on. She had heard nothing for several minutes, no movement. She was fairly sure the men had gone but couldn't be certain. She slowly unlocked the bathroom door and peered anxiously towards the living room. It was empty. She quickly went into the bedroom and put on a tee shirt. Back into the lounge, slowly, gingerly, watching for any danger. She reached the only exit door and turned the Yale lock slowly clockwise and gently pulled the door towards her. Another flash of lightning, followed by the thunder. No-one there.

Not bothering to shut the door, she put her head down and ran from the Lodge in her bare feet toward the Vicarage. She banged on the kitchen door as loud as she could.

"Help... help," she called.

A minute went by but seemed longer. She banged again. The kitchen light went on and the vicar was just fastening his dressing gown. He opened the door just as Denise came in to join him.

"Melanie...? What on earth's the matter?" she said.

"It's Michael... two men... they broke in... they're chasing him," she said. "We need to stop them... do something... Call the police," she said.

Denise looked at her husband and then at Melanie. "Come and sit down, I'll put the kettle on. You can tell us all about it."

"But... but... you don't understand... We need to do something," Melanie said almost in desperation.

"Yes... but for the moment we'll wait. This is something I know Michael wants to sort out and knowing him he will have a plan," said Denise.

"What do you mean?" said Melanie.

The vicar pulled out a chair from under the kitchen table and presented it to Melanie. "Here sit down," he said.

Melanie was bemused. "Aren't you going to help him?" she said.

"We are," the vicar said. "He would want us to keep you safe."

"I don't understand," said Melanie.

Denise handed her a cup of tea. "Has Michael told you anything about his background?" she asked.

"Not a lot... but I know those men want to hurt him," she said.

"Well I can't say much but I am sure Michael would want me to put your mind at rest. He is ex-special services, military," she clarified.

"Yes, I know he had something to do with the army. He told me," said Melanie.

"Well for a start they're very resourceful," said the vicar. "I used to be in the army, a few years ago now and I'm sure he'll be quite capable of looking after himself. But, you see, really we have no option. We don't know where they might have gone and the police will take an hour at least to get here from Stonington."

Melanie was beginning to see the logic.

"We need to protect Michael and the best way to do that is to sit tight and wait," said the vicar.

Denise served tea and as Melanie raised a cup to her lipsshe said, "But... we can't just do nothing," she said. "What if they come here? I mean I've seen their faces."

"Don't worry," said the vicar. "Nothing will happen to you and he left the room and came back a few moments later with a shotgun.

"You'll be quite safe," said the vicar.

Denise looked at her husband. "It's alright dear," he said, noticing the look on her face. "It is licensed," he said by way of reassurance. That was not what was concerning Denise.

Back along the path, Michael had reached the stile. Another flash of lightning lit up the scene. Jimmy and Brendan were still on his tail and Jimmy fired off another shot. It whistled by Michael as he jumped over the fence and headed for the woods. Brendan was first over the stile but was starting to feel out of breath. Jimmy leapt the obstacle like a champion hurdler and was now in front. Michael reached the trees and Jimmy followed. Even the lightning had difficulty penetrating the canopy.

Michael dropped down and watched as Jimmy stopped realising that he had made a mistake; one which was going to prove fatal. Michael was crouched low, just like the training missions a few years ago. Jimmy was highlighted against the slightly brighter background but from Michael's position he stood out like a beacon. Michael waited for a flash of lightning. He could see Jimmy trying to retrace his steps. Michael started to count and on five took aim and fired; Jimmy slumped to the ground. The sound was completely hidden by a violent crack of thunder. Even Brendan hadn't heard it. Michael could hear Brendan calling. "Jimmy where the feck are yers," he said.

Michael couldn't see Brendan. He had been concentrating on taking out Jimmy, the immediate threat, and had lost sight of his next target. It was now quiet. A rumble of thunder echoed around the trees; it was as though they had taken on a life-form, passing the noise from one to another like a football be kicked between players, mocking Michael's attempt to locate his prey.

Michael slowly crawled towards the last of the trees which had provided cover. He waited and watched. He could hear his own breathing. His senses primed only for survival, he was oblivious to the penetrating cold.

Another strobe-like flash illuminated the wood casting eerie shapes in the canopy. He could see the footpath which meandered back towards the stile and the border of the Major's estate. There was no sign of Brendan.

Then suddenly... "Jimmy will yer speak to us, yer crazy bastard."

Michael could hear Brendan calling somewhere to his left but still couldn't see him.

"Come on Jimmy... let's leave the fecker. We'll come back tomorrow and finish it," said Brendan. Michael moved slowly out of the cover of the woods towards the voice. Still no visual. He was in a crouch/walk position, his Browning poised at the ready. With the dark shape of the trees behind him there would be no silhouette to give him away.

Suddenly he heard a click and instinctively he dropped and rolled. Brendan was directly in front of him. He too had engaged his gun and it was pointing straight at Michael. A shot rang out, a miss... another shot. Brendan was aiming blindly now into the long, wet grass but Michael had already moved through the undergrowth. A flash of lightning lit the sky and this time Michael could see Brendan clearly still firing shots but in the wrong direction. Michael stood and with both hands steadying the barrel, fired at the shape. A body shot, always the best option in a hurry, less chance of missing.

There was a crack as the shot echoed around the valley but with everything else that was going on no-one would take any notice. The figure had gone. Had Michael hit him? He couldn't be sure. Brendan could have taken the same evading action that Michael had done. Slowly Michael crawled towards the last position. He winced as he slithered on his stomach through a patch of nettles, the stinging hairs attacking his skin like needles. Then he found him, lying face down. Michael did a quick check. He couldn't see where he had hit him but there was no sign of life. Brendan's gun was still in his hand. Michael took it and put it in the pocket of his shorts.

The rain kept coming, torrential now. The lightning was still overhead, thunder following at three. Michael looked up, it would pass, he said to himself... another few minutes.

Michael put his Browning down the side of his shorts and lifted the lifeless form of Brendan Monahan under the arms and dragged him backwards into the woods then along the footpath towards the lake. Sheet lightning lit the dark water, reflecting the fork as the remnants of the storm gave its last hurrah. It was back-breaking work, a dead weight sodden by the rain.

It took several minutes but eventually Michael reached the boat house and left Brendan, then went back for Jimmy. Michael suddenly remembered Jimmy's gun. Luckily, like Brendan, it was still in Jimmy's hand, his finger trapped by the trigger guard. Michael breathed a sigh of relief. If Jimmy had dropped it, there would be no way he would be able to find it in the darkness. He applied the safely catch and put the Beretta in the other pocket of his shorts.

It seemed to take an eternity but again Michel reached the boathouse with Jimmy's lifeless body.

The rowing boat that had capsized almost drowning William, was next to the boathouse upturned on its back. Michael managed to right it and hauled it to the waterside, then pushed it into the lake.

He secured it to the bank then went back and dragged Brendan to the boat and man-handled him face up into the bottom. Then did the same with Jimmy. He went to the back of the boat house and searched around. He found what he was looking for and picked up two heavy rocks. He went back to the boat and put those in as well. Another flash of lightning; then a more distant rumble. The oars were leant against the wooden hut and Michael picked them up and took them to the boat. He placed them on top of the bodies and Michael got in. The boat swayed; it was very low in the water. Michael picked up the oars and started rowing slowly towards the middle of the lake. From his discussions with Frank on the fishing trip he knew exactly where the deepest spot was. From the centre the ambient light was sufficient for Michael to have reasonable vision despite the rain. He checked his bearings. The next part was not easy. He unzipped Brendan's waterproof and slipped the first boulder inside and zipped it up again checking it was secure. He took off the belt from Brendan's trousers and tied it tight around the Irishman's neck which would secure the rock further. He lifted the body up and gently rolled him over the side. The boat tipped with the weight but didn't over-balance. There was a ripple as his body floated for a moment before drifting down the thirty feet to the bottom.

Jimmy was going to be more of a problem; he only had a pair of jeans and a hooded top. Again Michael undid the zip and secured the stone tight to Jimmy's chest, then refastened it. Michael took his own tee shirt off and ripped it in half. Then pulled the two ends so it stretched sufficiently to tie it around Jimmy's midriff, Michael tied it off and checked the knot to make sure it wouldn't give way. He didn't want the stone slipping out and allowing Jimmy's body to float to the top which it would do until all the air had been expunged.

Michael held his breath and repeated the process, gently tipping Jimmy over the side. There was relief as he watched the body slowly disappear out of sight. He took the two Berettas and cleaned them on his shorts then threw them randomly towards the centre of the lake. Michael took the Browning from his belt and looked at it. It had saved his life but he knew he had to dispose of it. He wiped it clean as best he could and then dropped it over the side into the dark gloom of the lake.

He started shivering in the unrelenting rain as he rowed back to the shore. The adrenaline was still pumping through his body but shock was starting to set in.

Michael reached the wooden pontoon in front of the boathouse, threw the oars onto the bank and made a grab for the docking post. He pulled himself out. He took hold of the bow of the boat and with an energy-sapping final effort managed to drag it out of the water. He caught his breath for a moment then hauled it the short distance to the side of boathouse. There would almost certainly be traces of blood in the bottom but Michael hoped the rain would have washed most of it away. He turned it on its side to wash the water out then on its back as he had found it. The oars again, he leant against the wall more or less in the same place; it wouldn't matter.

He walked back through the wood then once out of the trees started to jog back to the Lodge to keep himself warm and help dissipate the effect of shock.

The clock struck two as he walked to the front door. It was open. He walked into the house; there was no sign of Melanie. He could see a light on in the Vicarage and walked down the path to the kitchen and knocked on the door.

"Michael?!" said Melanie looking at Denise.

The vicar lifted the barrel of his shotgun; there was a 'click' as it engaged. He was ready. He nodded to Denise.

She went to the door and slowly opened it.

"Michael! thank goodness," she said and let him in. The vicar broke the shotgun and let out a sigh of relief.

Michael stood there, his hair matted and lank, his body flecked with mud and scratches, blood was oozing out of the deeper cuts and streaking down his chest and arms. Melanie rushed forward and flung her arms around him.

"God you're freezing," she said.

"Are you alright?" said Denise. "You had us really worried."

She handed him a towel and Michael started wiping off the moisture, a mix of sweat, blood and rain, then wrapped it around his neck; he was starting to shake.

"God look at you," said Melanie. "You're bleeding."

"Only scratches," said Michael.

"Do you want to use the downstairs bathroom to wash?" asked Denise. "I'll get you something to put on."

"Yes please," said Michael.

"I'll help," said Melanie and she followed him into the bathroom and started dabbing his wounds.

"These are quite deep," she said as she wiped away the blood. "Just a minute."

Michael just watched.

Melanie put her head around the door and shouted. "Have you got any antiseptic and a couple of plasters?"

Denise replied. "Yes, I'll bring them through," and she handed Melanie the medical chest she always kept for emergencies.

After a few minutes of running repairs Michael and Melanie returned to the kitchen and Denise presented Michael with one of the vicar's shirts which he put on. There were several sticking plasters stuck around his chest and arms. He was still shivering

"Have you called the police?" asked Michael, Melanie was holding on again.

"No," said John. "We thought it for the best."

"Good," said Michael.

"But what happened?" asked Melanie.

"Let's just say we've sorted out our differences. They won't be troubling us anymore," he said.

The vicar intervened. "I think we should leave it there, don't you?" he said.

Melanie looked quizzical.

"Well, if you say so," she said. "Just as long as you're alright," she added, looking at Michael.

"What's that on your shorts?" asked Denise. "Are you hurt?"

Michael looked down there was a red stain on the side of his thigh.

"No, I'm fine," he said.

"Let me have those in the morning and I'll put them in the wash," she said.

The vicar went up to Michael and shook his hand warmly.

"So glad you managed to sort it," he said. "It will always be our secret. Now how about a little something to celebrate," he said and went to the cupboard and produced a bottle of whiskey. Denise took some tumblers from the cabinet and the vicar poured four generous measures.

"Here's to a fresh start," said the vicar.

"I'll drink to that," said Michael and the four of them clinked glasses.

It was gone three before Michael and Melanie returned to the Lodge. Denise had to give them a spare key as Michael had left the house and slammed the door behind him without thinking.

Michael went over to the living room window and secured it as best he could. The broken glass he could do nothing about.

"I'll fix that in the morning," he said to Melanie.

In bed Melanie held onto Michael. "I hope that is the end of it Michael. I couldn't stand another night like this. I thought you were going to die," she said.

"Aye," said Michael. "It's over."

The following morning was difficult for Melanie; sleeping had

Alan Reynolds

not been easy and she felt rotten; her period had started.

"Why don't you call in sick?" said Michael.

"Can't do that, I've got my clients to see to," she said as she put on her work clothes.

Michael got up and made them both some tea and watched Melanie go to the salon at eight-thirty. It was cooler following the storm and the ground was wet, puddles everywhere.

A few minutes later there was an urgent knock on the door. Michael opened it.

"Denise...?" he said. "Is everything ok?"

"Yes..." she said. "Have you heard the news?"

"News...? What news?" he said.

"It's just been on the radio... Lord Ansty," she said.

"What about him?" said Michael.

"He's dead... This morning... IRA. Car bomb they said... It really is over, isn't it?"

Epilogue

Later at the White Hart concern was growing about the missing Irishmen. Their beds hadn't been slept in and their car was still in the car-park. Gladys Gable, the house manageress reported the matter to the manager, Gavin. "We'll give it till lunch time," he said.

Tony Rollinson was just arriving for duties and overheard the conversation.

"What's the problem?" he said.

"The Irishmen in eleven and twelve, gone missing," said Gladys.

"How odd," said Tony.

A little later Gavin had left on business and Tony went up to Gladys.

"Have you got the room keys, Gladys?" he said. "Just want to have a look round."

"Yes, but don't go touching anything. I'll lose my job," she said.

Tony got the keys, went upstairs and let himself into room eleven, Jimmy's.

He went inside and looked around. There were a couple of hold-alls which he rummaged through, nothing of any note; bathroom was clean, just a tooth brush and toothpaste on the sink top. He left and tried next door, Brendan's room.

There was a folder on the dressing table next to the small TV. Tony opened it and saw the pictures of Michael together with some notes from a firm of private investigators in Liverpool. He put the folder under his arm, then had a quick look through Brendan's hold-all which was on the bed, just washing and clean clothes. He opened the drawers of the dressing table; the left hand one contained the Gideon Bible, the right, an envelope. He looked inside there was a number of twenty pound notes. Tony had a feeling he would not be seeing the guests any time soon. He peeled off five and put them in his pocket. No-one would notice.

There was nothing else of any interest and he left the room and went to the small staff room and put the folder in his locker, then gave the room keys back to Gladys.

The following Monday when Michael came to start the maintenance work Tony made a point of catching him in the car park as he was unloading his tools from his trailer.

"Thought you would like this. The Irishmen left it behind and I believe it has nothing to do with anyone else" he said, and presented Michael with the folder.

Michael opened it and thanked him, then secured it in one of the panniers. He would dispose of it later.

It was three days before the police were called and an investigation started on the missing guests. With Brendan and Jimmy having both used aliases there was no record of their names or addresses. They had no ID in their rooms. The car was towed away to the police pound until the hire company came and claimed it. They too had no accurate records of the customers, different names again. The police had drawn a blank.

Another investigation had begun in Liverpool into the murder of Barry Springer. His assistant, Kathy Metcalf could offer no information that would help the police. She decided she would say nothing about the Irish clients for fear of reprisals. Again the investigation stalled.

In Belfast, Brendan Monahan's wife declared him missing when he had not returned home after four days. She had begun to worry when she hadn't received a phone call from him after the arrival in England. Before he left he had said he was going to be staying in a hotel but not where... or why. "Just some business," he had said. Ferry records were checked but no tickets were purchased in the name of Brendan Monahan or Jimmy Rafferty.

The day after the incident, Michael went to see the Major. He had discussed his decision with Denise and the vicar; they were delighted. He told Melanie when she returned home that evening and invited her to join him in the cottage on the estate when he took over as gamekeeper, if she would like. She accepted without a moment's thought.

Melanie's divorce went through and eventually at a trial in Gloucester Crown Court her husband, Mark was found guilty of manslaughter and sentenced to ten years in prison.

Tina Ashworth got her leading role in the TV series and moved to London; Ridge Cottage was sold for £1.2 million later that year. In the early 90's she was involved in another scandal when police raided her house and found a quantity of 'suspicious substances'. She was arrested and as part of her 'punishment' she booked herself into a clinic to try to cure her addiction. The adverse publicity sent her acting career into free-fall and she dropped out of the limelight. In 1998 an exclusive in a Sunday Newspaper found her in a squalid bedsit in Balham.

At the end of August after Michael had completed his contract with the White Hart and serviced what seemed like most of the central heating boilers in the village, he was officially appointed gamekeeper to the Manor estate. The Major was thrilled to get his man. Michael had some help from Frank in settling in, but unfortunately his condition deteriorated quickly and he died just three weeks after Michael had taken over.

Michael made an important decision and broke cover. He

phoned his handler in London and explained his change of circumstances. A more formal protection scheme was put into operation whereby Michael officially became Michael Beresford, the name on his passport. His Army Record was reinstated with new files added indicating his work in West Germany between 1977 and 1986. He was formally discharged as a Lieutenant and received a full army pension. He was given a National Insurance number and opened a bank account, everything was above board. He had received an informal and unregistered commendation from his commanding officer for his role in breaking up the Glenbar Gang. No questions were ever asked about Monahan and Rafferty, although their disappearance in Belfast had not gone unnoticed by agents there.

June 2006, twenty years since Michael's summer. The vicar was seventy eight but still lived with Denise in the village. After he had retired eight years earlier he was given one of the church cottages to see out his days.

Michael and Melanie had set up home together in the gamekeeper's cottage and got married in 1988. They have two children, Jack and Kimberley aged fifteen and thirteen both are doing well at Stonington Grammar School.

Melanie too has new responsibilities. When Mrs Audley retired in 1993 she took over managing the salon and eventually became the proud owner.

In his role as gamekeeper, Michael was left to his own devices; the Major was as good as his word. It has to be the best job in the world, he had said on many occasions in the White Hart where he was quite a regular. As time went by Michael became very close to the Major who treated him like the son he never had and the children became surrogate grandchildren spending a great deal of time at the Manor House with the Major and his wife who both doted on them.

The Major lost his beloved Memsahib in 1994 and his health too deteriorated quickly after she had died.

One day, shortly after his wife's funeral, the Major called on Melanie and Michael at the cottage and made an announcement. He was leaving the estate to Michael. There was a condition attached, that Michael would not sell it but run the estate as a going concern as the Major had done. Michael was more than happy with that, he had several ideas.

The Major died the following year and Michael inherited the estate as had been promised. He soon made changes and launched a new 'farm produce' grocery range called 'The Manor House'. He bought a substantial property just outside Stonington and converted it into a corporate Head Quarters. Sales quickly increased and it now turns over in excess of five million pounds, including exports to the Continent. With forty employees he is an important figure in the local community and is now on the Church and Parish councils.

He gives little thought to his past life and his whole purpose is to ensure the smooth running of the business. Both children are taking an interest.

He rarely has time for fishing but the lake is still made available to selected people, including important clients. There is a new estate manager - a title Michael prefers to 'gamekeeper', a graduate from Cirencester Agricultural College who keeps the lake stocked and maintained.

On Sunday 11th June 2006 two local lads had paid for their day permit and were trying their luck for eels from the boat. Eel fishing is different from fly or normal course fishing as you don't use a float or fly but 'dredge' along the bottom with a weighted hook and worm or some other lure. It was just after seven a.m. when one of the boys felt a pull on the line. He immediately jerked the rod upwards to ensure that the hook engaged in the fish's mouth. But there was no fight just a weight.

"What is it?" said his friend.

"Don't know, feels heavy though."

THE END

Alan Reynolds

…story left me with a racing pulse, jangling nerves and a real want for a follow up book.
- *Jacque Gerrard*

"**This book has everything**. The characters really come to life and I cannot wait for the next in the series!
-*Sara Seastron*

Brilliant read, thoroughly enjoyed it. Just waiting for your next publication.
- *Sarah Knight*

..one of those books you cannot put down… gripping tale.
- *Anna-Marie Dreyfus*

…currently reading Flying with Kites **CAN'T WAIT TO GET HOME TO READ MORE!**
- *Keeley Edge*

…David is raving about Flying with Kites. He's half way thru and already sees it's potential for a film…
- *William and Victoria Restaurant - Harrogate / book club*

… It will make you gasp, sigh and laugh out loud… Alan Reynolds has the ability to make this happen all on one page, absolutely superb… **a definite five stars!**
- *Lynette Machin*

A Brilliant Read... I'm never normally gripped so much by storylines but this kept me in suspense throughout. Just couldn't put it down!

- Anita Flowers

Gripping stuff... This story had me hooked from the outset. I'm sure that my pulse rate must have increased as I progressed through it and circumstances, decisions and fate all began to take effect. I recommend this book to fans of Ruth Rendell and I don't think for one moment they will be disappointed.

- Anne Ulah

Awesome read... I don't read very much at all and it's not the type of story I would have chosen but I could not put this book down. The whole story is totally believable. Towards the end I just could not leave it and sat all night reading to find out what happened.

- Claire Setchel

I recommend it as a must read book... Having read Flying with Kites I was eagerly waiting for Reynolds next book to be published. It was well worth the wait. Psychological thrillers are my favourite genre and this is one the best I've read for some time.

- 'Snow Leopard'

I couldn't turn the pages fast enough to find out what was going to happen... After reading Flying With Kites I was excited to read Alan Reynolds new novel, Taskers End, and I wasn't disappointed.

- Heather McLaren

...recommended. Having worked in the banking system I can relate to the background culture that was prevalent in 1990s / 2000s, and in other sectors, and I feel I have met the characters. ...a roller coaster of emotion, excitement and despair, hedonistic fun and shattering.
- *Richard King*

A riveting read... Alan's writing is very engaging and keeps you enthralled from start to finish. Would definitely recommend for anyone with a curiosity about the inner workings of branch banking.
- *Sally Turgoose*

I couldn't put the book down... Larger than life" characters are portrayed set in a ruthless and stressful environment; but are there elements of truth here? One is left wondering, particularly in the light of the recent banking crisis and recession! This book would lead to an interesting discussion in any book club.
- *CBL*

Brilliant and insightful... It would probably have been less risky to have taken our money to the casino than to the bank. Brilliant and insightful into just what was going on from the government downwards. No wonder we finished up in the mess we did."
- *John Leach*

This book is one I could not put down... As the title suggests, the storyline is set within a banking background. By the time I had finished, the reason the banks hit a crisis sending us into economic free fall became much clearer!"
- *Kate Goddard*

If you love an intriguing plot, this book is for you...
- *Lynn Newhart*

Can't wait for the next!... Loved it, such easy reading with a gripping story line, this is yet another book from Alan *Reynolds that has enthralled me!*
- *Chris Wren*

...captivating read from the first chapter... A thriller that draws you into the Muslim ways and how different factions of that faith interpret the Koran and how the jihad martyrs justify the killing of innocent people. The author gives you an insight into what it must have been like during the war in Iraq and also the war on terrorists in our own communities at home. I found the book to be a thought provoking read and as with his other books I didn't want to *put it down.*
- *Sarah K*

I look forward to reading more of Mr. Reynolds fine work... Alan Reynolds propels the reader deep inside the world of Islamic jihad conditioning and culture in this wonderful novel about war and its long-term social consequences. Reynolds literary prose and timing are impeccable as he takes you from the deserts of southern Iraq to an oil platform off the coast of Britain. What makes a young person (Tariq) become so enamoured in sacred ideals that he is eager to commit suicide to strike a blow against what his religious faction deems a Great Evil? It is my customary habit to read one chapter a night from my bedside table before sleeping. The Sixth Pillar lengthened my reading time to four or more chapters per night before I finished... always a good sign.
- *Randall R Peterson*

Lightning Source UK Ltd.
Milton Keynes UK
UKOW04f0606260216

269120UK00001B/3/P